# IRRESISTIBLE

# Mary Balogh

BERKLEY SENSATION, NEW YORK

**THE BERKLEY PUBLISHING GROUP**
**Published by the Penguin Group**
**Penguin Group (USA) Inc.**
**375 Hudson Street, New York, New York 10014, USA**
Penguin Group (Canada), 90 Eglinton Avenue East, Suite 700, Toronto, Ontario M4P 2Y3, Canada
(a division of Pearson Penguin Canada Inc.)
Penguin Books Ltd., 80 Strand, London WC2R 0RL, England
Penguin Group Ireland, 25 St. Stephen's Green, Dublin 2, Ireland (a division of Penguin Books Ltd.)
Penguin Group (Australia), 250 Camberwell Road, Camberwell, Victoria 3124, Australia
(a division of Pearson Australia Group Pty. Ltd.)
Penguin Books India Pvt. Ltd., 11 Community Centre, Panchsheel Park, New Delhi—110 017, India
Penguin Group (NZ), 67 Apollo Drive, Rosedale, North Shore 0632, New Zealand
(a division of Pearson New Zealand Ltd.)
Penguin Books (South Africa) (Pty.) Ltd., 24 Sturdee Avenue, Rosebank, Johannesburg 2196,
South Africa

Penguin Books Ltd., Registered Offices: 80 Strand, London WC2R 0RL, England

This is a work of fiction. Names, characters, places, and incidents either are the product of the author's imagination or are used fictitiously, and any resemblance to actual persons, living or dead, business establishments, events, or locales is entirely coincidental. The publisher does not have any control over and does not assume any responsibility for author or third-party websites or their content.

IRRESISTIBLE

A Berkley Sensation Book / published by arrangement with the author

PRINTING HISTORY
Jove mass-market edition / October 1998
Berkley Sensation mass-market edition / October 2007

Copyright © 1998 by Mary Balogh.

ISBN: 978-0-425-22103-7

BERKLEY® SENSATION
Berkley Sensation Books are published by The Berkley Publishing Group,
a division of Penguin Group (USA) Inc.,
375 Hudson Street, New York, New York 10014.
BERKLEY SENSATION is a trademark belonging to Penguin Group (USA) Inc.
The "B" design is a trademark belonging to Penguin Group (USA) Inc.

PRINTED IN THE UNITED STATES OF AMERICA

10   9   8   7   6   5   4

# ONE

THERE WAS ALWAYS A SENSE of pleasurable anticipation attached to entering London even though one had to travel through the poorer, more crowded outer areas before reaching Mayfair and its splendid mansions and thoroughfares. There was an indefinable air of energy about the city and the promise it gave of busy, varied activities to fill every hour of every day of one's stay.

It was even more exhilarating to be arriving at the very beginning of the spring Season, when all the beau monde would be converging on the city, supposedly so that their menfolk might take their seats in one of the two Houses and conduct the nation's business. But that was only a small part of the reason—an excuse, if one would—for the general exodus from country estates and smaller popular centers and spas.

Members of the *ton* came to London during the spring to enjoy themselves. And enjoy themselves they did with a dizzying array of balls and soirees and concerts and Venetian breakfasts and garden parties, not to mention attendance at theaters and pleasure gardens and walks and rides in fashionable Hyde Park or excursions to see the sights, like the Tower of London, or simply to shop on Bond Street or Oxford Street.

It was a special bonus, perhaps, to be arriving on a sunny spring day. The journey from Yorkshire had been a long and tedious one—and much of it had been accomplished in dull, cloudy weather, with even the occasional rain shower to slow their progress. Mud on the roads was always to be respected, even when one was eager to end a long journey. But although the morning had been cloudy, the sky cleared off during the afternoon and the sun beamed down.

"Is this really it, Nathaniel?" Miss Georgina Gascoigne asked, her voice awed as she leaned closer to the window. "London?"

It was a foolish question, perhaps, since they had long known that they were close and there was no mistaking London for any village along the route. But Sir Nathaniel Gascoigne recognized it as a largely rhetorical question and smiled at his sister's awed expression. She might be all of twenty years old, but her experience of the world had been limited until now to their Yorkshire home and the few miles surrounding it.

"This is really it," he said. "We are almost there, Georgie."

"It looks dirty and disagreeable," the young lady who sat beside Georgina said, sitting very upright on the seat and looking disdainfully from the window without leaning closer to it.

Lavinia. Their maternal cousin, Miss Lavinia Bergland, and Nathaniel's ward despite her advanced age—she was four and twenty—and his own relatively young age. He was one and thirty. Lavinia was his cross to bear, he often thought. She might have used that second epithet—disagreeable—to describe herself.

"You will change your mind when we reach Mayfair," he assured her.

"Oh, Lavinia," Georgina said without turning her head

from the window, "look at all the people and all the buildings."

"The streets are not paved with gold," Lavinia said. "But then we have not arrived at Mayfair yet. You must not be disappointed too soon, Georgina."

Nathaniel pursed his lips. His cousin was not without her own brand of caustic wit.

"I can scarce believe we are actually here," Georgina said. "I really thought you were funning us when you first suggested it after Christmas, Nathaniel. Will we receive *many* invitations, do you suppose? At home you have enormous consequence, but here you are but a baronet, after all."

"I am a gentleman of wealth and property, Georgie," he told her. "It will suffice. We will be invited everywhere. By the end of the Season, I will have found suitable husbands for both of you, never fear. Or Margaret will have done so."

Margaret, their eldest sister, two years his senior, was the wife of Baron Ketterly. She too was coming to London with her husband with the express purpose of sponsoring and chaperoning her second youngest sister and her cousin, the only two remaining unmarried females in the family. There had been six of them, counting Lavinia. Two of them had been married before Nathaniel returned home two years before, summoned by his ailing father. He had been away from home for years before that, first as a cavalry officer with Wellington's armies during the Peninsular Wars and Waterloo, and then for another year after he sold out, indulging in every imaginable extravagance and debauchery with his friends.

But he had gone home, albeit reluctantly, had buried his father a mere three months later, and had proceeded to take up the life of a country gentleman and to run his estate, which had been somewhat neglected during the last years of his father's life. He had married two of his sisters to respectable suitors, and had been left with just these two. At Margaret's suggestion, made over the Christmas holiday, he had considered bringing them to London, to the great marriage mart.

It was going to feel very good indeed to have the last of them married and respectably settled, to have his home and his life to himself at last. One of his main reasons for purchasing his commission had been his desire to escape from a home that was beset by females. Not that he was not fond of his sisters. But there were limits to a man's endurance. He had certainly never imagined that he would spend several years of the prime of his life organizing matches for his sisters—and Lavinia.

"I am sure, Nathaniel," Georgina said now, "there will be scores of ladies lovelier than I—and younger. I cannot imagine that I will attract many suitors."

"Do you wish to attract *many,* then, Georgie?" he asked with a smile and a wink. "Would one wealthy, handsome one not be enough—and one who loved you and whom you loved?"

The anxiety went from her face and she laughed. "Yes, such a one would suffice very nicely indeed," she said.

Georgina, he rather suspected, had had her heart broken at one time. Their youngest sister had married almost a year before. But her husband, a personable young gentleman of some fortune who had leased a property not far from Bowood a few months before Nathaniel's return there, had apparently directed his attentions to Georgina before turning them on Eleanor. Georgie, a young lady of tender heart and strong loyalties, had often stayed at home instead of attending assemblies and other entertainments with her sisters. She had stayed in order to give her company to their ailing father, who had always seemed to grow worse when his girls were planning some outing. And so her suitor had chosen to pay court to the more easily accessible Eleanor.

Twenty was an advanced age for a young lady to be making her come-out. But not too advanced—certainly not for a young lady of Georgina's delicate prettiness and sweet disposition. And she would have a more than adequate dowry. Nathaniel had no real fears for her.

Now, Lavinia . . .

"You need not look at me like that, Nat," she said as soon as his eyes turned in her direction and long before they could have assumed any expression that might be referred to as *that*. "I agreed to come. I even agreed quite readily as I wished to see London and to visit all the galleries and museums. I will even concede that there will be some pleasure in being outfitted by a modiste who will probably know what she is doing—Margaret has always spoken highly of her, anyway. And of course it will be interesting to attend balls and to witness all the follies of human nature as exhibited by its wealthiest and most privileged members. But nothing will prevail upon me, I warn you—*nothing*—to take my place in the marriage mart. Thank you kindly, but I am not for sale."

Nathaniel sighed inwardly. There was nothing delicately pretty about Lavinia. She was a ravishing beauty, a surprising fact when she had sported carroty red hair as a child and had shot up to a gangly and quite shapeless height before he had left home, with freckles and large teeth that did not fit her face. But he had returned home to find that her hair had been interestingly transformed to a shining flame red, that the freckles had disappeared, that her teeth, strong and white and even, now belonged with her face and enhanced its loveliness, and that shape had more than caught up with her height.

She had over the years—and she was *four* and twenty—refused probably every eligible gentleman, and a few ineligible ones, within a fifteen-mile radius of home, not to mention several who had happened into the neighborhood for one reason or another and would have liked nothing better than to happen out of it again with a red-haired bride.

She had no intention of marrying *anyone ever,* Lavinia always declared. Nathaniel was beginning to believe her. It was a gloomy thought.

"You need not look so glum," she said now. "You could be rid of me in a flash, Nat, if you would just not be so stuffy and release my fortune to me. I am four and twenty, for God's sake.''

"Lavinia," Georgina said reproachfully. Georgie was always the perfect lady. She never took the Lord's name in vain.

"And am not entitled to manage my own fortune until I marry or turn thirty years of age," Lavinia continued. "If Papa were still alive, he should be shot for including such a Gothic clause in his will."

Nathaniel tended to agree. But he could not change the will. And though he could, he supposed, arrange for his cousin to set up her own home somewhere under his supervision—something she longed to do, though he believed the supervision part did not appear large in her imagination—he would prefer to see her married to someone who could handle her and perhaps bring her some happiness. She was not a happy young woman.

Georgina gasped before he could reply—though in truth there was nothing to say that he had not said ad nauseam over the past two years—and drew their attention to the window again.

"Oh look!" she said. "Oh, Nathaniel!" Her hands were clasped to her bosom and she was gazing out at the streets and buildings of Mayfair as if they really were faced with gold.

"I must confess London is improving with every furlong," Lavinia admitted.

Nathaniel drew a deep breath and let it out slowly. He had found himself unexpectedly content with country life, but it felt good to be back in town. And though his sister and his cousin believed that he had come for the sole purpose of giving them a Season and finding them husbands, they were only partly correct.

His three closest friends were also coming to London and had written to beg him to come too. They had been cavalry officers together and had developed a deep friendship based on shared experiences, shared dangers, a shared need to make light of all the dangers and discomforts and to live their lives to the full—both on the battlefield and off it. One fellow officer had dubbed them the Four Horsemen of the Apocalypse for their tendency to be always in the spot where the fighting was thickest and most intense. They had sold out together after Waterloo and had celebrated their survival together for several months after that.

Kenneth Woodfall, Earl of Haverford, and Rex Adams, Viscount Rawleigh, were now married. Each had one son. Both spent most of their time on their country estates, Ken in Cornwall, Rex in Kent. Eden Wendell, Baron Pelham, was single and unsettled, the only one of them still to feel the restlessness and the need to grasp at every pleasure life had to offer that had consumed them all at first. Nathaniel had not seen any of them for almost two years, but they stayed in close communication with one another. The other three were to spend the spring in London. It did not take Nathaniel long to decide that he would join them there, especially since he had already been toying with Margaret's suggestion.

And there was yet another reason for his coming to town. He felt a strong aversion to the idea of marrying even though there were several eligible young ladies in the neighborhood of his estate and he had plenty of female relatives eager to play matchmaker. Indeed it was Margaret's declared intention not only to find husbands for Georgie and Lavinia in London, but also to find a wife for her brother.

But he had been beset by women for the past two years. He was longing for the time when his home would be his own, when he might come and go as he pleased, be as tidy or as untidy about the house as he pleased, put his booted feet up on the desk in his library if he pleased, or even on the best sofa in the drawing room, for that matter. He looked forward to the time when he might walk into any of the dayrooms in the house without looking about him in fear of seeing yet another new piece of embroidery or crocheting adorning tabletops or backs of sofas or arms of chairs. He looked forward to the time when he might bring one or two of his favorite dogs into the house if he pleased.

He had no intention of replacing sisters and a cousin with a wife, who would of necessity be with him for the rest of his life, managing his home for his supposed comfort. He intended to remain a bachelor—at least for a good number of years to come. Time enough to marry when he was in his forties, if at that time he found himself unable to quell the guilt of not having even tried to get an heir for Bowood.

But although his mind was quite set against a wife, he felt an almost overpowering need for a woman. Sometimes it amazed and even alarmed him to realize that he had not had one for almost two years. Yet all through his years with the army he had been as lusty as any man and a good deal lustier than most—he and Rex and Ken and Ede had never lacked for willing partners. And those months after Waterloo had been one continuous orgy—or so it seemed in memory. He supposed he must have taken a few nights off for sleep. Though perhaps not.

It was next to impossible in the country to satisfy his very natural male appetites without at the same time saddling himself with a wife. But London was a different matter. Georgie and Lavinia were without a doubt his primary responsibility. But they would not take all his time. There would be all sorts of activities that were for ladies only, and Margaret was sure to be a diligent chaperon. Besides, his nights would be his own except on those occasions when there was a ball—though they would be frequent enough, he realized.

He intended to slake his appetites quite thoroughly while he was in town. Eden would be sure to have a suggestion or two on the topic.

Yes, it definitely felt good to be back. His carriage drew to a halt before a tall, fine-looking house on Upper Brook Street. It was the house Nathaniel had leased for the Season. It was, he knew, not far from Park Lane or from Hyde Park itself. It was in one of the best neighborhoods of Mayfair.

He vaulted out of the carriage even before his coachman had put down the steps, and looked up at the house. He had always taken bachelor lodgings when he had stayed in London. But with a sister and a cousin to bring out, of course, a house was necessary. It felt good to stretch his legs and to breathe in fresh air. He turned to hand down the ladies.

Early the following morning a lady sat alone at the escritoire in the sitting room of her home on Sloan Terrace, brushing the feather of her quill pen across her chin as she studied the figures set out neatly on the paper spread before her. Her slippered foot smoothed lightly over the back of her dog, a collie who was snoozing contentedly beneath the desk.

There was enough money without dipping into her woefully meager savings. The bills for coal and candles had been paid a week ago—they were always a considerable expense. She did not have to worry about the salaries of her three servants—they were taken care of by a government grant. And of course the house was hers—given to her by the same government. The quarterly pension money that had been paid her last week—the coal and candle bills had been paid out of it—would just stretch to pay off this new debt.

She would not, of course, be able to buy the new evening gown she had been promising herself or the new half boots. Or that bonnet she had seen in a shop window on Oxford Street when out with her friend Gertrude two days ago—the day before she had been presented with this new debt.

*Debt*—what a sad euphemism! For a moment there was a sick lurching in her stomach and panic clawed at her. She drew a slow breath and forced her mind to deal with practicalities.

The bonnet was easily expendable. It would have been a mere extravagance anyway. But the gown . . .

Sophia Armitage sighed aloud. It was two years since she had had a new evening gown. And that, even though it had been chosen for her presentation at Carlton House to no less a personage than the Regent, the Prince of Wales, was of the dullest dark blue silk and the most conservative of designs. Although she had been out of mourning, she had felt the occasion called for extreme restraint. She had been wearing that gown ever since.

She had so hoped this year to have a new one. Although she was invited almost everywhere, she did not usually accept invitations to the more glittering *ton* events. This year, though, she felt obliged to put in an appearance at some of them at least. This year Viscount Houghton, her brother-in-law, her late husband's brother, was in town with his family. Sarah, at the age of eighteen, was to make her come-out. Edwin and Beatrice, Sophia knew, hoped desperately that they would find a suitable husband for the girl during the next few months. They were not wealthy and could ill afford a second Season for her next year.

But they were kindness itself to Sophia. Although her father had been a coal merchant, albeit a wealthy one, and Walter's father had resisted her marriage to his son, Edwin and Beatrice had treated her with unfailing generosity ever since Walter's death. They would have given her a home and an allowance. They wanted her now to attend the grander events of the Season with them.

Of course, it could do them nothing but good to be seen in public with her, though she did not believe they were motivated by that fact alone. The truth was that Walter, Major Walter Armitage, who had fought as a cavalry officer throughout the war years in Portugal and Spain, always doing his duty, never distinguishing himself, had died at Waterloo in the performance of an act of extraordinary bravery. He had saved the lives of several superior officers, the Duke of Wellington's included, and then he had gone dashing off on foot into the thick of dense fighting in order to rescue a lowly lieutenant who had been unhorsed. Neither of them had survived. Walter had been found with his arms still clasped protectively around the younger man. He had been in the act of carrying him to safety.

Walter had been mentioned in dispatches. He had been mentioned personally by the Duke of Wellington. His deed

of valor, culminating in his own death while trying to save
an inferior, had caught the imagination of that most soft-
hearted of gentlemen, the Prince of Wales, and so, a year
after his death, Major Armitage had been honored at Carlton House and decorated posthumously. His widow, who
had shown her devotion by following the drum throughout
the Peninsular campaigns and Waterloo, must not suffer
from the death of so brave a man. She had been gifted with
a modest home in a decent neighborhood of London and
the services of three servants. She had been granted a pension which, though modest, enabled her to achieve an independence of either her brother-in-law or her own brother,
who had recently taken over the business on their father's
death.

Walter himself had left her almost nothing. The sizable
dowry that had persuaded him to marry her—though she
believed he had had an affection for her too—had been
spent during the course of their marriage.

Life had been rather pleasant for a year after that appearance at Carlton House. For some reason the event had
aroused considerable interest. It had been reported in all the
London papers and even in some provincial ones. Sophia
had found that in the absence of Walter himself, *she* had
become the nation's heroine. Although the daughter of a
merchant and the widow of the younger son of a viscount,
a lowly person indeed, she was much sought after. Every
hostess wished to boast of having the famous Mrs. Sophia
Armitage as her guest. Sophia grew accustomed to telling
stories about the life of a cavalry officer's wife following
the drum.

Even last year, when she might have expected her fame
to have waned, it was suddenly revived when Lieutenant
Boris Pinter, a younger son of the Earl of Hardcastle, and
a fellow officer whom Walter had not even liked, had arrived in London and chosen to regale the *ton* with the story
of the time when Walter, at considerable risk to his own
life, had saved Pinter's when he had been a mere ensign

and had got into danger through his own carelessness and naïveté.

The *ton* had been enchanted. Their love affair with Major Armitage's widow had continued unabated.

And then she had been presented with the first of the great debts, as she had come to think of them. She had been innocent enough to believe it was also the last. But there had been another, slightly larger, one month after that. That time she had *hoped* it was the last. Hope had blossomed over the winter, when nothing else had been forthcoming.

But it had happened again. Just yesterday. A new debt, slightly larger than the second had been. And this time she had understood. She had spent a sleepless night pacing and understanding that her comfortable world had gone—perhaps forever. This time she was without hope. This would not be the last of such demands. Not by any means.

She knew she would go on trying to pay. She knew she must. Not only for her own sake. But how would she pay the next one? With her savings? What about the next after that?

She set down the pen and bowed her head. She closed her eyes in an attempt to ward off the dizziness that threatened. She must live life one day at a time. If she had learned nothing else during her years with the army, she had learned that. Not even always one day at a time. Sometimes it had been reduced to hours or even minutes. But always one at a time.

A cold nose was nudging at her hand and she lifted it to pat her dog's head and smile rather wanly.

"Very well, then, Lass," she said just as if the dog had made the suggestion, "one day at a time it is. Though to borrow some of Walter's vocabulary, I find myself in one devil of a pickle."

Lass lifted her head to invite a scratching beneath the chin.

The door of the sitting room opened and Sophia raised her head, a cheerful smile on her lips.

"Aunt Sophie," Sarah Armitage said brightly, "I could not sleep for a moment longer. What a relief to find that you are already up. Oh, do get down, Lass, you silly hound. Dog paws and muslin do not make a good combination. Mama is to take me for a final fitting for my new clothes later this morning, and we are to ride in the carriage in the park this afternoon. Papa is to take us. He says that *everyone* rides in the park at the fashionable hour."

"And you cannot wait to return home so that all the excitement may begin," Sophia said, getting to her feet after putting the paper with its figurings inside one of the cubbyholes at the back of her desk.

Sarah had been so restless with pent-up excitement the afternoon before that Sophia had suggested a walk back to Sloan Terrace and an evening and night spent there. Sarah had accepted the treat with alacrity. But now, of course, she was terrified that she would miss something. Soon— two evenings after tomorrow—all the activities she so eagerly anticipated would begin with the first major ball of the Season at Lady Shelby's.

"Shall we have some breakfast and then walk back through the park?" Sophia suggested. "It will be quiet and quite enchanting at this hour of the morning. And it looks to be as lovely a day as yesterday turned out to be. You need not dash about the room with such exuberant glee, Lass. There is to be breakfast first and you are not going to persuade me otherwise." She led the way to the dining room, her collie prancing after them, since Sophia had been unwise enough to use the word *walk* in her hearing.

How wonderful it would feel to be eighteen again, Sophia thought, looking wistfully at her niece, and to have all of life, all of the world, ahead of one. Not that she was ancient herself. She was only eight and twenty. Sometimes she felt closer to a hundred. The ten years since her marriage had not been easy ones, though she must not complain. But now, just when she had achieved some measure of independence and had made a circle of amiable friends and had expected to be able to make a life of quiet contentment for herself . . .

Well, the debts had arrived.

It would have been so very pleasant, she thought with an unaccustomed wave of self-pity, to have been able to afford a new gown, to have been able to afford to have her hair trimmed and styled, to have been able to convince herself that though not beautiful or even pretty, she was at least passably elegant. She had *never* felt passably elegant or frivolous or lovely. Well, not at least since the days of her youth, when she had deluded herself into believing that she was pretty enough to compare with anyone.

The truth was that she was dumpy and frumpy and unattractive and—and in a sorry state of self-pity indeed. She smiled in self-mockery and set herself to amuse Sarah with her conversation. She ignored Lass, who sat beside her chair breathing loudly and gazing unwaveringly into her face.

# TWO

His friends had arrived in town before him, Nathaniel discovered as soon as he entered the house on Upper Brook Street. There was a note awaiting him, written and signed by Rex but obviously composed when all three of them had been present, suggesting that if he arrived as planned on that particular day, he meet them for an early-morning ride in Hyde Park the following day.

The day, as he saw when he had awakened and crossed his bedchamber to throw back the curtains to look out on it, stretching as he did so, promised well. The sky was clear of clouds and from the look of the trees there was very little wind. He went into his dressing room and rang for his valet.

He was the first to arrive at the park, though his friends were not far behind him. There was a great deal of hand-shaking and backslapping and laughter. There was no friendship quite like that of one's long-standing male friends, Nathaniel decided. They had shared danger and discomfort and victory and life itself together for a number of years. The bonds would be lifelong.

Yes, it certainly felt good to be back in town. Not that Hyde Park in the early morning felt particularly urban. Its sweeping lawns and thick groves of trees and interlacing paths, its grazing animals and chirping birds could easily have beguiled the beholder into imagining himself to be in the park of some grand country estate. But there was something about Hyde Park, something intangible, that proclaimed it quite unmistakably to be at the center of the busiest, the grandest, the most dynamic city in the world.

There was that energy he had felt yesterday when his carriage had entered the streets of the city. It was London.

After the initial flurry of greetings, they rode for a while without a great deal of conversation, exercising their horses by giving them their heads, though a race inevitably developed and ended with much laughter.

"Now, what was the wager?" Eden asked. "One hundred guineas each to the winner, I do believe?" Eden had won the race, of course.

"Are all your dreams as pleasant, Ede?" Nathaniel asked.

"You had a start of a good length and a half over me anyway, Eden," Kenneth said, "and beat me by a length. By my reckoning that makes me the winner. Yes, I believe I heard one hundred guineas too."

"Have you heard the rumor that all Cornishmen are mad, Nat?" Rex asked. "I begin to think it is more than rumor. It must be the sea air in that part of the country. Ken used to be as sane as the best of us."

"Which is not, when you come to think of it," Eden said, "saying a great deal, Rex."

They rode onward at a more leisurely pace, enjoying their surroundings and one another's company.

"Well, Nat," Rex said after a while, "how have you enjoyed playing dull and respectable country squire for the past two years?"

"It is the old case of the pot and the kettle," Eden said, cocking one eyebrow. "You scarce stir from Stratton Park these days, Rex."

"But at least Rex has the excuse of being an old married man." Kenneth grinned as he held up a staying hand.

"As am I, Eden, of course. But Rex has been busier, one must confess. Moira and I still boast only one son, whereas Rex . . . Well, it may not be two *sons*. The second one could be a daughter. There is no knowing yet, is there? We will be kept in suspense for another—what? Four months, Rex? Five?"

"Closer to five." Rex chuckled. "Catherine has convinced herself that with the fashion for loose-fitting, high-waisted gowns, her condition will have gone quite undetected. I hope none of you will have the indelicacy to utter some pointed witticism in her hearing."

"Are you indelicate, Nat?" Eden elevated the second eyebrow to balance the first. "Do you utter witticisms, Ken? You are never looking at me, are you, Rex? Me, the soul of discretion?" Then he sighed and changed the subject. "Just three years ago there was Waterloo still to be fought and we dreamed, the four of us, of what we would do with our lives if we should survive."

"Sheer unalloyed, twenty-four-hour-a-day pleasure," Nathaniel said. "Every excess and debauchery known to man. You must admit that we gave it a good run, Ede. I swear we did not look at the world through sober eyes for six months or longer."

"We needed the release after all the tensions and dangers that had gone before," Kenneth said. "But it did not take long to discover that pleasure for its own sake quickly loses its appeal."

"You speak, of course," Eden said, his voice deliberately bored, "for yourself, Ken? I do believe I am the only one of us who can keep a vow. Nat, now, is up to his eyeballs in women."

"The devil!" Rex said, laughing. "It sounds like a single man's dream."

"Not," Eden said, "in *women,* Rex, but in ladies—relatives. Sisters, cousins, aunts, great-aunts, grandmothers. I warned him—I did, did I not, Nat? Two years ago when he insisted on going home, I warned him how it would be. Twenty unmarried sisters and thirty unmarried female—and resident—cousins. No dream, Rex—it is every man's nightmare.''

''The number increases every time you refer to them,'' Nathaniel said. ''I have five sisters, Ede, two of whom were married before I went home. And only one resident cousin, though sometimes she seems more like thirty, I must confess. And I have already succeeded in finding husbands for Edwina and Eleanor. There are only Georgina and Lavinia left. A Season in London should do the trick nicely.''

''And what about you, Nat?'' Kenneth looked at him with raised eyebrows. ''Once you have disposed of all your female dependents, will you take a wife? Is that part of your plan in coming to town? Moira and I will start to play matchmaker, will we? It is a role I rather fancy playing. Do you wish to help, Rex?'' He was grinning broadly.

Eden groaned. ''They are envious of us, Nat,'' he said. ''With all due respect to Moira and Catherine, they are envious. Hold out against them, my lad.''

But Nathaniel chuckled. ''You are looking at a confirmed bachelor, my friends,'' he said. ''No leg shackles for me, thank you kindly.''

Eden cheered with a whoop that would have been embarrassing, loud as it was, had the park not been deserted—or almost so. There was a workingman hurrying along a path not far distant, a maidservant, walking a dog almost as large as she, had passed them a minute before, and two females were approaching on foot from a distance, also with a dog.

''But not a celibate bachelor, it is to be hoped,'' Eden said. ''I have some delights in store for you the like of which you have rarely experienced before, Nat. Rex and Ken are no longer eligible. Just you and I. Starting tonight. Why waste even one more night of your stay in London, after all? You had better take a nap this afternoon, my lad. You are going to need all the energy you can muster.''

''Dear me,'' Rex said faintly. ''Were we ever this young or this jaded, Ken?''

''I think perhaps we were, Rex,'' Kenneth said. ''Once

long, long ago in the dark ages. I can even remember a time when we would have winced at the thought of respectability. And positively blanched at the very idea of a monogamous relationship.''

Splendid, Nathaniel thought. Tonight. Trust Eden not to waste time. There were all sorts of duties to be performed, of course, even today. This afternoon and during the next few days he would have to pay calls at all the right houses, leaving his card and making his presence known. Tomorrow Margaret and John were expected to arrive in town and there would be all the upheaval of getting Georgina and Lavinia ready to face the whirlwind. He would have to be seen with them. He would have to escort them everywhere. He had no intention of neglecting his responsibilities while he engaged in the sort of excesses and debaucheries that had left him feeling curiously dissatisfied two years before. He was Sir Nathaniel Gascoigne, baronet, now. He was a brother and a cousin first and foremost.

But there would be a few days of relative quiet. He would not, after all, have to accompany the girls to modistes and milliners and shoemakers, and all the rest. He would merely have to pay the bills. He could allow himself some time for personal enjoyment—for rides like this in the park with his friends, for visits to White's Club and Tattersall's and the races. For women. His need had been held at bay while he was at Bowood. Now it was not to be denied. In the future, he decided, he must make frequent visits to town. Two years was just too long a time.

But he had been woolgathering. The two females who had been approaching them on foot for some time, their black-and-white collie dashing about exploring while never losing sight of them, had drawn closer and Eden was whistling under his breath.

''A diamond of the first water, would you not agree, Nat?'' he said quietly. ''Now, if one were in the market for a bride . . .''

The younger and taller of the two ladies was indeed both pretty and elegant, and she was finely clad in a high-waisted walking dress of a pale blue color that complemented her very blond hair and fair complexion to perfection. She was also an extremely young lady—probably younger even than Georgina.

"But one is not, Ede," he said firmly. "And if one were, one could do better than rob cradles."

Eden chuckled.

But Kenneth was exclaiming loudly enough to be heard by the ladies. "By Jove," he said heartily, "it is! Just see who it is, fellows."

The other three looked more closely at the two ladies. The second one, smaller, older, less elegant, less fashionably clad than her companion, had at first appeared almost invisible beside her. But it was on this second lady that their eyes all finally alighted—and they looked at her with equal astonishment and pleasure.

"Sophie!" Rex exclaimed. "By all that is wonderful!"

"Sophie Armitage!" Eden said simultaneously. "Devil take it, but you are a sight for sore eyes."

Kenneth swept off his beaver hat and smiled dazzlingly. "What a wonderful pleasure this is, Sophie," he said.

"Sophie, my dear." Nathaniel leaned down from his horse's back and stretched out his right hand toward her. "This is a pleasant surprise to greet a fellow on his first morning in London in two years. You are looking well."

She shook his hand, her handshake as firm as a man's, as it always had been, Nathaniel remembered, and smiled at each of them in turn with genuine warmth. "The Four Horsemen," she said. "And all in company together, looking as handsome and as dashing as ever, just as if three years had not passed. But it is early morning and perhaps I am dreaming." She was laughing. "Do you see four gentlemen on horseback here, Sarah? Four of the handsomest rogues in England? Or am I imagining them?" But even as she spoke she was busily shaking hands with the other three.

Dear Sophie. She had been in the Peninsula with them. Her husband had been another comrade of theirs, and she had traveled everywhere with him, tougher, more resilient than most of the men. She had quietly looked after her husband's needs and had taken all his fellow officers under her wing too, tending wounds, mending tears in uniforms, brushing out stains, sewing buttons back on even though there had been valets and batmen enough to perform the tasks for them. Her hands might as well be busy while she listened to their nonsense and their idle chatter, she had always said when they had thought to protest. She had cooked for them sometimes too, though none of the other officers' wives would have so demeaned themselves. They had wangled many an invitation to sit at Walter Armitage's table.

Strangely, Nathaniel thought now as he smiled down at her, genuinely glad to see her again, as they all were, they had never really thought of Sophie as they had thought of other women in her position. They had not thought of her as frail and in need of their chivalrous gallantry. Yet she must have been very young indeed when she went to the Peninsula with Armitage and she was small enough to arouse the male protective instinct. But she had always seemed more like a comrade than a mere woman, someone with whom they had all been thoroughly comfortable. Even Armitage had seemed to treat her more as a friend than as a wife. Though there was no knowing, of course, what sort of a relationship they had had within the privacy of their own billets.

Poor Sophie had listened to many a story that would have caused other ladies to swoon quite away—and told in the sort of coarse language that would have caused additional fits of the vapors. She had never flinched and had never reproached them—neither had her husband. It had never occurred to them to modify either their language or their topics of conversation around her. Not that they had not respected her, but—well, they had respected her as an equal.

Everyone had liked Sophie. Perhaps because Sophie had always appeared to like everyone. It would have been hard to find a more cheerful soul. And she was beaming up at them now with all the old good humor, all the old air of camaraderie, even though she had been a widow for almost three years. And the old slight shabbiness of clothing. And the old untidy wisps of curly brown hair escaping the brim of her bonnet. Damn but it was good to see her again.

"We are real enough to bellow *ouch* if you pinched us, Sophie," Nathaniel said, "as are you, by Jove. Are you still basking in the glory of Walter's fame?" Perhaps, he thought too late, the words had been too carelessly spoken. Perhaps she grieved too deeply to do any basking. But one could not somehow imagine Sophie distraught with grief—certainly not after three years.

"Oh, yes indeed," she said, smiling. "I thought people would forget within a fortnight. But it has been almost two years now since my day at Carlton House and still people remember what a great hero he was. Doors are still wide open to me despite my extreme lack of presence. And now Sarah and Lewis are here for the Season with their mama and papa and *they* are being received with deference because they are Walter's niece and nephew. It is most gratifying. Walter would be thrilled—and amused, I daresay." Her eyes twinkled with merriment.

"Everyone loves a hero—and a heroine, Sophie," Nathaniel said.

"Walter would be genuinely pleased for you, Sophie," Kenneth said. "And what is this about your lack of presence? You are as conceited as you ever were, I see."

Sophie laughed and then sobered. "Oh, pardon me," she said, turning to the young lady half hidden behind her. "May I have the honor of presenting my niece? Walter's niece, that is. Sarah Armitage, daughter of Viscount Houghton, here for the Season with her parents and her brother. Four of your uncle Walter's dear friends, Sarah." She presented each of them in turn while her young niece—she could not be a day over eighteen, Nathaniel decided—blushed and curtsied and peered shyly up at them.

"Your horses are eager to be moving," Sophie said with great practicality after they had all made their bows to the girl and gazed at her appreciatively, "and I daresay you all are too. And my dog is eager to find new trees to sniff. It has been a great pleasure to meet you again. I do hope you enjoy your stay in town. Good morning to you."

"But we must see you again," Rex said, laying one arm across the neck of his horse and leaning forward. "We cannot simply lose you again after finding you, Sophie. My wife and I are entertaining some friends at Rawleigh House the evening after tomorrow. I believe you qualify. Will you come? I will have my wife call upon you with a formal invitation if you wish."

"Oh, you are married, of course," she said, smiling warmly at Rex. "I had heard that. I would not have set wagers on your being the first, Rex, I must say, but you were, were you not? Well, Lady Rawleigh is a fortunate woman to have such a handsome, charming husband, though one can only hope that she is of suitably strong character—she also has a rogue for a husband. I have not forgotten you." Her eyes were twinkling again. She was wagging one finger at him.

"Now, Sophie," he said, sounding aggrieved, "I shall rescind my invitation if you intend regaling Catherine's ears with tales from my past."

"Me?" she said, laughing. "My lips are firmly buttoned, I promise you. You need not send Lady Rawleigh on a formal visit, though. I daresay she has enough to do without calling upon me. I would be delighted to attend your gathering of friends."

"Do you keep a carriage, Sophie?" Eden asked. "If not, I would be pleased to take you up in mine and escort you to Rawleigh House."

"Now, a carriage," she said, lifting the forefinger she had just been wagging, and laughing at the same time, "is one thing the government did not think of granting me. Perhaps if Walter had saved the life of the Prince of Wales . . . But poor Walter, he is not here to enjoy the joke and he really *would* have enjoyed it. Thank you, Eden, that would be remarkably civil of you."

"And I shall escort you home again at the end of the evening," Nathaniel said. "It would be my pleasure, my dear."

She beamed at each of them in turn before firmly taking her leave. She had not changed. She had never pressed her company on anyone. It was always they who had pressed theirs on her. It had never occurred to any of them to wonder if sometimes Sophie would not have preferred more privacy or more time alone with Walter.

"I feel ashamed of myself," Rex said as they rode onward. "I remember reading all the reports of the honors paid poor Armitage—half with amusement, I must confess. One would have sworn that every other British soldier on the battlefield was lounging at his ease, twiddling his thumbs, and that only Armitage, like an avenging angel with glittering sword and flashing eyes and ginger mustaches—though those last were not mentioned in any of the reports—was saving them from the froggish brutes led onto the slaughtering fields by the Corsican monster. Those reports, as I distinctly remember, *did* overflow with all those clichés as well as every other known to man. But then I believe Sophie is amused by it all too—she always had the best sense of humor of almost any woman I have known— or any man, for that matter. Anyway, I remember reading about the London town house. Yet it has never occurred to me to call upon her when I have been in town."

"Or to me either, Rex," Eden said, "though I have spent a great deal more time in London than any of you during the past two years. And I have never run into her until today. Good old Sophie. She was one of the best comrades a man ever had. I am glad you invited her to Rawleigh House."

"I want Catherine to meet her," Rex said. "They will like each other, I believe. And Moira too, Ken."

They were all smiling cheerfully, Nathaniel noticed. As who would not on a lovely morning in lovely surroundings and in company with close friends? But Sophie had always had that affect on the men with whom she had been surrounded. She had always made a day seem just a little brighter—though perhaps they had been unconscious of exactly who or what it was that had made them more cheerful. It would be good to meet her at greater leisure at Rex's and to have a chat with her. It would be good to reminisce.

He *had* written to her on the occasion of Walter's posthumous decoration and had had a very civil reply. He had not written after that. He was a single man and it had suddenly occurred to him that she was now a single lady and it was not proper for them to exchange letters. But he had not forgotten her in the intervening years, as the others appeared to have done—it was so easy to forget people who had been really quite close friends during the war. He had fully intended calling upon her, taking Georgina and Lavinia with him. Though he had not been certain that she would be in town or at the same house. He was glad to discover that he had not lost touch with her and would see her again.

But that was two nights hence. In the meantime there were tonight and tomorrow night—and he intended to savor to the full all they had to offer. He supposed he would allow Eden to choose the exact place and mode of entertainment. It was, after all, almost two years since he had been in town himself. He guessed that all the old brothels still flourished and perhaps even some of the same girls. But Eden could be relied upon to have more up-to-date information. And Eden could be trusted to choose the best.

There was enormous pleasure in anticipating the night ahead. And he positively refused, Nathaniel thought, to react to his own anticipation as the staid country gentleman he had become. He refused to think about the dubious morality of employing a whore for the night. He was going to enjoy himself.

Deuce take it, but it had been a long time. Too long. Far too long.

"Breakfast at White's?" Eden suggested. "And a morning of looking at the papers and perhaps wandering over to Jackson's boxing saloon? This feels quite like old times."

"Not quite, Eden," Kenneth said. "Moira would have my head if I absented myself for the whole morning. Besides which, it would give me no great pleasure to absent myself. We are going to bring Jamie for a romp in the park before it gets too busy this afternoon."

"We dull married fellows, Eden," Rex said, laughing. "You will have to join our ranks one of these days and find out what all the attraction is."

Eden shuddered theatrically. "Many thanks for the thought, old boy," he said, "but no thanks. And do you have to return to the twenty sisters too, Nat?"

"Not even to the one sister and one cousin," Nathaniel said. "They both expressed their intention of sleeping until noon after the tedium of the journey. Lead the way to White's."

What an exhilarating morning it was turning out to be, he thought. He did not doubt that he would be happy enough to return to Bowood for the summer—alone, he hoped—but while he was here he was going to enjoy everything that town and society—and the demimonde—had to offer.

# THREE

SOPHIA ARRIVED HOME feeling utterly depressed and really rather shaken. But she could not immediately close the door on the world. There was her manservant to be smiled upon and to be listened to. Her servants had a habit of sharing all their household and personal woes with her, though they always handled any problem with perfect competence. It was as if they needed the reassurance of her approval. This morning there had been some problem with the coalman, who had tried to deliver enough coal for a winter month when it was already April. The manservant had put him firmly in his place, Mrs. Armitage would be pleased to know.

"You did the right thing, Samuel," Sophia assured him. "Next month he will be sure to be more careful."

"Yes, ma'am," he said, making her a deferential bow. "Shall I have tea sent up to your sitting room?"

"That would be lovely, thank you," she said with a smile. "And you might as well have Lass's dish sent up too, as she thinks she is genteel people and hates eating in the kitchen."

"Yes, ma'am." Samuel allowed himself an almost conspiratorial smirk.

And so even after Sophia had arrived in her sitting room

after taking her outdoor garments to her dressing room and patting her hair into something resembling order, she had to hold herself together until Pamela had arrived with the tray and had explained that the cup Mrs. Armitage usually used in the mornings had unfortunately slipped to the kitchen floor from Pamela's own hands and been smashed into a thousand pieces.

"For which Cook says as how you may dock my wages, ma'am," Pamela, the maid-of-all-work, said, sounding both aggrieved and anxious. "Though it were not my fault. If Samuel had not yelled out 'Oi!' quite so loud when the coalman come and tried to pull one over on him, ma'am, I would not have dropped the cup. I am very sorry, ma'am."

"We will blame the coalman," Sophia said cheerfully. "I am sure he has broad enough shoulders, Pamela. Though I do not suppose we can dock *his* wages, can we? This is a pretty enough cup. Prettier than the broken one, in fact."

"Yes, ma'am." Pamela curtsied. "But I am right sorry about the other one."

"Think no more of it." Sophia was desperate to be alone.

She reached for the teapot as soon as the door had closed behind the maid and she had set down the dog's dish. She poured tea into the ugly green-and-gold cup that had replaced her dainty pink rosebud one, then sat back and closed her eyes. Alone at last!

Sarah had been thrilled to meet the Horsemen. She always was, of course, when she met new gentlemen, something she had only recently begun to do, as she had been in the schoolroom until her eighteenth birthday just after Christmas. She looked upon every gentleman as a prospective suitor. But she had been excited by her meeting with these four, as what lady would not be? They were all, without exception, extraordinarily handsome men. The women in the Peninsula—women of all ages and social rank and marital status—had often amused themselves with trying to decide which one was the most handsome. Kenneth was the tallest—though they were all above the average in height—and he had the distinction of his very blond hair and aquiline features. Rex had been blessed with very dark hair and dark, compelling eyes and had, in addition to these assets, a devastating charm. Eden had the distinct advantage of very blue eyes, which he knew well how to use to effect, and he had a devil-may-care attitude to life that women always found attractive. Nathaniel Gascoigne had his slumberous gray eyes and his wonderful smile. As one of the women—a colonel's wife—had once remarked, one could not look at him without imagining his head on a pillow—next to one's own.

The women had all had their favorite, as had Sophia.

Though they had all been quite unashamedly in love with all four.

They had been so full of energy and humor and daredeviltry. They had always been in the thick of battle with their men, never sending enlisted men into dangers they were not willing to face themselves—and always leading the way. If there was danger in a part of the field that was none of their concern, they rode there anyway. They had been in their commander's ill favor as often as they were being congratulated by him. They should be thankful that they were officers rather than enlisted men, he had been fond of telling them—and they had been equally fond of reporting to their friends. They would have been almost constantly at the whipping triangles otherwise for failing to follow orders.

It was Walter who had first called them the Four Horsemen of the Apocalypse. It was ironic that Walter was the one to have so distinguished himself at Waterloo. Not that there had ever been anything of the coward about him. But he had been an unimaginative man, who had fought by the rules, going where he was sent, accomplishing the tasks he had been set.

At Waterloo there must have been innumerable cases of heroism to equal Walter's. It had simply been a case of his being in the right place at the right time—if one considered fame of primary importance. Or in the wrong place at the wrong time if one considered survival of some significance. Walter had died. The Four Horsemen had survived.

Sarah had been delighted to meet them and severely disappointed to be told that two of them were married and that the other two were perhaps a little old for her.

"Oh pooh," she had said. "Older gentlemen are so much more handsome, Aunt Sophie, and so much more *attractive*. Young gentlemen invariably have spots."

Sophia had chuckled. But none of the Four Horsemen would do for Sarah. She might have felt sorry that she had been forced into presenting her niece to them if she had not been convinced that they would be uninterested in so young a girl. They had all had a great deal of experience with life itself and with sexual matters in particular. There had been an endless stream of Spanish and Portuguese beauties all clamoring to share their beds.

Sophia had refused to stay for a second breakfast at Portland Place. She had been eager to get home, to be alone, to digest the morning's unexpected encounter.

She rested her head against the back of her chair and closed her eyes. Coming so closely as it had after the events of yesterday . . . it seemed that the past was never to be put behind her. All the time she had spoken with them, genuinely—oh yes, genuinely glad to see them again, she had been thinking to herself, How would they look at me if they knew? With disgust, contempt, pity? And she had known that the answer mattered to her. Even though she had not seen them for three years and perhaps would never see them again after two evenings hence.

It mattered.

She might try to convince herself that she had accepted those debts—*why* did she persist in calling them that?—for the sake of others: for the sake of Edwin and his family, for the sake of her own brother and his family. And it was true. But she had done it for her sake too. She would not be able to bear . . .

The feeling of safety at seeing them and talking and

laughing with them had been almost overwhelming. Here was safety in solid human form, multiplied fourfold. It had been almost a conscious thought as well as a feeling. But they could offer her no safety, no help. Quite the opposite.

She merely had one more secret to withhold from them. There had always been secrets. Always had, always would. It had become the story of her life. The burden must be carried alone. No one could help.

But there was the illusion of safety when she was with them. She knew that from experience, and it had not always been just illusion. Walter had not been a neglectful husband, but even so, there had been times when danger had threatened and she had had to move quickly from their billet when he was away at his duties—often in adverse weather conditions. She had never done so alone or even with just servants to help. One or more of the Horsemen had always turned up when they were most needed to help and escort her, to point out to her the funny side of the most unfunny situations.

Nathaniel had laughed at her once when they were escaping at reckless speed through a sea of mud and she had fallen from her horse's back when it had slipped. She had been caked with wet, foul-smelling mud, but Nathaniel had hauled her up in front of him, ruining his scarlet jacket, and held her bracketed in the circle of his arms.

"You know, Sophie," he had said, "ladies in London and Paris use mud packs to improve their complexions. They would kill to look as you do now."

She had laughed heartily and tried to mop the mud from her face with an equally muddy glove. "I should be beautiful all over by this day's end, then," she had said. "Walter will not recognize me. He will disown me."

"Never mind, Sophie," he had said. "We will take you in. My coat is going to need a good brushing after it dries."

She had laughed again and felt perfectly safe despite the physical discomfort and the very real dangers posed by traveling at speed through oozing mud and of knowing that

French troops were somewhere in the vicinity. Kenneth and Eden had been close by too. Kenneth had rescued her horse and was leading it beside his own.

Sophia opened her eyes and reached for her cup and saucer. She was parched and there was nothing more soothing than tea.

It had been undeniably good to see them again. How she would have rejoiced if there had not been yesterday. As it was, she was not at all sure she wished to see any of them again. Would she go to Rex's evening of friends at Rawleigh House the evening after tomorrow? Meet them again? Talk with them? Meet Rex's wife? And Kenneth's?

But she knew she would go. The prospect of such an evening was just too seductive to be denied. Besides, Eden was to take her up in his carriage and she did not know where he lived to send a note to tell him not to come.

Of course she would go. In the meantime she must settle this other thing, this *debt*—and hope that it would be the end of the matter. It would not be, of course. It would continue for a number of years. It was impossible to guess just how many letters there had been, to be redeemed now one by one. Where was she to find the means . . .

"Sometimes, you know, Lass," she told her collie, who had finished her meal and had come to lie at her feet, her chin resting on Sophia's slippers, "I wish Walter were still alive so that I might have the pleasure of wringing his neck. Are you shocked?"

If Lass was, she gave no indication.

"I played my part to the very end," Sophia continued, "though it was never easy, Lass." She laughed softly. "The understatement of the decade. Was it too much to expect that Walter play his part? Apparently it was. Men know very little about self-denial. I am thankful you are female, though perhaps I will change my mind when you present me with a litter of puppies one of these days."

On the whole, she thought treacherously, she did not really wish Walter were still alive.

"Thank heaven for your presence, Lass," she said with

rueful humor. "You add respectability to the deplorable habit of talking to oneself."

The next few days were busy ones for Nathaniel. He made what seemed to be endless calls, making his presence known in town, and—more important—the presence of his sister and his cousin, who would need invitations to all the more glittering parties and balls the Season would have to offer. He was only a baronet, after all, as Georgina had reminded him. News of his arrival would not spread as quickly of its own volition as it would have had he been of higher rank. Though it was true that he was a man of wealth and property, and both girls had more than competent dowries.

Some of the calls were more to his liking than others— and not even necessary, perhaps, for the procuring of invitations. Though even at those houses he met other people, and every contact was important. He called upon his friends' wives, for example, entirely from inclination. He called upon his elder sister the day of her arrival, taking Georgina and Lavinia with him, and nothing would do but he must escort them all to Bond Street without a moment's delay. Lord Ketterly, his brother-in-law, had been wise enough to withdraw to his club and was not expected home before dinner. And then Lavinia demanded to be taken to Hookham's Library to take out a subscription. And Georgina remembered that one of her bosom friends at home had told her to be sure to see the Oxford Street shops as soon as she arrived in town—yet two days had passed already. Would dear Nathaniel mind very much . . .

But invitations started to arrive, and appointments had been made with various modistes so that the ladies could be suitably outfitted for what lay ahead, especially for their presentation at court. Fortunately Margaret had assured her brother that his presence would not be necessary on those occasions, though he might escort the girls to Ketterly's town house on each of the appointment dates if he would be so good. Oh, and come to fetch them later, of course.

There was little time left over for more congenial male activities. And life in town after the tranquillity of the country was enormously tiring, Nathaniel was finding.

If he had used his nights for sleeping, of course, he might have found the daytime pace less hectic. But the nights were as busy as the days. Not that he enjoyed the night at the brothel nearly as much as he had expected. Eden had picked out quite unerringly, of course, the very best house and the very best girl for his friend's entertainment. She was very good indeed. Too good, perhaps. Nathaniel felt dazed and slightly out of control of his own bodily reactions—as well as marvelously satiated—after she had brought him to explosive completion for the third time in fewer hours. He left after regaining sufficient energy, even though he had paid for a full night's entertainment and the girl was already showing signs of renewed eagerness to earn every penny. It was a treat, she had told him in her throaty voice after the first time, to have a young and handsome gentleman.

He felt enormous relief at having had a woman again—and equal relief at being away from her and the brothel. He felt somehow soiled, though in deference to his servants he did not follow his first instinct, which was to hurry home and demand that bathwater be brought to his room—at three o' clock in the morning. Instead he joined a card party that he knew Eden had been planning to attend after his own shorter stay at the brothel.

They both wagered modestly and won modestly and drank sparingly. They spent a great deal of time talking and laughing, just being friends together. They went their separate ways well after dawn.

And then the night before Rawleigh's party they went, the two of them, to the theater, joining Kenneth and Moira, Rex and Catherine in Rex's box. He did not fancy a brothel again that night, Nathaniel had told Eden over dinner at White's, or any other night if it was all the same to his friend. He would prefer to employ a mistress for the Season and set her up somewhere where he could visit her at his leisure. The idea of having a different girl every night had lost its appeal sometime during that orgy they had indulged in after Waterloo.

Eden had laughed at him but had suggested the theater and the green room afterward. There were doubtless several dancers who would take Nat's fancy, and if he was in luck at least one of them would be currently without a protector. Eden himself had cried off long-term mistresses ever since the last one, who had been with him for over a year and had been devilish difficult to cast off.

"I felt somehow responsible for her, Nat," he said. "It was almost like trying to shed a wife. It was only by a remarkable stroke of good fortune that I discovered the minx was earning a bit on the side with old Riddings. He is so decrepit with age and riotous living that it is surprising he can still get it up, and maybe he cannot, but he paid well—in diamonds. As far as I know, he is still paying and Nell doubtless does not have to work near as hard as she did when she had me." He chuckled. "But I am not getting myself into that sort of pickle again. No entanglements is my new motto. None whatsoever. A one-nighter suits me admirably."

There *were* some pretty dancers, particularly a tall, lithe, auburn-haired beauty with long legs. And they did visit the green room after the performance—and after discreetly seeing their married friends and their wives drive away in Rex's carriage, having loudly declared their intention of walking together to White's. Rex had grinned and Ken had winked at that announcement, of course, but there had been ladies' sensibilities to consider. A few of the dancers were free, though most of them were in conversation with would-be protectors. The long-legged dancer was one of them, and though she appeared bored when Eden and Nathaniel joined the group of gentlemen surrounding her, she perked up noticeably on sight of them. It was not difficult, Nathaniel found—it was amazing how the old skills came back to one after so long—to cut out the opposition so that soon he was in private tête-à-tête with the girl.

And she was clearly very willing indeed. She had lips his own ached to kiss and a body he unclothed garment by garment in his imagination. She had legs a man would dream of having entwined about his own. She was clean and smelled good. Someone had given her elocution lessons with the result that she did not murder the English language as soon as she opened her mouth. She would be expensive—but he could afford her. She would also be good. She could satisfy all his hungers during the coming months.

He took her hand in his after talking with her for half an hour, bowed over it, raised it almost but not quite to his lips, favored her with his most charming smile—and then saw himself as if from the outside, a mere observer. What was he *doing*? Why was he trying to recapture an unsavory past he had deliberately and gladly given up some years before?

He bade the dancer good night.

"She said *no*, Nat?" Eden asked when they were outside the theater. "I do not believe it. She was devouring you with her eyes. Is there already a protector who would cut up nasty if she defected? Hard luck, old chap. We must try again tomorrow after we leave Rex's. Damn, but I could have sworn—"

"I did not ask her," Nathaniel said.

"Eh?" His friend frowned at him. "She almost tempted *me*, Nat, though she is doubtless angling for something a little more secure than one night. I would have at least tried, though, if you had but signaled your lack of interest."

"I was very interested," Nathaniel said, "Until . . . it is just . . . well, never mind."

"It is just what?" Eden was still frowning.

"She probably has no choice," Nathaniel said. "She probably came to London with the dream of being a great actress. She finds herself instead a mere dancer in a chorus, unable to support herself sufficiently on her wage. And so she must take the obvious additional employment. Poor girl."

"Poor girl?" Eden looked quite mystified. "Nat, my lad,

I never saw you perform, but I can well remember the be-sotted looks all your women shared when they emerged from your bedchamber. Any one of them would have gone back for a second session between your sheets without pay. You do not imagine that country living has made you lose your touch, do you? Eva complained last night? Or looked bored? Or tried to get through the night with the least number of performances?''

"They need the money," Nathaniel said. "We need sex. I am not sure it is a fair exchange, Ede. I suppose I have developed something of a conscience. I am not sure I can do it any longer."

"Well, devil take it, old man," Eden said. "You will have to marry, then."

Nathaniel grimaced. "Hardly," he said. "It is not a strong enough reason for marriage, is it? The simple need for sex?'' They were wandering in the direction of White's, he noticed. Good. A safe, male haven. They would doubt-less end up playing cards again.

"Why do men marry, then?" Eden asked. "*Is* there an-other reason?"

Nathaniel chuckled while his friend grinned. "Proba-bly," he said, "though I'll be damned if I can think of a single one at the moment. I'll not be marrying, Ede. I can-not imagine wanting the same woman living in my home and managing both it and me for the next forty years or so. And to be fair, I cannot imagine any woman wanting to put up with me and my foibles for that same length of time. I have no intention of becoming a monk, of course. There has to be some solution. An *affaire de coeur,* perhaps? They are common enough, are they not? An affair between equals?''

"A married woman?" Eden said. "I would not advise it, Nat. Pistols at dawn can be injurious to the health."

"*Not* a married woman," Nathaniel said quite firmly. "The very idea, Ede."

"And definitely not a young virgin," Eden said. "Irate papas are just as capable of hoisting pistols as injured husbands are. And—worse—they can nudge one quite determinedly into matrimony. Some lovely and lively widow, then. She should not be difficult to find. You have merely to pick one, smile nicely at her, and wait for her to signal that she has accepted the invitation. We will have to put it to the test. This adds considerable piquancy to the idea of attending balls, by Jove. I can hardly wait. In the meantime I shall search my mind for likely prospects. They must be legion—though the chosen one must be both lovely and lively. I insist upon it.''

Nathaniel was laughing. And yet the idea was not without its appeal now that he and Eden between them had thought of it. An affair between equals. Satisfaction for both. The exploitation of neither. It sounded very civilized and very satisfactory. The distaste he had felt a short while ago in the green room had taken him by surprise. But he knew he would not be able to go back there or to any brothel.

And he certainly was not ready—he doubted he ever would be—to start any courtship.

Yes, an affair would be ideal. Though he did not share Eden's optimism about the prospects being legion.

It did not matter, he decided. He was enjoying the company of his friends and he must remember that his primary purpose in being here was to introduce Georgina and Lavinia to polite society and to find them husbands.

He had, after all, had a woman again after two years. Three times. He grinned to himself. At least he knew he could still do it.

He turned into White's with cheerful steps.

# FOUR

S OPHIA  FOUND  HERSELF
after all looking forward with some eagerness to the evening at Rawleigh House. She looked over her array of
gowns suitable for such an occasion and sighed in some
frustration. There were pitifully few and none of them were
new or anywhere near in the first stare of fashion. But she
had known that before she looked. There was no point in
upsetting herself or telling herself that she would send her
excuses to Rawleigh House.

Rex would not mind if she looked shabby and dowdy.
Neither would the others. When had she looked much different, after all? In Spain and Portugal she had always
dressed more for comfort than for elegance or fashion. And
Walter would have smiled as cheerfully and spoken as
heartily to her whether she had worn the finest silks or a
coal sack. He had never noticed her appearance. She had
just been ''Sophie, old girl'' to him.

She sighed. There was no way of being beautiful. Why
imagine that if only she had pretty clothes . . .

She would still be just ''good old Sophie'' to the Four
Horsemen. She would wager a quarter's pension that Lady
Haverford and Lady Rawleigh were extraordinarily beau-
tiful women.

"And then there is me, Lass," she said with a laugh to her collie, who was sitting—against the rules—on her bed.

And so she prepared for the evening at Rawleigh House with calm practicality even though she grimaced at the sight of herself dressed in her dark green silk gown—the one Walter had bought her for the Duchess of Richmond's ball in Brussels before Waterloo—with the inevitable pearls, her only adornment of any real distinction. Her brown hair, thick, very curly, and too long for sense, had been tamed into something resembling respectability, but it was a disaster even so. She had begun to notice lately that short hair was fashionable. She was tempted to have hers cut, but what if her hair cut short turned out to be just as unruly as it was long? What would she do with it then? At least now she could twist it ruthlessly into a topknot.

She smiled ruefully at her image. Nobody looking at her now would guess that her father had been a wealthy man, that Walter's chief inducement to marry her had been her dowry—as hers to marry him had been the simple desire to wed a respectable, decent man.

Walter had had his pride, at least—and he *had* been decent. After a certain—*confrontation* early in their marriage, he had declared his intention of caring for her entirely on his officer's pay, taking not a farthing more from her father. And he had done it too. She had never gone hungry or cold or companionless.

"Oh, Walter," she murmured, fingering her pearls, his only frivolous gift to her—just after their confrontation.

But she turned determinedly from the looking glass and gathered up her shawl and reticule from the bed. Eden would be arriving at any moment and those glorious blue eyes of his would sweep over her before smiling with the rest of his face. He would see—Sophie. Good old Sophie.

Well, there were worse things to be than good old Sophie. And than being the friend—the pal, the chum, the comrade—of the Four Horsemen of the Apocalypse. She looked forward immensely to seeing them again, to conversing with them, to listening to them. And to meeting the two wives.

But she sighed one more time before leaving the safe haven of her own room and making her way downstairs. Why was it that age made handsome men even more attractive? It was not fair to her sex. It definitely was not fair at all. They looked more dashing, more gorgeous than ever, the four of them.

She was eight and twenty years old. She grimaced. Where had the time gone? Where had she misplaced her youth? What was ahead for her? What was there to look forward to? Especially now . . .

She gave herself a mental shake. One day at a time. And this evening she was to spend at Rawleigh House.

Nathaniel had left his sister and his cousin at home in a fever of excitement. At least, he had left *Georgina* in a fever of excitement. It was quite beneath Lavinia's dignity to admit to any such emotion. She had been apparently engrossed in the pages of one of her library books. But even she, he suspected, was excited at the prospect of her first London ball the following evening. Tomorrow their Season would begin in earnest. But for him there was this evening during which to relax and enjoy himself with his friends.

He was going home early tonight, he had told Eden. To sleep. Gone were the days when he could survive and even have a functioning brain on no more than an hour or two of rest night after night. But he certainly had enough energy left for the evening. And he knew everyone, he discovered when he arrived. Apart from Ken and Moira, Eden and himself, Rex and Catherine had invited several other mutual friends and a few relatives, including Rex's identical twin, Claude Adams, and his wife, Clarissa; Rex's sister Daphne, Lady Baird, and her husband, Sir Clayton; and Catherine's young brother, Harry, Viscount Perry. And Sophie was there too, of course, looking very slightly disheveled and very slightly shabby and altogether familiar and dear.

Catherine took her arm and led her about as soon as Eden had escorted her into the drawing room and presented the two women to each other. Moira was with them by the time they had circled the room, talking to everyone as they went, and had come eventually to where Kenneth and Eden stood with Nathaniel.

"Well, Sophie," Kenneth said, "our fate is in your hands—at least Rex's and mine are. What stories are you burning to share with Moira and Catherine?"

"Oh, none at all," she said. "One would hate to be a bore in company, and what would be duller than a recitation of how perfectly respectable and upright and sober you always were, Kenneth? And Rex too, of course."

They all laughed.

"Especially when I know it to be true already," Moira said, "and have never been in any doubt whatsoever."

"But there must be some interesting stories about Nathaniel and Eden," Catherine said. "You must regale us with those sometime, Sophie. Is your name Sophia, by the way, and these men have taken the liberty of shortening it?"

"I am Sophie to my friends," she replied, smiling warmly about her. "And I believe I am among friends."

"Sophie it is, then," Catherine said. "Rex came home after meeting you a few mornings ago and talked about you all through breakfast. How I admire you for following your husband to the Peninsula and cheerfully enduring all the discomforts and dangers there. You really must tell us some stories. Will it embarrass you? Or bore you? Are you always being asked to entertain fellow guests in such a way?"

"Not at all," Sophie said. "But you must not let me go on and on. Stop me when you have heard enough. Have you heard of the time when Nathaniel and Eden and Kenneth rescued my horse and me from a muddy grave?"

The men all chuckled. "The only part of you that was not a shiny brown, Sophie," Eden said, "was the whites of your eyes. And I am not even quite sure about those."

"Nat's scarlet regimentals suffered irreparable harm," Kenneth said.

"Not so. Sophie brushed them clean when they were dry," Nathaniel said. "It was the least she could do, of course."

Trust Sophie, he thought, to begin with a story that showed her in such a disadvantageous light. He remembered the incident vividly—the slippery ooze of her as he had hauled her up onto his horse before him. The unpleasant smell of her. Her good-natured laughter when almost any other woman would have been having a first-class fit of the vapors.

Rex joined them before she finished that story, and they spent a whole hour unashamedly reminiscing. They did a great deal of laughing, Sophie as heartily as the rest of them. Catherine and Moira moved away after a while, summoned to the pianoforte to accompany some impromptu singing.

It was only after they had left that Nathaniel noticed the contrast between their appearance and Sophie's. They were both taller than she, both elegantly dressed and coiffed in styles that were fashionable and becoming. But Sophie's lack of elegance had never detracted from their fondness for her. She had an inner beauty that needed no outer adornment.

He did wonder, though, now that he had noticed the contrast, why Sophie looked almost *shabby*. Did she care so little about her appearance? Or was her pension smaller than a grateful government had had any right to offer her? Or had Walter left debts? But Walter had not appeared extravagant. He had not played deep at the tables. Besides, he had an elder brother—Viscount Houghton—who would surely have taken care of any debts.

It was really none of his business, Nathaniel thought, bringing his mind back to the conversation. Sophie might look as shabby as she pleased and still look good to him and be pleasant company.

It was a wonderful evening, Nathaniel decided as it progressed. He would never make the mistake—none of them would—of glamorizing those years of war, of imagining that they had been a happy time. War was not a happy thing. It was their understanding of that fact that had led them all to sell their commissions after Waterloo. But they had made much of life during those years, more aware than they had been either before or since that life could end at any moment. And there had been some enjoyable times or some less enjoyable ones that they had nevertheless chosen to look upon with a sense of humor—and to remember in the same way.

And it was during those years that they had made the enduring friendships that they celebrated tonight. Life would be altogether less rich if he had never known Eden or Ken or Rex. Or Sophie. Strangely Sophie had seemed more of a friend than Walter, who had always been quiet and somewhat aloof. One had never felt one quite knew him, though he had been an amiable enough fellow. And Sophie had been devoted to him.

"Well, Nat," Rex said at last, "when do you begin your brotherly matchmaking maneuvers in earnest?"

Nathaniel grimaced. "I hope that will be more Margaret's task than mine," he said. "But tomorrow night, actually. The Shelby ball. I have been assured it will be one of the great squeezes of the Season. I shall escort the girls, of course. Ede has promised to dance with them both."

"On the strict understanding that Nat will not slide a pair of marriage contracts under my nose immediately afterward," Eden said with a grin.

"Who would want you as a brother-in-law anyway, Eden?" Kenneth asked, raising his quizzing glass to his eye.

Nathaniel looked at Sophie. "One of my sisters is still unmarried," he told her, "and so is a cousin who is my ward. I have brought them to town with the express purpose of finding husbands for them."

"Nat has been tamed, Sophie," Rex said. "Would you have believed it of him?"

"And you do not know the half if it, Rex." Eden winced theatrically. "Nat came to town after being incarcerated in the country for almost two years, simply panting for a taste of all the joys freedom can bring, and yet after just one night of pleasure—the object of his pleasure handpicked by none other than myself, I would have you know—he has declared it to be against his conscience or his religion or something ever again to employ a—"

"Ede!" Nathaniel said sharply. "There is a lady present."

"Nonsense!" Eden laughed. "Sophie is not—well, actually she is, of course. But she is also a good sport, are you not, Sophie? Have I offended you?"

"Of course you have not," she said cheerfully. "I heard a great deal that was far more explicit in past years."

"Well, I certainly object to having my sexual peccadilloes discussed in a lady's hearing, Ede," Nathaniel said, deeply mortified. "My apologies, Sophie."

"You could make a fortune in blackmail if you set your mind to it, Sophie," Kenneth said with a grin.

Sophie lost her good-natured smile. "That," she said sharply, "is not even a good joke, Kenneth. Nathaniel's apology was unnecessary. But I will hear yours now, if you please."

Nathaniel gazed at her with interest while Eden and Rex grinned and Kenneth apologized with exaggerated abjectness. She was serious. He had forgotten that side to her character. Almost eternally good-natured, she had very occasionally surprised them by scolding them and demanding apologies from them. There was the time, for example, when they had been joking about a fellow officer who had been cuckolded by a superior on whom he had been fawning for months in the hope of advancement. There was nothing amusing, she had told them in just the voice she had used now, about infidelity in marriage or about an unhappy man's misery.

They had all given the demanded apology—with considerably more sincerity than Ken was showing now.

Their group broke up then with the announcement of supper. Rex's twin came to lead Sophie in and she declared that it was eminently unfair to the rest of mankind that there should be two such identically handsome men in the world. Nathaniel offered his arm to Daphne and she took it with a smile.

"How pleasant to see you again," she said. "You have brought some sisters for the Season? I daresay they are beside themselves with excitement."

"Oh, indeed," he said. "It is one sister and one cousin, actually. I shall be escorting them to the Shelby ball tomorrow evening."

"Splendid," she said. "I shall keep my eyes open and send Clayton over if there should be any danger that one of them is facing the dreadful misfortune of having to sit out a set."

"Thank you," he said. She was laughing, but he knew she meant it.

The guests began to drift away quite soon after supper since no special entertainment had been arranged for the evening. Catherine and Rex had been determined, apparently, that it be an informal evening for friends to converse with one another.

Nathaniel handed Sophie into his carriage well before midnight. He was glad of it. He was feeling tired and would welcome a good night's sleep, especially when there was the ball to face the following evening. He yawned and realized how unmannerly he must appear. Sometimes one forgot to behave with Sophie as one would with any other lady.

"You are tired," she said.

"A little." He took her hand and drew her arm through his. "Town life is a great deal more tiring than country life. Do you live here all year?"

"Yes," she said. "But I do not go to parties and balls

every evening all year round, you know. I live a rather quiet life."

"Do you?" He looked at her in the near darkness. "Are you ever lonely, Sophie? Do you miss Walter? Pardon me, what a very foolish question. Of course you miss him. He was your husband."

"Yes." She smiled. "I do not miss that way of life, though. It was uncomfortable when all is said and done. And I am not lonely. Not really. I have some good friends."

"I am glad," he said. "I would have expected you to go to live with Houghton or with your own family. But of course a town house was part of what the government coughed up after Walter was decorated. You like it well enough to live there all year?"

"I am more grateful than I can say," she said, "to be able to live independently of either my brother-in-law or my brother, Nathaniel. I am very fortunate. Walter did not leave me well-off enough to live alone, you know."

And she was a proud woman too, he thought. She preferred modest independence to comfortable dependence on wealthier relatives. Her own family was very wealthy indeed, he believed.

The carriage stopped. They had arrived at her house already? He was feeling very pleasantly tired, though he repressed the urge to yawn again.

"Invite me in for tea?" he asked, smiling.

"When you are just about asleep?" she said, laughing.

"I am too tired to go home to bed," he said. "Ply me with tea and talk, Sophie, and then I shall walk briskly home and be fast asleep before my body hits the bed."

"You are as mad as you ever were." She clucked her tongue, though she was still laughing. "Come along, then. Though I must persuade you to drink chocolate rather than tea. Tea keeps a person awake, as does coffee."

"Does it?" he said. "I must remember that the next time I am suffering from insomnia."

He really must be mad, he thought a couple of minutes

later as he followed her inside her house, having dismissed his carriage. He listened to her instruct the manservant who had opened the door to have a pot of chocolate sent up to the sitting room before going to bed. She would lock up after Sir Nathaniel had left, she told the man.

He followed her to the sitting room. It was very much as he might have expected—small, cozy, tasteful without being in any way fussily feminine.

"This is pretty, Sophie," he said as she stooped to pat her dog, who had jumped up eagerly from the hearth to lick her hand and fan the air with its tail.

"Thank you." She smiled. "I had so much pleasure furnishing a home of my own after all those years of moving from billet to billet, trying not to accumulate one belonging more than was necessary. It is so lovely to be always in one place."

"Yes," he agreed. "It is. I went home, you know, only because my father was too ill to manage without me—I had left and bought my commission in order to get away from unrelieved domesticity. But you are right. It feels good to belong and to be surrounded by one's own things."

"It is strange," she said, fingering a porcelain ornament, "how things can come to be part of one's identity. I would not go back if I could, Nathaniel. Would you?"

"No," he said. "Not for a moment. It is good to reminisce. It is good to renew old friendships. But I like my life as it has become."

They smiled comfortably at each other before she gestured to a love seat and sat on a chair some distance away. The dog, with a sigh of contentment, had resumed its place on the hearth.

"I like both Catherine and Moira," she said. "They did tell me to call them by their given names, you know. I approve of them."

"In what way?" he asked. "They are both beauties, of course."

"They are both strong women," she said. "Or so it appeared to me on such short acquaintance. Rex and Kenneth need strong women, women of character. You all do.''

He smiled at her. ''You saw us at our worst, Sophie,'' he said. ''I am almost ashamed to remember.''

''Yes,'' she agreed. ''And at your best too. Tell me about your sisters. You have more than the one, do you not?'' The chocolate had arrived and she poured him a cup and carried it across to him.

''Come and sit beside me,'' he said. ''My eyes are too tired to focus on you at such a distance. Yes, five, and Lavinia, who easily counts for five people on her own.''

She brought her cup and saucer and sat beside him on the love seat. ''Lavinia is the cousin?'' she asked. ''She is a handful? Poor Nathaniel.''

''She refuses even to think about the necessity of taking a husband,'' he said.

''Oh dear.'' She sipped her chocolate.

''And her father, my uncle, was insane enough to decree that she could not come into her fortune until her thirtieth birthday,'' he said.

''Ah. One of those,'' she said. ''One hopes for your sake that Lavinia is not a scant eighteen or younger.''

''Four and twenty actually,'' he said. ''But six years sound like a very long time, Sophie. The girl has an opinion on everything.''

''I would not be surprised,'' she said, ''if Lavinia does not resent hearing herself called a girl. Is that why you do it, Nathaniel, or was it a slip of the tongue? And I would guess that perhaps she has some intelligence if she has the effrontery to have opinions of her own. I would like to meet her.''

''You shall do so,'' he said. He grinned at her. ''I remember now, Sophie, that way you have of scolding so gently that one scarce realizes one has been scolded.''

''I did not scold,'' she said, lifting her eyebrows. ''I do not have the right.''

''Lavinia hates being called a girl,'' he said.

She hid her smile in her cup as she sipped.

"I will probably never call her that again," he said. "But you asked me about my sisters."

He told her about them and she told him about her life since Waterloo. She described the reception at Carlton House with a great deal of humor—much of it directed against herself. She particularly amused him with a description of the turban she had worn on top of her newly washed and therefore doubly unruly hair. He could almost picture its determination to spring clear of its perch and her desperate attempts to keep it where she had placed it. He laughed outright.

"Walter would have loved it all," she said, placing her empty cup and saucer on the table beside her. "I wonder if he realized what an act of bravery he was performing— and for whom? Did he even recognize the Duke of Wellington? I wonder. Is one conscious of a brave deed in the midst of battle, Nathaniel?"

"Not really," he said. "One acts from instinct as much as anything. Doing one's best to save a friend or a comrade comes quite instinctively. There is little leisure for rational thought when one is engaged in a fight."

"I would imagine," she said, "that the instinct to run away is quite strong too."

"Before battle begins," he said. "Every time, in fact. The more battles one has fought, the stronger the urge. But not once it has started. One learns—or one learned—to will the guns to start their cannonade just so that the butterflies might disappear from one's stomach."

He should go. He had stayed long enough. Too long. He must have been there for at least an hour. But he was warm and cozy and sleepy again. And there was something particularly pleasant lulling his senses. He had been largely unconscious of it. He breathed in deeply, moving his head a little closer to her.

"That perfume," he said. "You always wore it, Sophie. I have never smelled it on anyone else before or since."

"I wear none." She smiled. "It is soap you smell."

"Then other women should discover your secret," he

said. "It is the most enticing perfume I have ever smelled."

They smiled at each other again, just as they had a dozen times during the past hour. Except that this time something happened. A mere moment of silence. A locking of eyes. A sudden tension.

A sudden shockingly unexpected *sexual* tension.

He broke eye contact and turned, embarrassed, to set his cup on the table beside him. He turned back to her, intending to thank her for the chocolate and to bid her a good night. But she had reached out one hand and set it lightly against the lapel of his coat. She watched her hand as it brushed lightly back and forth there and then came to rest over his heart. He could scarcely feel its weight. He could scarcely breathe.

He licked his lips. He should turn the moment. It could be done quite easily. He could say something, move, get to his feet. Instead he dipped his head closer to hers, paused one moment to give *her* a chance to turn the moment, and then closed his eyes and found her mouth with his own. He felt dizzy. He waited for her to pull away. She stayed quite still for a few moments and then her lips pushed back against his own.

He traced them with his tongue, prodded at the seam, and when she opened her mouth, tentatively, as if she did not know quite what he asked of her, slid his tongue deep. He had turned her, he realized, so that her head was against the back of the love seat.

It was a long and a deeply intimate kiss.

"Mm," he heard himself say as he drew his tongue back into his mouth and lifted his head to look at her.

She looked back and said nothing. She did not push at his chest or try to move away. She simply looked at him.

The tension had not lessened at all. Quite the contrary.

"Are you going to slap my face?" he asked her. "Or are you going to invite me to bed?"

"I am not going to slap your face," she said calmly.

He waited.

"I am inviting you to bed," she said just as calmly after several silent moments.

He got to his feet and held out his hand for hers. She looked at it and then placed her own in it.

# FIVE

SHE WAS THE ONE WHO HAD said it. *I am inviting you to bed.*

Just like that. Just as she had always dreamed of doing. Always. Sometimes her attraction to him had been almost painful. It was very pleasant, of course, and not really something to arouse a great deal of guilt, to be half in love with a handsome man even when one was married to someone else. She had been half in love with all four of them. But sometimes she had suspected—she had never allowed herself to know for sure—that it was more than that with Nathaniel. Sometimes it had hurt.

And she had never forgotten him, as she had half forgotten the others. He had always hovered in her memory. The unforgettable one. She had kept his letter, she remembered now. Of all the letters she had received and later destroyed, his had been the one she had kept.

She was going to go to bed with him. She was going to commit a wicked sin with him, though it would not be adultery, of course. She could never have done that. She never had and never would have done that even if Walter had lived to an old age. There were some moral principles that were not negotiable with one's conscience.

But this was a sin she could and would commit. No one would be hurt by it—except her.

She expected that it would be somewhat embarrassing to undress when they reached her bedchamber. But it was not. He unclothed her, kissing her as he did so—on the lips, on the throat, on the breasts. He touched a nipple with the tip of his tongue and she felt a sharp stab of raw desire all the way from her throat to her knees.

She unclothed him at the same time, though she could not quite bring herself to touch his breeches. She could see, though, at a single shocked glance, that he was fully aroused.

She was going to go to bed with him. It would still be possible to stop, she supposed, though it would be impossibly embarrassing. But she had no wish to stop. It had been so long. So very long. Years. And even then, so few times and so very disappointing. Worse than disappointing. Nightmarish.

She almost pushed him away in panic when she remembered how it had been, but she was naked and his arms had come about her. His mouth had found hers again and he was putting his tongue into her mouth again. She would never have imagined that such a shockingly unexpected intimacy could possibly be pleasant. It was. She sucked on his tongue and he made that sound in his throat again—the one he had made downstairs before asking if she was going to slap his face.

The sound made her feel desirable. She had never felt desirable, she realized. Never. Quite the opposite, in fact.

"Take me to bed, Sophie," he murmured against her lips, and she took him, folding down the bedcovers neatly, almost as if she were a maid, before lying on her back and reaching up her arms for him.

She should be embarrassed by her own nakedness, she thought—she had never been naked with a man before and had long ago lost confidence in her own beauty. But she would not be embarrassed, though he was perfect in every way—even the scars of old wounds only seemed to contribute to his perfection. He wanted her. That was perfectly obvious. She was excited by her own desire—and by his.

The candles were still burning, she realized as he came down directly on top of her, pressing his knees between hers until she straddled him. She did not care.

"Come," she said, wrapping her arms about him.

"Sophie." His mouth found hers again, and he whispered her name between feathered kisses. "I should take time to give you pleasure. But I want to be in you—now. Stop me if you are not ready."

Ready? She was bursting with readiness. She had been ready for years, or so it seemed.

"I want you in me too," she said, looking into his wonderful heavy-lidded eyes. "I am ready." Even now she could scarcely believe the evidence of her own senses—that he *wanted* her. But he did. Ah, dear God, he did.

He thrust almost before she stopped speaking and her mind exploded in shock. He was hot and hard. She felt stretched in every direction. Gloriously stretched.

He was Nathaniel, she found her mind telling her foolishly. Dear God, he was *Nathaniel*. He was in her bed, in her body.

She pressed into him, even though her first instinct had been to draw away lest she be hurt by his size and by *him*. She lifted her knees and hugged his sides tightly. She moaned.

"You are hungry?" he asked, his voice low against her mouth. "As I am, Sophie?"

Hungry? She was ravenous. Starved.

"Yes," she said. "So very hungry."

"Let us savor every moment, then," he said. "Let us enjoy the feast."

She did not quite comprehend his meaning. All that was left now, she knew from bitter experience, was the brief convulsive jerking. She wished this moment of stillness could last forever. Why could a single moment of time not be transformed into an eternity?

He withdrew slowly and she sighed aloud with disap-

pointment and braced herself. But it did not matter. She
would always have the memory of this moment. It would
become her greatest treasure. She knew without a doubt
that it would.

He pushed in slowly again and withdrew slowly. She lay
open beneath him in wonder, feeling the building of a slow
rhythm, feeling the increasing comfort of wetness, hearing
the accompanying rhythmic squeaks of the mattress. She
had not realized that sound could be erotic. Or that *this*
could be. A feast, he had called it. She braced her feet flat
on the bed, lifted her hips slightly, let her body feel the
rhythm, and moved with him.

For a long time. Until they were both hot and sweating
and panting with the exertion. Until she was almost mindless with the ache of a crescendoing desire. Almost. But
not quite. She would not allow herself to give in to pure
sensation. She wanted to know. She wanted to feel. She
wanted to experience every moment. She wanted to understand with every thrust and withdrawal that he was Nathaniel. That she was in bed with him. Loving him. Loving
him openly and at last with her body and with all of herself.

And feeling like a woman. Feminine. Normal. Incredible,
wonderful feelings. *Because he found her desirable.*

After what must have been several minutes the rhythm
quickened. And then deepened. And then broke altogether
as his hands came beneath her and held her still while he
pushed deeper than deep. She felt the hot gush of his seed
as he sighed against the side of her head and then relaxed
his weight onto her.

"Ah, beautiful," he murmured. "Beautiful."

She knew that he spoke of the experience more than of
her—and it had been beautiful. But she felt beautiful too.
For the first time in a long, long while.

They were both still hot and panting. Her body was still
humming with undefined aches and yearnings. But she was
living through one of those moments that occurred only
rarely and only briefly in life, she knew. She was utterly,
totally happy.

He moved off her and lay beside her on his back, one arm thrown over his eyes while his breathing quietened and she felt the thudding of her own heart grow fainter in her ears. He would get up and go away in a few moments, she supposed even as the last of the candles flickered and went out. And perhaps tomorrow he would be sorry—perhaps they both would. But for now she was consciously happy. And for the rest of the night after he was gone she would relive what had happened. She would not allow the bed to feel empty once he had gone. She would move over and lie on his side of the bed. She would keep the warmth there with the heat of her own body. Perhaps the smell of him— of that musky cologne he wore and of *him*—would linger. She would imagine that it did even if it did not do so in fact.

And she would not allow herself to feel guilty. She *would* not.

He reached down to pull up the bedcovers and turned onto his side with a sigh. He slid one arm beneath her neck and drew her onto her side against him. He kissed the top of her head as he tucked the covers warmly about them both. And then, just like that—she could tell unmistakably from his breathing—he was asleep.

She could have cried and almost did. But if she did, she would wet his chest and then need a handkerchief in which to blow her nose. She would have to move and that would wake him and send him on his way. She bit her upper lip again and breathed deeply of the warmth and the smell of him.

She would not sleep. *She would not sleep.* There were more moments—more blessed moments to savor.

Perhaps he would stay all night.

Oh, she had so little experience, she thought, with what love and marriage might have been. With what tenderness might have accomplished. Almost everything about tonight had been a surprise—just as if she were a raw innocent. Would that she were!

•   •   •

Nathaniel awoke feeling warm and comfortable and rested, though it was still dark. He was not in his own bed. He was with a woman. For one disoriented moment he could not remember with whom.

But for one moment only.

She moved her head away from his chest and looked up at him. There was enough light in the room after all to see her face quite clearly enough.

Sophie.

With her always wild hair loose and in tangled disarray about her face and over her shoulders and down her back—his one arm that was beneath her head was entangled in it—she looked unfamiliar. She also felt womanly, enticing, beautiful. Not that he had ever thought of her as being *un*womanly. It was just that he had never particularly thought of her in sexual terms. She had been a married woman.

She was gazing silently at him—Sophie. By God, he had made love to *Sophie Armitage*. And felt stirred again by her unmistakable womanliness.

"Have I outstayed my welcome?" he asked her.

"No," she said. That was all. For one moment, gazing back at her, he could almost imagine that she was not Sophie after all. He had never had this sort of fantasy about her. Never. He had always had very strict notions about married women. She had always been just a friend. Though a particularly dear one, he had to admit.

He moved his free hand over her body. Her skin was smooth and silky. She had small breasts. But not too small. Her nipples were rigid. He rubbed his thumb lightly over one before pinching it not ungently between the thumb and forefinger. Her eyes closed and her teeth clamped onto her lower lip. He lowered his head, took the nipple into his mouth, and suckled her, rubbing her with his tongue at the same time. She moaned and her fingers twined in his hair.

She had a shapely waist and hips and nicely rounded buttocks. He had never particularly noticed her shapeliness. Perhaps it was the dresses she always wore. They were almost invariably ill-fitting and in dark colors that did not suit her. Though he had never been critical of her appearance either. She had always looked rather dear to him— but as a friend.

She had slender thighs. He set his mouth to hers as he moved his hand between them and explored her lightly with his fingertips. She was invitingly hot and wet. He rubbed his thumb with featherlight strokes over a certain spot until she hissed an inward breath, drawing air from his own mouth. He slid two fingers up inside her. Her inner muscles clenched tightly and invitingly about him as he moved them slowly in and out.

"Invite me inside again, Sophie," he whispered to her.

"Come inside." She spoke out loud—unmistakably in Sophie's voice. He felt as if he were in the middle of a disorienting dream. He felt a moment's thankfulness that he had never been fully aware of her attractions while Walter was still alive.

He lifted her leg over his hip, positioned himself, and slid deep into her wetness as they lay on their sides pressed together.

"Oh," she said—a sound of surprise and pleasure.

He worked her slowly again so that they could enjoy at their leisure the physical sensation of coupling as well as the rhythmic sounds of the most intimately physical act of all.

"Is there a lovelier feeling?" he asked her.

"No," she said.

She was moving with him, he noticed, as she had the first time, enjoying as much as he did what they did together. Was she as amazed as he, he wondered, to find herself here—with him? He was reluctant to finish. He prolonged the exertion as long as he could before holding her motionless and ejaculating deep inside her.

He moved her leg away from his hip after he was fully finished and rubbed it lightly to work any cramps from it. But he did not uncouple them. It must be very late—or very early, depending upon one's point of view. Once they were uncoupled he must make a move to leave. He was reluctant to do so. Not just because he was warm and comfortable where he was—and sleepy again too.

No, not just because of that.

He was awake, of course. He had been awake when he had come to bed with her and had her the first time. But he had the uncomfortable feeling that once he left her house, once he breathed in fresh air, he was going to *really* come awake. And he did not care to contemplate what his thoughts might be when that happened.

For as long as he was here he could perhaps convince himself that she was simply a woman and he was simply a man and they had simply enjoyed a night of good sex. They had coupled together—really together—two separate times. They had both enjoyed the experience. Immensely. But the trouble was that she was not just any woman. She was Sophie.

He did not know quite how either of them was going to feel about all this tomorrow. But he suspected that life was going to appear far more complicated in the morning than it had before he asked Sophie to invite him in for tea. Had he been mad? Had he really expected that he could treat her like a comrade tonight as he had always used to do? And how was she going to feel? Betrayed? He winced inwardly.

He set a hand beneath her chin, lifted her face, and kissed her lingeringly and openmouthed. Her softly parted lips pressed warmly back against his.

"Sleepy?" he asked.

"Mm," she said.

"I am going to draw out of you," he said, doing so regretfully, "and get dressed. Stay there where it is warm until I am ready to leave. Then you can slip on a robe, let me out of the house, lock the door behind me, and be back here before the bed has cooled. You will be asleep before I have reached the end of the street."

She watched silently as he dressed in the dark, and then she got out of bed and walked naked to a wardrobe to withdraw a woolen dressing gown. She had a pretty body, he thought, his eyes moving over her before she drew on the garment and belted it about her waist. Not voluptuous, just—pretty. Her hair billowed down her back almost to her bottom. She led the way downstairs, holding the single candle she had lit in the bedchamber, and slid the bolts back quietly on the outer door. She turned and looked up at him without saying anything.

"Good night, Sophie." He touched his fingertips to one side of her jaw. "And thank you."

"Good night, Nathaniel," she said. She sounded like the Sophie of old, calm and cheerful and practical. "I hope all goes well with your sister and your cousin. Remember not to call Lavinia a girl."

"Yes, ma'am." He smiled at her, but she did not smile back.

He did not kiss her again. He was already feeling awkward about the whole thing. He stepped out into the chill early-morning air and walked away briskly. He did not look back.

Chill indeed. What the devil had he got himself into?

Viscount Houghton and his wife and daughter had persuaded Sophia to go to the Shelby ball with them. Sarah had declared her intention of simply dying if Aunt Sophie refused.

And so she would go. She would wear her best dark blue silk—the Carlton House gown. It would have to do for another year—probably longer. She simply must have new evening gloves, though. The old ones, which had been threadbare at the fingers for some time, had finally sprung an undarnable hole in a place where it could not possibly be hidden from view.

And so she would go shopping during the morning. She would call to see if Gertrude wished to accompany her. Although part of her wished to remain alone at home, she knew that fresh air and exercise would feel good once she had forced herself out. And Gertie's constant chatter—always witty and interesting—would be good for her in a different way.

But as she was on her way downstairs, her bonnet tied beneath her chin, one glove on, the other half on, her manservant was opening the door in answer to a knock. There was no time to retreat out of sight even if she had wished to do so.

She smiled—her usual cheerful smile. "Good morning, Nathaniel," she said.

He was immaculately dressed in what was surely one of Weston's creations, a blue formfitting coat. He wore even more formfitting pantaloons with shining, white-tasseled Hessians. He looked handsome and elegant. He was unmistakably one of the Four Horsemen of the Apocalypse, those almost godlike cavalry officers she, together with almost every other woman in Wellington's armies, had secretly admired.

Last night seemed quite unreal. Especially now that she was seeing him again in the light of day.

She saw from his expression when he looked up and locked eyes with her that it seemed unreal to him too.

"Sophie." He made her a bow. "You are going out?"

"It is nothing that cannot be postponed," she said. "Will you come up? Samuel, will you have coffee sent to the sitting room, if you please?"

"No." Nathaniel held up a hand. "No coffee, thank you. I have just come from breakfast. But I would appreciate a word with you if I might, Sophie."

She was not sure if she had expected his call today or not. Perhaps she had been afraid to expect it. Perhaps an unconscious wish to avoid it had given her the energy to plan her shopping expedition. How aghast he must have been this morning to remember with whom he had lain last night. As aghast as she should have been. She should have remembered who she was—a respectable widow—and who he was. She should have remembered that they had always been friends, with no hint of anything else between them. She should have been embarrassed at the very least to remember what indiscretion being alone together late at night had led them to.

But she would not lie to herself. She was not sorry for last night. She did not even feel guilty. No one had been harmed—except perhaps her.

She turned and led the way upstairs, drawing off her gloves as she went and untying the ribbons of her bonnet. She set them on a small table just inside the sitting-room door.

"Do have a seat," she said, and gestured toward the love seat before she could stop herself.

But he had not noticed. He had crossed the room and was standing at the window, looking out. His hands, clasped at his back, were not still. She wished she could have avoided this. If she had only been five minutes earlier . . .

"I have no excuse, Sophie," he said after a short silence. "And an apology would not even begin to suffice."

She wondered if he really regretted what had happened. Probably he did; but *if* he did, she hoped he would not say so. A woman needed some illusions. Perhaps just one in her life. Surely it was not too much to ask. One would suffice.

"Neither an excuse nor an apology is necessary," she said, seating herself on the chair that had been too distant from the love seat last night for the focus of his eyes.

He lowered his head and she heard him draw an audible breath. "Will you do me the honor of marrying me?" he asked.

"Oh no!" She leaped to her feet and was across the room without giving her reaction a moment's consideration. She set one hand on his shoulder. "No, Nathaniel. This is not necessary. Believe me, it is not."

He did not turn. She removed her hand when she realized where it was and closed it into a fist, which she set against her mouth.

"I debauched you," he said.

"What a perfectly horrid way to describe what happened,'' she said, putting on her usual manner with an enormous effort of will. ''You did no such thing. I actually found it rather pleasant.'' *Rather pleasant!* Just the most gloriously wonderful experience of her life. ''I thought you did too. I did not expect to find you so conscience-stricken today.''

He turned to look at her and she could see that his face was quite drained of color. She smiled cheerfully at him.

''You are my friend, Sophie,'' he said. ''You are Walter's wife. I never dreamed I could be capable of treating you with such disrespect.''

''Friends cannot sometimes go to bed together?'' she asked him, though she did not wait for an answer. ''And I am not Walter's wife, Nathaniel. I am his widow. I have been a widow for almost three years. It was not adultery. Or seduction, if that is what you fear. I asked you, if you will remember.''

''You are so cool and practical about it,'' he said. ''I might have guessed it, I suppose. I feared I would find you distraught this morning.''

She smiled. ''How foolish,'' she said. ''I am not a woman of loose morals, you know. I have never done before what I did last night. But I cannot feel distraught about it or even mildly upset. Why should I? It was pleasant. Very pleasant indeed. But hardly a catastrophic event that necessitates a marriage proposal and a hasty wedding.'' *Oh, Nathaniel, Nathaniel.*

''Are you sure, Sophie?'' He was searching her eyes.

Foolishly, she realized as soon as he asked the question, she had been hoping against all reason that perhaps he had asked because he had *wanted* to ask. Very foolishly.

''Of course I am sure.'' She laughed. ''I am the last woman in the world you would wish to be marrying, Nathaniel. And I have no wish to marry anyone. I have Walter to remember and I have this house and my pension and my circle of friends. I am perfectly happy.''

''I have never known anyone as serene and cheerful as you, Sophie,'' he said, tipping his head to one side as he continued to regard her closely. "You really are contented as you are, are you not?"

"Yes." She nodded. "Of course."

The color was visibly returning to his face. He was not good at dissembling. His sense of relief was patently obvious.

"I will not press my addresses on you, then," he said. "But what happened will not affect our friendship, Sophie? I would hate to find next time we meet that there is an awkwardness between us."

"Why should there be?" she asked him. "What we did we each did freely. We are adults, Nathaniel. There is no law that says a man and woman may no longer be friends once they have been to bed together. How would any marriage survive if that were so?"

He smiled for the first time. His slow, wonderful smile that had enslaved countless women.

"If you put it like that," he said. He looked beyond her to her bonnet and gloves. "May I offer my escort to wherever it is you are going?"

She hesitated. She wanted desperately to be alone, but if she refused, then she would be setting up the very awkwardness she had just assured him would not exist between them.

"Thank you," she said. "I am walking to the home of a friend just two streets away. I shall be grateful for your escort."

She put her bonnet and gloves on again, her back to him as she tied the ribbons. And suddenly it seemed unbearable that it was all over almost before it had begun—her wonderful fling with a man around whom she had weaved painful dreams for years. All over.

One night—one glorious night—was more than she could ever have expected.

But it was not enough. If she had convinced herself that one night would be enough, she had been foolish indeed.

One night was far worse than none at all.

She turned to him with her usual smile and took his offered arm. "I am ready," she told him.

# SIX

THERE WAS SOME AWK-
wardness between them after all as they walked, a certain
difficulty in fixing on a topic of conversation. He commented on the weather—cloudy, a little chillier than it had
been, though dry at least and with almost no wind—but
there was very little she could say in response to his de-
tailed report.

She really was small. Her head reached barely to his
shoulder. He could not see her face beneath the brim of her
plain, serviceable bonnet. He was very aware of her—phys-
ically aware. It felt strange to look down and see his friend
Sophie, to remember the cheerful, placid, sensible way she
had received him this morning. And yet to feel an awareness of the woman in whose bed he had spent several hours
of the night before. It was strangely disorienting to know
that the two women were one and the same.

He had realized almost as soon as he had left her last
night, of course—or perhaps even before he had left—that
he must come back and do the honorable thing this morning. He had enjoyed the night with her more than he could
remember enjoying a night with any other woman, and he
certainly liked her more than he had ever liked any other
woman. But the thought of marriage with her had frozen

his heart. And the prospect of having to force marriage on her had made him heavy with guilt. But he had no choice.

Trust Sophie to have treated the whole situation with her usual cheerful good sense. It had been very pleasant, she had said. Dear Sophie—he might have felt offended if he had not been so enormously relieved. *Very pleasant.* She had admitted that she had never before done such a thing, and he believed her. But she had found it only *very pleasant*?

"You have changed," she said now.

"Have I?" He bent his head closer to hers. He wondered in what way she saw him differently.

"You have grown up," she said. "So have Rex and Kenneth, I believe. Eden has not. Not yet."

"Because I have become a staid country squire, Sophie?" he asked. "Because I have taken it upon myself to escort my sister and my cousin about town?"

"Because you are no longer comfortable with paying women for their favors," she said.

The devil! Trust Sophie to come right out and remind him of that embarrassing moment at Rex's. "I should have slapped a glove in Ede's face," he said. "In the Peninsula it was a different matter, Sophie. But in a genteel drawing room it was unpardonable of him to say what he said in your hearing."

"But you are not ready for marriage, are you?" she said.

He grimaced. "I would readily—" he began.

"Oh yes, I know," she said. "You are a man of honor, Nathaniel. Of course you would readily have married me once you had—oh, *dishonored* me, I suppose you would call it. But you are not ready for matrimony yet, are you?"

Did she wish him to persuade her? He did not believe so. He tried to see her face, but she kept her head down.

"You do not wish to marry," she continued, "and yet you can no longer bring yourself to take the alternative."

He stopped walking and drew her to a halt beside him. "Where is this leading, Sophie?" he asked.

When she looked up at him, she looked so much her

usual self that he thought perhaps he was still sleeping and in the middle of one of those utterly bizarre dreams.

"I am not beautiful," she said, "and I am not particularly attractive, though I do not believe I am exactly an antidote. Certainly you did not find me so last night. You enjoyed the experience as I did. Did you not?" For the first time she flushed.

He could not pretend to misunderstand her. "Sophie." He dipped his head closer to hers. "Are you offering to be my mistress?"

"No," she said calmly. "A mistress is a kept woman. I am my own mistress, Nathaniel. But I found it pleasant, I believe you did, and . . ."

"And?" He raised his eyebrows. Thank heaven, a part of his mind thought, they were standing on a deserted street.

Her lips moved without producing sound. But she pulled herself together. "You will be in town for a few months," she said. "You will be busy. So will I. But just occasionally . . . Perhaps it would not be a bad idea . . . I am not in search of a husband, Nathaniel, any more than you are in search of a wife. But—but I am a woman with a woman's needs. Hungers. Sometimes. Not enough to send me endlessly in search of lovers. But . . . But if you wish . . . If it would solve a problem for you . . ."

He understood in a sudden flash despite her seeming inability to complete a sentence. How easy it was to see Sophie's good nature and not realize that there were deep and real feelings behind it. But he remembered asking her the night before if she was hungry as he was—hungry for passion. She had said yes. Her body had said yes.

"My dear." He covered her hand on his arm with his own. "You miss Walter dreadfully, do you not? And we—the others and I—have made jokes of his posthumous fame. How heartless we have been. And insensitive. Do forgive me."

She merely gazed into his eyes. "Shall we do it, then?" she asked him.

He wanted to, he realized in some surprise. It would be that affair between equals he had hoped to find and not really expected to find. He could have it with a friend, with someone he liked and respected and found attractive. It would be a relationship they would both find pleasant—he smiled inwardly. He would hope they would both find it more than just that. It would be a relationship that would hurt neither of them.

"Last night *was* good, Sophie," he said.

"Yes." She nodded.

"It would certainly bear repeating." He smiled at her.

"Yes."

He felt a sudden and unexpected amusement. He laughed and she smiled her usual cheerful smile. "Sophie, you are a bold minx," he said. "You are bent on corrupting me. Did you *plan* this?"

"Only as the words were coming from my mouth," she said. "Have I forced you into something you may regret? Would you like to take time to consider?"

"Would you?" he asked her.

"No." She shook her head.

He thought of Walter's lovely and lively widow. And he thought of the woman who had lain beneath him last night, riding to the rhythm his own body had set. Sophie—lovely and lively. It was hard to believe that this enticing woman had been there all the time in the Peninsula, but he had seen her as only a friend. Perhaps it was just as well.

"I believe, Sophie," he said, "I would be honored to be your lover."

For one very brief moment she closed her eyes and bit her lower lip. Then she looked about her, the old Sophie again. He noticed in the same moment that there were two people coming up behind them, still from some distance away.

"Gertrude's house is just there," she said, pointing a short way ahead of them.

They approached it without speaking again until he took his leave of her after knocking on the door for her and waiting for a servant to open it. He bowed over her hand and bade her a good morning.

"Thank you for your escort, Nathaniel," she said, and disappeared inside the house.

He stood staring at the closed door for all of two minutes before moving on.

"Ah. You look very nice, Sophia," Beatrice, Viscountess Houghton, said kindly. "It is the Carlton House gown, is it not?"

The Carlton House gown must be nationally famous by now, Sophia thought with wry humor. Beatrice looked extremely elegant in a new rose-red silk gown with matching turban. She was all ready for the ball. The carriage had just arrived at Portland Place, bringing Sophia—she had refused the invitation to dinner on the grounds that there would be enough excitement in the house without the added distraction of a dinner guest.

Sarah, of course, looked youthful and lovely in the obligatory white gown, which was all delicate simplicity, allowing the beauty of its wearer to speak for itself. Sophia recognized Beatrice's guiding hand in the choice of design. Sarah danced around in a complete circle before hugging her aunt.

"What do you think, Aunt Sophie?" she asked artlessly. "Do you think I will be the loveliest lady at the ball? Papa says I will, but Lewis only snorts."

Lewis, as blond and slender as his sister, but with an altogether more masculine effect, grinned. "If I found you the loveliest lady at the ball, Sare," he said, "there would be something decidedly wrong with me. I did concede that you look pretty enough."

Sarah tossed her glance ceilingward.

"Brothers," Sophia said with a laugh, "have a way of being brutally honest. You look breathtakingly wonderful, dear. And you look very nice too, Sarah."

Lewis roared with laughter and Sarah went off into fits of giggles and any incipient sibling quarrel was averted.

"The Carlton House gown always was elegant, Sophia," her brother-in-law said, handing Beatrice her wrap and organizing everyone for departure. "But a new one would enable you to be in the forefront of fashion again. Bea and Sarah have spent days educating me on what is currently fashionable. Will you go with them the next time they visit the modiste? I would not notice the cost of one extra gown among all of theirs, I do assure you."

"You would look lovely in a pale shade of blue, Sophia," Beatrice said, "and in a lightweight fabric for summer. Oh, do come with us. It would be such *fun*, would it not, Sarah?"

Sophia smiled at them. "If we do not move toward the door soon," she said, "Edwin is going to be bellowing at someone. I really do have all the gowns I need. And dark colors are so much more serviceable than pale. As for a lightweight fabric, Beatrice, why would I be so foolish when I live in an English climate?"

Lewis offered her his arm and she took it, noticing with approval the varying shades of dove gray and white in which he was dressed. There were going to be a dozen or more young ladies falling all over their slippers to secure an introduction to him. And Sarah's theory was not true of her own brother. Although he was only one and twenty, there was not a single spot in evidence on his face.

"Some people," Edwin said as he escorted his wife and daughter into the hall and nodded to the servant on duty there to open the outer door, "are as stubborn as the proverbial mule."

"And some people," Sophia said cheerfully as Lewis handed her into the carriage, "will be eternally grateful that they have the means with which to live independently." She smiled at Edwin as he settled on the seat opposite to show him that she meant no offense by her words.

Though she wished she had not spoken them just then. They only served to remind her of how very precarious her independence was. She had paid off the newest debt—why was she never willing simply to call a spade a spade, even in her mind? She had dealt with the latest round of *black-mail*—there, she had verbalized it in her mind at last. But she had left herself panting for breath and trying desperately to hide the fact from her family. She had given in to blackmail three separate times now and knew she was merely getting herself deeper and deeper into a black hole from which there would be no escape. However would she cope with the next demand? There was no money left. . . .

*One day at a time.*

"Will *anyone* wish to dance with me?" Sarah asked suddenly, panic in her voice. "What if no one does, Mama?"

"Young Withingsford is to lead you into the opening set," Edwin reminded her.

But Sarah only pulled a face. Young Withingsford, Sophia understood, was merely a neighbor and so scarcely counted as a conquest in Sarah's mind. Perhaps the poor lad even had spots.

"Invitations have been pouring in at flattering speed," Beatrice said. "Everyone will know, Sarah, that you are Uncle Walter's niece. Aunt Sophie is with us."

Sarah's eyes focused on her aunt. "Do you suppose, Aunt Sophie," she asked, "that Lord Pelham and Sir Nathaniel Gascoigne will ask me to dance? They are sure to come and pay their respects to you, are they not? And then they will remember that they have been presented to me. Will they *dance* with me?"

"Sarah talked of no one else all day after that walk in the park," Edwin said with a chuckle. "They are both eligible, Sophia? I will not ask if they are respectable. I am sure they are if you claim an acquaintance with them and if you judged it proper to present them to Sarah."

"They are both unmarried, if that is what you mean," Sophia said, "and both wealthy, I believe. And handsome, of course. I am sure Sarah did not fail to mention that detail."

"The most handsome men in London," Lewis muttered. "Or was it in all England, Sare? Or all of Europe? Or the world?"

"I believe I said merely that they are handsome," Sarah said, on her dignity. "There is no need to snicker at everything I say, Lewis."

"And are they young, Sophia?" Beatrice asked.

"They are probably both about thirty," she replied.

"A good age," Edwin said.

Beatrice smiled. "One can only hope that they are at the ball now that we have ascertained that they are eligible in every way," she said. "You will present them to Edwin and me, Sophia?"

"Of course," Sophia said, "if they are there tonight." *She knew they were going to be there.*

"Well," Edwin said with a chuckle. "After tonight we will have Sarah happily settled and you and I may retire to the greater comfort of the country again, my love."

"Papa!" Sarah, who rarely recognized a joke when it was subtly made, looked alarmed. "Nothing will be settled in *one* evening. We cannot go home yet."

Beatrice laughed and patted her hand.

Nathaniel was going to be at the ball with his sister and his cousin, Sophia thought. Perhaps he would not wish to bring them anywhere near her. Not now that she was his— no, she was not. Absolutely not. She would not even begin to think of herself in that demeaning way. But even so, he might feel awkward about presenting her to his relatives or asking her to present him to hers. She really did not know how such affairs were conducted. But of course he had already met Sarah. Would he dance with her? Would Edwin and Beatrice try to net him for their daughter?

The thought was absurd—and horrifying. Nathaniel was far too old in both years and experience for Sarah. Besides, he had no wish to marry. And even if he did, he would not have the poor taste to choose the niece of his lover.

But examining her feelings, Sophia recognized that there were both jealousy and possessiveness there. And a huge lack of confidence in her ability to hold his interest. She *hated* her lack of self-esteem. It had not used to be there, but though she knew there was no real need to doubt herself, damage had been done when she was young and impressionable. It was difficult to recover belief in oneself once it had been lost—or robbed.

*Last night was good, Sophie.*

*It would certainly bear repeating.*

He had meant the words. She must believe them. She had as much to offer their relationship as he did. She must believe that. She *would* believe it.

"Perhaps, Aunt Sophie," Sarah was saying, "Lord Pelham and Sir Nathaniel will dance with you. It would not be surprising, I am sure."

"You are indeed very famous, Sophia," Edwin said, a twinkle in his eye.

Sophia laughed. "And well past my dancing years," she said. "I shall be perfectly content to find a quiet corner in which to sit and watch Sarah's triumphs. And Lewis's too."

In all the regimental balls throughout the war years she had never sat out a single set. It was not a matter for conceit. It had happened, of course, because the gentlemen had always far outnumbered the ladies. *None* of the ladies had ever sat out a set. But each of the Four Horsemen had always danced with her. They had not always danced with the other ladies. She had felt young on those occasions and attractive and exhilarated—but they had been very rare.

How wonderful it would be tonight if . . . But probably not with Nathaniel. Doubtless they would keep well away from each other. And even the faint chance of being able to dance with one or more of the others did not quite make up for the fact that the two of them would probably treat each other like strangers. She hoped she would not find herself in the awkward position of having to present him to Edwin and Beatrice. Oh dear, she thought, and they had convinced themselves that there need no longer be any awkwardness between them. She dreaded seeing him again in public.

Would he come to her later tonight? she wondered. Or tomorrow? Or never? Last night it had happened without planning. This morning an affair had seemed possible. This evening it did not. It was something that would somehow never be spoken of between them again, she was suddenly sure—especially as the carriage had slowed and then stopped behind a long line of carriages and she could see far ahead all the glitter of the other guests getting down from their carriages.

All she had really done this morning, she thought— though perhaps last night had made it inevitable—was lose a friend. One of the dearest friends a woman ever had, even if she had not seen him for three years before this week and had had only that one precious letter from him.

Sarah was chattering nervously and the others were all checking their appearance preparatory to making their public appearance at the door of the Shelby mansion. The carriage inched forward.

Georgina looked quite perfectly turned out for her first London ball. Or so her brother thought fondly as she sat beside him in his carriage. She was dressed in white satin and lace, as was proper, she had white ribbons threaded through her fair and elaborately styled curls, and she was glowing with pleasurable anticipation. There was the suggestion of a tremble in the hand that rested lightly on his sleeve.

Georgina was his favorite sister, though he would not have admitted to any living soul that he had favorites. He wished fervently for her success tonight and during the coming weeks. He felt almost as nervous as he knew she was. Her next words confirmed his suspicion.

"Nathaniel," she asked, almost in a whisper, perhaps in the vain hope that Margaret and Lavinia would not hear her from the seat opposite, "are you *quite* sure my appearance is not just a little vulgar?"

Apparently she had found herself in a tussle with Margaret and the modiste over the low-cut bosom of tonight's ballgown. Margaret and the modiste had won after insisting that her gown, far from being vulgar, was in extreme danger of being too conservative.

Lavinia, Nathaniel saw in the semidarkness, was engaged in the characteristic gesture of tossing her glance at the roof of the carriage. Margaret drew breath to speak, but he held up his free hand.

"I am quite, quite sure, Georgie," he said. "You look extremely beautiful. If Margaret has to exert herself even slightly in an effort to find you partners tonight, I will be very surprised indeed."

"Lord Pelham is to dance the opening set with me," she said. "But that is because you asked him to, of course."

"I most certainly did not," he assured her. It had been all Eden's idea to meet the girls during the afternoon and to reserve a set at tonight's ball with each of them. His notice could do them nothing but good. Eden was a baron, after all, and both well-known and popular with the beau monde.

"Lord Pelham was kind enough to ask Lavinia for the second set," Margaret said, "and she refused."

As if any of them needed reminding!

"I was there when it happened, Marg," Nathaniel said ominously. "It was one of the more embarrassing moments of my life. I have explained to Lavinia that one does *not* refuse a dancing partner unless there is a *very* good reason for doing so—"

"There was," Lavinia said, interrupting him midsentence. "I told you so at the time, Nat, when you took me aside in order to favor me with a tongue-lashing."

"—such as not having been formally presented to the gentleman in question or like not having a free spot on one's card," he continued as if she had not spoken. His voice was rising, he noticed, as it so often did with his cousin. "You had been presented to Lord Pelham, one of my closest friends, by me, Lavinia, in my own drawing room, and *every* spot on your card was free."

"I informed him that I was not a charity case," she said, looking at his sister just as if Nathaniel did not exist. "He was so *condescending,* Margaret. One could see at a glance that he had decided as a favor to Nat that he would ask these awkward little country bumpkins to dance—they would doubtless swoon quite away at the honor being accorded them. He has the *bluest* eyes, Margaret—have you met him?—and clearly expects every female at whom he deigns to direct them to fall into a mindless dither.''

''I have met Lord Pelham,'' Margaret said. ''He is a handsome, dashing, charming gentleman. And very eligible, of course.''

''Then I certainly did not play my cards right,'' Lavinia said. ''Had I known he was *eligible,* Margaret, I would have danced with him and he would have come tomorrow to see Nat and offer for me, and all Nat's troubles would be at an end. I, of course, would have lived happily ever after.'' Being Lavinia, instead of looking flushed and irritable after delivering this tirade of sarcasm, she merely smiled dazzlingly at Nathaniel.

He raised his eyebrows and absently patted Georgina's hand. This was not going to be easy—but had he ever expected that it would be? And Lavinia's gown was a bright turquoise, most unsuitable for an unmarried young lady who was making her come-out. White, yes. A pale pastel shade, perhaps. But bright turquoise? Even the combined forces of Margaret and the modiste had not been able to prevail upon Lavinia to conform. She was *four and twenty,* she had been quite unembarrassed to remind them. The best they had been able to do was dissuade her from choosing a scarlet satin for tonight's all-important first appearance before the beau monde.

''Now, that other chit,'' Eden had said this afternoon when he was leaving—he had just complimented Nathaniel on the prettiness and sweetness of his sister, ''should have been taken over someone's knee years ago, Nat—preferably someone with a large, heavy paw—and given a sound walloping. I suppose you feel it is too late now. One cannot imagine you spanking a full-grown woman. I pity the poor fellow who is going to have to face that sharp tongue across the breakfast table for the rest of his life.''

Nathaniel had sighed. ''I fear it might be me, Ede,'' he had said. ''Who in his right mind would have her even if she were not loudly declaring that no one ever will?''

''You could not lock her up in a convent?'' Eden had suggested. ''No, wrong historical era. A pity.''

But Lavinia was not beyond showing the occasional sign of being almost normally human. The carriage at first slowed and then came to a full halt at the back of a long line of carriages waiting to draw up before the carpeted pavement and steps leading to the Shelby mansion on Grosvenor Square. Lavinia lifted her fan to her face and plied it quite vigorously despite the fact that it was not a particularly warm night.

She was nervous. Good. It would serve her right if she had not a single partner all night, Nathaniel thought uncharitably. But he would, of course, dance the opening set with her himself. And he would present some of the friends and acquaintances she had not already met to her as partners and hope fervently that she would not repeat her ridiculous statement about being treated as a charity case. If she did, that was that. She was going home tomorrow to stay at the rectory with Edwina, his second eldest sister, until he returned home. She would hate it. She considered the Reverend Valentine Scott, Edwina's husband, to be the dullest, most pompous man on earth, and Valentine considered that she should spend altogether more of her time in pious reflection and in the performance of good works.

One false move tonight, Nathaniel decided, eyeing her across the width of the carriage, and he would hint to her the consequences of being rude to his friends.

''It is amazing, Nat,'' she said, her fan stopping abruptly in mid-wave, ''that any battles at all had to be fought against Napoleon Bonaparte. If someone had just had the wisdom to seat you across from him so that you could glare at him like that, the poor man would simply have folded his tents and gone home to Corsica.''

"But you," he said, "are made of sterner stuff."

She smiled again suddenly and quite dazzlingly, reminding him that she was a considerable beauty—one tended sometimes to forget that fact. "Nat," she said, "you are quite lovely when you are rattled. I am doing you a great favor, you know. All the ladies at the ball, married and unmarried alike, I daresay, will pull out all the weapons in their arsenal in an attempt to attract that stern glance their way. I would wager that you will find a wife long before Georgina finds a husband—not that it will take *her* a great deal of time."

Which speech, intended to antagonize him further, merely reminded him of one particular lady, married and widowed, who was going to be at the ball. It still seemed unreal to him that *she* had offered *him* carte blanche this morning and he had accepted. Sophie, the minx! He felt both awkward and eager at the prospect of seeing her again this evening.

"Well, that silenced him at least," Lavinia said, bringing his mind back to the present and the slow-moving line of carriages. "Are you dreaming of your future bride, Nat?"

"Actually," he said, "I was dreaming of your wedding day, Lavinia, and the personal happiness the occasion will bring me." He raised one eyebrow and grinned at her.

She smiled back, looking genuinely amused. Her fan was fluttering before her face again. Out of the carriage window, he saw a red carpet come into view. The carriage in front of theirs was disgorging its passengers and a liveried footman had appeared outside their door.

Somehow, he thought, despite the myriad frustrations of being Lavinia's legal guardian, it was quite impossible to dislike her.

He turned his head to smile reassuringly at Georgina, who surprisingly looked to be the calmer of the two.

# SEVEN

T HERE WAS SOMETHING UN-
deniably exciting about being at the Season's first great
squeeze of a ball, Sophia had to admit to herself as she
stood with her in-laws, looking about her at all the splen-
didly fashionable and bejeweled guests. She certainly felt
like someone's poor aunt, though she was not ignored. A
flatteringly large number of people bowed to her and even
spoke to her. Two years after the Carlton House affair she
had still not sunk into total obscurity. But perhaps, she
thought with wry humor, if she were ever to appear at an
evening event in a different gown, no one would even recognize her.

Rex and Kenneth and their wives had arrived before her
party. They were in a larger group at the other side of the
ballroom. Eden too, she saw after a few moments, was
there. He was using those blue eyes of his, the rogue, to
charm a particularly attractive young lady, who was blushing and plying her fan.

Sophia looked carefully all about her. The ballroom was
already crammed so full of people that it was difficult to
see everyone. But there was one person—one man—she
did not see. Her heart, she realized, was thumping uncomfortably against her rib cage and even in her throat. He

might arrive later, of course, but he was definitely not here yet. Perhaps he would not come at all. She drew a few steadying breaths.

And Nathaniel was not here yet either. But he arrived just minutes after her own group. He was with three ladies, and another gentleman joined them at the door and took the arm of the eldest lady. They must be Nathaniel's sisters, the husband of the eldest, and his cousin, Sophia guessed. She looked away from them. Tonight he was a family man, the head of the family, responsible for the launch into society of his young charges. But she felt all atremble and breathless—like a young girl with her first infatuation. How ridiculous! He looked extremely handsome tonight—but then, when did he not? While many of the other gentlemen were wearing darker, more fashionable colors for evening, he was wearing a pale blue coat with silver waistcoat and gray knee breeches and white linen. And he was smiling. Ah, that smile. Sophia wondered how many other female hearts were turning over at the sight of it.

The first set was about to begin. She did not, of course, dance it herself—she did not expect to dance at all—but she smiled to see young Mr. Withingsford lead Sarah out and to note with some pride that her niece compared very favorably with all the most lovely young ladies present. She would surely do well despite the fact that it was now clear why she did not approve of her first partner. He was very young, very thin, and undeniably spotty, poor gentleman. He would improve with age. Gentlemen usually did. And of course he was heir to a baron's title and property.

Sophia noticed that Eden was dancing with one of Nathaniel's young relatives—his sister at a guess. She looked too wide-eyed and demure and was too conservatively dressed to be the rebel cousin. The other young lady—the one dancing with Nathaniel—must be the cousin. She was extremely lovely with her slim, proud bearing and her flame-colored hair. She was also dressed quite daringly in bright turquoise. But then she was already four and twenty, was she not? Sophia approved of her decision not to try to appear like a young girl.

Sophia tried not to watch them dance. She feared catching his eye. And she was more than ever aware—and hated the fact that it *mattered* to her—of how terribly dull she looked. She was only four years older than his cousin. She felt at least a century older.

Eden came at the end of the set and smiled and bowed to both Sophia and Sarah. ''Sophie,'' he said, ''will you do me the honor of presenting me to your brother- and sister-in-law?''

She did so, including Lewis in the introductions, and listened with a smile while they all talked briefly about Walter. He would ask Sarah to dance, Sophia thought, pleased. A dance with someone like Eden could do wonders in drawing a young girl to the attention of other gentlemen. And Sarah was gazing almost worshipfully at him. But it was to Sophia he turned when the second sets began to form.

''Will you dance with me, Sophie?'' he asked. ''You were always the best dancer in the army.''

''If I remember correctly, Eden,'' she said, enormously pleased at the prospect of actually dancing, ''I had very little competition.'' She set her hand in his.

''And with your mother's permission, Miss Armitage,'' he said, inclining his head to Sarah, ''perhaps you would reserve the next set for me?''

Sarah curtsied, all smiles. The plumes of Beatrice's turban waved her acquiescence.

''You have made Sarah very happy,'' Sophia told him as they took their places in the set. ''But you will remember, Eden, how young she is and how very innocent?''

He chuckled. ''Yes, ma'am,'' he said. ''I have asked her to *dance,* Sophie, not to kiss and cuddle with me in some murky corner.''

''I am happy to hear it,'' she said, joining in his laughter despite herself before abandoning herself to the exhilaration of performing the steps and patterns of a vigorous country dance.

"Well, Sophie," he said later during one of the short intervals when they were close enough to converse, "I suffered a fine tongue-lashing on your account this afternoon when I had thought merely to engage in a very civilized social call. Nat was incensed at what I almost said in your hearing last evening."

"All of you said a lot worse when we were in the Peninsula together," she said. "I have thick skin, Eden."

"Which is exactly what I told Nat," he said. "Not the thick-skin part, of course. But about your good sense and your good humor. But I was given strict orders to make my apologies to you and to look sincere when I did it. I do so most humbly. I certainly meant no disrespect." He grinned again. "Nat has grown disturbingly respectable, Sophie."

"It comes of having family responsibilities," she said. "It is something you have not yet experienced, Eden." She smiled and then laughed as he deliberately winced. "I accept your apology."

They were separated by the patterns of the dance.

"I feel a definite obligation toward Nat," he said when they came together again. "I do believe I am going to set up as a matchmaker, Sophie."

"Heaven help us all," she said.

"I am going to match him up," he said. "Oh, not with a bride, Sophie. Is that what you thought? It would go against all my finer principles to marry off the poor fellow. Besides, according to Nat himself, he has had quite enough of females in his home to last him for a lifetime or two. No, what I intend to do is match him up with a, ah . . . Oh, Lord, I can feel the necessity of another apology coming on." He chuckled and used his eyes on her quite shamelessly.

"Your meaning is crystal clear," she told him before they completed the pattern of the dance with different partners. She gathered that Nathaniel had not told him about last night, then—or about this morning. She had wondered. Men, she knew from experience, loved to discuss their amatory conquests with one another. She could not have borne . . . but of course Nathaniel would have done no such thing. He was too honorable a man.

"Do you know anyone suitable, Sophie?" Eden asked her a couple of minutes later. "You must know a considerable number of females of suitable age and marital status. She has to be someone respectable, of course. And lovely and lively too. Nat's own words."

*Oh!*

"If you expect me to help you matchmake in such a cause, Eden," she said tartly, "you must certainly have windmills in your head. I beg to decline. Why do we not discuss the weather?"

He chuckled as they were separated again.

When the set was ended he did not, as she expected, lead her back to her own party. He took her toward Kenneth and Moira, Rex and Catherine, who were in a group with Rex's brother and sister and their spouses and with Catherine's brother. Sophia would have preferred to return to Beatrice's company. But at least Nathaniel was not part of the group.

"We called on you this morning, Sophie," Moira said, "did we not, Catherine? We were going to drag you off to the shops with us to find some frivolity to buy. But you were not at home."

Samuel had not told her she had had other visitors. How fortunate that they had not arrived when she had been there alone with Nathaniel. The very thought of her narrow escape turned her uncomfortably hot. What would they have made of it?

"Will you dance the quadrille with me, Sophie?" Kenneth asked. "Or have you promised it to someone else."

"How foolish!" she said. "Of course I have not."

"Sophie," Rex told the group at large, his voice languid, his quizzing glass in one hand, "was always the most conceited lady of our acquaintance. 'How foolish! Of course I have not.' " He did a creditable imitation of her voice.

They all laughed and she felt herself flush before joining in. "Thank you, Kenneth," she said. "That would be delightful."

It was too. She would dance two sets in a row—with two of the most handsome gentlemen at the ball. She would be fortunate indeed if her head fit through the doorway by the time she wished to leave. Kenneth was bowing formally and extending his arm for hers.

In the event it turned out to be *three* sets in a row. Kenneth took her back to his group after he had finished dancing with her because Moira, who had been dancing with Mr. Claude Adams, was smiling and beckoning. She wished to make plans for a shopping trip the afternoon after the one following—most of her mornings and Kenneth's, she explained, were set aside for the entertainment of their son. And then Rex asked Sophia for the next set and out she went for yet more country dances.

"I feel young and giddy again," she told him, laughing and breathless as they danced down the line together.

"You *are* young, Sophie," he said. "You are younger than I, I believe, and I do assure you that I consider myself young, despite marriage and paternity. But you were never giddy. There was never much chance to be in the Peninsula, was there? Perhaps it is time you were now. Time you enjoyed yourself." He winked at her when her eyes met his.

Had Nathaniel *told* him? No, he would not do that to her.

Rex too took her back to his own group at the end of the set just as if she fully belonged there, and indeed the others all received her as if she did. She just hoped that Mr. Adams or Sir Clayton Baird or Viscount Perry would not now feel obliged to ask her to dance. She would feel mortified. But she was saved—if *saved* was the correct word.

"It still seems somewhat comical to see Nat playing the part of devoted brother," Kenneth said with a grin, looking over Sophia's shoulder. She realized, with an uncomfortable lurching of the stomach, that he must be approaching. A glance behind her showed her that he had a young lady on each arm.

Did he know she was here? How dreadfully embarrassing—though why it should be so she would have been unable to explain even to herself. She wished she could duck out of sight, return to her own group. But it was too late.

Nathaniel had noticed her almost from the moment of his arrival in the ballroom. But she did not notice him. Or so he thought at first. After a while it seemed unlikely, despite the great squeeze of guests, that she just had not seen him. She was deliberately avoiding him, then.

Why?

Had she changed her mind? It seemed very possible. Or was it just that she was embarrassed to see him in public after the events of last night, and after the agreement they had come to this morning? She was with her family—Walter's family. Perhaps she did not want them to suspect. Indeed, it seemed the likeliest explanation for her behavior.

He had expected to be a little embarrassed himself at sight of her. But he was not. She looked so endearingly familiar—not just as last night's lover, but as Sophie Armitage. Her gown was a dreary color. At first he thought it was black, but it was not. It was a very dark blue. Its high-cut square neck and its shapeless elbow-length sleeves were quite unfashionable—had they ever *been* fashionable? Her hair had been carefully dressed into a topknot and confined curls, but as always, so many feathery curls had sprung loose from the coiffure that they formed a sort of dark halo about her head. She was smiling her placid, cheerful smile.

Last night seemed unreal again until he remembered that hair loose and wild about her face and shoulders and billowing down her back all the way to her bottom. And her dreamy, passion-filled eyes. And the slim beauty of her body.

Oh, Sophie. Someone had once shown him a picture of

a vase—except that the vase had disappeared and two human faces in profile had replaced it when he changed the focus of his eyes. He could see both pictures after that but never simultaneously. There was always either the vase or the faces. His view of Sophie was somewhat like that this evening. He could see dear Sophie, his friend, who warmed his heart and brought an involuntary smile to his lips. And he could see and feel—and smell—last night's lover and know beyond any doubt that he wished to continue the liaison. But it was difficult to see both women at the same time.

After it had become clear to him that she really was avoiding even looking at him, Nathaniel decided that he must take matters into his own hands. It would be remarked upon if he was the only one of the four friends to fail even to pay his respects to her. Besides, he *wished* to talk with her. And he wanted Georgina and Lavinia to meet her—he had always intended to take them to call on her. Georgina at least would like her, he was sure. And so between sets he offered an arm to each and led them to where Sophie was standing with Ken, Rex, Eden, and their retinue.

His three friends had already met his sister and Lavinia. Rex and Kenneth had called with their wives during the afternoon, just after Eden had left. Indeed, Rex and Ken had each danced a set with both young ladies. Lavinia had not refused either of them, Nathaniel had been interested—and relieved—to find.

There was a great buzz of greetings and conversation as the three of them joined the group. Catherine took it upon herself to present Georgina and Lavinia to her brother and to Rex's relatives. She seemed to assume they must have met Sophie.

Nathaniel turned to her at last and smiled. If she was feeling embarrassed, she was not showing it. She stood quietly, as she always had, neither pushing herself forward nor cowering away out of sight.

"Hello, Sophie," he said. "Are you enjoying the ball?"

"Oh, yes indeed," she assured him. "I did not expect

to dance at all, you know. But I have danced three sets in a row—with three of the Horsemen of the Apocalypse, no less. I believe I might say that my evening—my whole Season—has been an unqualified success.'' She had always had that ability, he remembered, quietly and cheerfully to mock herself.

''May I have the honor of presenting my sister and my cousin to you?'' he asked.

''Yes, please,'' she said.

''My cousin Lavinia Bergland,'' he said, ''and my sister Georgina.''

She looked at them each in turn and smiled kindly.

''Mrs. Sophie Armitage,'' he continued. ''A very dear friend of mine who was in Spain and Portugal and Belgium with her husband during the wars. He was unfortunately killed at Waterloo but not before distinguishing himself in a quite extraordinary fashion.''

''How distressing for you, Mrs. Armitage,'' Georgina said, curtsying.

''You followed the drum, Mrs. Armitage?'' Lavinia said, her voice bright with interest. ''How splendid of you. How I envy you.''

''Sophie, please,'' Sophia said. ''Yes, I suppose I am to be envied. I was fortunate enough to be able to spend almost every day of my short married life with my husband.''

''Sophie.'' Lavinia reached out her right hand like a man and shook Sophia's hand. ''How lovely it is to meet you. I am going to like you. How fortunate that you are one of Nat's friends. We will meet again, then. There will be someone sensible to talk with.''

Sophie laughed. ''I do hope I can live up to your expectations,'' she said.

''But you must never offer to take her walking or shopping, Sophie,'' Eden said in the bored voice he used whenever he wished to ruffle someone's feathers. ''Or she will accuse you of treating her like a charity case and look at you with such marked disdain that you would feel your shirt points withering, if you ever wore them.''

Eden, Nathaniel thought, had been offended this afternoon. And who could blame him? Lavinia had been unpardonably rude.

Lavinia gave Eden the look he had just described and then smiled at Sophie with contrasting charm. "I would *love* to go walking or shopping with you, Sophie," she said. "Preferably walking so that we may talk uninterrupted. Shopping can be such a bore. I shall have Nat escort me to your house one day, if I may—does he know where you live?—and we can proceed together from there. May I?"

"Of course," Sophie said. But she darted a glance at him, Nathaniel saw. It would never occur to Lavinia to wait for an invitation, to wonder if her desire for friendship was reciprocated. But then Lavinia did not have many female friends. She thought most women silly.

The orchestra was tuning up again.

"Miss Gascoigne." Young Viscount Perry, Catherine's brother, was bowing to Georgina. "May I take you for some lemonade? This is a waltz and you may not dance it yet, I suppose."

Perry, Nathaniel could not help thinking, was heir to the Earl of Paxton. He was also a wealthy and personable young man and doubtless attractive to the ladies. Georgie was blushing and setting her hand on his arm. Fortunately she always looked her prettiest when blushing. Nathaniel caught Catherine's eye. She raised one eyebrow and half smiled at him.

"Is there *really* truth in that ridiculous story?" Lavinia asked of no one in particular. "One may not waltz until some old dragons say that one may?"

"It is a good thing none of the dragons are within earshot," Eden said, "or you might be waltzing for the first time on your eightieth birthday. Nat wants to waltz with Sophie. You had better come with me to the refreshment table, Miss Bergland, or you are going to look suspiciously like a wallflower."

Nathaniel raised his eyebrows. Ede really must have been

offended. It was unlike him to speak to any lady without his customary charm. Indeed, he had been downright rude. However, Lavinia took his offered arm without bristling noticeably.

Nathaniel turned to Sophie. Eden had read his wishes correctly. And it was to be a waltz. He could not have planned it better.

"It would be a shame, Sophie," he said, "if you could not dance the fourth set with the fourth Horseman and so complete the quartet. Will you dance it with me, my dear?"

"That would be very pleasant." She set her hand on his arm.

The music was already beginning. And which Sophie was he seeing now? he asked himself as he set one hand at the back of her waist—why had he never noticed in the past how alluringly slender it was?—and took her hand with his other. He could smell her perfume—no, her soap.

She smiled up at him as she set her free hand on his shoulder. Sophie Armitage's cheerful, comfortable smile. And the small, supple body of last night's lover.

# EIGHT

THE SURGE OF PHYSICAL awareness that assailed Sophia as soon as she touched him, as soon as he touched her, took her completely by surprise. She had been consumed by embarrassment—would not all their mutual friends and acquaintances *suspect*? And by the awkwardness of finding herself being presented to his relatives. And by her dismay at Lavinia's eagerness to strike up a friendship.

And by annoyance that she was somehow seeing herself as a . . . what? A mistress? A fallen woman? How foolish! How very middle class, Walter would have said. But then she *was* middle class.

But now she felt only awareness—and the sudden memory that just last night, not even twenty-four hours ago, they had been naked and intimate together. She raised her eyes to his. He was looking steadily at her from those heavy-lidded eyes of his that always made him look enticingly sleepy.

"Was it proper?" she asked him.

"Is that what troubled you?" he asked her in return. "Do you feel like a kept woman, then, Sophie?"

"No, of course not." And it was the truth, she told herself firmly. She did not.

''Then why is it improper,'' he asked, ''for you to meet my sister and my cousin? For me to meet your niece? What we do in privacy together and by mutual consent concerns no one but us, Sophie.''

She wondered—had wondered all day—if that was really true. Even though she believed it.

He moved her into the dance then and for a while she forgot all else but the glorious exhilaration of dancing with him, of waltzing with him. There had never been any waltzes at the regimental balls—it had been too new, too controversial a dance. She felt his body heat though their bodies did not touch, smelled his cologne, shared his rhythm—and felt her cheeks grow hot at the memory of another shared rhythm.

She was mad, she thought. Insane. How would she survive the inevitable end of the coming months? But how, after last night, could she survive without them?

He was still looking at her when she glanced up again. He was half smiling too. ''You were born to dance, Sophie,'' he said.

Strange words. She did not ask him what he meant. But suddenly she felt wonderfully feminine. She so rarely felt this way. She thought back to her youth and Walter's brief courtship—she had been only eighteen. He had never been a particularly handsome or charming man, but she had liked his bluff good humor. At that time she had still thought herself passably pretty and attractive. When she had accepted him and married him, she had anticipated great happiness. She had had confidence in herself as a woman. She had looked forward eagerly to being a wife, a mother. It was all she had ever wanted of life.

It had not taken long—not long at all—to lose all confidence in her beauty and charms. She had quickly learned to be content with being Walter's ''old girl'' or ''old sport'' and with being ''good old Sophie'' to the Four Horsemen and others—though now she came to think of the matter, she did not believe that Nathaniel had ever used that particular phrase.

She did not know whether it was good for her to hear that she had been born to dance. But she smiled back at Nathaniel before lowering her eyes so that she could concentrate on sheer sensation again. She had waltzed before, but it had never been like this—like dancing in a dream or on a rainbow or on clouds or among the stars or any of those other clichés, all of which seemed suddenly quite fresh and altogether appropriate.

She realized finally that the waltz must be coming to an end. She looked about her, trying to hold the memory, wishing again that it were possible to freeze a moment in time. She looked beyond Nathaniel's shoulder—and froze indeed. She completely lost her step with the result that her slipper ended up beneath Nathaniel's shoe. She winced and he hauled her right against him for one moment.

"Sophie, my dear," he said, stopping dancing and looking down at her in dismay. "I am so sorry. How dreadfully clumsy of me. Did I hurt you?"

"No," she said, flustered, her mind flying off in all directions. "No, it was my fault. I am quite all right."

"You are not," he said. "Come. Let us move over here and stand by the windows. Are you hiding crushed toes inside that slipper?"

"No." She shook her head and bit her lip—she felt as if she had *five* crushed toes—and darted a glance to the doorway. He was not there. Had he come farther inside? Had he gone away again? Had she imagined that he had been there at all? She knew she had not imagined it. Their eyes had met.

"Let me find you an empty chair," Nathaniel suggested.

"No." She grabbed his arm. "No, let us finish the waltz."

He dipped his head and looked more closely into her face. "What is it?" he asked her. "You stopped dancing, did you not? Not that it was not still my fault. It is a capital offense, I do believe, to tread upon one's partner's toes. What is it, Sophie?"

There it was again, that illusion of safety that was not

safety at all. She imagined telling him and seeing his look of concern turn to one of disgust. She would not be able to bear it.

"Nothing," she said, smiling. "Just screaming pain. You must weigh a ton, Nathaniel. Perhaps two. But the pain has gone now. Let us dance."

"May I come to you tomorrow night?" he asked her, his head still dipped toward hers.

Her stomach lurched with unmistakable desire. "About midnight?" she said. "I will watch for you. My servants will be in bed."

"Would you prefer that it be somewhere else?" he asked her. "I could rent a house."

"No," she said quickly. "That would be intolerable."

"Yes," he agreed. "It would. But I would not wish to cause problems with your servants."

"They need not know," she said. "And even if they do, I am my own mistress, Nathaniel."

"Yes," he said. "I think you always were, Sophie."

Strange words again. Comforting words. And true to a large degree. She had always—almost always—controlled her own life. She would continue to do so even though there were several things to fear over the coming months. Financial ruin or exposure. Losing Nathaniel when the Season was over. Finding life too frighteningly empty.

"Let us dance," he said, taking her hand in his.

Nathaniel returned Sophie to her own group. He should have gone earlier, he knew, to pay his respects to her niece, since he had been presented to the girl in the park. Doing so, of course, would mean having to be presented to her parents too. But then Houghton was Walter Armitage's brother. It was only right that he make the man's acquaintance. There was no reason to keep his distance because he was bedding Sophie—the idea still seemed dizzyingly strange. There was nothing immoral in what they were doing—he had convinced himself of that during the course of the day. And there was nothing distasteful about it, provided they were discreet and kept the affair strictly private.

And so he went with Sophie, bowed to and smiled at Miss Sarah Armitage and complimented her on her appearance, and secured an introduction to her parents and her brother. Houghton, he discovered, had none of Walter's ruggedness of build or floridity of complexion. He looked far more refined. They all talked about Walter for a few minutes and then, because Miss Armitage had stood close to him and gazed at him the whole while with the result that any prospective partners must have assumed she already had one, he felt obliged to invite her to dance the set with him.

*That* seemed somehow improper, especially as the girl had that way of looking at him, he remembered from the year after Waterloo, when he and his three friends had quickly come to realize that they were being seen as very eligible young men. He had forgotten. Because he had come to town with the express purpose of shepherding Georgina and Lavinia about and finding husbands for them, it had not struck him that perhaps women—both mothers and daughters—would be looking at *him* as a prospective husband.

Miss Sarah Armitage was looking at him that way. So had her mother before he led the girl out. And of course Miss Armitage looked quite exquisitely lovely. He set himself to talking as little as possible—the intricate patterns of the dance discouraged conversation—and to confining his few remarks to dull, safe topics. But fate had conspired against him. It was the supper dance, and so he was obliged to offer the girl his arm when it was over and to lead her into the supper room and secure her a place beside him. He was obliged to talk with her, to smile at her, to give her the courtesy of his undivided attention.

He must be so terribly brave, she told him. He simply must tell her all about his courageous deeds in battle. She could not believe that her uncle Walter had been the only brave officer. He told her a few of the more amusing incidents he could remember, like the time when Major Hanley, an avid sportsman, had taken out his dogs and his cronies and had had such success at the hunt that they had come riding back to camp whooping and shouting and doing nothing to quell the exuberant barking of the dogs. Their colonel, who had been sleeping off the effects of a hearty dinner washed down by large quantities of liquor, had woken up startled and befuddled, had assumed a surprise French attack was about to descend upon his head, and had bellowed out commands that had thrown the whole camp into panic and confusion.

"But there was no French attack?" Miss Armitage asked after a short pause, her eyes wide with alarm.

He smiled gently at her. "There was no French attack," he said. "Only Major Hanley and his friends and his dogs."

"Oh," she said. "He ought not to have been making so much noise, ought he? I daresay he might have alerted a French force had one been near. And then you and Uncle Walter and—everyone would have been in grave danger."

"You are quite right," he said, deciding that he must turn the conversation to bonnets or some such topic with which she would feel more at home. "I do believe Major Hanley was severely reprimanded and was contrite and never did it again." He was about to add that the colonel had sworn off drink from that moment on, but he did not want her to believe she was being made fun of.

"And Aunt Sophie would have been in grave danger," she added as an afterthought.

"Your uncle was there to keep her safe," he said. "And all of us who did not have wives looked out for the ladies too, you know, as gentlemen must always do. Sophie was a particular favorite with my friends and me. We always kept an eye out for her whenever your uncle was on duty."

"I am sure," she said, gazing at him with what appeared to be real worship in her eyes, "she must have felt perfectly safe if *you* were close by, Sir Nathaniel."

He smiled at her and looked about the room to find Sophie. She was sitting some distance away with her sister-in-law. But a gentleman came up behind her even as Nathaniel watched, and touched her on the shoulder. She turned her head, her customary smile on her lips, and—and something happened. She did not stop smiling. She proceeded to speak to the man and to listen to him and then turned to her sister-in-law, apparently to present the gentleman to her.

But there was something wrong. Nathaniel was reminded of the way she had suddenly stopped dancing an hour ago and caused him to step heavily on her foot. It had been something very fleeting, and something she had denied afterward. But something had definitely happened. She had seen someone unexpectedly, perhaps.

He could not see the man's face to identify him until he turned to make his bow to Viscountess Houghton and appeared in profile. He looked familiar, though Nathaniel could not immediately put a name to the face. And then he did remember—how could he have forgotten? The man was no longer in regimentals, of course, and therefore he did look quite different. Pinter. Lieutenant Boris Pinter. Always a weasel, ingratiating himself with superiors even at the expense of his fellow officers, dealing with subordinates with unutterable cruelty in the name of discipline, Pinter had been liked by no one and hated by many. He had been the only officer of Nathaniel's acquaintance who had actually enjoyed watching a formal whipping and had hated to see any other man promoted.

Walter Armitage had once opposed Pinter's promotion on grounds that had never been made public—and had won his point. Pinter never had made the rank of captain. Apparently he had not had the funds with which to buy the promotion although his father was an earl.

And Pinter was now talking with and smiling at Sophie—and being presented to Walter's sister-in-law. Nathaniel frowned. And he could see now what was wrong with Sophie—the outer evidence of what was wrong anyway. Her smiling face was quite without color. He half rose from his chair.

But his view of Sophie was suddenly cut off by the appearance of young Lewis Armitage, who had come to take the empty chair opposite his sister.

"Oh, Lewis," Miss Armitage said, "Sir Nathaniel is telling me *such* stories about French attacks and hunting dogs and sleeping colonels."

Young Armitage grinned at Nathaniel. "I trust, sir," he said, "that you have included no gory details to give Sarah nightmares for the next six months."

"Indeed, I would never forgive myself if I had," Nathaniel said.

"Oh silly, Lewis," Miss Armitage scolded. "Sir Nathaniel has been just *entertaining* me. But seriously, I would just *die* if I had to follow the drum like Aunt Sophie did."

Ken and Eden had gone to the rescue, Nathaniel saw after shifting his position so that he could see across the room again. They were standing on either side of Pinter, smiling, perfectly at their ease, talking with him, talking with her. He might have trusted them to notice too that she was in distress. He relaxed a little.

"Actually, sir," young Armitage was saying, a flush of color in his cheeks, "I was wondering if you might do me the honor after supper of presenting me to the young lady in white whom you are escorting—your sister, I believe? With your permission, I would like to lead her into a set."

He must be one or two and twenty, Nathaniel thought. He was blond and slender, very like his sister. He seemed to have a deal more sense than she—though she was not without a certain sweetness, he must confess. Armitage was heir to a viscount's title and property. Probably not a wealthy one, but certainly respectable. He was not asking to marry Georgie, of course, merely to dance with her. But even so, the responsibility of bringing a sister out was a serious one. One would not wish her to make ineligible connections.

"I shall return Miss Armitage to your mother's side when supper is over," Nathaniel replied. "I would be happy then to take you to meet my sisters."

"Thank you, sir," the young man said.

Moira had crossed the room to Ken and the two of them were leading Sophie out, one on each side of her, each with one of her arms drawn through theirs. They were laughing and talking. Eden had taken the empty seat beside Viscountess Houghton and was engaging her in conversation. Pinter was looking around him, a half smile on his lips. For one moment before Lewis Armitage moved and cut off the view again, his eyes met Nathaniel's.

The wars might be over and Walter might be dead, Nathaniel thought, but Sophie was still their friend. They would still watch out for her safety, the four of them, and protect her from the impertinences of the likes of Pinter. It made no difference that Nathaniel was now also her lover—certainly the other three would never know that fact. They could all be trusted to watch over her.

Was it Pinter she had spotted when she was dancing with him? But why would the mere sight of him have had her faltering and then denying that anything was wrong? Would she not have simply grimaced and said something like—"You will never guess whom I just saw"? She could have shared her distaste with him. They had both known the man, after all.

And why had she presented Pinter to her sister-in-law—even if he had asked? It would have been far better if she had merely inclined her head to him with icy courtesy and turned back to the table. He would have got the message and left her alone in the future.

Well, he would leave her alone in the future if he knew what was good for him.

Miss Armitage, Nathaniel noticed with sudden amusement, was describing to him in great detail the bonnet her mama had helped her pick out just that morning. It was apparently the most darling bonnet ever fashioned and worth every penny of the exorbitant price.

"Papa may disagree when the bill arrives on his desk, Sare," young Armitage said with a chuckle.

"Well, there you are wrong," she said, on her dignity.

"Papa said that no expense is to be spared in showing me to very best advantage this spring."

And then Nathaniel was further amused when another young man touched Lewis Armitage on the shoulder and proceeded to speak softly but quite audibly to him.

"I wonder if I might prevail upon you to present me to your sister, Armitage," he said.

The young Viscount Perry, Rex's brother-in-law. The gentleman who had taken Georgie for a lemonade during the waltz. He and Armitage were close in age and obviously knew each other.

Armitage performed the introductions and Perry secured the next set with Miss Armitage. She looked at the young man, Nathaniel was interested to note, with as much bright worship in her eyes as she had shown to himself. She was perhaps a young lady of some sense after all. She had come to London to find a husband. She was going to consider all her possible choices at least during her first ball.

She could do a great deal worse than Perry. But then so could Georgie.

This marriage-mart business could easily give a man a permanent headache, Nathaniel thought. He looked forward with some longing to the following night. Midnight, she had said. Twenty-four hours away. An eternity.

"Lean a little more heavily on my arm if you wish, Sophie," Kenneth said. "It will be cooler in the ballroom. We will find you a seat in a moment."

"Are you going to faint, Sophie?" Moira asked, her smiles and laughter gone now that they had left the supper room behind. "Kenneth will carry you if you are."

"What nonsense!" Sophia said, pulling herself together. "But thank you both anyway. The supper room was very stuffy. This is very foolish. I never faint." She laughed shakily.

"It is not foolish," Moira said. "I was sitting with Rex and Clayton and Clarissa. Rex saw you with that man and muttered something that should have had me blushing at the very least, and he started to get up. But Kenneth and Eden had reacted faster. Who *was* he?''

''A particularly unpleasant former lieutenant,'' Kenneth said. ''All of us, almost without exception, had some quarrel with him, but he had a particular grudge against Walter Armitage, Moira, because Walter—with the concurrence of several more of us, I must add—blocked a promotion he had been expecting. He had no business approaching you like that, Sophie. He was fortunate the setting was so very public. One of us would have planted him a facer.''

''I feel better now,'' Sophia said. ''Really, it was just the heat. I did not mind so very much Lieutenant Pinter's greeting me.'' She could not repress a shudder at the memory of turning to find that it was *his* hand that was resting on her shoulder.

''But one could see that you did, Sophie,'' Kenneth said. ''And so you should have. He even trapped you into presenting him to Walter's sister-in-law. I might plant him that facer yet.''

''It is really quite all right,'' Sophia said.

''Some of your color is returning,'' Moira said, patting her hand. ''Poor Sophie. Have you seen him since your husband's passing?''

''Yes,'' Sophia admitted after a moment's hesitation. She smiled. ''He is responsible, I do believe, for my continued fame. It was he who came forward last year to inform the *ton* that Walter risked his life to save his when he was a mere ensign and Walter was a major. He even painted himself in a less than glorious light with the result that Walter appeared correspondingly more heroic.'' She swallowed. ''It was very obliging of him.'' It was no such thing, of course. She knew very well why he had told such a blatant lie.

''The devil!'' Kenneth muttered. ''That was Pinter, Sophie? And now he believes he has a perfect right to accost you before the whole *ton* whenever he pleases?''

''I do not often appear before the whole *ton*, Kenneth,''

Sophia said. "I live a very quiet life. Do not make a deal of what happened just now, I beg you. Really it was nothing."

"You are too good-natured by half, Sophie," he said. "We will keep an eye on you from now on, you may be sure. He will not bother you further."

"You have four champions, Sophie," Moira said with a chuckle. "Nathaniel was getting up too at the same moment as Rex. I saw him."

"The Four Horsemen of the Apocalypse as my devoted knights," Sophia said gaily. "What more could any woman ask of life?"

"That is the spirit, Sophie," Kenneth said. "Do you still need a chair? You are looking much better."

They had been strolling about the almost deserted ballroom, though a steady stream of guests was beginning to return.

"I am perfectly fine," she said, releasing her hold of their arms. "Thank you so much. I am fortunate to have such good friends."

"If he bothers you again, Sophie, when none of us are present to rescue you," Kenneth said, "you must let us know. One of us will pay a call on Mr. Boris Pinter. Or perhaps all four of us. That would put the wind up him!"

Sophia laughed lightly. She had no doubt at all that Mr. Boris Pinter would be appearing in her sitting room the very next morning, another letter—another *love* letter—in his pocket. And another price—a higher price—on his lips. Tonight's humiliation would doubtless raise that price even higher. How would she pay it? She drew a slow breath to quell the panic.

"There is Beatrice returning with Eden," she said. "I shall go and join her. Thank you again." She smiled at both of them before making her way toward her sister-in-law.

Nathaniel had been getting up to come to her rescue too, she thought. She wished it were tonight he was coming to her. But tonight would be over by the time the ball came to an end, of course. Tomorrow seemed an eternity away. Between now and tomorrow night . . . No, she would not think of it.

Eden was smiling. His very blue eyes looked searchingly into hers. ''Sophie?'' he said. ''You have recovered from your near faint?''

''Yes, thank you,'' she said. ''It was very silly of me.''

Beatrice was turning away to watch Sarah come toward her on Nathaniel's arm, Lewis with them.

''If you ever need a pair of fists to be put to use on your behalf, Sophie,'' Eden said, leaning closer to her and speaking for her ears only, ''mine are always available.''

''Thank you,'' she said, laughing. ''But it was merely the heat, you know.''

She could see that he did not believe her any more than Kenneth had.

# NINE

NATHANIEL HAD BEEN UP
and out riding early, but he joined his sister and his cousin
for a late breakfast.

Georgina, as might have been expected, was glowing
with memories of the ball the night before. She had missed
dancing only two sets, and both of those had been waltzes.
And the first of them she had spent with Viscount Perry
and the second with Viscount Rawleigh, who had agreed
to allow her to visit his nursery and play with his infant
son. Of course it was beaux more than children, though she
passionately loved them, that were on Georgie's mind this
morning. She marveled at how many gentlemen had been
kind enough to dance with her. She could scarce believe
that two of last night's partners had actually sent her posies
this morning. And she was to go driving in the park this
afternoon with the Honorable Mr. Lewis Armitage.

She was very pleased with life this morning, and Nathaniel was pleased for her.

Lavinia was a different matter, of course. She too had
had a partner for every set except the second—Margaret
had made it very clear to her that having refused Lord Pelham's offer for no good reason, she could not then dance
with any other gentleman. But she had attracted a good deal

of notice—some of it from gentlemen who were very eligible indeed. She had received one posy and two huge bouquets during the morning. But she chose to think it all silly nonsense.

"They probably sent flowers to every lady with whom they danced," she said of the three gentlemen concerned. "They have nothing better to do with their money, I suppose."

And having dismissed so carelessly three prospective suitors—one of them was the same gentleman with whom she had refused to drive in Hyde Park this afternoon—she turned her conversation away from the ball.

"I wish to call upon Sophie this afternoon," she announced. "She will go walking with me in the park, I daresay, and we will have a far more interesting and sensible conversation than I might expect from any of the gentlemen I met last evening. You will escort me to her house, Nat?"

Nathaniel raised his eyebrows. "Would it not be better to send a note and suggest another day?" he asked. "Perhaps she will be busy or even from home this afternoon, Lavinia."

"Well then," she said, "we will return here and be none the worse off except that we will have had some air and a comfortable drive. She said I might come."

Sophie was altogether too good-natured, Nathaniel thought, sighing and getting to his feet. He would not wish Lavinia on his worst enemy—and Sophie fit very high in the opposite category. But he wanted to see her himself, he had to admit. He would see her tonight, of course, but he wanted to reassure himself before then that she was none the worse for last evening's unpleasant experience. Ken had told them this morning that she had made light of the fact that Pinter had forced his attentions on her, that she had claimed the stuffiness of the room as the cause of her near faint. Ken did not believe it for a moment. Neither did the rest of them. But Ken had also said that Pinter had spread stories to enhance Walter Armitage's fame—and his own— the year before. That would explain the fact that Sophie had not given him the cold set-down he had deserved. Doubtless she felt she owed him something.

She did not, of course. As Rex had pointed out, Pinter had never been an ensign in the Peninsula. He had been a lieutenant when he had arrived there. And none of them was aware of any occasion when Armitage had saved his life. Pinter, in his usual opportunistic way, had merely shouldered his way into someone else's glory.

"We will take the carriage to Sloan Terrace, then," Nathaniel said to Lavinia. "If Sophie is not at home, we will walk back and you may have all the air and exercise you wish for, Lavinia."

She smiled dazzlingly at him. "If you think that is a threat, Nat," she said, "you are doomed to disappointment. Of course the walk would be in your company, which somewhat diminishes its attraction, but we would both probably survive the experience."

"Perhaps," he agreed, setting down his napkin. "Will one hour be sufficient time for you to get ready?"

"More than enough," she said amiably. "And for you, Nat?"

He had long ago conceded her need to have the last word in their verbal exchanges. He merely pursed his lips and left the room.

They arrived at Sloan Terrace an hour and a half later. Nathaniel left Lavinia in the carriage while he got down to knock on the door and ask if Sophie was at home and receiving. But the door opened above him just as he was setting his foot on the bottom step, and he looked up to discover that Boris Pinter was leaving the house, looking elegant and confident and even handsome in a certain oily, toothy way.

The devil! Nathaniel's hand closed more tightly about his cane.

"Ah, Major Gascoigne," Pinter said, smiling broadly. "You too are calling upon the charming Sophie?"

"Pinter?" Nathaniel inclined his head very slightly and assumed his frostiest manner. It was in his mind to demand what the man was doing here and to question the familiarity of his reference to a superior officer's widow. But he restrained himself. He would need to talk to Sophie first. Perhaps she had not even admitted the man.

"You will find her looking her usual lovely self," Pinter said.

Nathaniel found the handle of his quizzing glass and raised it indolently to his eye. "Indeed?" he said faintly before turning away to hand the waiting butler his card. "Ask Mrs. Armitage if she would be so good as to receive Miss Bergland and Sir Nathaniel Gascoigne," he said, stepping inside.

He did not watch Pinter walk away. They must pay a call on the man if he had the presumption to press his attentions upon Sophie again, Ken had said during the morning ride. All four of them—he had chuckled at the suggestion. It would be his distinct pleasure, Nathaniel thought now. And if by some good fortune there were any fisticuffs to be engaged in, he was going to be first in line.

Mrs. Armitage, the butler informed him, would be delighted to receive her visitors.

Lavinia was chuckling when Nathaniel went back to hand her down from the carriage. "Far be it from me to compliment you in the normal way of things, Nat," she said, "but that was a stellar performance. I expected to see icicles hanging from his chin and his eyebrows by the time you had finished with him. What a deadly weapon a quizzing glass can be. Who on earth *was* he?"

"No one you would care to know," he said.

Sophie came to meet them at the door of her sitting room, her comfortable smile on her lips, her hands extended to take Lavinia's.

"You did come," she said. "I am so glad."

She looked her usual cheerful self.

"I have been all alone," she said, "and just longing for a companion with whom to go walking. It is such a glorious day. I was about to take my maid, but she hates walking anywhere farther than from the kitchen to her bedchamber on the upper floor. Lass, get down. That is far too fine a dress for you to rest your paws on.''

''Oh, but he is such a lovely dog,'' Lavinia said, fondling the dog's alert ears. ''No—*Lass*. *She* is such a lovely dog. May she come walking with us?''

''Try to stop her,'' Sophie said with a laugh—and darted a glance at him, Nathaniel saw. She was wondering, of course, if he had seen Pinter leave her house, and was hoping he had not. Or at least that was how he interpreted her enthusiasm and her lie—she had *not* been alone—and her failure to look fully at him.

''You are not busy, then, Sophie?'' he asked. ''I may safely leave Lavinia in your care?''

''In her *care*?'' Lavinia exploded into sound. ''I am four and twenty, Nat. Sophie is not exactly eighty. Can you not simply concede that you are leaving us in company together?''

Sophie's smile looked far more genuine now as she turned it on him—and very amused. ''She has a point, you must admit, Nathaniel,'' she said. ''But do run along. We three *girls*—Lass, Lavinia, and I—will do very nicely together. There are very few bandits in the park, I have been assured.''

They were in feminine league against him, he could see. Laughing at him. Even the dog was prancing about the two of them and ignoring him entirely.

He grinned and then chuckled. ''Come back with Lavinia for tea, Sophie,'' he said. ''Rex and Catherine are coming and Margaret and John. I will be able to send you home later in the carriage.''

''Maybe,'' she said. ''Thank you. I shall have to run upstairs for my bonnet, Lavinia. I shall be only a moment.''

He was dismissed. He left the house and climbed back into his carriage after giving his coachman directions to take him to White's.

Why did she not want him to know that Pinter had called? Perhaps she really had not admitted him? Or was she just afraid that he would make a fuss as Ken had last evening? But if Pinter was calling on her in her own home, it was high time someone made a fuss—someone with the sort of persuasive powers a man like Pinter would understand.

He would confront her about it tonight. This was something she did not need to handle alone. But Sophie was so damned independent.

Tonight. He closed his eyes. Eden had been talking this morning about some card party he assumed Nathaniel would attend with him. He had chuckled quite derisively when his friend had pleaded the necessity of having a decent night's sleep after last night.

He could hardly believe how much he looked forward to tonight, Nathaniel thought, how much he longed for Sophie again. He laughed softly to himself. He hoped his appetites would have quietened down somewhat by the time he must return home to Bowood for the summer.

Sophia did not go in to tea at Upper Brook Street, even though she walked there with Lavinia and was tempted to accept the invitation. Perhaps, she thought before rejecting the notion, she could take the rest of just this one day for herself.

She stooped down to attach Lass's leash to her collar and straightened up to smile at Lavinia. "This has been so very pleasant," she said. "I shall look forward immensely to our visit to the library tomorrow morning."

"And so shall I," Lavinia said fervently. "You cannot know how I have been starved for sensible friends, Sophie. I hope I do not presume too much. I am sure Nat believes I do." She rolled her eyes skyward.

"I am as delighted as you," Sophia said. "Oh yes, Lass, standing around is very tedious, I know. Until tomorrow then, Lavinia."

And she went striding off along the street. She had something to do, and she wanted it done now, this afternoon. She would know no peace until it was accomplished.

She would have enjoyed her long walk with Lavinia immensely, she thought, if that other thing had not been hammering constantly against the back of her consciousness. But she was becoming almost accustomed to the feeling. She *had* enjoyed the walk regardless. She liked Lavinia very much indeed and felt that she had just made a friend who could become very dear to her if the friendship was given a chance to blossom.

It was strange really that Lavinia admired her—for following the drum and enduring all the discomforts of life with a constantly moving army as well as all the very real dangers. She admired Sophia for living independently now when she might have chosen to spend most of her time in the homes of her male relatives.

"And all this you have done before your thirtieth birthday," Lavinia had added with a sigh.

It was strange because Sophia as a girl had wanted only marriage and motherhood. She had been no different from almost any other young lady of her acquaintance both then and now. It was only circumstances that had shaped her and strengthened her and made her into the sort of woman who could and would stand alone—though that might change very soon, she thought with a sharp intake of breath. She hauled back on Lass's leash, judging that the four large horses pulling a ponderous carriage along the street must be allowed to take precedence over one eager collie.

"Sit!" she commanded, and Lass sat, tongue lolling, and watched the horses go by.

Lavinia felt no general hatred of men despite some bitingly witty remarks about several of the gentlemen who had tried to pay court to her at last evening's ball. She even conceded that she dreamed of one day finding that one and only man with whom her soul as well as her body could mate—she spoke her mind quite boldly. But he would have to be someone, she explained, who would recognize that in addition to being a woman, she was also and first and foremost a *person*.

"Sometimes, Sophie," she had said quite candidly and quite without conceit, "I think it a curse to be beautiful.

Especially a beautiful redhead. One is expected to be strong-willed and fiery-tempered when one has red hair, of course, but you would not believe the flights of wit on which gentlemen take wing with the accompaniment of the most odious smirks when they speak of dousing fires. They believe I am waiting with trembling hope for the advent of some man strong enough to tame me.''

"Yet all you are really waiting for," Sophia had said, "is some man strong enough to allow you to be you."

"Exactly!" Lavinia had said, stopping on one of the paths of Hyde Park and gripping Sophia's arm while she smiled dazzlingly at her. "Oh, Sophie, that is *exactly* it and no one—absolutely no one until now—has understood it. Oh, *how* I like you!"

But Sophia was not able to bask in the pleasure of a new friendship. There was too much else crowding out her memories of a pleasant walk in bright, warm sunshine and of the interesting, intelligent conversation of Nathaniel's cousin.

Had Nathaniel seen Boris Pinter leave her house? At the time she had convinced herself that if he had, he would have said so immediately. But the more she had thought of it since, the more she was convinced that not enough time had elapsed between the departure of Mr. Pinter and the arrival of Nathaniel and Lavinia. Surely the two men must have seen each other. And yet Nathaniel had said nothing. And she had foolishly lied. She had told them she had been alone and bored.

What if he mentioned it tonight? It was none of his business, of course. She might say anything she pleased to any question he chose to ask or even nothing at all. But she did not want to lie further to him or have him think she was keeping secrets from him—she laughed aloud and then looked about self-consciously to see if anyone on the street had noticed. *Keeping secrets from him!*

Boris Pinter's visit had not been unexpected, of course. Indeed, she would have been surprised if he had not come today. And the price had not been totally unexpected, though her knees had grown weak beneath her when he had named it.

"Where do you expect me to find such a sum?" she had asked him before she could stop herself. One could not expect compassion from a blackmailer, and she had resolved never to beg, never to show weakness to him.

"Why, Sophie," he had said, smiling and revealing those large, white, perfect teeth of his—she always found herself looking idly to see if his eyeteeth had yet grown into fangs, "you have a brother-in-law with estates in Hampshire and a brother who, though no gentleman, is said to be rich enough to buy up all of Hampshire with the loose change in his pockets. Is it not time one of them was called upon to support old Walter's widow?" She and Walter had been "sir" and "ma'am"—with the accompaniment of a salute or a deferential bow—during the war years, of course.

She had looked at him with cold contempt. It might come to that, of course—in fact, it undoubtedly would—but not until she was quite desperate. *And that would be next time.* an inner voice had said loudly and clearly. But she would not involve Thomas in something that was really not his concern unless she had no alternative, and she hated the thought of involving Edwin, of telling him . . .

"I just happened to find this one more letter, Sophie," Boris Pinter had said, taking it from his pocket. "It had fallen down behind a drawer just when I thought I had returned them all to you. It makes one shudder to realize that I might have left it there to be discovered by a future tenant of the house, who might immediately feel it his duty to make it public, does it not? You really would like to have them all, would you not, Sophie, as a final memento of old Walter?"

He had always brought one of the letters with him. He had always put it into her hands, while hovering close enough to be sure that she could not destroy it before it had been paid for. She had read the first one from beginning to end. It had been unmistakably in Walter's hand. She had found herself strangely relieved to discover that there was no vulgarity in the letter, nothing shockingly graphic. Only a deep, poetic tenderness—she would never have suspected that Walter was capable of anything approaching poetry. It had been perfectly obvious that Walter had been passionately, irrevocably in love. She had looked at the name at the top of the letter, at his signature at the end. She had not read any of the subsequent letters in detail. She had only glanced at them to ascertain that they were indeed love letters written by Walter.

"I always had a great respect for old Walter," Boris Pinter had said that first time—and every time since, "and for you too, Sophie. I knew you would not wish this letter to get into the wrong hands and so I have brought it straight to you. In light of the extreme bravery of his final act and the grateful adulation of a nation, it would be sad indeed if it were suddenly learned that for a full two years before his death he was, ah, *unfaithful* to his wife."

It was always the same speech, give or take a word or phrase.

"You will have your money," she had said earlier this afternoon. "Within one week, you said? You will have it long before then. You will leave now."

"No offer of tea, Sophie?" he had asked. "But I can understand how upsetting it must be to discover that Walter preferred someone else to you—though not nearly as lovely as you, of course. One can only wonder at his poor taste. You do realize, of course, that old Walter's *Four Horsemen of the Apocalypse* would be the very last to offer you sympathy if they could take one glance at any of these letters?"

"You will leave now," she had repeated quietly.

And a scant five minutes later—perhaps not even as long—Samuel had appeared at the sitting room door with Nathaniel's card and a request that he might be received with Lavinia.

It would have taken a miracle indeed for him not to have seen the other man.

Sophia found the jeweler's shop she was looking for and went inside after tying Lass's leash to a post outside the door. She had at first intended to go to a pawnshop, but she had rejected the idea for two reasons. She did not believe she would be able to get enough money at a pawnshop. And there was no point in giving herself false hope. There was no chance that at any future date she would be able to redeem her pearls. No, she must sell them.

She emerged from the shop ten minutes later, untied Lass, who was standing and eager to be on her way, tail waving in the air, and proceeded to take the shortest route home.

"Well, Lass," she asked her dog briskly when they came to the familiar streets close to home and she had bent to remove the leash, "what is the best story to tell Beatrice and Sarah and anyone else who is likely to notice my bare neck at the next evening entertainment and remark upon it? I broke the string and am having it mended? How long does it take to have pearls restrung? I misplaced the pearls? How long would it take to search my house from attic to cellar? I forgot to wear them? I am tired of wearing them? I lent them to Gertrude? Poor Gertrude."

Lass had no suggestion to make. She was sniffing at the boot scraper outside someone's door. Sophia waited for her to resume the journey home.

And how am I going to explain *that*? she asked herself silently, half withdrawing her left glove and seeing in some dismay her bare finger, the base of it shiny and pale and indented from the impress of the ring she had never removed since her wedding day—until this afternoon. How foolish she was. She had expected that the pearls would bring a far greater price than they had. She had hoped there would even be some money left after the payment of this new demand. But what she had actually got for the pearls and the wedding ring combined would only barely cover it.

Well, she decided, she would simply tell anyone who asked that after three years it was time to put her marriage and her memories behind her. That might sound heartless. She would say, then, that it had become too painful to be reminded of Walter every time she looked down at her hand. That would sound too extravagant.

She would think about her answer when the question came. For now she had the money she needed. But she had nothing left except the bare wherewithal to make it through to the day of her next quarter's pension. And that in its entirety would not nearly cover the cost of the next letter.

She wondered exactly how many of them there were. She had never suspected that Walter was a letter writer. Or that he could write so eloquently of his deepest emotions. She bit her lip hard. But then there was a great deal about Walter she—and most other people—had not known. She had not suspected the affair, though clearly it had flourished for two whole years before his death—two of those difficult years during which she had scrupulously kept her end of their agreement.

She had even felt mildly guilty about the infatuation for the Four Horsemen that almost every other military wife had shared with her. She had been definitely troubled by the secret love for Nathaniel Gascoigne that she had always refused to call love—and she had never allowed herself to indulge in any except very mild fantasies or to flirt with him in any way at all.

Yet all the time Walter had been writing those letters—during the times when he had been unable to indulge his sexual passion in deed. And he obviously had done that plenty—the letters, though not graphic, made that very clear. His affair had been flourishing all the time he had been taking her, Sophia, his "old sport," wherever Wellington's armies went.

"Sometimes, Lass," she said as her dog trotted ahead of her and turned without having to be told up the steps to her house, "I am so filled to the brim with pent-up anger that I think I might explode into a million pieces. Poof! Gone! No more Sophie. No more troubles." She smiled as Samuel opened the door, and hoped he had not heard her voice when she had no one with her except Lass with whom to converse.

But she did not want to die, she thought, even though the idea of oblivion was sometimes enticing. She ran lightly up the stairs, Lass panting at her heels, undoing the ribbons of her bonnet as she went. She had the money this time. Last year there had been only two letters. This year there had been two already. Perhaps he planned to space them out over a number of years, two a year. Perhaps there would be freedom at least for a few weeks or months. She did not believe he would have come as soon this time if it had not been for the irritation of last evening.

She would live as if she were free for a while. *One day at a time.* And she had tonight to look forward to. Nathaniel was coming. She should feel guilty, she supposed. There was something ever so slightly—or perhaps ever so greatly—sordid about what they were embarking upon. But she would not feel guilty. For years and years—for her whole youth—she had kept herself strictly disciplined in order to keep up appearances, in order to be respectable.

There had been so little joy in her life.

But the night Nathaniel had spent with her had been joyful.

And tonight would be joyful. She *would not* consider morality. And she would not think ahead to the end of the spring and the nightmare his departure for home would bring her.

Joy was always a fleeting thing. Life and experience taught a person that. It could not be grasped and held on to for a lifetime. She would no longer deny the little joy that was offered her.

*One day at a time.*

# TEN

I<small>T</small> FELT A LITTLE AWK-
ward, Nathaniel found. He had kept mistresses occasionally
in former years and had visited them by appointment. There
had never been anything awkward about it. He had called
on them for one purpose only. Neither he nor the woman
concerned had expected anything else or thought anything
else necessary.

It was somewhat different with Sophie. She was not his
mistress. She was his friend. She opened the door for him
before he had a chance to knock. She was wearing a long
loose dressing gown over her nightgown and her hair was
down, though it was caught back with a ribbon at the nape
of her neck. But she greeted him with her usual smile and
bade him good evening before turning to lead the way upstairs, a single candle in a candlestick in one hand.

He had not known whether to bend his head and kiss
her. He had not done so. She had not looked as if she
expected it. He half expected that she would pause at the
first landing and lead him to the sitting room, but she continued on her way to the next floor and took him to her
bedchamber. Her dog, lying on the rug before the hearth,
thumped its tail several times in greeting and made not even
a token objection to his appearance there. That collie, he

thought, would win no prizes as a watchdog or as a sheep-dog—it would doubtless welcome the wolf into the fold.

There was another single candle burning on the dressing table—she set hers beside it. The bedcovers were turned neatly back from the bed. The scene had been carefully set.

It had not felt awkward the first time. That had not been planned. This had. And it felt damned awkward. He did not know whether to engage her in social conversation or to proceed to the business at hand. They had not exchanged a word since their initial and rather formal greetings at the door.

"This does not feel right, Sophie," he said, running one hand through his hair after he had set down his hat and cane and removed his cloak. He smiled ruefully at her.

"You would prefer to leave, then?" she asked quite calmly. "You may do so, Nathaniel. I shall not protest."

She thought he did not want her.

He reached for her hand and drew her closer to him. She watched him with steady eyes and expressionless face. He lifted his other hand and untied the ribbon at the back of her neck before dropping it to the floor.

"I find it hard to treat you only as a woman I wish to bed," he said, "although I *do* wish to bed you. I see you as Sophie, someone I have liked and respected for years."

She half smiled before closing the distance between them and setting her face full against the folds of his neckcloth. He could hear her drawing a slow breath. He could smell her hair. She must wash it in the same soap she used on her skin. He could see it in tight, heavy ripples all down her back.

She looked lovely, he thought suddenly. And it was not only her hair. He realized what it was then. Her dressing gown was a very pale blue. The nightgown beneath it was white. She looked different—delicate, very feminine—in light colors. Not that she ever looked unfeminine, but . . .

He lowered his head, turning it so that his cheek rested against the top of her head. He set his hands on her shoulders.

"What do you want?" he asked her. "Straight to bed? Straight into action, so to speak?" He did not believe he would be capable of going into action if she answered in the affirmative. He wondered if this was going to become downright embarrassing.

She lifted her head and looked into his face only inches from her own. "This is a mistake, is it not?" she said, sounding like the sensible, practical Sophie he had long known. "I thought it would feel like the other night. It does not. Yet I do not want you to leave."

No, he did not want to leave either, though he could not feel sufficiently aroused to do what he had come to do. She was not—*damn it all!*—his mistress.

He touched his lips to hers. She made no move to deepen the kiss, though she did not draw away either.

"Let us just lie down, shall we?" he suggested. "There are no rules for relationships of this sort, you know. There is no rule that says our bodies must be joined within five minutes or half an hour or an hour of my arrival. Or at all in fact."

"No." She bit her lip. "You would not prefer simply to leave, Nathaniel? You are not staying because I said I wished you to?"

"Let us lie down," he said after kissing the end of her nose. "I will blow out the candles, if I may, and remove some clothes."

It was in some way laughable, he supposed. She removed her dressing gown; he stripped to his breeches. She climbed in on one side of the bed; he climbed in on the other after dousing the candles. They were behaving just like a couple of virgin newlyweds. He reached across and took her hand in his. Their fingers curled about each other's and clung. The collie on the hearth heaved a deep sigh.

"Tell me about your day," he said, and then wished he had not started with that particular request. He did not wish her to think he was prying about Pinter's afternoon visit. Not yet.

But she proceeded to give him an account of her walk

in the park with Lavinia—Lavinia herself had declined to say more than that it had been by far the most pleasant afternoon yet of her stay in town—and to tell him how very much she liked his cousin.

"I felt guilty," he said, "as if I had foisted her upon you, Sophie. She is not an easy companion with whom to have to spend a whole afternoon."

"She is quite delightful," she said, her voice warm and very obviously sincere. "She is an acquaintance I very much hope will develop into a close friend. We are only four years apart in age, you know. We are peers and share a great many ideas and opinions."

"Sophie," he said, unconsciously lacing his fingers with hers, "what am I to do with her? She is four and twenty, almost past marriageable age, and yet she will not recognize the urgency of finding a husband. I must confess that my concern is partly for myself—I do not know how I will endure her company for another six years—but mainly it is for her. How can she ever be happy if she never marries? Spinsterhood is a dreadful fate for a woman. And in her case there is no need of it. She is wellborn, wealthy, and damned lovely in the bargain—pardon my language. I forget myself."

"What are you to do with her?" she asked. "Nathaniel, you do not have to *do* anything. Lavinia is an adult, and an intelligent one. She knows what she wants. She cannot yet do it because her father's will has kept her fortune from her, but she knows. Perhaps you should simply trust her."

"Trust her to turn down every respectable offer until there is not one unmarried man left in England to make one?" he asked.

She laughed softly. "Yes, if necessary," she said.

"And what kind of advice is that?" he asked her, exasperated.

"Wise advice, I hope," she said. "Most women by the time they leave the schoolroom wish for nothing but homes and husbands and families of their own. Your sister Georgina is one of them, I believe. She will be happily married before Christmas, I dare predict. I was one of them too. I met Walter, he offered for me, I accepted, and I thought that at the age of eighteen I had achieved everything necessary for my life's happiness. But there are some women who are different, who feel that there has to be more to life than marriage to the first man who offers—or even perhaps to the one hundred and first. Lavinia is such a woman. Trust her.''

It was such very sensible advice that it was hard to admit to himself that he had not really considered the idea before. But trust Lavinia? She would make a disaster of her life if left to herself, would she not? But then he respected Sophie's judgment. He had heard something else that had distracted his mind from Lavinia's problems, however. He raised himself on one elbow, propped the side of his head against his hand, and looked down at her—his eyes had grown accustomed to the dark.

''Poor Sophie,'' he said. ''You thought to have had a lifetime's happiness with Walter and yet all you had was— what? Six years? Seven?''

''Seven,'' she said.

''And no children.'' He had never really thought of Sophie's childlessness until now. He smoothed the fingers of his free hand through the hair at her temple. ''Did you long for them?''

''At first,'' she said. ''But we could not have subjected children to the kind of life we led and it was important that I stay with Walter.''

A thought struck him. Actually it was a thought that had been niggling at him ever since the night before last. ''You know a way of preventing it from happening, then?'' he asked her.

She smiled at him. ''All army women know a dozen ways,'' she said, ''though most of us would not admit it even under torture, in normal circumstances.''

''I would not wish to get you with child,'' he said.

''You will not.'' She was gazing calmly back into his eyes.

"If I did—if I *do*—you would have to marry me, Sophie," he said, "like it or not. I would not allow any argument."

"It will not happen," she told him.

He wondered then why she had not married again, why she had told him the day before that she had no wish to do so. Had the dreams of her eighteen-year-old self died in the ten years since then? Did she no longer want the home and husband and children that would have brought her lifelong happiness? Or was it just that the dream could never now come true since Walter was dead? She had seen to it that she did not conceive during the years of her marriage because it had been important to her to be with Walter. Did she wish now that there had been at least one child after all?

But he could not ask her. The question was too personal. He did not have the right. He was only her friend and her temporary lover.

He bent his head and kissed her, lightly at first, prepared to draw back his head if it became apparent that she was still not ready for intimacy. Her lips softened and parted beneath his. He slid his tongue past her teeth and deep into her mouth. She sucked gently and he could feel himself harden into arousal.

"I think we should remove a few more layers," he said.

"Yes." She waited for him to remove her nightgown but she lifted first her hips and then her arms to help him. She did not help him remove his breeches.

The awkwardness had gone. They had talked for perhaps half an hour, something that he would have expected to make the situation of their being in bed together more awkward still. But it had not. It seemed the most natural thing in the world now to turn to each other and begin the play that would bring them both sexual pleasure.

Not that Sophie knew a great deal about play. He supposed it was understandable that a respectable married woman would not even if she *had* been married for seven years. A man perhaps would not think of teaching his wife to give or receive pleasure. A marriage bed, after all, was seen by most men as the place where his children were begotten. Most men did their playing elsewhere. Though Sophie's marriage bed had not been for that—Walter had died too soon, before they had had a stable home of their own. And Walter was definitely not the sort to have kept a fancy piece on the side.

But Walter was the last person he wanted to be thinking of at the moment. Indeed, he did not want to be *thinking* at all.

He gave her pleasure with his hands and his mouth. He knew soon enough by her tautened nipples and her soft sighs and the wetness between her thighs that she was pleased. He would not be demanding tonight, he decided. He would not bewilder her. He would teach her on another occasion how to use her own hands for both their pleasure.

"You are ready for me?" he asked her eventually, his mouth against hers. He parted folds with his fingertips, pushed one a little way inside her, and felt her close about him. "You want me, Sophie? Here? All the way inside here?"

"Yes." She twisted against him, parted her thighs without coaxing as he came over her, made a cradle of them as he lowered himself, and lifted her legs to twine about his own. She thrust her breasts upward to rub her hardened nipples against his chest. Her eyes, he noticed when he looked down at her, were closed. Her mouth was open in an agony of wanting.

He had given her more than pleasure, he realized in that moment. He had aroused desire and need in her. He had seen it feigned in countless women. This was unmistakably the real thing.

He positioned himself carefully at the entrance to her body and pressed hard inside, watching her face all the while. She moaned and tipped her head back against the pillow.

Sophie. Oh dear God, Sophie.

He had intended to work her slowly as he had done two

nights before, in order to give her more pleasure before he allowed his own release. But he realized suddenly that she was going to come to climax herself—if he gave her what she needed. But he had no experience . . .

He pumped hard and repeatedly into her, giving her his full length, driving past the tightness of her inner muscles. But she could not seem to let go and he did not know how to help her.

Oh yes, he did, though.

He slid one arm down between them, found the small area that he knew would help her, and rubbed his thumb very lightly over it.

Her climax came violently. She shouted out his name and shuddered against him quite out of control. He held still and deep in her, lowered most of his weight onto her, clasped both her hands tightly in his own, and set his cheek against the side of her head.

*And this was Sophie?* he said to himself in wonder over and over again. *This was Sophie?*

The collie was sniffling and whining softly beside the bed, he half noticed.

When she was quiet and relaxed and—yes, asleep beneath him, he lifted some of his weight off her again and worked to his own quieter, but utterly satisfying release. Before disengaging and moving to her side, he saw that her eyes were open, watching him sleepily.

"Sophie?" He took her hand in his and raised it to his lips. "It was good?"

She did not answer him. The side of her head burrowed warmly against his shoulder. She was asleep again.

This, he thought, lifting the bedcovers carefully with one leg and one hand so as not to disturb her, was vastly different from what he had anticipated. In accordance with his age and his present status as a respectable country gentleman with family responsibilities, he had expected a quiet affair, short on passion, long on coziness and comfortable satisfaction. Especially with Sophie.

When was it he had thought of Sophie as a woman incapable of deep passions? After he had bedded her that first time or before? Either way, he had still believed it when he had come to her tonight. He had been eager, yes, but he had not been expecting—this.

He was not even sure he wanted this.

There was something a little disturbing, a little frightening about it. There was the element of the unknown about it. And yet it was only his mind that felt unease. His body was wonderfully satiated. He turned his head and kissed the top of hers. Her fingers curled more warmly about his and she burrowed closer with soft sounds of satisfaction. She was still asleep.

The dog had returned to the hearth again and sighed almost in unison with its mistress.

It felt good, Nathaniel thought, to be just lying here like this, relaxed and warm and sleepy after a long cozy talk and after thoroughly good sex. With a friend—he half smiled. He felt more at ease than he had felt in months—years, perhaps.

Except that this was a little different from what he had planned for himself. This was not just sex. Not even just *good* sex. This was a relationship. And the thought was somewhat disturbing. But he was far too tired and far too contented to explore the thought now. He would think of it tomorrow.

"Come here, Sophie." It was not a command exactly, although he had reached out a hand toward her. The words were softly spoken, almost as a question.

She had pulled her nightgown back on while he dressed and put on her dressing gown over it. She had not had a chance to tie back her hair again. It must look a dreadful mess. He looked immaculate again and somehow remote, as if he could not possibly be the same man who had been in bed with her most of the night.

He was standing by the window of her bedchamber fully clothed, though not so many minutes ago he had finished coupling with her again, slowly, thoroughly, wonderfully,

the way he had done it two nights ago. Unlike the first time
tonight. She did not know quite what had happened then.
It had been wonderful beyond imagining but also embarrassing in memory. What must he have thought of her? She
had completely lost control of herself. Was it about that he
wished to speak? Or did he merely intend to kiss her good
night—or good morning—before leaving?

She went to him and took his hand and lifted her face
to smile at him. They had not lit the candles again, though
it was still dark outside, but she could see him clearly. He
was looking at her with those lovely slumberous eyes.

"Sophie," he said, "tell me about Boris Pinter's visit
here yesterday afternoon."

Ah.

Her stomach lurched. He *had* seen. Of course he had.
How could he not have? And why had she been so gauche
as to have lied? It had been so unnecessary.

"Oh that." She laughed. "He came to pay his respects.
He does so occasionally. He did not stay long. He would
not even take tea with me."

"Why do you receive him?" he asked.

She raised her eyebrows.

"Do you feel obliged to do so," he asked, "because he
made up those ridiculous lies last year to enhance Walter's
fame? He did it only to ingratiate himself with the *ton,*
Sophie."

"Lies?" she said.

"When he came to the Peninsula," he said, "Pinter was
already a lieutenant, Sophie. He was not an ensign."

Ah, she had not realized that.

"Then it must have been *Lieutenant* Pinter, not Ensign
Pinter, whom Walter saved," she said. "Does it matter?"

"Only in that you owe him nothing," he said. "He was
never a pleasant character, Sophie. He had a particular
grudge against Walter. You must stay away from him and
certainly not receive him here. Ken told you last night, quite
rightly, that any of the four of us will protect you anytime

Pinter chooses to bother you. It would be our pleasure to be of service to you—mine in particular.''

It was Kenneth's ''protection'' last evening that had cost her her wedding ring this afternoon, she thought. The price would not have been quite so high otherwise. And next time the price would be higher again—impossibly high.

She drew her hand away. ''And since when,'' she asked, ''have you had the right to direct my behavior, Nathaniel? To tell me whom I may or may not receive in my own home? Since you became my lover? Do you now see me as your mistress despite your earlier denials? I am *not* your mistress, and I am *not* either Lavinia or Georgina to be given orders you expect obeyed instantly and without question. How dare you!''

She never lost her temper with people. Never. Not with anyone. She listened to herself, to the cold control of her voice, and knew very well what was happening. The terrible anger that was bottled up inside her was finding a small outlet. Nathaniel, who wanted only to protect her, was bearing the brunt of it. Appalled, she found herself even hoping that he would give her an argument.

He did not.

He tipped his head a little to one side and looked searchingly into her face. He glanced down at her hands, which were clenched into tight fists at her sides.

''You are quite right, of course,'' he said, no anger, no hauteur, no chill of hurt pride in his voice. ''I do beg your pardon, Sophie. Please forgive me?''

She nodded and closed her eyes briefly, letting the anger seep away.

''I do not see you as my mistress, Sophie,'' he said quietly. ''That was why I could not—make love to you when I first came tonight. You are my friend and my lover.''

Damn him—she unashamedly borrowed in her mind one of Walter's phrases. She had wanted to have a screaming quarrel with him—but how did one conduct a screaming quarrel? Now she wanted only to sag against him and cry into his neckcloth. Independence could sometimes be a

heavy burden. And gentleness and tenderness could sometimes undo one far more effectively than anger or arro-
gance.

She smiled at him.

"Promise me something?" he asked her.

She lifted her shoulders.

"Promise to come to me if you are in any kind of need,"
he said. "Promise not to be too proud or too independent
to ask."

"That is two promises," she said.

"Promise me?" He was not to be diverted.

*Would you kindly lend me a princely sum of money with
which to purchase the rest of the passionate love letters
Walter wrote so indiscreetly to someone else? On the understanding, of course, that I will pay back every penny,
though it may take me another sixty or seventy years to do
so?*

"Sophie?" He sounded hurt now. "Cannot you do even
that much to set my mind at ease? Or go to Rex or Ken or
Ede if you would prefer. But one of us, Sophie."

"Your mind does not have to be uneasy over me, Nathaniel," she said. "I will promise to call upon you on any
matter in which I believe you may help me. How is that?"

He reached out and took both her hands in his. He
squeezed them tightly. "You minx, Sophie," he said.
"You have promised nothing at all. Do you wish to continue with our arrangement?"

She felt that lurching of the stomach again. "You do
not?" she asked him, scarcely able to get the words past
her lips.

"I do." He moved his head closer to hers. "But you will
never let me forget, Sophie—and quite rightly too—that
this is a relationship of equals. I will not take anything for
granted, then. May I come again?"

"Yes." She smiled. "It is pleasant, Nathaniel. I would
like it to continue."

"Good." He closed the gap between their mouths and
kissed her.

She led the way downstairs a few minutes later, Lass padding along behind them, and he unbolted the outer door quietly.

"Good night, Sophie," he said before opening the door. "And thank you, my dear."

"Thank *you,* Nathaniel," she said.

She saw his lovely smile in the light from the street as he opened the door. "And good night to you too, Lass," he said.

Then she was closing the door behind him, bolting it slowly so as not to make too much noise.

"Back to bed, then, Lass," she said. Back to recapture the warmth and the smell of him, to relive the events of the night—all of them, not just the physical parts.

She was not at all sure, she thought as she climbed into bed and lay where he had lain, pulling the bedcovers right up over her head, that she would have suggested this affair if she had known it would be more than the actual couplings. Those she might recover from—she had lived without them all her life, after all, except for that dreadful first week of her marriage.

But there had been more than that tonight. They had lain side by side, their hands clasped, and simply talked as friends, as equals. And then after that wildly wonderful— and embarrassing—coupling, they had slept together for several hours. She had half woken a few times and felt him against her side, warm and relaxed and asleep.

*And no children. Did you not long for them?*

Somehow those words, more than any others, echoed and reechoed in her mind. No, no children. Had she longed for them? Not really. Not under the circumstances. She had quelled her needs as a woman so ruthlessly that she had almost forgotten that most primal of all feminine needs. And did she long for them now? She was only eight and twenty. Sometimes she forgot that she was still young.

*If I did—if I do—you would have to marry me, Sophie, like it or not. I would not allow any argument.*

Oh, Nathaniel. Her heart ached and ached.

When Lass jumped onto the bed and set her chin across Sophia's legs, she was not ordered to get down as she normally would have been. Her living presence felt infinitely comforting.

# ELEVEN

"You really ought to have been there, Nat," Eden said after regaling them for several minutes with an account of last night's card party. It seemed that one young lord, newly sent down from Oxford for what had been euphemistically dubbed as "wildness," had lost a large estate, to which—fortunately for his purse, unfortunately for his honor—he was still only the heir. He had been tossed out on his ear, or so Eden claimed. And then another young lord—London seemed to teem with them this year, Eden commented—challenged old Crawbridge to a duel over the tone in which the latter had mentioned a courtesan twice the young lord's age. Crawbridge had merely looked the youth over from head to toe and offered to tan his backside with his bare hand before sending him home to his mother. The duel had been averted.

"Yes," Nathaniel said with a chuckle, "it sounds as if I missed a thoroughly genteel entertainment, Ede. Rex and Ken will be bitterly regretting that they are married men. Or perhaps they should have taken their wives to join such a refined gathering."

"Think of what we missed, Ken," Rex said. "And all

we had in exchange was an evening at Claude's with music and conversation.''

"And cards, you must confess, Rex," Kenneth said. "I went home half a crown poorer than when I went. Your wife went home richer by a corresponding amount."

"And she won a shilling from Clayton too," Rex said. "We are a wealthy family this morning."

They were riding in the park again, the four of them. It had become something of an early-morning ritual with them. The sky was overcast with a suggestion of rain in the damp air, but they were all agreed that fresh air of any description was a necessary component of the beginning of a new day.

"If I might return to my original point," Eden said, "*if* you are all done with your witticisms at my expense, that is." He paused but had nothing but grins in response. "Lady Gullis was there, Nat."

"Lady who?" Nathaniel raised his eyebrows.

Rex whistled. "Miss Maria Dart as was, Nat," he said. "Remember? Before Waterloo and afterward too?"

"The one with—the bosom?" Nathaniel asked, waggling his eyebrows.

"And the hips and the legs and the ankles," Rex said. "Not to mention the lips and the eyes."

"Cupid's Dart?" Kenneth said. "We all agreed, I do believe, that if we were in the business of shopping at the marriage mart, we would probably have a mass falling-out and come to fisticuffs and never be friends again."

"Yes, I remember, of course," Nathaniel said, laughing. "She married old Gullis with his millions and his gout."

"Old Gullis's tombstone has been decorating a church-yard for well over a year," Eden said, "and our Maria is a wealthy widow with a roving eye, Nat."

"And it did not light on you last night, Eden?" Kenneth asked, tutting and shaking his head. "You need to polish up those blue eyes of yours, old chap. You must be losing your touch."

"As a matter of fact," Eden said, "I sat out a hand and

talked to the lady. She did everything except come right out with a bald invitation for me to take her home to bed. But alas, she made it clear that she had in mind an arrangement to last until she embarks on a planned tour of the Continent later in the summer. I was sorely tempted, I tell you, since there would be a definite period to the liaison and the lady's charms are enticing, to say the very least. But I am not in the mood to take any risks. Besides, there is a new girl at Harriet's I mean to try.''

''I believe, Nat,'' Rex said, ''the lady rejected him.''

''I hate to admit it, Rex,'' Nathaniel said, ''but I do believe you are right.''

''The devil!'' Eden said, hot with indignation. ''What I am trying to say, if a fellow could but get a hearing, is that I put in a good word for you, Nat. I talked about you and about how so much of your time is given to shepherding your sister and your cousin about that you have almost none left during which to look to your own interests. There is nothing more calculated to win female sympathy.''

''This sounds interesting,'' Kenneth said. ''I do believe Eden has been as good as his word and has been matchmaking for you, Nat—though not with matrimony in mind, of course.''

''She remembers you, Nat,'' Eden said. ''When I started to talk about you, she set a hand on my sleeve and said, 'Lord Pelham, is he the one with the *eyes*?' ''

They all roared with laughter, Nathaniel included. Eden had done a fair imitation of a husky contralto voice.

'' 'And is he the one with the—lovely smile?' '' Eden continued. ''Note that pause, Nat, my lad. It was not simply 'Is he the one with the lovely smile?' It was 'Is he the one with the—lovely smile?' And her voice dropped an octave during that pregnant pause. Did I make that clear?''

''Well, there you have it, Nat,'' Kenneth said after they had all laughed heartily again. ''A mistress just waiting to be engaged for the rest of the Season. And a shapely armful to boot. Not to mention one capable of pregnant pauses.''

''And you can have the best of both worlds, Nat,'' Rex

said. "She could be had only with a wedding ring and a vast fortune three or four years ago. Now she can be had on a temporary lease at the price of *eyes* and a—lovely smile. Dash it, that was only half an octave. I am not as good as Eden."

"She is going to be at Mrs. Leblanc's soiree this evening, Nat," Eden said triumphantly. "I happened to mention that you would be there too."

"With Georgina and Lavinia," Nathaniel said dryly. "Not to mention Margaret and Ken and Rex's wives and—and Sophie."

"If you cannot court a mistress discreetly under the very noses of the *ton,* Nat," Eden said, "then the past two years must have changed you sadly. You should be able to woo her and bed her and keep her without even the three of *us* knowing if you so choose."

"Is it going to make up its mind to rain in earnest?" Nathaniel asked, looking upward and holding out a hand palm up. "The mention of Sophie reminds me, by the way, that there is something odd going on with Pinter."

"Do tell me he has been pestering her again," Kenneth said. "I would enjoy nothing better than a little conversation with the man. I regret I did not have it the night before last. I was too concerned with taking Sophie out of the way."

"He was coming out of her house as I was going in with Lavinia yesterday afternoon," Nathaniel said.

"That does it." All sign of levity was gone from the group. Kenneth was clearly annoyed. "I certainly hope she turned him away with a flea in his ear."

"She did not," Nathaniel said. "She got decidedly frosty when I asked what he had been doing there, and downright angry when I suggested that she ought not to receive him."

"Sophie?" Rex said with a frown. "Angry? I have never seen her really angry."

"She was angry," Nathaniel said. "She told me—quite rightly, of course—that I had no business telling her whom she may or may not receive in her own home."

"What the devil?" Eden was frowning too. "She *welcomed* Pinter's visit, Nat? She looked pale enough to faint when Ken and I went to her rescue at the Shelby ball."

"She did not say why he was there," Nathaniel said, "except that he had gone to pay his respects, as he has done before, and would not stay for tea."

"What *is* he about?" Kenneth asked. "Trying to feed off her fame? Though that has waned somewhat this year. And Pinter is the son of an earl. He does not need her to get him entrée to *ton* events. And I do not imagine Sophie is wealthy, is she? She does not *look* wealthy. What does the bastard want with her?"

"Whatever it is," Rex said, "he is not going to be wanting it for much longer. We all noticed the effect the sight of him had on her the night before last, and we were not even all sitting together. She certainly does not like him—for which fact one can only applaud her good taste. When shall we pay the former Lieutenant Pinter a visit? Can it be squeezed in today? I would hate to waste a single moment."

"I am with you, Rex," Eden said grimly. "It is time the bounder discovered that Sophie has loyal friends."

No," Nathaniel said. "It cannot be done. Not that way, much as I wish it could. Sophie told me to mind my own business. Pinter did not do anything openly outrageous at the Shelby ball. He was received at Sloan Terrace yesterday just as Lavinia and I were—he did not force his way in. And Sophie did not complain of his visit. We have no right to act on her behalf by calling on Pinter and warning him away from her."

"Actually, Nat," Eden said, "I would be acting on my behalf as much as on Sophie's."

"She would never forgive us," Nathaniel said. "We have no right to interfere in her life."

"Damn," Rex said.

"Why did you bring up the subject, then, Nat?" Kenneth asked.

Nathaniel frowned and thought back to that scene in her

bedchamber earlier in the morning. He had seen her annoyed before. She was human, after all, and no one could be unfailingly cheerful. But he had never seen her angry. But she had been angry this morning—quite furiously angry even though she had not raised her voice or used those fists that had been clenched at her sides. Far angrier than the provocation seemed to have called for. Merely because he had shown concern for her? Merely because he had unwisely couched advice in the form of a command? He had been wrong, of course—he had realized it as soon as she spoke. His apology had been quite genuine.

But she had not been simply indignant. She had been *furious*.

Sophie? Furious?

He shook his head. "There was something wrong," he said. "She was—frightened? Was she? Is that what was behind her anger? I do not know what was wrong, but something certainly was."

Or perhaps her anger had been occasioned simply by the fact that his timing had been rotten. He had started to give orders to her immediately after having spent the night bedding her. As though he thought he owned her. He had not meant it that way, but he could see how his behavior might have been interpreted thus.

"Damn," Rex said again. "Is this worth pursuing? Sophie is an independent woman, after all. We have not known her for three years and have only just become reacquainted with her. She has her life; we have ours. She told Nat to mind his own business. Perhaps we all ought to do just that. After all, Pinter was only ever a sleazy nuisance, was he not? If Sophie is prepared to tolerate him, who are we to object?"

"There was the night before last, though, Rex," Kenneth said. "She did not just have a pale face, you know. She leaned so heavily on my arm when Moira and I led her out of the supper room that I was bearing almost her whole weight. Only that indomitable willpower we were all once well acquainted with held her upright."

"Damn!" That was Rex again.

"What makes a woman like Sophie faint?" Eden asked, frowning in thought.

"Fear," Nathaniel said.

"Devil take it, Nat," Eden said, "she would have been unconscious the length and breadth of the Peninsula, then."

"A different type of fear," Nathaniel said. "Not a physical fear."

"Any suggestions?" Kenneth asked.

"No." Nathaniel shook his head. "He called her 'Sophie' and made references to her lovely and charming self. This was out on the steps when he was leaving and I was arriving—fortunately I had left Lavinia in the carriage until I was sure Sophie was receiving. Did Pinter ever call her Sophie in the Peninsula?"

"A lieutenant call a major's wife by her first name?" Rex said. "Never."

"Why would she receive him the very day after the sight of him made her nearly faint?" Nathaniel asked. "And then become downright angry when I offered our services in her defense?"

"An independent spirit?" Kenneth said. But he answered his own question. "No. Not Sophie. She was always accepting our help in the Peninsula as we were always accepting hers. We all knew that the motive was friendship, not condescension or the conviction that she was weaker than we and could not cope with life without our male assistance. There is something going on, then, you think, Nat?"

"But not something we can solve in the obvious and most satisfactory manner," Rex added. "I would dearly love to thrash Pinter. How dare he even raise his eyes to Sophie?"

"I think we should watch them both as much as we possibly can without interfering with Sophie's independence," Nathaniel said. "We need to find out why she is frightened of him yet will not confide in us. If she *is* frightened, that is."

"Oh, she is, Nat, surely," Kenneth assured him. "It takes a great deal to rattle Sophie, but she was rattled two nights ago. And yet she let him into her *house* yesterday?"

"She is to be at Mrs. Leblanc's tonight?" Eden asked of no one in particular. "I wonder if Pinter will be there too. I will stay close to her. Rex and Ken, you have your wives to think of, and Nat is going to be busy courting the widow under your very noses without seeming to do so— not to mention squiring his young relatives about. Leave Sophie to me, then. I'll maybe take her about with me in the coming days and weeks too. It will be no hardship after all, will it? One cannot imagine more congenial company than Sophie's, even if she is not the world's most ravishing beauty."

Nathaniel found himself wishing it were appropriate to pop his friend a good one to the nose, but it was not and so he held his peace.

He was not at all sure he had done the right thing this morning. He felt almost as if he had betrayed Sophie. What she did in her own home was, after all, no one's concern except hers. But Ken was right. Her reaction to Pinter at the Shelby ball had not been one of simple dislike. And her anger last night—or this morning—had not been simple indignation. There was definitely something wrong. And it seemed the natural thing to turn to his friends with the problem. They were her friends too, after all. And this was something that concerned their friendship. It had nothing to do with Sophie's being his lover.

Except, he admitted, that that fact made him more protective of her than ever. And more worried. If she would not confide in a lover, then there must be something indeed. And of course, there was that other fact he had been unable to tell his friends without revealing that he had been twice to her house yesterday. At his first call she had pretended that Pinter's visit had not even taken place. She had not wanted him to know at all.

"White's, Nat?" Eden was saying. "Breakfast?"

"Not today," Nathaniel said. "I have been informed that

I am to escort Lavinia to Sophie's this morning—they are to visit the library together. And I have been asked to take Georgina to Rawleigh House. It seems she is to call upon a certain Master Peter Adams.''

''Ah yes,'' Rex said. ''My son will be delighted to acquire yet another female admirer. He has altogether too many of them in town. His nose is going to be severely out of joint when a brother or sister joins him in the nursery in a few months' time.''

The conversation moved on into other channels, but Nathaniel was satisfied—and also a little uneasy—that he had allies in his determination to protect Sophie from whatever it was that was upsetting her usual placid cheerfulness..

Sophia almost did not go to Mrs. Leblanc's soiree. It had never been her way, even at the feverish height of her fame and popularity, to attend more than a select few of the Season's entertainments. And though she had realized that this year would be different because of Edwin and Beatrice's presence in town and Sarah's come-out, she had not intended to go everywhere with them. Perhaps she would accept one invitation a week, she had thought, and even that seemed somewhat excessive. The soiree was only two evenings after Lady Shelby's ball.

But she succumbed to the lure of friendship—and of something else too. First Lavinia, during their morning visit to the library, begged her to be sure to attend. What would she do for sensible conversation if Sophie were not there? she asked.

It felt good to be wanted—not just as a sister-in-law or as an aunt or chaperon, but as a friend. Their reading tastes were remarkably similar, they discovered. Both of them liked to read books of history and travel and art. Both of them liked novels in moderation but shunned the more spectacular Gothic romances that pleased so many ladies of their acquaintance. Both liked poetry, though Sophia loved Blake and Wordsworth and Byron, while Lavinia preferred

Pope and Milton. It was a wonderful morning with a great
deal of conversation—and of laughter too.

And then during the afternoon Moira and Catherine, who
had come to bear Sophia off to the shops, expressed their
disappointment over the fact that she was not quite certain
she would attend the soiree. She simply must reconsider,
they both told her. They were determined to know her better now that they had discovered her.

There was that other lure, of course. Nathaniel would be
there. It was the very fact that should keep her away. They
had spent two of the last three nights together; she had
danced with him at the ball; she had received him, however
briefly, in her sitting room yesterday afternoon. She must
be very careful not to presume upon their relationship. She
must be even more careful not to arouse even the smallest
suspicion in any of their friends and acquaintances—or in
any other member of the *ton* for that matter.

But she had loved him for many years. And now they
were lovers—for a brief moment in time. For one springtime out of her life. And she found, to her alarm, that she
craved even a single sight of him. Even if they did not
come close enough to each other at the soiree to exchange
a greeting, even if she just saw him from afar and did not
hear the sound of his voice . . . Even that would be better
than not seeing him at all.

Or so she told herself. Though she was not sure she believed herself.

She wore her dark green second-best gown—the one she
had worn to Rawleigh House. She simply must *not* give in
to the temptation to attend many more entertainments, she
thought as she gazed at her reflection with a sinking heart.
How could she when she had only two very dull gowns to
wear? And not even a string of pearls with which to dress
them up? She touched a hand to her bare throat. She felt
half-naked without them.

And of course it was the first thing Beatrice noticed after
they had arrived at Mrs. Leblanc's and their cloaks had
been borne away and they had entered the drawing room.

"Oh, Sophie, dear," she said just when Rex and Catherine were converging on them, a smiling Viscount Perry with them—he was smiling at Sarah, of course, "you have forgotten your pearls."

"And so I have," Sophia said, touching her left hand to her neck and trying to look surprised. "Oh dear." Oh dear indeed! What was she going to say next time?

"Oh, Sophie!" Beatrice's voice was more than dismayed this time—it was horrified. "And you *wedding* ring too."

"Oh." Sophia stared at her hand. The shiny white rim at the base of her finger looked far more noticeable than the ring ever had, she thought. "Well, I do not suppose another living soul will notice, Bea. At least I remembered my gown. Rex, did you approve of the bonnet Catherine bought this afternoon? I promised to use my influence with you if you were cross. It was positively made for her, you know. There is no one else who could wear it to such advantage."

"Your influence, Sophie?" he said with a grin. "Were you one of the culprits who talked her into its purchase, then?"

"Absolutely," she said.

"Then I must thank you," he said, taking her hand in his and raising it to his lips. His eyes laughed into hers. "The bonnet *almost* does its wearer justice."

It was so delightful, Sophia thought, to know that Rex had made a love match and to see that Catherine was his equal in every way that mattered. Rex had always been the biggest rogue of all of them, the one most adept at using his charm to get whatever—or whomever—he wanted. With Catherine, she suspected, he had been outcharmed, with fortunate and happy results.

Her pearls and her wedding ring seemed to have been forgotten. And she was not sorry she had come this evening. All her particular friends were present, she could see. Her debt had been paid off today and tonight she might relax. Perhaps Nathaniel would even . . . No, she must not come to expect it every night. It did not matter. The memories of last night were good enough on which to live for a few days to come. She might expect a few weeks of freedom in which to enjoy this brief springtime of her life, even though she knew very well that the freedom would not last. There would be other letters.

But for now, for tonight, for the few days and weeks to come, she would simply enjoy herself.

*One day at a time.*

He was wearing dark green tonight, with gray and silver and white. Nathaniel, that was. He was the first person she had seen on entering the room, though she had not even yet looked directly at him.

She was going to enjoy herself.

# TWELVE

LADY GULLIS CLEARLY FELT
that she had paid her dues to society and was now entitled
to please herself. At the age of twenty she had married—
or *been married to* was probably a more accurate description of that transaction, Nathaniel supposed—the enormously wealthy Lord Gullis, who had been more than three
times her age. He had lived to enjoy his marriage for only
a little longer than a year. He had not lost his infatuation
with his bride in that time. He had left her everything that
had not been entailed on his heir.

Now, still very young, even more beautiful than she had
been before her marriage, she was in search of personal
gratification. She was not in search of a second husband,
Nathaniel would have suspected even if Eden had not told
him as much, but of a lover with whom to satisfy herself
until she left during the summer for a year or so of travel
on the Continent.

Eden had clearly performed well his self-imposed task
of matchmaker the evening before. The lady soon maneuvered matters at Mrs. Leblanc's soiree that she was in
a small conversation group that included Nathaniel. He had
already been deserted by his female relatives, Georgina
having been invited by young Lewis Armitage to join a

group about the pianoforte, and Lavinia having stridden off without a word of explanation to join Sophie. Margaret, with no immediate chaperoning to attend to, had wandered off with her spouse to exchange news and gossip with a group of acquaintances.

And that left him with the widow, Nathaniel thought in some amusement. Soon enough the number in their group had dwindled to just the two of them. Lady Gullis, he thought, was a lady who knew both what she wanted and how to get it—or so she seemed to believe. She was extremely lovely, of course, though *lovely* was a tame word to describe her charms. She was quite simply stunningly voluptuous. She also had some conversation and wit to balance the effect of her physical presence. She was not just a pretty ninnyhammer.

Eden had been as good as his word, Nathaniel saw. He was with Sophie and Lavinia, though the latter was no doubt making him feel unwelcome. There was something about Ede that aroused decided hostility in Lavinia. Perhaps she sensed that he was not the type of man who took relationships with women seriously, though he enjoyed using his charm—and his blue eyes—on them. Yes, he was just the sort of man to set her teeth on edge.

Lady Gullis was asking his impressions of Spain, which was to be one of her intended destinations during the coming year. She was intelligent enough to realize, of course, that a country in wartime must appear vastly different from the same country in time of peace. He answered her questions while part of his mind was elsewhere.

If Eden thought it necessary to brave Lavinia's wrath and deny himself the company of other beauties in order to be at Sophie's side, he thought, there must be good reason. That reason could only be the presence of Boris Pinter at the soiree. Nathaniel had not seen him, but there were three adjoining rooms being used for the evening, and each of them was crammed with a great squeeze of people. Rex and Ken had gone with their wives into the music room next to the drawing room, but they came back after just a short while and took up a position not far from Sophie. They were not part of her group, but they were close.

Yes. Nathaniel smiled at a remark Lady Gullis made about the discomforts of travel. If she could but have her own house set upon wheels and take it with her, she said, and smiled too, she would be entirely happy. Yes, Pinter must be here. And Rex and Ken and Ede would do their best to discourage him from drawing close enough to Sophie to spoil her evening as he had done at Lady Shelby's ball. Perhaps he too . . .

"Do let us chase that tray," he suggested, indicating a servant a short distance away, "so that I may get you a fresh drink. It is rather warm in here, is it not?"

She set a hand on his sleeve, her long, well-manicured fingertips touching the bare flesh of the back of his hand. He maneuvered them closer. He hoped Sophie would not suspect what was up. She would probably be annoyed, as she had never used to be, to know she was under the close protection of the Four Horsemen of the Apocalypse.

He had noticed the absence of her pearls as soon as she came into the drawing room with her family. They had not been a grand piece of jewelry and he had never consciously noticed them. But he noticed their absence. Her dark, almost shabby gown looked drearier than usual. Her neck looked bare. He tried to remember what she usually wore there and remembered that it had always been a single string of pearls. Always, for every evening function she had attended as far back as he could remember.

But not tonight.

He had deliberately looked for her wedding ring, though it was difficult to see across the room if she wore it or not. She had not worn it last night. He had thought at the time that perhaps she had removed it out of deference to him. He would not have thought of looking for it tonight if he had not missed the pearls. But he did look. He was almost sure she was not wearing it.

Something, he thought—and he was quite convinced he

was not simply overreacting to a trivial circumstance—
something was wrong.

Lady Gullis kept her hand on his arm even after he had
removed her empty glass from her hand and taken a full
one from the servant's tray to replace it. Her fingertips
played as though absently against the back of his hand. She
was asking, in the throaty voice he did not remember from
three years before, how a gentleman who had lived life so
fully as a cavalry officer in the wars could find enough
entertainment from merely bringing out his sister and his
cousin. She was, he thought, moving in for the kill.

It struck him that if this had happened a mere few days
before, he would have been ecstatic. She was everything he
had dreamed of finding—wealthy and independent in her
own right, desirous of only a few months' diversion, very
lovely, beddable in the extreme, and flatteringly interested.

"There are, of course," he told her, "my clubs and the
races and my friends, not to mention all the entertainments
at which I may delight in the conversation of companions
other than my relatives."

He remembered too late what seemed to be the general
female opinion of his smile. He was smiling at her and she
was flushing at the compliment she was taking to herself.

Damn Eden.

Though that was not really fair. He might spend tonight
in this woman's bed if he so chose, Nathaniel thought. He
might have her for a bed partner for the rest of the spring
if he pleased her—and he had never heard a single com-
plaint of any past performances of his. He had no doubt at
all that she would be an interesting and a vigorous lover.
And he would have Eden to thank. Even as he thought it
and looked at his friend, he found Eden winking broadly
at him. And Kenneth, behind Moira's back, was raising his
eyebrows and pursing his lips.

They approved, damn them. Even Ken.

What he *should* be feeling, Nathaniel thought suddenly,
was frustration that this had happened too late. He could
have had this woman and avoided the entanglement with

Sophie. He glanced at her while Lady Gullis asked him if he had seen Kew Gardens yet this year and told him that if he had not, they were certainly not to be missed—in company with someone who could appreciate their beauty with him, of course.

In appearance Sophie compared unfavorably with Lady Gullis, who was dressed fashionably and expensively, her neck and ears and wrists and even her blond hair glistening with jewels. Sophie was neither elegantly nor becomingly dressed. She never did dress to advantage—except in her bedchamber, he thought. In her pale dressing gown and with her hair down she was lovely. Without clothes at all she was perfectly beautiful. In manner she was placid and cheerful and quite without the arts and charms of the woman on his arm. She was also, he remembered, capable of glorious passion.

He smiled at Lady Gullis and told her that he really must try to find time to see Kew Gardens before he returned home for the summer—if the busy round of *ton* entertainments and the weather permitted, of course.

He heard Eden's laugh and then Sophie's and Lavinia's as he spoke and realized that he would far prefer to be in that group than where he was. He would prefer to be smelling Sophie's soap and to be looking down at the untidy halo of escaped curls about her head. He would prefer to be listening to her sensible voice saying things that could not in any way be construed as flirtatious. He would prefer not to have to weigh every word he spoke and every smile he smiled, careful not to give the wrong impression.

And if he was to spend the night in any woman's bed, he thought, he would prefer to spend it in Sophie's. It had surprised him during the course of the day to realize that he remembered the first part of the night, when they had simply lain side by side talking and holding hands, with as much warm satisfaction as he remembered their two couplings.

Being Sophie's lover was comfortable as well as sensually satisfying. He would not have expected to find both in the bed of one woman. But he had. And he remembered that feeling he had had after their first coupling last night that what they had started was a great deal more serious than he had ever intended. He remembered without the unease he had felt at the time.

There was something special about Sophie. He had always known it, of course—they all had. They had never taken any other officer's wife beneath their collective wing as they had Sophie—yet Walter had not even been a particularly close friend of theirs. But there was something special too about his new relationship with her. Special in a way impossible to put into words.

He met her glance suddenly and they half smiled at each other. He wondered if she would think him impossibly demanding if he went to her again tonight. He would find a moment later and ask her, he decided. He would also remind her that she was quite at liberty to say no. He hoped she would not say no.

"I did not bring my companion with me this evening," Lady Gullis was saying. "One has to have a companion for appearance's sake, you know. She was once my governess, but she has grown deaf, poor dear, and tires easily. I promised I would be quite safe without her this evening, and persuaded her to go to bed early. She sleeps like the dead." She laughed lightly. "I am sure I *will* be safe on the streets of Mayfair alone in my carriage later tonight, will I not, sir? I have a stout coachman and footman."

Some situations were quite unavoidable. "I am sure my sister and brother-in-law will be happy to see my charges safely home," he said. "I will be pleased to set your mind at rest, if I may, ma'am, and accompany you in your carriage."

"You are most kind," she said, and for a brief moment her fingers curled beneath the frill at the cuff of his shirt-sleeve.

But his attention had been quite effectively distracted. Boris Pinter had appeared in the open doorway between the drawing room and the music room. He stood there for a few moments, looking about him, assessing the situation, a smile of what appeared to be genuine amusement on his lips.

Nathaniel removed his arm from beneath the lady's playing fingers, set his hand against the back of her waist, and propelled her firmly in the direction of Eden and Sophie and Lavinia.

Sophia, having decided that she was going to enjoy herself, was doing so. The necessity of moving about the rooms, working her way into a group, had been taken from her. It was something she was perfectly capable of doing, but something she never enjoyed. She always imagined— and was never quite convinced that she was not *merely* imagining it—that the members of the particular group she chose did not want her there. Which was absurd, of course. Every single guest at every single entertainment was doing the same thing she was doing.

This evening she did not even have to move from the spot where she had first come to a halt inside the drawing room. While Sarah had been borne away by Viscount Perry—there seemed to be a genuine spark of mutual interest there, Sophia thought—and Beatrice and Edwin decided to stroll through all three rooms to see who else was present, she herself was immediately detained by Lavinia, who came to inform her that she had read some of Blake's poems, on Sophie's recommendation, and had been amazed and delighted by them.

And then Eden joined them and amused them with a slightly naughty story about a duel that had been narrowly averted last evening at a card party he had attended. At least Sophia suspected there was naughtiness behind it, since it seemed very unlikely that the cause of the quarrel had *really* been an uncomplimentary remark the elder man had made about the younger's mother—although that was Eden's laundered version of events. In the Peninsula he would have told the story with all its bald and sordid details. Tonight he was on his best behavior—for Lavinia's sake, of course. Though Lavinia was not taken in for a moment.

"It is so gratifying," she said, smiling sweetly at Eden, "to be treated like a half-wit, Lord Pelham. Is it not, Sophie? Was the, ah, *mother* at least worthy of the quarrel, my lord?"

Eden merely grinned at her and reminded her that there were certain things of which a true lady pretended to be quite ignorant.

"I daresay," Lavinia said, her sweet smile considerably more dazzling, "you would be willing to call me no true lady in Nat's hearing, my lord?"

"Oh, the devil!" Eden said quite outrageously. "Nat always had a quite wicked sword arm. *Did* I call you no true lady? Did I, Sophie? My memory has become shockingly unreliable. I have no recollection of saying any such thing. But if I did, I do most humbly apologize, ma'am."

They were, Sophia realized after the first few minutes of suchlike conversation, greatly enjoying themselves. She looked from one to the other of them with considerable interest. They were probably both convinced that they thoroughly disliked each other.

*He* was not here, she thought after a careful perusal of the drawing room. And so she might relax and allow the evening to take its own pleasant course. There was, however, the sight of Nathaniel with Lady Gullis to be contended with. At first they were in a group together, but soon enough they were in a tête-à-tête, and not long after that they were even touching. She had a hand on his sleeve, but it was not properly positioned. Her fingertips dipped over the edge of his cuff to touch his hand.

Lady Gullis was a wealthy and lovely widow with a growing reputation as a flirt. Her riches and her position in society preserved her respectability, of course. Tonight, it was as clear as if a majordomo had appeared in the room and announced it in stentorian tones, that the lady had set her sights on Nathaniel. And of course they looked quite startlingly beautiful together.

"I believe," Eden said in Sophia's ear at a moment when Lavinia's attention had been taken by a passing acquaintance, "our Nat is captivated, Sophie."

"And you are looking decidedly smug," she said. "I suppose you set it up, Eden?"

"But of course." He grinned wickedly at her. "I am a matchmaker extraordinaire, Sophie. At your service, ma'am. Whom may I find for you?"

"You, Eden," she said, tapping him sharply on the arm, "may mind your manners and your own business too."

"Now, Sophie," he said, looking comically aggrieved, "the happiness of my friends *is* my business. Are you not my friend?"

Fortunately Lavinia turned her attention back to them at that moment.

She was horribly jealous, Sophia thought, and despised herself. What did she have with which to compete against the likes of Lady Gullis? Not one single solitary thing, that was what. And how silly it was even to think of competing. She had no claims on Nathaniel, and the sooner she put any illusions to the contrary from her mind, the better.

But even as she was thinking such sensible thoughts, she glanced to the doorway between the drawing room and the music room and froze.

How very wrong to have assumed that just because he had not been in the drawing room he was therefore not in the house. He was standing there, looking directly at her, his amused, mocking smile on his lips. And then he looked about at the people close to her. Eden was right beside her, of course. But by some unhappy coincidence both Kenneth and Rex were close by too. And so was Nathaniel.

He would not fail to notice that and be inflamed by it. He might even think it was deliberate, that she had gathered them about her as guards. Would he truly believe she could have done anything so insane?

And then her stomach lurched with alarm as Nathaniel, just at the worst possible moment, joined her group and

proceeded to present Lady Gullis to both Lavinia and herself.

*Go away,* Sophia wanted to screech at both Eden and
Nathaniel. *Move back,* she wanted to cry out to Rex and
Kenneth. *I cannot bear to have him antagonized.* She had
counted so much on having a few weeks of freedom.

She was aware, even as she smiled at Lady Gullis and
uttered some courtesy she would not have been able to
recall one minute later even if she had tried, that Boris
Pinter was approaching at leisurely pace. She was aware
too that both Eden and Nathaniel had stepped closer to her
on either side—bringing with them the illusion of safety.

Oh, it *had* been planned. Damn Nathaniel! Damn him all
to hell and back.

Nathaniel kept talking. Lady Gullis, with charming condescension, complimented Lavinia on her appearance and
asked her if she had yet received vouchers for Almack's.

Nathaniel hoped Sophie would not realize they were deliberately protecting her. Rex and Ken were showing every
sign of joining their group. But that would look just too
obvious. It should be unnecessary anyway. Pinter would
surely take the hint and refrain from upsetting her as he
had two evenings before.

But Pinter did not take the hint. And when all was said
and done, there was very little Sophie's friends could do
about it short of drawing unwelcome attention her way by
creating a scene.

"Sophie." Pinter bowed to her, favoring her with his
very white smile. "I am hurt that you have sought out your
other friends before me." He reached out and took her left
hand in his. He glanced down at her ring finger and then
placed his lips to the very spot where her wedding ring
usually rested.

Yes, Nathaniel saw, the finger was definitely bare.

"Mr. Pinter," she said—in her usual steady, cheerful
voice.

"Pinter." Eden was using his most haughty, languid

voice. His quizzing glass was in his hand and halfway to his eye. "Just the chap who will know where I might find the card room. Do come and show me."

But Boris Pinter was not to be distracted. "Sophie," he said, lowering her hand but not releasing it, "you are with some of your dearest friends. Some of them are our mutual acquaintances. But there is one young lady I do not know. Will you present me?" He turned his head and smiled at Lavinia.

For one moment Nathaniel's eyes met Sophie's. She was—smiling. Her usual placid, comfortable smile. She was surrounded by friends, any one of whom would be willing to shed blood in her defense. She must realize at this moment that they had all stayed deliberately close to her to protect her from just such unwelcome attentions. She might quite easily have snubbed Pinter without in any way drawing general attention her way. Instead she was smiling and beginning to extend a hand in Lavinia's direction. In another moment—less—she would be making the requested introductions and that bounder would be able to claim an acquaintance with Lavinia.

Not if he could help it!

"Excuse us," he said abruptly, grasping Lavinia's arm. "Lady Gullis? Sophie?" His half bow took in both ladies. "We must be joining my sister and brother-in-law." He whisked Lavinia past Rex and Kenneth, who must surely have heard what had passed.

What he had done, Nathaniel thought, was humiliate Sophie. And he was not sure his snub had gone unnoticed. All the members of Rex and Ken's group seemed to have turned to watch him go. But he was still too furious to care greatly.

Lavinia hauled back on his arm as they approached the doorway. "Nat?" she said angrily. "Unhand me this instant. What was that all about? Who *is* he that you must be so abominably rude? And do not tell me as you did yesterday that I would not wish to know. Who is he?"

He drew a deep breath. "Boris Pinter is the name," he

said. "A son of the Earl of Hardcastle. And Sophie Armitage's friend. You are to have nothing to do with him, Lavinia. Do you understand? And nothing more to do with Mrs. Armitage either. And that *is* a command."

"Nat." She finally succeeded in pulling her arm free when they were inside the music room. "Do try not to be quite, quite ridiculous. And if you are considering translating that murderous look into any act of violence against me, I give you fair warning. I shall not take it meekly."

The sense of her words penetrated the fury that seemed to have taken over his mind. He licked his lips and clasped his hands at his back. He forced a whole lungful of air inside himself before he trusted himself to speak again.

"I have never yet used violence against a woman, Lavinia," he said. "I do not plan to start with you. Forgive the look. It was not really directed against you."

"Against whom, then?" she asked him. "Against Mr. Pinter? Or against Sophie?"

He closed his eyes and tried to get his whirling thoughts under control. Why exactly was he so furious? Pinter was a thoroughly unsavory character and doubtless had not changed in three or four years. But Sophie was a free and independent woman. She was free to befriend whom she wished. But why Pinter? And why had she not wanted him to know of Pinter's visit yesterday and then made light of it? Tonight she had smiled at him and had been prepared to introduce *his* niece to the man without his permission.

Tonight there had been no sign of fear—they had probably all imagined that at the Shelby ball too. Tonight she had been her usual cheerful self.

Perhaps, he thought, he was feeling sorry that he had started an affair with a woman of such poor taste that she could befriend a man like Pinter, a man whom her own husband had abhorred.

"Perhaps against myself, Lavinia," he said, answering her question at last. "Let us find Margaret."

"I want," Lavinia said, looking closely at him, "to know more about Mr. Pinter. But you are not going to tell me more, are you? I am just a delicate female. He is an earl's son and he seems charming enough. And yet you were abominably rude to both him and Sophie merely because he wished to be presented to me. Are you jealous of him, Nat?''

''Jealous?'' He looked at her, stunned. ''Jealous? Of Pinter? And why, pray, would I be jealous of him?''

''No, I suppose not,'' she said, frowning. ''You are as handsome as they come, Nat, I will give you that. You can attract any woman you want. You do not imagine, I suppose, that I have not seen how the wind blows with Lady Gullis this evening? Sophie is not the sort of woman who could make you jealous, is she, more is the pity. But she is my friend, and her friends are mine.''

''My arm,'' he said curtly, offering it to her. ''I see that Margaret is over there beyond the pianoforte.''

She took his arm without another word, but her jaw, he saw at a glance, was set in a familiar stubborn line.

He was beginning to wish that after all he had stayed at Bowood.

Or that he had not gone riding in the park that first morning.

He wished he had not met Sophie again. Or at least that he had not become her lover. What on earth had possessed him to do such a thing? With Sophie!

Now, damn it all, he felt responsible for her. Did he not have enough females for whom to feel responsible?

# THIRTEEN

SOPHIA COULD NOT HAVE felt more shocked or more humiliated if her face had been slapped. Or more guilty. She had been about to present Boris Pinter to Nathaniel's niece when Nathaniel himself had been standing there to be applied to to perform such a service. But she had been about to comply merely because he had asked it of her—just as she had presented him to Beatrice at the Shelby ball.

Nathaniel had taken Lavinia's arm, bowed frostily, and spoken with great clarity. His words and his actions had caught the attention not only of their group, but of the group next to it too—the one that included Rex and Kenneth and their wives. A sizable number of people had witnessed her humiliation. He had cut her quite ruthlessly.

How she hated Nathaniel in that moment.

And how she hated herself.

Was this what she had come to? Was she now a puppet on a string? Was she to be one for the rest of her life? How far would she allow herself to be pushed? A limitless distance?

But there was no time to stand and think. She smiled and held out an arm for Boris Pinter's.

"Sir," she said, "will you be so good as to escort me

to the refreshment room?'' She inclined her head to Lady Gullis and to Eden, who was looking intently at her, though he made no attempt at further interference on her behalf.

Pinter gave her his arm.

"Sophie," he said when they had stepped outside the drawing room and were on the wide landing that extended the length of the three rooms in use for the soiree, "I do believe our mutual acquaintances do not like me."

"Enough of this," she said briskly. "If you enjoy playing the part of cat, sir, I certainly do not enjoy the role of mouse. I will not play it any longer."

"You would prefer another role, Sophie?" he said, chuckling. "Pariah of a nation, perhaps?"

It was not even a great exaggeration, she feared. But she might risk even that if she were the only one who would be affected. But she thought of Sarah and Lewis and of Edwin and Beatrice. And even Thomas, her own brother, would not be immune. His business success depended a great deal on the preservation of a good name. And he had three young children and a fourth on the way.

"I have allowed myself to become your victim," she said. "I have paid for four letters, and of course there are several more which I will be asked to buy at your convenience. That is one thing, sir. This is another—this *stalking*. What is the purpose of it, pray?"

"When I joined the cavalry, Sophie," he said, "I dreamed as every young officer does of doing my duty, of distinguishing myself, of earning rapid promotion. I am unfortunate enough to have a father who dislikes me, who was willing to purchase my commission in order to be rid of me, but who was unwilling to purchase any further promotion for me. An unnatural father, would you not agree? All proceeded according to plan until, as a lieutenant, I sought a captaincy. Your husband blocked that promotion simply to indulge a personal grudge. I was still a lieutenant when I sold out."

"That was between you and Walter," Sophia said. "Or between you and the army. It had nothing to do with me."

"And now you, Sophie," he said, "a mere coal merchant's daughter, have become a favorite of the *ton*. And a favorite of those favored beings, the Four Horsemen of the Apocalypse. Perhaps you have your sights set very high indeed. Pelham is a single man, as is Gascoigne—a baron and a baronet. Either one would be a step up from the mere brother of a viscount."

Oh, Nathaniel. "How ridiculous!" she said scornfully. But she was getting the point. He wanted a little revenge as well as a great deal of money. Her social life was to be ruined, as were her friendships, to console him for the spoiling of his military career.

And was her wonderful springtime to be ruined too? She could not forget the coldness in Nathaniel's eyes as he had looked into hers and read her intention of presenting Boris Pinter to his niece. And yet only a few minutes before that their eyes had met and a smile, hardly perceptible on their faces, had passed between them. A sign of awareness, even of affection.

Now it was to be all spoiled. No, it was not a future thing. It had been spoiled.

"I see," she said. "I am to stay away from my friends, stay away from *ton* events. Is that what you wish? And what will you do, sir, if I ignore your warnings? Shout your knowledge from the rooftops? Send a letter or two to the papers? You will have created a glorious scandal, but all your power over me will be gone. I wonder which you would prefer?"

"Either one, Sophie," he said, "would give me great satisfaction."

Yes, she believed him. And she understood too, though perhaps he did not intend her to know it, that he would eventually have both—all the money she could scrape together from her own resources and from her relatives and Walter's, and their eventual disgrace and ruin too. The beau monde would not take kindly to having been so shockingly duped.

"I am going to leave you now, sir," she said, "in order

to find my sister-in-law. If I were you, I would not be too hasty. You might ruin your own fun far too soon. All scandals die eventually, you know. Then you would have to find something new—or someone—with which to amuse yourself.''

''Sophie.'' He took her hand in his and bent over it, though he did not set his lips to it this time. ''You are almost a worthy adversary, my dear. Walter did not deserve you. Though I suppose that when you have soot beneath your fingernails, you cannot be too fussy, can you?''

''Good evening to you, sir.''

She smiled at him for the benefit of the other people strolling out on the landing and turned back to the drawing room. She hated to walk in there again, to imagine—and not be sure that it *was* imagination—curious glances directed her way. Kenneth and Moira were still there. She ignored them and went in search of Beatrice. She had fully intended to plead a headache and ask if the carriage might take her home. But she changed her mind. She would not play the coward.

She saw Nathaniel a little later. He was having a tête-à-tête with Lady Gullis again, bending toward her the better to hear her over the loud hum of voices. He was smiling his wonderful smile. And even as Sophia watched, the two of them left the room, not for one of the other rooms, but for the landing and the stairs. They did not return.

Well, she thought, she had known it was to be a very temporary thing, her affair with him. She had hoped for longer, for a few months perhaps. But she was not sorry it was over so soon. She had known from the start that she was playing with fire, that there was only heartbreak ahead. She would never have succeeded in convincing herself that her infatuation with him would have played itself out after a vigorous affair of a few months' duration. The opposite would have been true.

She had spent two nights with him. At least she had those to remember for the rest of her life. But the affair had not gone on long enough to leave her truly bereft. It was better this way.

She wondered five minutes after his departure how it would feel to be truly bereft. Could it possibly feel worse than what she was feeling now?

Nathaniel did not go out for the usual ride with his friends the following morning. He was lying in bed, though he was not sleeping. He had lain down only an hour before he usually got up, convincing himself that he would sleep, that he needed sleep.

He had spent most of the night walking the streets. He might, he supposed, have gone to Sophie's since that was where he had wanted to go earlier. Or he might have spent the hours in Lady Gullis's bed—he had escorted her home but had made the excuse for not going into the house with her that he did not wish to compromise her reputation with her servants. She had been flatteringly disappointed, but it had been an argument with which she could hardly argue. Or he might have sought out Eden or some other of his male acquaintances, many of whom made a practice of remaining up all night and returning home only with the dawn.

He might even have come home and gone to bed.

But he had walked the streets and had even had the intensely satisfying experience of beating off a would-be thief with his cane.

He was feeling disgruntled, he found, because this business with Sophie was not developing in any way as he had expected. He had wanted peace and comfort—and good sex—after the past few years, when he had shouldered the responsibility of settling a whole family of females. He exaggerated, of course. But it had seemed that way. He had looked forward this spring to seeing to his own contentment as well as to finding husbands for Georgina and Lavinia.

Sophie had seemed the perfect choice after his initial surprise at finding that he was attracted to her in *that* way— and that apparently she reciprocated his interest.

But Sophie had changed. Despite the outward sameness of both appearance and demeanor, she had developed a mind and a life of her own. It was not surprising, he supposed, when he had not seen her for three years. And it was not undesirable in a woman who lived independently. She also had some sort of secret—he did not doubt that—that she chose not to share.

She was no longer that placid, comfortable Sophie who was always there to cater to a man's need for pampering and a man's need to protect. The latter need might have been satisfied, he guessed, but she chose not to avail herself of his protection. And so the relationship had become troublesome to him, uncomfortable. It was just the sort of thing he had come to town to escape.

He thought with regret of the two nights they had spent together, of that cozy feeling of companionship as they had lain side by side talking, of her unexpected passion, of the intense satisfaction he had got from all their couplings. He thought too about that uneasy feeling he had had after the second night—just last night—that it was a more serious affair than he had looked for.

Last evening it had become downright ugly. For reasons of her own—her need to assert her independence, perhaps?—she had chosen deliberately to thumb her nose at them all. She must have *known* that they had stayed close to her, the four of them, so that she would not have to acknowledge Pinter or endure his attentions. She had shown them that she did indeed reserve the right to make her own friends.

It did not help his mood of irritation to realize that she was perfectly right. After an affair of less than a week's duration he was already thinking of her almost as he thought of his sisters and Lavinia, as someone who needed his protective, guiding hand on the reins of her life. Almost as if he owned her.

It was over between them. Over before it could become serious indeed. It should never have started. An affair between friends must surely always be disastrous. Friendship was one thing and sex was another. It was foolish to try to blend the two, except perhaps in marriage. That was a different matter. But then he was not in search of a marriage partner.

It was over. The only thing he had not decided during his sleepless night was whether he ought to tell her so, make a formal visit just for that purpose, or whether it was enough merely to let the whole thing lapse.

He was going to begin an affair with Lady Gullis. Although she was intelligent and witty and charming, there would really be only one function to their liaison. It would be better that way. He had made an appointment to take her to Kew Gardens two days hence. He would bed her after that. Probably the best plan would be to rent a house. She would not want him in her home, though she had invited him there last night. *He* would not want to go to her home. Word would inevitably spread, and though no one would condemn either one of them since all would be conducted with enough discretion to satisfy the scruples of the *ton,* it was not the sort of notoriety he cultivated. Those days were over.

He tried to sleep even though daylight flooded the room. But he kept seeing Sophie's bare hand with the mark apparent on the third finger where her ring had always been. And her bare neck. No pearls. No ring. There were numerous explanations, none of which was any business whatsoever of his.

*Sophie* was no business of his.

He tried to think of Lady Gullis, to imagine . . .

Finally he threw back the bedclothes, got up in a thoroughly bad humor, and rang for his valet.

Sophia did not sleep all night, though she did try lying in bed for two full hours before getting up and curling into the greater comfort of the chair beside the empty fireplace. She certainly could not sleep on that bed—not tonight. She had fancied she could smell him on the pillow next to her own—and had rolled onto her stomach to bury her nose in the memories before rolling back again, furious with herself, furious with him, furious with everyone and everything.

She hated the feeling of helplessness. She hated feeling trapped at every turn. She had to *do* something. There was precious little she could do, though in her anger last evening she had been prepared at first to defy Boris Pinter, to break loose from his power, to dare him to do his worst.

But Sarah had been with Viscount Perry, looking young and innocent and happy. . . .

There was *something* she could do, though, and she was going to do it. She was no longer in Spain. Those days were long over. She was a different person now. She had been on her own, ordering her own life for three years. Did they not realize that? It was high time they did.

She had been so very *happy* to see them. She had thought old times could be recaptured, but they could not. Her life had only become more complicated, and much more unhappy.

Very much more.

She remembered the time of the morning when she had met them in the park with Sarah. She wondered if they rode there at the same time every morning. She rather believed they did. Someone had mentioned it at Rawleigh House that first evening. It would be very much more convenient if she could see them all together and soon. Then at least she could begin to put part of her life back together again.

She would perhaps have the illusion of control for a short while. Until he "discovered" the next letter and she was forced to face the reality of the fact that there was no money with which to pay him and nothing to sell.

She would think of that when the time came. *One day at a time.*

And so Sophia went walking early and alone in the park, except for Lass, of course. Samuel had asked if she wished him to summon Pamela to accompany her and looked disapproving when she said no, but her servants were not her keepers either. She would take charge of her own life and she would do it today.

It was all illusion, of course.

She had been walking for all of three quarters of an hour before she saw them off in the distance, riding toward her—three horsemen, not four. She wondered which one was absent and prayed silently that it was not Nathaniel. She did not wish to have to talk separately with him.

But it was Nathaniel. Fate was against her, it seemed.

They had seen her, of course. They were all smiling gaily when they came close just as if last evening had not happened. But then to them, perhaps, it had not seemed such a momentous incident after all. She would not let that possibility deter her, however.

"Sophie," Kenneth called while Lass pranced all about them just as if the horses and riders were her long-lost friends. "Good morning. And a fine one it is for a change."

"All alone, Sophie?" Rex asked, looking about him as if he expected to see a maid bob up from behind the closest bushes.

"You will notice, Sophie," Eden said, grinning down at her, "that we are all present and accounted for except Nat. As are you. You will help us tease him, no doubt. He escorted *Lady Gullis* home from last night's soiree." He winked at her.

"For which piece of information Sophie will be eternally grateful, Eden," Rex said dryly. "You had better not be planning to share it with Catherine too."

"Sophie is made of sterner stuff," Eden said. "And I have to boast of my matchmaking skills before someone who will appreciate them."

They were all mightily pleased with themselves and with the absent Nathaniel, Sophia noticed, given the circumstances of his absence.

She stood looking up at them, unsmiling. "We are not in the Peninsula any longer, Eden," she said. "I am no longer Walter's wife, no longer *good old Sophie*. Those days are gone and I would thank you for remembering the fact.''

Kenneth grinned. Eden looked embarrassed.

"Oh, I say, Sophie," he said. "I am most awfully sorry. I thought you would enjoy the joke."

"I have not enjoyed it," she said. "Neither have I enjoyed your determination to treat me as someone who cannot possibly live her own life or think her own thoughts or choose her own friends." She was looking from one to the other of them, and they were all serious now. "I do not appreciate unsolicited interference in my life."

"You refer to last evening," Rex said after an uncomfortable silence. "We did not wish a repetition of what happened on the night of the Shelby ball, Sophie. We did not want him frightening you."

"I was not frightened," she said curtly. "The supper room was stuffy and I almost fainted. Mr. Pinter is a friend of mine. None of you ever liked him in the Peninsula. Neither did Walter. I am me, Sophie, and I like him. I choose to have him as a friend and I deeply resent the embarrassment of last evening, when you made it apparent to both him and me that you saw yourselves as my bodyguards to keep him at a distance from me. I will not have it."

"Sophie—" Eden began, but she whipped around to glare at him.

"I *will not* have it," she repeated. "If I must choose between the four of you and him, then I choose Mr. Pinter. He has done nothing to offend me. You have. Perhaps you have meant well, but you have treated me as a child. No, worse than a child. You think, Eden, that I enjoy your ribald remarks, that I am just a jolly fellow. I am not. I am a woman with a woman's sensibilities just like Catherine or Moira or any other *lady*. I may not be a lady, but I do have the same feelings as one."

"Sophie—" It was Eden again, sounding quite distressed now. "My dear."

"I am not your dear," she said. "I am nothing to you, Eden. I am nothing to any of you. I believe it would be as well for you all to remember that. We were once friends, and I have enjoyed meeting you all again. I enjoyed reminiscing at Rawleigh House, Rex. I thank both you and Kenneth for presenting me to your wives. But times have changed. I want no more dealings with any of you.''

They all stared fixedly at her as if, she thought, they expected her to burst into song at any moment or explode into dance.

Kenneth was the first to straighten up. He touched the brim of his hat with his whip and inclined his head to her. ''My deepest apologies, Sophie,'' he said. ''Good day to you.''

The other two murmured something similar and the three of them rode away. None of them looked back, which was just as well, Sophia thought, or they would have seen her both rooted to the spot and shaking like a new sapling in a stiff breeze.

She had not intended to say half of what she had. She certainly had not intended to go for Eden's throat with her accusations of ribald vulgarity. And she had accused them all of treating her as less than a lady merely because she was *not* a lady. She had never even *thought* that. The words had seemed to come from nowhere.

She had intended to end the friendship in a perfectly calm and rational manner—if it was possible to end a friendship in that way.

Now she felt bereft, she thought, trying to bring her limbs and her heartbeat under control. *This* was what it felt like. Did it feel better or worse than last night's misery? But she could not make the comparison. She had not yet talked to Nathaniel. It seemed a cruel fate that this morning of all mornings he was not with his friends.

He was with Lady Gullis. He had spent the night in her bed, doing to her and with her the things he had done with *her* the night before. It was a horrifying realization, not just because of the intense jealousy it aroused—though to her mortification there was that too—but because it made her feel cheap.

He had been in London just a short while, yet already he had spent a night at a brothel—had not Eden said that at Rex's?—two nights with her, and one night with Lady Gullis.

And she had thought there was something beautiful, something special about their nights together? She had even humiliated herself by suggesting that they have a long-term affair. How he must have laughed at the ease of his conquest of her.

How she hated him. And herself. Herself most of all. Would she never learn that dreams—or the fulfillment of dreams, anyway—just were not for her? She was just too plain and ordinary and unexciting. Unfeminine. She *hated* her lack of self-esteem.

And when she did dream of a man, she chose a blatant *rake*. He had never been anything else. Had she learned nothing in her years with the army?

Should she assume that her morning's task was now completed? she wondered. Would they go and tell Nathaniel what she had said? She did not doubt that they would. She did not need to subject herself to any more of this.

But no. Perversely, there had been something marvelously satisfying to her bruised heart in that confrontation. It would be even more satisfying to hurl her defiance and her scorn in Nathaniel's face. She could still see his cold eyes boring into hers last evening just before he turned away disdainfully with Lavinia, leaving her with one hand outstretched, a smile on her face, and her mouth open to begin the introductions.

*Nathaniel, how could you have done that to me?*

She turned her steps determinedly in the direction of Upper Brook Street.

# FOURTEEN

NATHANIEL HAD GONE IN for an early breakfast, discovered that he was not hungry, and considered going to White's to read the morning papers. He did not feel like reading the papers. To see if any of his acquaintances were there, then. Ede, for example. He did not want to see Eden—he would want to know all about last night and what had happened with Lady Gullis.

But it was a lovely morning, he saw, standing at the breakfast-parlor window, looking out. It would have been perfect for a ride. He should have got up and gone as usual—he had not slept anyway. But he did not want to see his friends. They would *all* want to know about last night. And they would want to discuss Sophie.

There was nothing to say about Sophie.

"Yes, what is it?" he asked when his butler came into the room behind him and cleared his throat. One could always tell by the throat clearing the nature of the message. This was an embarrassed throat clearing.

"There is a lady to see you, sir," the butler said. "Unaccompanied, sir. I asked if she wished to speak with the young ladies though they are still abed, but she said no, sir, that she wished to speak with you."

A lady? Alone? Lady Gullis? But she would not be so

lost to propriety, surely—or so willing to appear more eager than he.

"And does this lady have a name?" he asked.

"Mrs. Armitage, sir," his butler said.

*Sophie?*

"Thank you," he said. "I will come. Show her into the visitors' salon, please."

"Yes, sir." His butler bowed and withdrew.

Sophie? What the devil? He frowned. Well, he had wondered if he needed to talk to her, to put a definite face-to-face end to their affair. Now the decision had been taken from him. He could do it now. But why had she come here—and so early and alone? Was there trouble? Had his first instinct—and that of his friends too—been right and it was fear that had impelled her last night as it had at the Shelby ball? Had she needed their help after all? Did she need it now?

He strode from the breakfast parlor to the visitors' salon.

She was standing across the room from the door, facing it. She had removed her bonnet. It lay on a chair beside her. She looked as usual—neat and plain and practical in a mid-blue walking dress, her hair slightly disheveled. And she looked different from usual—far from appearing placid and comfortable and cheerful, she looked determined and almost belligerent.

She looked beautiful, he thought, bending absently to scratch the ears of the collie, which had come trotting across the room to greet him with wagging tail and lolling tongue—though he did not take his eyes from his visitor.

"Sophie?" he said. "May I summon a maid?"

"No," she said.

"Did you come to see Lavinia?" he asked. "You are at least a couple of hours early, I am afraid."

"No," she said. It sounded almost like a declaration of war. Was she going to *quarrel* with him? he wondered, his interest piqued.

"What is it?" he asked, taking a few steps closer to her and clasping his hands at his back. "How may I be of service to you, Sophie?" He listened to his own words with some inner amusement. Was he the man who had decided quite firmly to finish with her? But when all was said and done, she was still his dear friend.

"I believe," she said, and her head went back and her chin jutted and she looked even more hostile, "I owe you an apology. I ought not to have tried to present Mr. Pinter to your niece. I should have directed his request to you."

It sounded very trivial now that it had been put into words, the incident that had so angered him last evening and that had kept him awake all night determining to be finished with her.

"Sometimes," he said, "we are taken by surprise and do not have time to think out a wise course of action. I drew attention to you by reacting as I did. I should perhaps have simply spoken up. But I would have refused. I do not consider Pinter a suitable acquaintance for Lavinia."

"You accept my apology, then?" she asked, her cheeks flushed.

"Of course," he said. "And will you accept mine?"

He had drawn his hands from his back. He was about to reach them out to her. They would clasp hands and perhaps they would kiss and the whole business of her acquaintance with Pinter—which really was none of *his* business—would be forgotten about for the present. Perhaps, after all, the Season had not been ruined.

"No, I will not," she said quietly.

He raised his eyebrows and returned his hands to his back.

"I believe," she said, "you think you own me, Nathaniel. Rather as you think you own Georgina and Lavinia. There is perhaps a little more justification in their case, though not a great deal more. You do not *own* anyone. They are merely in your care. They are persons. I am a person. But just because I am a woman and you have been—inside my body, you think that I am your possession, your responsibility. You think you can choose my friends and freeze out those of whom you disapprove. I have never given you that power over my life. I did not give it with my body—I gave only my body. You have interfered against my express wishes.''

He felt rather as if a whip were lashing all about him.

''I wanted to protect you from harm, Sophie,'' he said. ''We all did.''

''From harm?'' she said. ''From Mr. Pinter? He is my friend. He was deeply humiliated last evening. So was I. And you were the one most responsible. I cannot blame you for taking Lavinia away. You were acting, rightly or wrongly, out of your sense of responsibility to her. But I can blame you for being where you were at the time. You had been quite intent on conversing with Lady Gullis until Mr. Pinter stepped into the room. You should have stayed where you were with her. I did not ask you and Eden or Rex and Kenneth to close ranks about me.''

She was right, of course. They had presumed. But from the best of intentions. And those had been stronger than a simple dislike of Pinter. All four of them had seen her reaction to him in the Shelby dining room, and he had seen more. He had seen her falter in the waltz and come to a complete and sudden halt so that he had trodden on her foot. She had been *horrified* to see Pinter. Not only displeased, but—frightened. Was that too strong an interpretation of what they had seen?

He did not believe that Pinter was her friend.

But he had no right to argue with her. If she chose not to tell him the whole of it, then that was her prerogative.

''No, you did not,'' he said. ''Pardon us for caring, Sophie.''

''Your caring caused me deep embarrassment,'' she said.

''Sophie.'' He gazed at her, his head tipped slightly to one side. He had spent all night thinking about his own anger, his own grievance against her. He had not really thought of the humiliation he had caused her. ''It will not happen again, my dear.''

''No, it will not,'' she said, ''as I have just finished telling your friends in the park.''

"You saw them there?" he asked her.

"I told them what I am telling you now," she said. "I want no more interference in my life. Not from any of you. I do not want your friendship any longer. Or even your acquaintance."

The words seemed to come at him one at a time. It took him several moments to fit them together so that they had meaning. While he did so, he watched her eyes falter for the merest moment and then look steadily into his again.

"We should all have been content with that one meeting in the park," she said, "the morning I was with Sarah. I should not have gone to Rawleigh House. I should not have allowed you to escort me home. I should certainly not have invited you inside, Nathaniel. It was a mistake. All of it."

It was what he had been thinking all night. His heart felt like a heavy, giant ache in the center of his chest.

"Our friendship is a thing of the past," she said. "It flourished under a certain set of circumstances and was precious at the time. It is still precious in memory. But that was a long time ago. We have all changed, and we all have lives of our own now—very separate and very different lives. I cannot fit you into mine and I will not allow you to try to fit me into yours. Go back to Lady Gullis, Nathaniel. She can offer you what you need better than I can."

"Go *back* to her?" He frowned.

"I know where you spent last night," she said, flushing again. "And your face this morning tells a story of a sleepless night. It does not matter. I have no claim on you and have renounced any small claim I had. I wish you well. And I will bid you a good morning."

The collie, sensing an end to the visit, clambered to its feet from its reclining position before the fireplace, looking eager. Sophie bent and picked up her bonnet.

"You cannot so easily kill a friendship, Sophie," Nathaniel said. "You can stay away from me and mine, ignore me when you do see me, live your life without any interference or any caring attention from me—we have a difference of opinion, you see, on what happened with Pinter.

You can behave as if we are not friends, as if we never have been. But it is there, you know—the concern, the affection, the lifting of the spirits at the mere sight of the other. If this is the end of our friendship, it is so as a result of a one-sided decision.''

And yet she had merely said what he had been planning to say—and what he never could have said, he realized now, once he had seen her again.

''*Damn* you, Nathaniel,'' she said, shocking him both with the unladylike language and the vehemence of her tone. Her eyes were suddenly swimming in tears. ''*Damn* you. If you cannot keep chains about me, you will use silken threads instead. I will not have it. Oh, I *will* not.'' She was trying to tie the ribbons of her bonnet into a bow beneath her chin with visibly shaking hands.

The collie was standing at the door, whining eagerly, its tail a waving pendulum.

''Allow me to escort you home?'' he asked quietly, averting his eyes at last so that she could the more easily complete the task.

''No!'' she said. ''No, thank you. I want no more dealings with you, sir.''

It should have been a mutual, rational decision, he thought. But suddenly he could not bear the thought of life without Sophie—which was an alarming realization. For three years he had been quite content neither to see nor to hear from her—except that one letter in response to his own.

''Don't upset yourself, then,'' he said, taking her hand in his and raising it to his lips. ''I will not argue. But if you have need of me, Sophie, I am here.''

She snatched back her hand, caught up the side of her dress, and whisked herself past him. He stood with his back to the door, listening to it open, listening to the scratching sound of her dog's paws on the marble floor of the hall, and then listening to the silence that succeeded the closing of the door.

They had not even said good-bye.
He had kissed her left hand—her *bare* left hand.

Eden had gone to White's alone for breakfast. But he
might have saved himself the trouble, he thought as he left
there an hour or so later. He had not been hungry and Nat
had not shown up. Perhaps he could have cheered himself
up if he could but have listened to an account—a strictly
expurgated account, of course—of Nat's successes the
night before. But then he would have had to tell Nat about
the meeting with Sophie in the park—a meeting that had
disturbed and even upset them all considerably.

Sophie had acted in a way so damnably unlike Sophie—
and had left them all feeling like whipped and guilty
schoolboys. Damn it, they had been trying to help her—
because they *liked* her and Walter was no longer around to
do the helping.

Eden had walked to White's after riding home. He was
glad to be on foot as he took a path back through the park.
A brisk walk would perhaps blow some cobwebs away. He
was trying to decide whether to call at Upper Brook Street
to see if Nat was home yet. It would be very interesting
indeed if he was not. But then he probably was. Nat had
become damnably respectable and he had those young relatives of his to fire off into marriage—though who would
take the·prickly redhead heaven alone knew. And perhaps
even heaven did not have the answer.

And then he frowned and stopped walking. Talk of the
devil! There were several people out and about in the park,
it being well into the morning by now. But the one walker
in the middle distance was quite distinctive. For one thing
she strode along like a man, though even from this distance
it was very obvious that there was nothing else whatsoever
about her that looked masculine. For another thing, she was
quite, quite alone. There was no escort, no companion, no
maid, no footman this side of the horizon. And for a third
thing, she was Lavinia Bergland or he would eat his hat.

Eden changed direction and increased his pace. He set

out on a collision course with her and it almost came to that too, since she was so intent on reaching her destination, wherever it might be, that she was not looking where she was going. She jerked to a halt when he appeared before her, sweeping off his hat and making her a mocking bow.

"Oh," she said, "it is you, is it?"

"It is I," he agreed. "I must advise you, ma'am, to slow your pace so that your maid might puff into view."

"You might try not to be ridiculous, my lord," she said.

"Yes, I might," he conceded, "but it would be tedious. I take it there *is* no maid?"

"Puffing along behind me?" she said. "Of course not. I am four and twenty, my lord. Good morning to you. I must be on my way and cannot stand here chatting."

He thought for a moment that she was about to proceed straight through his chest, but she lost her nerve at the last moment when it became obvious that he intended to stand his ground. She stayed where she was. She raised haughty eyebrows and assumed a sour expression that suited her admirably.

"Excuse me," she said.

"Certainly," he said. "Might I ask your destination, Miss Bergland?"

"My destination is absolutely none of your concern, my lord," she told him.

"Then I suppose," he said, "it must be Upper Brook Street. I had half made up my mind to go there myself. Do take my arm." Upper Brook Street lay in the exact opposite direction from the one she had been pursuing.

"Of course the wolves of Hyde Park will all eat me up if I proceed alone," she said. "I am not going home, Lord Pelham. I am going to see Sophie."

Ah.

"I suppose," he said, "Nat waved you on your way." After whisking her away from Sophie and Pinter just the evening before.

She tossed her glance skyward. "Nat looks this morning as if he had not a wink of sleep last night," she said to

Eden's intense satisfaction, "and he has the mood to match. I merely mentioned Sophie's name to him and he *barked*. I am going to see her."

"Is it wise?" he asked. "One was given the distinct impression last evening that Nat considered it inappropriate for you to have an acquaintance with Sophie's, ah, friend."

"But I am not paying a call on Mr. Pinter," Lavinia said. "I am visiting Sophie. *My* friend, sir. And what does Nat have to say to the matter?"

"Ah, let me see." He frowned. "Everything?"

She made an impatient and utterly derisive clucking sound. "I am not going to cut my acquaintance with Sophie merely because Nat has a grudge against Mr. Pinter," she said. "Are you planning to stand there all morning, my lord? If so, I shall turn around and take another path. Unless you plan to detain me by force, of course. But I must warn you before you decide upon that course that I shall embarrass you horribly by squawking very loudly."

He did not doubt that she would do it too. And on another occasion he might have been delighted to put the matter to the test. But not this morning. He had a choice—perhaps two. He might step out of her way. He might sling her over his shoulder and carry her forcibly back home to Nat. Or he might at least see her safely to Sophie's. It would be interesting to discover how Sophie would deal with her female friends—Miss Bergland, Catherine, Moira. He executed an elegant bow and offered his arm again. "Shall we compromise on our difference of opinion?" he suggested. "I will escort you to Sophie's."

She gave the matter some consideration and then nodded curtly. "Thank you." She took his arm.

"I understand that you do not like Mr. Pinter any more than Nat does, my lord?" Lavinia asked after they had walked in silence for a while.

"We had an acquaintance with him in the Peninsula," he explained. "He was a lieutenant, two ranks below us— and Walter Armitage. Walter—Sophie's husband, that was—blocked his promotion to captain on one occasion.

Need I add that he had no fondness for Major Armitage after that?''

"Oh pooh!" she said. "Boys' games. War is a game for unruly boys who have not grown up, you know."

"Yes," he said. "Thank you for the compliment."

Nat should be a candidate for sainthood, he thought. All gallantry aside, Eden was not sure that if she were *his* ward he would not have bent her over his knee long before now and given her a good walloping. Not that he approved of woman beating. But she certainly knew how to get beneath a man's skin like an annoying itch.

He wondered as they approached the house on Sloan Terrace if Sophie would receive Lavinia Bergland. He would wait around and see, he decided, though he would not, of course, try to gain admittance himself. Sophie had made herself very clear just a few hours before.

But less than a minute after Lavinia had sent her name up with Sophie's butler, he came back again with the request that she follow him. Eden bowed and would have bidden her a good morning but she had stridden off toward the stairs without a word or a backward glance.

Well, Eden conceded as he left the house and settled his hat firmly on his head again, she had not *asked* to be escorted, had she?

Sophia had had a hearty good cry as soon as she had arrived home. She had virtually collapsed facedown on her bed and given in to abject self-pity. But she had got up again after less than half an hour, bathed her face in cold water, and smiled rather ruefully at her red-faced image in the glass.

The end of the world, she decided, had not quite come. Not yet, anyway.

Little more than a week ago, apart from worry over the renewed demands concerning the letters, she had been quite content. The worry had been no small thing, of course, but she had been living quite happily without *them*. Without *him*.

She would be happy again. She had a very pleasant circle of friends and just enough social activities to prevent her from feeling her loneliness or turning her into a hermit. There was nothing in those people or those activities to arouse the spite of an evil man, surely. It had been a shock last evening to discover that he meant to take away her peace of mind, her enjoyment of *ton* events, and her past friends as well as her money.

Well, she still had not been destroyed and would not be.

*You cannot so easily kill a friendship . . . it is there, you know—the concern, the affection, the lifting of the spirits at the mere sight of the other.*

Sophia grimaced. Trust Nathaniel to have been so much more than just the gentleman. At least the others had had the grace to tip their hats to her and ride away, the perfect gentlemen, as soon as she had said her piece. But he had refused to accept her severance of their friendship. Not that he had raged at her or argued with her. He had done worse. He had been gentle and kind and dignified.

*Did* his spirits lift at the mere sight of her?

She hated him today for the very qualities she loved in him—had always loved. Even though she had not really been conscious of it before, she could see now that he had always been a little less selfish, a little more genuinely caring than the others. Perhaps it was why she had found him irresistible, why she had always loved him whereas she had only ever been *half* in love with the other three.

But she did not want to think of any of them any longer. She had released herself of one complication in her life today and she must live with the resulting unhappiness and loneliness. She would not let either drag at her spirits.

The news that Lavinia was downstairs wanting to call upon her seemed particularly poorly timed, but she could hardly turn her away. Besides, she felt a painful lurching of pleasure to know that Lavinia had come—that she had come from *there,* from that elegant, unostentatious house on Upper Brook Street. And perhaps, she thought foolishly, Lavinia had brought some message from *him.*

She stretched out both her hands when her visitor was shown into the sitting room and squeezed Lavinia's hands. "I suppose," she said, "this is a secret visit. I do hope it will not get you into dreadful trouble."

"Lord Pelham came charging across the park like the cavalry officer he once was when he saw me walking alone," Lavinia said. "I informed him I would squawk very loudly if he tried to take me back home. Oh, very well, Lass. There. Now you have been noticed." She pulled the collie's ears and Lass, contented, padded back to her place before the fireplace. "Lord Pelham took fright and escorted me here instead. So I daresay if Nat needs to find someone to rip up at, it will be Lord Pelham." She smiled brightly.

Sophia laughed. "Lavinia," she said, "how delightful you are. And how very pleasant it is to see you. Come and sit down and I will ring for tea."

"Thank you," Lavinia said, removing her bonnet and setting it aside. "Now you really must tell me about your friendship with Mr. Pinter. He is actually rather handsome, is he not? I understand that Nat and his friends—and your husband too—did not like him, perhaps because he was an inferior officer and they saw him as an upstart. Men can be quite childish about such matters, as I just remarked to Lord Pelham. He did not like it above half—he looks deliciously toplofty when he pokers up. Anyway, what I wish you to know is that if Mr. Pinter is a friend of yours, Sophie, then he is a friend of mine too, and you may present him to me anytime you wish."

"Oh dear," Sophia said, sitting down. "I truly would not wish to do that, Lavinia. He really is not my friend at all."

"Oh?" Lavinia had sat down too. She leaned forward now, interest lighting up her face.

She ought not to have said that, Sophia thought. But how could she have encouraged Lavinia to defy Nathaniel on the question of an acquaintance with Boris Pinter when all the right of the matter was on his side? What was she to say now?

She smiled. "Mr. Pinter is not a well-liked gentleman," she said. "Despite his good looks he has an unfortunate personality that repels rather than attracts. Perhaps I feel a little sorry for him. Or perhaps I merely wished last evening to assert myself against Eden and Nathaniel, who had gathered close to save me from his attentions, and against Rex and Kenneth, who were only a few feet away with a similar purpose in mind. I have been too long independent to enjoy having men take me under their wing."

Lavinia seemed satisfied. "Men are an abomination," she remarked. "If I were you, I would gather the four of them together and treat them to a thorough scolding. I only wish I could be there to hear." She laughed.

"I have done it already," Sophia said. "I have gone further, Lavinia." She was going to know it soon enough anyway. "I have ended my friendship with all of them. I have told them I wish to have no more dealings with them."

Lavinia looked at her blankly.

"So I do not believe Nathaniel will encourage you to continue your friendship with me," Sophia said, pouring the tea, which had just arrived. "And you must not feel obliged to do so. He is, after all, your guardian, either until you marry or until you are thirty—all of six years in the future."

"You have broken off *entirely* with them?" Lavinia said just as if she had not listened to the last speech. "But, Sophie, they are so *fond* of you. And you of them. And annoying though they can be—Nathaniel and Lord Pelham anyway; I do not know the other two well—they are not . . . Well, I . . . That is, they mean well, surely. Oh, this is none of my business. Shall we talk of something else?"

"I have been reading Milton's *Paradise Lost,*" Sophia said. "It is heavy. But you are quite right, Lavinia. It is well worth reading."

"Poor Milton did not realize what a marvelous hero he was creating in Satan," Lavinia said.

"The quintessential rebel," Sophia said. "I am not surprised that you sympathize with him."

They settled into a comfortable chat. Sophia's mind did touch upon the dreadful problem she would be facing if Boris Pinter decided to call today, but she did not believe he would. He would wait a while before presenting her with the next letter. He would wish to savor last night's victory for a few days or even weeks.

*Did* Nathaniel's spirits lift at the mere sight of her? she wondered. As hers did at the sight of him?

# FIFTEEN

Coming to London for the Season seemed to be accomplishing one of its purposes at least, Nathaniel thought a week later. For his own part he would have been quite content to return to Bowood, since he was not enjoying himself despite the pleasure of seeing and spending some time with his friends again. But Georgina was happy.

She appeared to love everything about London—the famous sights, the museums and galleries, the shops, the parks, the social events. And she had gathered about her a group of admirers, two or three of whom might have been pursuing her with serious intent. His sister, Nathaniel discovered, was blossoming rather late into an extremely pretty and surprisingly vivacious young lady.

Young Lewis Armitage, Houghton's son, was a definite favorite. He was an amiable young man, eligible in every way. Nathaniel did nothing to discourage the growing attachment, even though he could have wished there was not the connection with Sophie. He had not seen her since she had called at Upper Brook Street. She had not made an appearance at either of the two balls her family—and his—had attended. But sooner or later, if Georgie and Armitage remained together, he was bound to see her again.

He did not want to see her.

She had indeed put an end to all connection with Rex, Ken, and Eden as well as with him. When Catherine and Moira had called on her, she had refused to receive them.

He wished he had never seen her again. She had put a blight on the Season he had looked forward to with such eager anticipation. He had danced with Lady Gullis twice at each of the balls in the past week, and he had walked in Kew Gardens with her and driven her in Hyde Park. He had accepted an invitation to dinner and the theater with her and four of her friends during the coming week. But he had not yet been to bed with her, though the invitation to do so had been stated in all but words. Indeed, the lady appeared to be becoming impatient with his scrupulous concern for her reputation.

Eden and the others, of course, assumed that the deed had already been done and a full-blown *affaire de coeur* was now in happy progress. Assailing him with ribald wit obviously afforded them enormous pleasure—they never tired of affecting great surprise when he joined them for their early-morning rides, and they always proceeded with a spirited discussion of whether he was up early or late. He had not bothered to disabuse them. It was easier to hide behind their assumption.

Sophie had left him feeling strangely hurt and bruised.

Lavinia was the only one with whose friendship she had not broken. Lavinia, as he might have guessed, had made no secret of the fact that she had gone alone to call upon Sophie the very morning of Sophie's visit to him. It was only later he had discovered—from Eden—that in fact she had had an escort most of the way to Sloan Terrace. He guessed that she had omitted that detail in order to shield his friend from his wrath.

But Nathaniel had not ripped up at her, except to scold her for not taking at least a maid along with her. Lavinia, he was beginning to realize at last, was not a child and was not going to conform to any comfortable pattern of his or society's devising. Even after just a couple of weeks in town, she probably could have had a veritable court of besotted followers. By the end of the Season she could probably be married ten times over if she so chose.

She did not so choose. She treated with careless grace those gentlemen who might have been serious about her; she treated with hauteur those few of high rank who would have condescended to her; she treated with humorous scorn those who would have become possessive; and she quarreled at every turn with Eden, who quarreled right back.

Sometimes it struck Nathaniel, though he kept the thought strictly to himself, that they would make an interesting couple.

But he had resigned himself to being stuck with her until she was thirty.

It happened at last, as was inevitable—the meeting with Sophie. They had been invited to an evening of music and cards at the Houghtons—an intimate gathering of friends, as Lady Houghton had described it. Nathaniel gathered that he qualified as a friend because of Lewis Armitage's interest in Georgina, just as Rex qualified because of Viscount Perry's interest in Sarah Armitage—Rex and Catherine were invited too.

And of course Sophie was there, looking very much as she always looked and behaving just as if they were not there.

It was hard to ignore her. Nathaniel played a few hands of cards, an activity he never particularly enjoyed, and stood for a while behind the pianoforte bench, watching a series of young ladies play and sing. Sophie sat the whole while in one of the remoter corners of the drawing room in conversation with several older ladies. The fact that she stayed there, identifying with them, annoyed him intensely. The fact that where she sat and what she did was absolutely none of his business only annoyed him further.

Lavinia joined her eventually and he was triply annoyed. Did Sophie continue with *that* friendship deliberately to wound him since he had humiliated *her* by refusing to allow her to present Pinter to Lavinia? He hoped she would

not try defying him to the extent of introducing the two of
them after all. Though on mature consideration he did not
worry about the result of such an acquaintance as much as
he had at first. Lavinia was a sensible young lady in many
ways. She would not easily be swayed by the veneer of
charm Pinter was capable of wrapping about himself.

Nathaniel left the drawing room for a couple of minutes,
having discovered that he had left his handkerchief in the
pocket of his cloak. It was not the sort of party at which
the guests wandered beyond the main center of entertainment. The hallway was deserted and lit by only two
branches of candles. But someone else was coming out of
the drawing room just as he was returning to it—someone
who was probably on her way to the ladies' withdrawing
room. He halted only just in time to avert a collision. She
stopped too and looked up at him, startled.

"Sophie," he said softly.

Her face looked thinner, he thought, her eyes more luminous. Her hair was surrounded by its usual dark halo of
escaped curls.

She did not answer him but stared at him as if speech
and movement had become impossible to her for the moment. And he could think of nothing else to say. He caught
a whiff of her soap smell and realized something suddenly—an explanation for his inability to put her from his
mind and put Lady Gullis there instead.

He still felt a strong sexual yearning for Sophie Armitage.

He might have kissed her, he thought with some embarrassment later, if two things had not happened to save him.
She spoke, and he caught a flutter of movement from the
doorway beyond her.

"Excuse me, please, sir," Sophie said in her calm, placid
voice.

Lavinia was with her.

"I do beg your pardon," he said, stepping smartly to one
side to allow them both to pass. A few seconds had passed
between the near collision and her speaking. A few seconds

of eternity that he hoped had passed with their usual speed and lack of significance to the two ladies.

It was time, he thought as he went back into the drawing room and responded to Lady Houghton's beckoning hand from the direction of the card tables, that he bedded Lady Gullis. If she could not drown out all other sexual cravings, then his was a hopeless case indeed.

Lavinia was up a little earlier than usual the next morning. Nathaniel looked up in some surprise from reading his steward's report, newly arrived from Bowood, as she came through the door of his study after knocking but not waiting for an answer. He got to his feet.

"Good," she said, waving him back to his chair and seating herself uninvited on a chair across the desk from him, "you have returned from your ride but have not gone back out. It is difficult to find you at home in the mornings, Nathaniel."

"If I had thought my absence distressed you, Lavinia," he said, sitting down again, "I would have made more of an effort to be available to you."

Her lips twitched. "Heaven forbid!" she said, to which remark Nathaniel only just stopped himself from adding a fervent amen.

"What may I do for you?" he asked, leaning back in his chair.

"I am worried about Sophie," she said. It was characteristic of Lavinia never to waste time discussing the weather or her own or her listener's health when there were more important matters at hand.

But there were some topics he did not wish to discuss and Sophie was one of them.

"Indeed?" he said. "I am afraid I no longer have an acquaintance with Mrs. Armitage and am therefore quite unable to discuss the matter with you."

"Nat," she said scornfully, "do try not to be ridiculous."

He merely raised his eyebrows.

*"Mrs. Armitage!"* she said, rolling her eyes. "At least have the grace to call her Sophie."

He remembered his impression that Sophie's face was thinner, her eyes brighter. "Why are you worried?" he asked.

"She behaved last evening as if you did not exist," Lavinia said, "or Catherine or Lord Rawleigh either. When she did run almost head-on into you outside the drawing room, she called you 'sir,' just as you now called her 'Mrs. Armitage,' and she would not talk about it afterward even when I tried to make a joke of it. She merely turned the conversation. Have I missed something, Nat? You were a little rude to her on that evening when you whisked me away—well, perhaps more than just a little. She has a friend whom you dislike. But why was that incident of such huge significance that she has broken all connection with you—and with Lord and Lady Rawleigh, Lord and Lady Haverford, and Lord Pelham too? She was so *fond* of you all."

Nathaniel sighed. "Sometimes seemingly small incidents are merely the tip of an iceberg, Lavinia," he said. "I suggest you not worry about it. I have not tried to cut off *your* friendship with her, have I?"

"Nat." She leaned forward in her chair and set both hands flat on the desk. "Don't treat me like a child."

"If I were doing that," he said, "I would have packed you back to Bowood by now. Perhaps she prefers Pinter to us, Lavinia."

"But she does not even *like* him," she said. "She told me as much when I said she might present me to him at any time if she wished. She told me he was not her friend."

He rested his elbows on the arms of his chair and steepled his fingers beneath his chin. He had *known* that. But Sophie had taken away from him—from all of them—the right to pursue the reasons for her behavior.

"Then perhaps," he said, "she merely wished to teach us a lesson, Lavinia. We were trying to protect her from him that evening—all four of us were, even though she had expressly told me, at least, that I had no business trying to tell her whom she might befriend or receive. We chose to interfere anyway and she was furious. You of all people should be able to identify with that." He smiled ruefully at her.

But she was frowning down at the hands she had spread on the desk. "I could understand and even applaud her ripping up at you, Nat," she said. "Indeed I urged her to do it before she told me she had already done so. But to completely break off all those friendships—and even with Catherine and Moira? And she is so miserable, Nat."

"Miserable?" He drew a slow breath.

"She smiled and talked last evening just as if she were in the most comfortable of moods," Lavinia said, "but she so very obviously would not look at or speak of either you or Lord Rawleigh or Catherine that it was clear she was very *un*comfortable and unhappy. What hold does Mr. Pinter have over her?"

There, it had been put into words—the very obvious idea that he and his friends had skirted about in conversation together and that his mind had shied away from. Pinter had some hold over Sophie. Nathaniel's eyes met Lavinia's and held them, and for the first time he looked at her as an equal, as someone who cared enough for a mutual friend to wish to help her.

"I do not know, Lavinia," he said.

"How can we find out?" she asked him.

"I have no right," he told her. "She does not want me to know."

"Perhaps she does," she said. "Perhaps she has been *told* that she is not to solicit your help."

He closed his eyes and pressed his chin down onto his fingertips. He had thought of that too—and had avoided the thought.

"You are her friend, Nat," Lavinia said, "as much as I am. Perhaps more so. You have known her longer, and I know you are fond of her. Fonder than the others are."

He opened his eyes and looked into hers. He pursed his

lips. She saw too damned much. But for once he did not feel annoyed with her.

"You think he has threatened her, then?" he asked. "Is that too Gothic an interpretation, Lavinia? Too melodramatic?"

"When I called on her three days ago," she said, "—I *did* take a maid, Nat—we heard someone knocking on the door below. She turned terribly pale and jumped to her feet and rushed to the window and said she must send me up to her dressing room as it was too late for me to leave without being seen. But before she could push me out through the door—she really was *pushing*—her butler came up to announce her friend Gertrude. We all sat down for tea and neither Sophie nor I referred to the strange incident again. Nat, who did she *think* it was?"

It seemed hardly a question that needed answering.

"Was it just that she wished to oblige you by not presenting me to him?" Lavinia asked.

"Or was trying to bundle you upstairs too excessive for that?" he said more to himself than to her.

"Nat," she said, "we have to help her."

"We?" He looked more closely at her, but he held up a hand, palm out, before she could reply. "Yes, we, Lavinia. Pardon me for being about to exclude you. Thank you for coming to me. You have forced me to face what I have been avoiding for longer than a week. Sophie *is* my friend even if I am not hers."

"Oh, you are," she said, sitting back in her chair. "Tell me about Mr. Pinter, Nat. Not just that he was an unpleasant officer in the Peninsula. Tell me all you know of him."

He certainly would not have said anything more than that to his sisters, he thought, looking consideringly at her. But Lavinia was different—a massive understatement. And he owed her his confidence.

"He enjoyed power," he said. "He used it cruelly. He seemed to spend much of his time trapping his men into committing small, insignificant misdemeanors and then ordering punishment for them."

"Punishment?" she said.

"Whippings mostly," he said. "Formal affairs conducted while the rest of the regiment stood on parade, watching. The offender would be stripped and tied to a punishment triangle to have his back flailed. We all used to hate it."

"Except Mr. Pinter?" she asked.

He nodded. Kenneth had used to say that Pinter derived a sexual thrill from watching a whipping. Nathaniel was not about to say *that* to Lavinia. But he did not need to.

"I daresay," she said, "it was his substitute for whores."

He jumped to his feet. "Lavinia!" he said, his eyes blazing.

"Oh, Nat," she said, looking decidedly cross, "do try not to be ridiculous. Did he like whores too?"

He sat down again, set one elbow on the desk, and propped his face against his hand. "I *cannot,*" he said, "continue this conversation any further."

"I am sorry," she said. "I have embarrassed you. But I would wager he did not. I believe we should find out as much more as we can about him, though, Nat. I shall ask Lord Pelham. He will sputter and poker up just as much as you, of course, and mutter darkly again that I am no true lady, but perhaps he will remember more. What you have said is very revealing, though."

"Lavinia," he said, "you must leave this to me—*please*. Poor Ede already thinks someone should have given you a good walloping when you were younger."

"He would," she said, sounding bored. "I suppose a heavy hand on the rear end scrambles the brains and causes a girl to grow into a suitably featherbrained lady. How convenient for men."

"You can do something for me, though," he said, drumming his fingertips on the desktop. He did not know quite where the idea had sprung from, but he supposed it must have been forming for some time in that deep part of his mind of which he was unaware. "You can come shopping with me—for a pearl necklace and a wedding ring.''

One of the first things he had noticed about Sophie the evening before had been the continued absence of her pearls and her wedding ring. He did not know quite why he had noticed or why their absence had taken on such significance to him.

''Why, Nat,'' Lavinia said, ''I did not know you cared.'' But despite the levity of her words, she was looking keenly at him.

''Sophie's are missing,'' he said. ''Until a week ago I had never seen her without her ring. And I had never seen her at a social function without her pearls. On the night of that soiree they were both suddenly missing.'' The ring had been missing the night before too, but he was not going to explain that meeting.

''Lost?'' she said. ''Stolen?''

''Or pawned,'' he said. His mind had still not verbalized the final ugly word, but it did so now with crashing though silent clarity.

*Blackmail.*

But what the devil could she have *done*?

''You want to try to find them?'' Lavinia asked.

''It might be a wild-goose chase,'' he said. ''And we will have to look somewhat impoverished, Lavinia, if we are to shop for a wedding ring at a pawnbroker's. Or perhaps at one of the lesser jeweler's, people who buy jewelry to resell. Pawnshops first, though—I do not believe she would *sell* her wedding ring. I could go alone, of course.''

But Lavinia had brightened considerably. She looked flushed and happy. Her eyes were shining as she leaned across the desk toward him.

''Oh, darling Nat,'' she startled him by saying, ''I adore you so very much, my love, that I would take you even without a ring or a wedding gift of pearls. And *of course* I will forgive you for gambling away all your fortune. I *know* you will never do it again. The power of my love will transform you into a nobler being.''

He chuckled. ''Minx!'' he said. ''But you might have to

act out the part for a number of days, and even then we may find nothing.''

"For you, darling,'' she said, batting her eyelashes at him, "anything." And then she looked like her old brisk, no-nonsense self again. "And for Sophie too."

But devil take it, Nathaniel thought, he did not know what the recovery of Sophie's property would do to help. All it would do was prove that she had needed money quite desperately.

She had *told* him not to interfere.

Apart from a few walks in the park with Lass at times of the day when she was unlikely to meet any acquaintances, and one visit to and one from Gertrude, and a couple of calls from Lavinia, Sophia had stayed home alone for almost two weeks—apart from that one evening at her brother-in-law's, of course.

It had been no grand *ton* entertainment, and she had allowed herself to go for that reason and because Beatrice had asked her especially to come. Foolishly, because she had been told it was to be an intimate gathering of family and friends, she had not expected to see any of the Four Horsemen there. She had forgotten the young people and their attachments.

Foolishly too she had expected the misery of the evening to be her only punishment. And it *had* been miserable—utterly so. Rex had carefully avoided her—to save her from embarrassment, she guessed. Catherine had glanced at her a few times and had looked hurt. And he—Nathaniel . . . She could still shudder, five days later, at the realization that, outside the drawing room, she had come very close indeed to taking that one step forward that would have buried her face against his neckcloth, against the warm, familiar, safe smell of him.

It had been pure agony to see him again and to know—she had *seen* them in the park, though they had not seen her—that he had been with Lady Gullis for longer than a week.

But that evening had not been punishment enough. He must be spying on her, she thought with another shudder— Boris Pinter, that was. He must have discovered that she had been to a *ton* party, albeit a modest one, and that Rex and Nathaniel had been there too. At least she assumed he must have found out. Or perhaps it was only coincidence that had brought a note two days later. He had, of course, "found" another of those love letters and knew that dear Sophie—he persisted in playing that ridiculous game of concerned friend with her—would not wish it to fall into the wrong hands. The sum he asked for was so exorbitantly large that perhaps fortunately her mind had frozen and had still not quite thawed three days later.

She was in her sitting room in the middle of an afternoon, doing nothing except sit smoothing her hand over the back of a contented Lass, who was stretched out across her lap. The warmth of the collie's body and the sound of her contented sighs somehow brought with them the illusion of comfort.

She had a few options—her mind was coming sluggishly back to life. She might simply let the deadline date, eleven days hence, go by and see what he would do. She would not, of course, take that option. She might try to sell the house. She did not know if she could. It had been a gift from the government, but she was not sure if it was a free gift or if there were some conditions attached. She supposed that she might find out, but if that was the option she chose, she must do so without much further delay. Or she could go to Edwin or Thomas—Edwin first, probably—and tell them all and allow *them* to decide on the best course of action. It would come to that eventually, of course, but she hated to burden them with her knowledge and the realization that it could at any moment become *public* knowledge.

And yet there would be such enormous *relief* to be no longer alone, to have someone else to bear the burden.

She closed her eyes and ignored Lass's cold wet nose nudging against her hand—she had stopped smoothing and scratching. If she sold her house, she would perhaps lose her pension too. She would be a dependent. She would have to live with Edwin and Beatrice or with Thomas and Anne.

But she must try to sell the house. She turned cold at the thought finally taking shape in her mind.

There was a tap on the door.

"Come in," she called.

Her butler had a card on his tray and brought it over to her.

She picked it up, looked at the name on it, and held it against her chest. Well, if there was a spy, now he would have something else to report.

"Tell Sir Nathaniel Gascoigne to go away, Samuel," she said. "Tell him I am not at home. Tell him that I never again will be at home. And if he comes again, save yourself the trouble of climbing the stairs."

"Yes, ma'am," he said with his conspiratorial smirk. She often wondered if he and the other servants knew that Nathaniel had spent two nights in her bedchamber with her. They probably did. Not much could be kept from the servants of a house.

"Samuel," she shrieked after he had left the room and closed the door behind him. Lass, startled, jumped down from her lap and sought a more peaceful refuge in front of the hearth.

"Yes, ma'am?" Samuel had opened the door again.

"Show him up," Sophia said.

"Yes, ma'am." The smirk had graduated to an expression that looked very like a self-satisfied smile.

Oh yes, they knew all right.

And what had she done now?

*What had she done?*

# SIXTEEN

Iᴛ ᴡᴀs ᴀ ᴄʜɪʟʟʏ ᴍᴏʀɴɪɴɢ, cloudy and blustery and trying its very hardest to rain. Sophie had a fire lit in the sitting room. She was standing before it, facing it, her hands stretched to the blaze. Nathaniel stood looking at her while her man closed the door behind him. Her collie nudged at his hand and he patted the top of its head.

"Sophie," he said.

She was wearing a faded muslin dress that looked light and pretty despite its obvious age. She had surely lost weight, he thought. She did not turn around.

"I believe I told you," she said, "that I wanted no more dealings with you, sir."

And yet she had admitted him.

"Sophie," he said again.

He tried to see her as he had always used to—as Walter Armitage's brave and practical and amiable wife, as a not extraordinarily lovely woman whose beauty lay mainly in her character. As simply a friend—dear Sophie. It could not be done. He could no longer see her with any objectivity. She had become someone he cared about—with his heart.

"If you have something to say," she said, "please say

it and leave. If you have nothing to say but my name, then why did you come?''

''Why is this happening, Sophie?'' he asked her, taking a few steps farther into the room.

''This?'' She turned to look at him at last—though not at his face. Her eyes were fixed somewhere below the level of his chin. ''I do not know, sir. You tell me.''

''Why have you spurned your friends who care about you?'' he asked her. ''Why have you spurned me? We have been lovers.''

Her pale, almost gaunt cheeks flooded with color. ''Hardly that,'' she said. ''I was your bed partner for two nights. Do you call all such women your lovers?''

''No,'' he said, trying to draw her eyes to his but failing. ''No, only you, Sophie. Why have you turned away from us?''

''Because you interfered in my life,'' she said, frowning. ''Because you made me unhappy.''

*Unhappy.* Did she mean all four of them? Or only him in the capacity of lover? But that was not the point now.

''Must caring for a friend, wishing to help and protect her be dubbed interference and punished so harshly?'' he asked. ''We are unhappy too, Sophie. I am unhappy.''

For one moment her eyes came to his. But she turned away again to gaze into the fire.

''I am sorry,'' she said. ''But I cannot think that I am of lasting importance to any of you. I wish you would leave.''

''Did he tell you to break off all connection with us?'' he asked her.

She whirled on him, her eyes wide with shock. *''What?''* she said.

''Or did you just fear that we would antagonize him and he would make you suffer more for it?'' He watched her closely. She was bringing herself under control. Her brow smoothed over; her eyes turned blank.

''Who is this mysterious *he*?'' she asked. ''Mr. Pinter? You are still determined to make a villain out of him, Na-

thaniel? Perhaps I can persuade him to go about in black
domino and mask, slinking from dark corner to dark corner.
Then you would be thoroughly satisfied. No. I will have to
persuade him too to carry me off, kicking and screaming,
to some damp, murky lair so that the Four Horsemen of
the Apocalypse can ride to my rescue and slay him.''

Her eyes slipped below the level of his chin again when
he did not immediately answer but just gazed at her.

''What power does he have over you, Sophie?'' he asked
her.

She clucked her tongue and made an impatient gesture
with one hand.

''Blackmail?'' he suggested.

''*No!*'' Her eyes blazed into his again. ''Get out of here,
Nathaniel. Get out!''

''What have you done?'' he asked her. ''What could you
possibly have done, Sophie, so bad that you would allow
him to have this power over you?''

She closed her eyes and drew breath.

''Fool!'' she said quietly. ''Oh, fool! Go away from here.
Leave this.''

''Tell me,'' he said. ''Let me help you. I do not care
what it is, Sophie. Was it an adulterous affair? Some—petty
theft, perhaps? I do not care. Let me share the burden with
you and help you.''

When she opened her eyes he could see that they were
bright with tears. ''You are a kind man, Nathaniel,'' she
said, ''but you have a vivid imagination.''

''Then why did you break off our friendship and our
other arrangement?'' he asked her.

''That was a mistake,'' she said, blinking her eyes.
''Look at yourself, Nathaniel. Look at yourself in a glass.
And look at me.'' She half smiled. ''And at Lady Gullis.''

''You believe I have lain with her?'' he asked her.

She turned her head away. ''I do not care,'' she said. ''It
is not my concern, Nathaniel. *You* are not my concern.''

''I have not,'' he said.

''Ah,'' she said softly, and said nothing else for a few

moments. She hunched her shoulders. "It was still a mistake. I was not made for casual affairs or for pleasure without commitment. I am sorry. It was my suggestion, I know. I made a mistake. I would like you to leave now, please."

So they had got into personal matters after all. He had not intended it.

"I *have* looked at you," he told her, "and I have looked at Lady Gullis. I prefer you, Sophie."

She smiled then and looked genuinely amused for a fleeting moment. "What shockingly poor taste you have, sir," she said, her voice bitter.

"Sophie," he said, "let me help you. Tell me what hold he has on you and I will put a stop to it. It is no idle boast. The Pinters of this world are invariably cowards as well as bullies."

She sighed. "I am afraid, Nathaniel," she said, "you are going to have to accept the fact that I have befriended someone you do not like and someone that Walter did not like. And that when you insulted him you insulted me. If you cannot accept the idea that anyone could possibly choose him before you, then maybe you have a problem with conceit. But it is not my problem. Will you please leave now? I would hate to have to ring for Samuel and have him throw you out."

"I would hate it too," he said. "Poor man. He would not have a chance. I will leave. I want to give you this first, though." He drew out the package he had placed in an inner pocket and held it out to her.

She looked at it warily. "No," she said. "No gifts. Thank you but no."

"Take it," he said, keeping his hand extended. "It is yours."

She came close enough to take it when it became obvious to her that he would not move until she did. She looked down at the small square package almost as if she believed it would explode in her hand. And then she opened it, removing the paper wrapping and then lifting the lid from the box.

Nathaniel watched her face as she stared down at her wedding ring surrounded by her pearls. She turned so pale that even her lips were white.

"Where did you get these?" She was whispering, her eyes on the contents of the box.

"From the jeweler to whom you sold them," he said. It had taken him and Lavinia three long and tedious days to find the right one after they had exhausted every pawnshop except those situated too deep inside some of the more dangerous rookeries.

Sophie's lips moved several times as if she would speak before she actually did. "This was foolish of you," she said. "I sold them because I no longer wanted them."

"No, Sophie, it will not do." He stepped forward, removed the ring from the box, took her cold, nerveless left hand in his, and slid the ring onto the correct finger. "I cannot force you to confide in me or allow me to help you. But you may not lie to me. It would be pointless, my dear." He raised her hand to his lips.

She was crying then with awkward, noisy sobs. Box and pearls went clattering to the floor as she reached for him, her arms coming up about his neck, her face burying itself against his neckcloth. He closed his arms about her and held her.

He thought back to the wars, to all the men he had killed in battle, many without faces, many with. They were faces that still sometimes swam about in his nightmares and probably always would. He thought back to a morning two years before, to another killing, in England this time, the result of a duel. Rex had done the killing, though the rest of them had been there and had approved—indeed, Nathaniel had had a pistol trained on the man after he had cheated and shot early, wounding Rex in the right arm. The dead man had been a rapist of more than one woman, but of Catherine in particular. Nathaniel remembered thinking at the time that there was an end of it, an end of all killing as far as he was concerned. He had found since that he could not even hunt on his land. War had made him value life, even that of wild animals and birds.

But he was going to kill Boris Pinter. Somehow it was going to happen. He closed his mind to the question that inevitably asked itself—was killing the only answer to life's worst problems? Perhaps the answer was yes. In this case it was yes. He was going to kill Pinter for Sophie.

Her face was warm and wet when he found her mouth with his own. He had intended to comfort her, but she responded with fierce passion, opening her mouth against his own, tightening her arms about his neck, pressing herself to him. It was the wrong time, he thought in some regret after a while—and after he had wondered if her servants ever entered a room unbidden. It was too mindless a moment. It was something they would both regret if they did not stop now.

He drew back his head from hers.

"Let me come to you tonight," he said. "I am no longer cut out for casual affairs either, Sophie." He was not sure quite what he meant by that—or perhaps he did not want to know. But he did know that he wanted her. Not just in bed, but—he wanted her back. He had been lonely without her.

She pulled away from him, found a handkerchief in a pocket, turned away, and wiped her eyes and blew her nose.

"Yes," she said then without looking at him. She bent to pick up the box and the pearls.

"I will not mention the other to you again, then, Sophie," he said, "unless you mention it first. But know that I am always here, that I will always listen, always help. If you are desperate for money—well, you would not come to me, would you? But know that you could, that matters are never so desperate that there is not that way out. There, I will say no more. Shall I come at midnight?"

"Yes," she said. "I will watch for you."

"Thank you," he said. And he turned without another word and let himself out of the room.

But he had a strong feeling that he had let himself into

something from which he would never free himself. And perhaps he would never want to. It was a bewildering and a thoroughly alarming thought.

Lady Honeymere's ball on Hanover Square was set for that evening. Even before setting out, Nathaniel had stated his intention of leaving early, but Georgina and Lavinia would be able to stay until the end, since both Margaret and John were to be there to chaperon them and accompany them home.

Lavinia would have been quite content to leave early with her cousin in the normal course of events. Although she enjoyed the social activities of the Season, she did believe they were conducted to excess. As she had told Sophia on a visit the previous day, one became mortally tired of seeing the same silly gentlemen wherever one went and hearing the same silly compliments and fielding the same silly advances. Did gentlemen not harbor an *un*silly thought in their heads?

She and Sophia had enjoyed a good laugh on the topic. But Sophie, Lavinia had not failed to notice, though she had made no mention of it, no longer attended *ton* functions, even though her brother and sister-in-law did.

On this particular evening Lavinia was quite happy to remain at the ball—once she had discovered that Nathaniel's early departure did not take away his friends too. She had thought that just might happen. They were very close, those four, and were very obviously enjoying a few months of one another's company. But he was the only one who left. Lady Gullis had not appeared at all at the ball, Lavinia had not failed to notice. Doubtless there was some connection.

She had been granted permission to waltz at Almack's the previous Wednesday. Having been utterly contemptuous of the strange rule ever since her first ball, and having threatened a dozen times to waltz whether she had been granted permission or not, she then, of course, had felt obliged out of sheer principle to refuse to waltz even after permission had been granted. But tonight she intended to waltz—it was the set before supper.

She sought out Eden before it began—he was standing with a group of people, mostly gentlemen, but Lavinia did not allow that fact to deter her. She tapped him on the arm with her fan. He turned toward her, his eyebrows lifting in surprise. He was very good at that look of hauteur, as she had conceded before tonight. Though if he expected to cow her with the look, he was going to be disappointed.

"I have been granted permission to waltz," she told him. Lavinia had decided years before that if there was a bush to be beaten about, doing so was a waste of time.

"Ah." His hand had gone to the handle of his quizzing glass. He had turned away from his companions to give her a little more privacy. "My most heartfelt congratulations, Miss Bergland."

"The next set is a waltz," she said.

"I do believe you are right." He had the glass halfway to his eye.

"I want you to dance it with me," she said.

If gentlemen knew how a quizzing glass enlarged one eye while leaving the other incongruously small, Lavinia thought, they would not use it so freely.

"Indeed?" he said. "I am your charity case, ma'am? You fear I cannot find a partner of my own?"

"Oh," she said impatiently, "how ridiculous men can be. Have you enjoyed that little piece of revenge?"

"I have been enormously tickled by it," he said, sounding decidedly bored. "Miss Bergland, will you do me the honor of waltzing with me?"

"If you can perform the steps without treading all over my toes," she said.

"Hmm." He dropped his glass on its ribbon and extended an arm for hers. "Are your feet that large, then? I am too well-bred to stare down at them."

He did not tread on her toes. Indeed, she had the strange feeling as he whirled her about the ballroom during the following half hour, making all the colors of gowns and coats and the glitter of jewels blur into a wondrous kaleido-scope, that her toes did not touch the floor at all. If she had but known that he danced this well, she thought, she she would have danced with him that very first time. No, she would not—he had been far too condescending and far too certain that those blue eyes of his would smite her into dithering incoherence.

They were quite gorgeous blue eyes, of course, but that was beside the point.

"Allow me to escort you in to supper," he said when the set came to an end—far too soon. "Or are you now about to assert your perfect confidence in being able to find a place for yourself and to fill a plate of your own?"

"I am not hungry," she said, taking his arm. "Take me into the garden."

His eyebrows shot up and his hand reached for his quiz-zing glass again. "Feeling amorous are we, Miss Berg-land?" he asked.

"I cannot answer for you, my lord," she said, "but I am certainly not. I wish to speak with you."

"Ah," he said. "Interesting."

The garden was very prettily lit with lanterns and set about with rustic seats. The evening was a little chilly but at least the garden was deserted, all the other guests doubt-less feeling ravenously hungry after the exertions of half an evening.

"I want to know more about Mr. Boris Pinter," Lavinia said when they were outside.

"I would not if I were you," Lord Pelham said: "Nat would have an apoplexy or two if you were to develop an interest in the man."

"Try not to be ridiculous," she told him. "He is black-mailing Sophie."

He was quiet for a few moments and his steps slowed. "You know that?" he said. "Has she admitted as much to you, then? She would not admit it to Nat when he returned her ring and pearls to her earlier today. But it would be as well anyway for you not to be involved in this. It might possibly become nasty.''

Lavinia clucked her tongue. ''I spent three days with Nat pretending to be besotted with him despite the fact that he had just gambled away his family fortune and could not afford to buy me a *new* wedding ring or wedding gift,'' she said. ''I simply must be granted either sainthood or involvement as a reward. I never did fancy being a saint—wearing a halo and plucking the strings of a harp would become a mite tedious after the first century or so.''

''Ah,'' he said, ''Nat did not tell us you had been his accomplice.''

''Now tell me all you know of Mr. Pinter,'' she said.

''So that your indignation against him can increase?'' he said. ''Nothing can be served by that. Nat wants simply to kill the bast—'' Lord Pelham discovered the necessity of clearing his throat. ''But we do not fancy watching him swing. If you have any influence with him, talk sense into him. Though perhaps I am commissioning the wrong person to do that.''

''Nat told me about Mr. Pinter's cruelty,'' she said. ''About his trapping men into doing wrong and then ordering them to be whipped—and watching the punishment with great enjoyment.''

''Mmm,'' he said noncommittally.

''He blushed and looked horridly embarrassed when I suggested that Mr. Pinter must have arranged all that rather than take a whore,'' she said.

Lord Pelham's cough was getting worse. ''I will be eternally thankful,'' he said when the spell had passed, ''that we are strolling in the dark. Is it just a malicious rumor that you are a lady?''

''Is it true, do you think?'' she asked him. ''Is he *peculiar*?''

''I hardly think—'' Lord Pelham was using his pokering-up voice and Lavinia was having none of it.

''Yes, yes,'' she said impatiently. ''But do you not *see*? One does not deal with a blackmailer by wagging a finger in his face and admonishing him to stop it and be a good boy. Neither does one stop it by killing him and then having to swing for it, as you put it. One stops it by matching fire with fire.''

"Meaning?" he asked her, stopping and turning to face her, though they could not see each other clearly since they were in among some trees from which no lanterns hung.

"Meaning," she said, "that we find something that *he* would certainly not wish to come into the light."

"Blackmail," he said.

"Of course," she said briskly. "What do you think I have been talking about? If he carries out any of his threats to Sophie—though what he could possibly have on her I cannot even begin to imagine—but *if* he does, even in the smallest of ways, then we let the world know about him. But first we let him know what the consequences of his behavior are to be."

"Good Lord," he said, "you are pure unadulterated poison, ma'am."

"In defense of my friends, yes," she said. "If it is true that Mr. Pinter derives enjoyment—*that* sort of enjoyment—from watching men stripped and whipped, and if we can find enough proof to worry him, then we can put a stop to this business with Sophie. Shall we do it?"

"We?" he said faintly.

"*We,*" she said firmly. "As in you and me. Nat would send me back to Bowood with instructions to the coachman to spring his horses if I made the suggestion to him."

"No," he said firmly. "We as in Nat and me and Rex and Ken, Miss Bergland. But I will grant you that it is a brilliant idea and I am ashamed we have not thought of it for ourselves. I daresay we are not devious enough."

She thought for a few moments. "Oh very well," she said finally. "But only provided I am given a full account of what happens. I do not want to hear when it is all over that the details are not fit for a lady's delicate ears."

"Yours?" he said, raising his quizzing glass even in the

near darkness and training it on one of her ears. "I daresay they are made of cast iron."

She smiled at him. "You are going to save Sophie," she said. "All of you. I would not wish to be in Mr. Pinter's shoes. I think the four of you pokering up all together would be quite a formidable sight."

They grinned at each other, in unusual accord.

"I suppose," he said, "if I were to kiss you I would have my face thoroughly slapped and would have to endure the embarrassment of reappearing in the ballroom with five red fingermarks across one cheek?"

She looked at him consideringly. "Do you *want* to kiss me?" she asked.

"The thought had crossed my mind," he admitted. "*Would* I be slapped?"

She thought again, taking her time about doing so. "No," she said finally.

"Ah," he said, and bent down and set his lips to hers. But he lifted his head almost immediately. "Child's stuff," he murmured, his arms coming about her. "If we are going to do this—and by some mutual madness it appears that we are—let us at least do it properly."

He did it properly.

Lavinia drew back her head when it occurred to her after some considerable time that perhaps she ought. She frowned at him. "Do all gentlemen kiss like that?" she asked him. She clarified. "With their mouths open?"

"I have absolutely no idea," he said, sounding surprised. "I have never crept up close and watched. But *this* gentleman kisses like that. Did you mind?"

"It had a strange effect on my insides," she said.

"Dear me," he said. "It was not by any chance your first kiss, was it, Miss Bergland? At *your* age?"

"Oh, you will not make me ashamed," she said, "and scrambling to lie and claim that I have been kissed so many times that I have lost count. I have never before *wished* to be kissed and so I have not been."

"But this time you did wish it?" he asked her.

She had not really intended to make that revealing admission, but she had talked her way into it and would not deny it now. "I suppose," she said, "you have had a great deal of practice, and if one is to experience something at least once in one's lifetime one might as well experience it with someone who knows what he is doing."

"Ah," he said. "Shall we try once more? Perhaps this time you might refrain from puckering up and try opening *your* mouth."

She followed his advice. And if she had thought the first time that strange things happened to her insides, well, the sensations were beyond thought the second time.

"Much more of this," he said sometime later, at which point she noticed that he was *withdrawing* his hand from about one of her breasts and was sliding it out from the low neckline of her gown, "and I am going to have to be paying Nat a formal morning call tomorrow. I am sure neither of us would want that to be happening."

"The very thought!" she agreed, shuddering and glancing down at herself to make sure nothing was showing that ought not to be showing.

"I will have a conference on that other matter with Nat and the others during our early-morning ride," he said. "Perhaps we can come up with something."

"There is to be no perhaps about it," she said, taking his offered arm in order to return to the ballroom with him—other guests were beginning to appear outdoors again and the members of the orchestra were tuning their instruments. "You must come up with something. Sophie is your friend and mine. Do it."

"Yes, ma'am," he said.

# SEVENTEEN

Sophia had had hot water hauled laboriously up to her dressing room, and she had soaked for all of half an hour in the deep tub after washing herself with the soap he had thought was perfume. She had washed her hair with it too and had then let it almost dry before brushing and brushing it until it crackled and shone. She had picked out her prettiest nightgown. With the dressing gown she had no choice. She had only the one.

She prepared for him as if she were a bride awaiting her bridegroom, she thought rather ruefully. But she was not deterred by the thought. There had been an hour, of course, after his departure when she wondered what madness had her in its grip and had almost dashed off a note to tell him not to come, never to come again.

But she had come to a decision, sitting there with Lass on her lap again. Or rather, before the decision, she had had a vision of herself. She had seen herself as she had become. In a sense she had been a victim ever since her marriage, but at least then she had made the best of circumstances. She had made something of her life. She could not say she had enjoyed those years in the Peninsula, in France, and in Belgium. But she had endured and even prevailed over dreadful conditions. She had had friends.

She had been liked and respected. She had respected herself.

And then she had had a taste of real freedom after Walter's death and the unexpected gifts and pension from the government. She had made a new life, a new circle of friends. She had been happy in a contented, placid sort of way. She had felt in control of her own life and destiny. She had begun to like herself.

Yet now what had she become? She had become a poor cringing thing, afraid to go outside her own house, afraid even to look from the windows lest she see him or his spies watching. She was afraid to attend any social function, especially a *ton* entertainment. She was afraid even to walk in the park lest she meet someone she ought not to meet— and someone else see her do it. She was afraid of every knock on the door below.

She had given up almost all communication with Walter's family, though they were puzzled by it and perhaps even hurt—Sarah was hurt. Sophia had refused to attend a garden party with them just the day before. And she had brought to a bitter end four of the friendships she had valued most in the course of her life—as well as the friendships she had begun with the wives of two of them.

She had cut short the spring love affair she had promised herself she would indulge in without any qualm of conscience.

In order to become an abject creature who jumped to the command of a villain and a bully. In order to be constantly afraid, afraid, afraid . . .

And why?

Because Walter had betrayed her yet she would not betray him. That was why.

And so her life had been ruined, and soon Edwin's life and that of the rest of his family would be ruined too, and perhaps Thomas's as well. And beyond the ruin—what? Scandal and disgrace? Very probably.

It was not only her life that had been ruined, she had realized, turning her head and laughing despite herself when Lass decided to lift her head and lick Sophia's cheek. It was her very self. Through to the very core of herself she felt worthless.

She would not allow it any longer. She simply would not. She had wondered from the start how far she would allow herself to be pushed. She had wondered if there was a limit beyond which she would not go and had feared that perhaps there was not. But there was. The limit had been reached. She would go no farther into degradation.

And so she had sat on, well after the time she would normally have rung for tea. She had planned what she would do, what she must do—three things. She would discover whether she could sell her house and proceed with the sale if she could. She would find the boxes in the attic that contained those belongings of Walter's that she had kept. And she would have her last, glorious night with Nathaniel. It would be glorious. She would see to that. And it would be the last.

She had had hot water hauled to her dressing room. . . .

She did not feel as nervous or as self-conscious or as awkward as she had that second time—or not nervous in the same way anyway. She was strung up with excitement, of course. She was ready soon after eleven and after that paced her bedchamber and her dressing room, peering out through the window every minute or so. She could not sit down. And for lack of anything else to do with her hands, she brushed her hair again as she paced.

Lass gave up trotting around at her heels and jumped onto a forbidden chair. She rested her head on her front paws, peered upward at Sophia as if expecting the usual command to get down, and closed her eyes. She heaved one deep sigh.

"Precisely," Sophia said. "Midnight will never come."

But *he* did. Seven minutes early. She flew down the stairs and pulled impatiently and as quietly as she was able at the bolts. Finally she had the door open.

"You are early," she said.

"Am I?" He stepped inside, removed his hat, and bent his head to kiss her. "Should I have waited outside until the stroke of midnight?"

She smiled at him, brimming over with happiness and excitement. "No," she said. "I was earlier. I have been waiting."

"Have you, Sophie?" He took the candle from her hand and lifted it higher. "You look very happy. Happy to see me?"

"Yes." She beamed at him before turning to lead the way upstairs. "Very."

She was not going to play any games of pretended indifference tonight. This night was for her and she was going to grasp all it had to offer. For once in her life she was going to be utterly selfish.

He set the candle down on the dressing table when they reached her room, glanced at Lass, who thumped her tail on the cushion and opened her eyes briefly, and turned to Sophia. Perhaps he expected a repetition of that other night when neither of them had known quite how to proceed. But tonight she was not going to allow any awkwardness. She had followed him to the dressing table. She reached up her hands and unbuttoned his coat. She pushed it off his shoulders and down his arms while he stood still, watching her.

"You are not wearing evening clothes," she said. "These are your riding clothes."

"Yes," he said.

She started on the buttons of his waistcoat. "There was a ball tonight," she said, "at Lady Honeymere's. Did you not go to it?"

"I went," he said.

His waistcoat was on the floor behind him, on top of his coat. She pulled his shirt free of his pantaloons and then began unwrapping his neckcloth.

"But you did not stay?" She had to reach behind his neck to complete the unwrapping.

"I had something better to do," he said.

And so he had gone home and changed into his morning

clothes. Did he intend staying all night, then? She hoped so. It was already past midnight. Time was running out on her. But she would not think of that.

He raised his arms so that she could lift his shirt over his head. She dropped it on top of his waistcoat, spread her hands over his chest, and set her face against him. He smelled faintly of some musky cologne.

"Sophie." He took her by the arms and held her away from him while those wonderful bedroom eyes of his roamed all over her. "You are so very beautiful."

"Oh." She laughed, embarrassed. "It is very kind of you to say so, Nathaniel, but you need not do so. I know I am not lovely. But"—she lifted a hand to set against his lips to stop him from saying what he was about to say—"thank you for saying it anyway. Every woman should be told that at least once in her life. You have suddenly made me *feel* almost beautiful."

And she would always, *always* remember that he had said it, that he had been that attracted to her.

But his eyes were looking quite intently into hers. "I have just realized something today," he said. "At some time in your life—I do not know when, perhaps even at the very beginning of it—you convinced yourself that you were not pretty. And so you set out to hide your beauty from yourself and from everyone else. You have been quite clever at it—with the style and fit and color of the clothes you have always worn, with your manner of dealing with other people. If someone had asked me even a week or so ago about your appearance, I might have described you as pleasant looking but not particularly lovely. And then you said those words this afternoon—about my looking at myself in a glass and looking at you and at Lady Gullis. The implication was that I would find you by far the most inferior of the three. And I realized that you had trapped me—always, ever since I have known you—into seeing you as you see yourself."

Once upon a time she had thought herself tolerably pretty. Sometimes, when she was feeling particularly vain, she had even thought herself beautiful. And then she had married Walter. . . .

She bit her lip and wished his hands were not still holding her where he could gaze at her. She wanted to put her face against his chest again.

"Sophie," he said, "you should always dress in light colors like these. You should always dress your hair not to confine its glory but to display it. And you should always smile as you smiled at me downstairs after you had opened the door to me tonight. You are surely one of the most beautiful ladies of my acquaintance—perhaps even *the* most beautiful, but then I am partial."

She had always told herself that beauty did not matter. And indeed she believed it. She had told herself that it was more important to be an amiable person, to have friends who liked her. She had told herself that it was better to be good old Sophie than to be a ravishing beauty.

But oh, it felt wonderful beyond belief to be told that to Nathaniel she was perhaps the most beautiful lady he had ever known.

She smiled at him—as she had smiled downstairs. "Thank you," she said. "Oh, I *do* thank you."

"Did Walter never tell you that?" he asked her.

She sobered instantly. Walter had never been able to bear to *touch* her.

His hands released her then, and his arms came about her, drawing her to him like iron bands. "I am sorry," he said, his mouth against the top of her head. "I am so sorry. Your marriage is none of my business. Please forgive me."

But she was not going to have her glorious night spoiled. She lifted her face to him and smiled again. "I do not want to think about Walter," she said. "I want to think about you, though I am not sure I wish to do a great deal of *thinking*."

"Sophie." He rubbed his nose against hers. "Ah, Sophie, I have missed you."

She put her arms up about his neck as he kissed her and abandoned herself to her night of love. Although she would not say so in words, she was not even going to pretend that for her it was not going to be just that. A night of love.

"Sophie," he said after a couple of minutes, "you are as hungry as I. Let's remove the rest of our clothes and lie down, shall we? Let's make love."

"Yes," she said, smiling at him as she undid the ribbon bow that held her dressing gown closed at the neck. She thought she might well burst with happiness. "Let's make love."

It was getting light outside. That happened early at this time of year, of course, but even so he must be going soon, Nathaniel thought regretfully. It would be very pleasant just to go back to sleep with her head pressed against his arm as it was now and one of her arms thrown across his chest. And to wake up with her later, perhaps make love to her yet again before they got up and had breakfast together and planned their day together.

He opened his eyes and stared upward. This was the part of a night spent with a woman when he usually felt cozy and regretful at having to leave the comfort of the bed— but he usually felt eager too to be gone, to draw fresh air into his lungs, to stride off homeward, to feel free again, his own person again. He did not usually think of breakfast with and the rest of the day with his bed partner.

But *usually* of course no longer applied to him. Nights like this past one were no longer usual with him.

And a night *just* like this last one was unique to his experience.

They had slept very little. They had made love over and over again—with fierce passion, with moaning tenderness, with quiet, shared pleasure. They had made love without clothes, without covers, without masks. They had given and taken and shared. They had exhausted each other and re- stored each other. They had been as one.

And he was not sure he was going to be able to let her go at the end of the Season. He caught himself in the thought but he did not push it instantly away. He held it and considered it. No, he was not at all sure.

He bent his head and kissed her mouth. She opened her eyes and smiled sleepily at him.

"Did I fall asleep?" she asked. "I wonder why I came to do that."

"I must be going," he said.

But she rolled closer and tightened her arm about his chest. "Not yet," she said. "Oh, not yet. It must be very early."

"I must have made you very sore," he said. "I have been insatiable, I am afraid."

"Not too sore," she said. "I feel wonderful—there. There, where you have been. Sore and sensitive and aching for more. Come there again."

She spoke—she had spoken all night—quite unlike the Sophie he knew. She had told him quite graphically what pleased her, what might please her more. She had asked in the same way what she might do to please him better and had done everything he had suggested, apparently quite unshocked by the more shocking intimacies he had been unable to resist asking of her.

He had been quite right in what he had said to her last night. She had been in hiding for as long as he had known her. Their small and seemingly rather plain Sophie, their cheerful, placid good comrade Sophie, was in fact a beautiful, slender, passionate, vibrant woman.

It was a startling discovery.

"If you absolutely insist." He turned onto her and slid deeply into her warm wetness while she wrapped herself about him and held tight. "I'll come to you again tomorrow night—or do I mean tonight?—if I may, Sophie, but I cannot promise that all my body parts will function efficiently. You may have worn them out for a while." He grinned down at her before lowering much of his weight onto her and going to work in her.

But she was not in the mood for a gentle loving with humor. She tightened inner muscles, increasing his own desire, and moaned to his every stroke. She climaxed very quickly and then lay still and relaxed while he completed his own act.

He wondered if *she* would be able to let *him* go at the end of the Season. Was he merely receiving the benefit of the long-pent-up sexual appetites of a passionate woman? Or was she making love to *him*?

One thing had become disturbingly clear to him. She had had anything but a good marriage with Walter Armitage. They had always seemed content with each other, but then perhaps that was the key word—*content*. Sophie was made for far more than mere contentment. And he had always admitted that there was no way of knowing what went on in a couple's relationship in the privacy of their own home.

It had not been a good marriage.

"Mmm," he said, realizing that he had allowed himself to relax the whole of his weight on her. "One squashed Sophie. You should have pushed me off."

But when he went to lift himself away from her, she tightened her arms about him again.

"Not yet," she said. "Not just yet. I like your weight."

He sighed and relaxed for a few minutes longer. But she did not relax, he noticed. Her arms held him to her as if she would never let him go.

Perhaps she would not let him go at the end of the spring either. And perhaps he would not mind. Perhaps it would be mutual, as everything that had happened this night had been.

"There," she said, letting her arms fall to her sides at last, "you must be eager to be gone. And it is time. Go then."

He kissed her and smiled before drawing free of her and lifting himself off her and off the bed. "Not eager," he said. "But it *is* time. I do not fancy bidding Samuel a good morning as I leave."

She had tears in her eyes as she let him out of the front door ten minutes later. But she was also smiling that radiant smile he had never seen on her face until last night.

"Thank you," she said. "Oh, thank you, Nathaniel. You

were always my favorite, you know. Always.''

He pondered those words as he walked along the street after kissing her one more time. Her favorite? Among whom? Ken and Rex and Eden—and Walter? All men? He had been her favorite. In what way? Sexually?

Yet she had only ever been a dear friend to him. How could she so effectively have hidden for so long? How could he not have seen in her from the start the woman who could mean more to him than any other woman, than any other person, who would feel as close to him as the beating of his own heart?

Was this, he wondered uneasily, what being in love felt like? Was he in love with Sophie? And did he also *love* her?

Could he live without her? That was surely the test. Could he live without the air he breathed? Could he live without the beating of his heart?

Could he live without Sophie?

''Nat had better keep his eyes hidden beneath the brim of his hat,'' Kenneth said. ''They are bloodshot.''

''The question is, Ken,'' Rex added, ''whether the ladies would consider they looked more than usually as if they belonged in a boudoir.''

''The lady who caused them to be that way probably does,'' Kenneth said, and the two of them chuckled as if they had been the authors of marvelous wit.

''One can merely hope,'' Eden said, reining in his horse so that he would not lose a tittle or morsel of the conversation, ''that Lady Gullis does not sport a similar beauty feature this morning. It would not suit her as well as it does our Nat.''

''One must similarly hope,'' Rex said, ''that no one but us made too much of the fact that the lady was absent from last night's ball while Nat left indecently early.''

''But everyone would doubtless be as charmed as we are,'' Kenneth said. ''Not that Moira is charmed, it is true. She believes you can do altogether better for yourself, Nat.

I was forced to remind her that you are not exactly setting up a *wife*. In her opinion, you ought to be ashamed of yourself.'' He grinned.

''I wonder,'' Nathaniel said at last, gazing about him at the trees and feeling nostalgic for the countryside, ''if everyone in town suffers from the same mathematical malady. Does everyone add two and two together and come up with five?''

His three friends simultaneously roared with laughter.

''Protecting the lady's reputation, are you, Nat?'' Eden asked. ''We are all agreed that you have impeccable taste, old chap.'' He cleared his throat. ''But I beg leave to remind all here present that it was I who selected the lady for you.''

''Doubtless,'' Nathaniel said, ''you will receive your reward in heaven, Ede.''

''I have an idea for how we may help Sophie,'' Eden said, changing the subject abruptly as he often did. ''At least, the idea was not mine exactly. It was your cousin's, Nat. She cornered me last evening and deprived me of my supper. But she had a deuced good idea.''

''I have the best idea,'' Nathaniel said grimly. ''I am going to pick a quarrel with the bastard and force him to challenge me. I can remember just how we all did it for Rex when there was Copley to deal with. I am going to kill him and it is going to be the one killing in my life that I will enjoy.''

Rex spoke up sharply. ''Don't talk yourself into thinking that, Nat,'' he said. ''I remember feeling the same way, and I still do not really regret shooting Copley instead of wasting my bullet on the air as I might have done if *he* had not shot before the signal. But I still see him in my sleep and probably always will. I still feel that I have him on my conscience even if my reason tells me that I did what was right. Pinter is guilty of blackmail, which is evil enough, I grant you. But not quite as evil as what Copley was guilty of. Besides, I did it for the sake of my wife. Sophie is only our friend.''

Nathaniel's lips tightened. "Nevertheless," he said, "I am going to kill him." He turned to Eden. "What did Lavinia have to say? I wish I had not allowed her to become involved in this. She helped me find the pearls and the ring, you know. It is hard to say no to Lavinia, and it was Sophie herself who made me see that perhaps I ought not simply because she is a woman."

"She thinks we should blackmail Pinter," Eden said.

Kenneth and Rex both laughed.

"With the threat that Nat will hang him and draw and quarter him if he does not leave Sophie alone?" Kenneth said. "It might work too, by Jove. Did you ever see an officer direct his men from *behind* them as often as Pinter did? He is undoubtedly a cowardly bastard. And even some stouthearted men would quail at the thought of having Nat let loose on them when his temper is up."

"But what the devil can she have *done*?" Rex asked of no one in particular. "One cannot imagine Sophie doing anything that might even remotely make her prey to a blackmailer."

Nathaniel had been thinking about it. The answer had been staring them all in the face, but then the answer seemed almost as unlikely as their first assumption.

"Perhaps it is nothing *she* has done," he said. "Perhaps it was Walter."

"*Walter?*" Eden sounded incredulous. "There was no one more solid, more respectable, more thoroughly dull than Armitage. He would not have recognized temptation if it had met nose to nose with him."

"Is it more unlikely than that it was something to do with Sophie?" Nathaniel asked.

"The whole thing is a mystery to me." Eden shrugged and turned his horse to begin the ride back to the park entrance. They all followed his lead. "But blackmailing Pinter, having him sweating and shaking in his boots appeals to my sense of justice. Not just the threat of Nat, though. Miss Bergland had me blushing from the tips of my toenails up when she blurted out her conviction that

Pinter got sexual thrills out of watching whippings."

"The devil she did!" Nathaniel was appalled. "And she actually said it to you, Ede? *Aloud?*" He grimaced.

"But she was right," Eden said. "We all knew it. I can remember Ken's saying it more than once. The thing is, can we gather enough of such muck to make him dread having us make our opinions public?"

"Do we need any more?" Nathaniel asked. "I could make a very colorful story indeed out of just that. With a little embellishment and a whole parcel of innuendo we might create a nice balance to whatever it was Sophie—or Walter—did."

"There might be more," Kenneth said with obvious reluctance, turning all attention his way. "A new recruit complained to me once that Pinter had made advances to him. Sexual advances, of course."

Silence succeeded his words.

"I had a talk with Pinter," Kenneth said, "and assured him that the boy had doubtless misunderstood and should probably be whipped for so criminally misunderstanding an officer—but it might be less humiliating to let it pass that one time and give the boy a chance to redeem himself. It seemed the only way to save the poor blighter from punishment on one of the usual trumped-up charges."

"And you never reported him?" Rex asked.

"Pinter?" Kenneth said. "No. I knew a few boys at school with the same preference, as you all probably did, and in the army too. The law notwithstanding, I never felt the need to hate them or root them out or bother them provided they did not make themselves obnoxious to me or anyone under my command. They were created that way, I have always thought, and no one can help the way he was created. The fact that Pinter was a thoroughly unlikable character did not seem excuse enough to report him."

"We have him, then," Nathaniel said grimly. "Dead to rights. It is a capital offense, by Jove."

"I rather think we do," Eden agreed.

"And so we save Sophie whether she likes it or not,"

Rex said. "She need not know it was us, need she? She can think for the rest of her life that the bastard developed a conscience. I wonder if she will ever talk to any of us again?"

"He threatened her to make her stay away from us, you may be sure," Eden said. "Especially in light of what you have just told us, Ken. He knows that you know *that* about him, or at least have reason to suspect, and that the four of us are close friends—and deuced fond of Sophie. Once we have explained his options to him and he has kept his distance from her for a while, I think she will realize that she can speak with us again. Good old Sophie. We will have to wait a while not to make it too obvious that we have interfered, as she puts it. But we should be able to start inviting her about again before the Season is over."

"We had better go about this in a way that will impress itself properly upon Pinter," Kenneth said. "Shall we agree upon tomorrow morning? Today I will write a few things down and we can all sign. I'll make several copies and we can all have one. We will have to make it obvious that he has a lot of us to get rid of if he is to be free to continue tormenting people like Sophie."

"I'll find some other way of convincing him of that," Nathaniel said. "I may not be allowed the pleasure of killing him, but by God, I'll be rearranging his features for him before I have finished with him."

"Perhaps you had better let me do it, Nat," Eden said with a chuckle. "Lady Gullis may not like you with a battered face."

"Perhaps we should draw for it," Kenneth said. "You two cannot horde all the pleasure to yourselves."

"If you all want a go at him too," Nathaniel said, "you are going to have to stand in line and await your turn, I am afraid. This one is going to be for Sophie, and I am going to be the one doing it. Just as Rex did for Catherine."

He spurred his horse into a gallop and left his friends temporarily behind him, looking after him in some surprise.

# EIGHTEEN

DESPITE A NIGHT OF VERY little sleep, Sophia spent a busy morning and felt invigorated and even exhilarated.

She did not go back to bed after Nathaniel had left, but dressed warmly against the early-morning chill and took Lass for a long and brisk walk in the park. She even played with the dog for a while, throwing a stick for her to fetch, then taking it from her when she brought it back and running with it, while the collie tore along after her, barking excitedly. And then she teased the dog with the stick, holding it out invitingly, lifting it just beyond reach as Lass came for it, waving it from side to side when the dog jumped, and laughing gaily the whole while. Then she hurled the stick once more, beginning the game all over again.

She had a hearty breakfast after returning home—far more hearty than usual—and engaged Samuel in conversation until he put an end to it by entertaining her with a monologue on his silent sufferings with an ingrown toenail on his left foot. Mrs. Armitage did not know what torments his cheerful outward demeanor hid day after day, he informed her. Sophia suggested various remedies and, looking down critically at his shoes, suggested that he might wish to try wearing ones that were wider at the toe. Having tramped over half a continent with an army, she told him kindly, she had seen her fair share of corns and blisters and ingrown toenails and . . . Well, yes, thank you, she believed she would have another cup of coffee.

She went out again after spending some time at her escritoire writing a few letters. She went first to see a lawyer, a man with whom she had done business before. She put the matter of the sale of her house into his hands, discussed another matter, and left, perfectly confident that he would handle everything for her. She was not going to worry or even think about what she had done.

Though she did think anyway, of course. How could she not? She had somehow assumed that she would live out the rest of her life in the house on Sloan Terrace. She had been happy at the prospect, happy with her life, with her limited prospects. She was only eight and twenty years old even now, but she had settled quite contentedly into a comfortable middle age.

It seemed unbelievable now that she had been willing to settle for quiet contentment. She was still *young*. She still had a great deal of living to do—and she was free to do it. Oh, yes she was. And besides all that, she was beautiful. She *felt* beautiful this morning, and more than that, she knew that she *was* beautiful. He had said so.

She did not go home immediately after visiting the lawyer. She went shopping. She had very little money in her purse and might well not have any more there for some time. She looked at the bracelets and necklaces and earrings in a jeweler's window and passed on by. She admired bonnets and fans and reticules and parasols but was content to look. But she could not resist the ready-made dress in a mantua maker's window—made for a customer who had changed her mind about purchasing it, Sophia guessed, and therefore on sale. It looked too small for her. It was of simple design in a light calico cotton fabric. It was the palest blue.

She went inside.

When she tried it on, she discovered that the dress was indeed smaller than her other clothes—she had got into the habit while following the drum of having clothes made to fit loosely so that they would also be comfortable. The dress draped itself attractively over her bosom and about her hips, revealing a figure that was feminine and nicely proportioned even if it was not voluptuous. It made her look dainty and pretty. When the modiste's assistant told her so, Sophia smiled and believed her.

She bought the dress, the blood hammering at her temples as she did so. It was not an expensive dress, but it was far beyond her means. And yet, as she left the shop, the parcel beneath her arm, it was not fear or guilt she felt but sheer delight. She had something pretty to wear. Her mood threatened to falter when she remembered that *he* would never see her wearing it, but she smiled and lengthened her stride. The sun was shining again this morning. She lifted her face to it.

She depended upon no one for a sense of her own worth. She had done that for long enough. She was going to go to Gloucestershire, where she had grown up, where her brother and his family still lived, and she was going to begin a wholly new life there. Perhaps in time she would even marry again. Someone would surely ask her—she was *beautiful*. Perhaps she would still even be young enough to have a child or two. She had trained herself years ago to stop thinking about children of her own.

When she returned home, she handed her parcel to Pamela with instructions to iron the creases from the dress, and she took one of the boxes of Walter's things she had found in the attic the day before into the sitting room, where she sat for a long time polishing with meticulous care the pistol that was inside. She had done it before. Not often, it was true. Walter, like most soldiers, had preferred to clean his own guns, and she had always been somewhat squeamish about handling them especially when she remembered that each of them had been used to kill and would be so used again. But occasionally she had done it. She knew exactly *how* to do it.

While she polished, she composed in her head the letters she would write when she was finished. The letter to Thomas, explaining that she was selling her house and moving back to Gloucestershire, asking him to expect her within the next week or so. The letter to Boris Pinter, informing him that she would call upon him tomorrow morning if he would be so good as to remain at home. She would have to strike just the right balance in that letter between courtesy and obsequiousness, she thought. And the letter to Nathaniel. But she found she could not even begin to compose that in her head.

It was not any easier to write it when she sat at the escritoire later, pen in hand, the other two letters already written. She brushed the quill back and forth across her chin as she thought. Crumpled-up pieces of paper, which she could ill afford to waste, dotted the floor about her. Finally she could only be brief and abrupt.

"Dear Nathaniel," she wrote, "I must thank you again for every kindness you have shown me." *Kindness* seemed somehow an inappropriate word, especially to describe the night before, but she could not think of a more suitable one. "You mentioned coming tonight. I beg you not to. I beg you not to come here again. I bear you no ill will. I will remember you fondly. But please do not come here again. Your friend, Sophia."

A brief letter, she thought, reading it over, very tempted to crumple it up and send it to join the others on the floor. Brief and yet repetitive. But it would have to do. There was really nothing else to say, and that one point needed to be repeated lest he believe she did not really mean it.

She did mean it. She knew that this morning she was being borne along on a strange sort of euphoria, that in some ways she was in a state of denial. She knew that when she returned to herself she was going to suffer dreadfully. But she knew too that she had been changed permanently for the better in the course of the past day and night. She had gained confidence in herself both as a person and as a woman—and of course he had been largely responsible for the latter.

She loved him desperately. And the memories of last night—not just the passion and the tenderness, but also the sheer *joy*—would haunt her for a long time to come, perhaps forever. But she knew that she did not *need* him except with her deepest emotions. She could live her life without him. She could live a new, exciting life without him. Certainly remaining for the rest of the Season merely to prolong an affair that would inevitably end at *its* end— she was the one who had suggested it—would do her no good at all. Only harm.

She sealed the letter and rang for Samuel to take all three and send them on their way, before she could change her mind. She had tea brought up.

And she sat in her favorite chair beside the fireplace, Lass heavy and contented across her feet, her cup of tea growing cold at her side, holding in her hands something else she had found in the box with Walter's pistol. Something she had put there determinedly after his death, though it had not been his. Something she had *almost* forgotten about, though she had looked eagerly for it as soon as she had opened that particular box.

She spread the folded linen handkerchief across her palm and with the forefinger of the other hand traced the smooth embroidery of the initial *G* across one corner. She lifted the handkerchief to her face. It smelled musty, though she had laundered it and kept it in lavender after he had handed it to her on that day he had taken her up before him on his horse, covered from head to toe with mud.

She had always told herself that she would return it to him, that she simply never thought of it when he was present, only when he was absent. But the truth was she had almost held her breath whenever she saw him for weeks afterward, fearing that he would ask for it.

She had used to take it out from between its lavender bags inside her small trunk occasionally—no, more often than occasionally—and hold it to her nose and her lips as she was doing now. And all the while she had convinced herself that she was only a little in love with him as she was with the other three, as every other wife and camp follower with the regiment were.

*Oh, Sophie,* she thought, *you have told yourself so many lies over the years. You have never been free.*

But now at last she was going to be free. She thought of the pistol wrapped in a clean cloth in the box and felt a fluttering of unsteadiness in her stomach. And she thought of the note on its way to Nathaniel.

She was going to be free. She closed her eyes and rubbed her cheek back and forth across the soft musty linen of the handkerchief with *G* for Gascoigne embroidered across one corner.

Nathaniel spent a busy day, even though he was anxious at every moment for it to pass. He returned invigorated from his ride in the park despite an almost sleepless night. Sleeplessness in a good cause, he thought with a grin as he took the stairs two at a time up to his dressing room to change for breakfast, did not make one tired as sleeplessness for any other reason invariably did.

He looked at his eyes in the looking glass. His friends had exaggerated. Indeed, they had seen only what they had wished to see. His eyes were not bloodshot at all.

He had promised to take Lavinia to the library during the morning.

He noticed as they walked how pleasant a day it was. He could hardly wait for tonight. Not that he anticipated a repetition of last night. They would simply not be able to find sufficient energy. But just to lie with her, to hold her close, to talk with her, to kiss her, and—best of all—to sleep with her and to wake to her. Yes, he could scarcely wait.

"You are looking very pleased with yourself this morning, Nat," Lavinia said, bringing him back to the present with a start. He fervently hoped that she was not good at reading minds.

"It is a lovely day," he said. "Did you enjoy last night's ball?"

She blushed. *Lavinia* blushing? His interest—and his hope—was piqued for a moment until he remembered what had happened at last evening's ball.

"Very well, thank you," she said.

"Eden told me you had him blushing from the tips of his toenails up," he said.

"Oh?" Her own blush spread to her neck. Nathaniel was glad to see that she had a conscience.

"You ought not to have cornered him like that, you know," he said. "He is, after all, almost a stranger to you."

Her eyes blazed. "I might have known," she said, "that he would be unable to keep his mouth shut about it. Conceited idiot!"

"Oh," he said, "he did not take credit for it, Lavinia. He was quite ready to admit that it was all your idea."

"Did he?" She bristled and then she stopped walking abruptly and stared at him with suddenly sagging jaw. "Nat—what are you *talking* about?"

"About your suggestion that we give Pinter a dose of his own medicine, of course," he said, frowning. "What did you think I was talking about?"

"Nothing," she said, making it sound like everything. "We were not talking at cross-purposes after all. Yes, that is what we talked about. And it is as clear as the nose on your face, Nat, that it will be easy. Mr. Pinter probably cannot do it with women, and so . . ."

"Stop right there," Nathaniel said hastily, holding up one hand and looking about him to make sure no other pedestrian was within hearing distance. "I just wish you had come to me instead of embarrassing poor Eden."

"You would have told me to run along and learn to be a proper lady," she said.

"No, I would not." He touched her hand on his arm. "I have learned a thing or two in the past few weeks, Lavinia.

I am still hoping that during the rest of the Season you will meet a man you can like and respect enough to marry. But if you do not, we will go back to Bowood for the summer and discuss together what *will* be best for you—what you wish to do, and what will allow me still somehow to carry out the responsibilities of my guardianship. We will have to try to come to some sort of mutually agreeable decision. A cottage in the village or on the estate, perhaps, somewhere close so that I can feel reassured, but far enough away that you can feel independent. I might in time even be prevailed upon not to call on you more than two or three times in a day.'' He smiled at her.

She cocked her head to one side and regarded him closely before startling him by throwing her arms about his neck and kissing one cheek with a resounding smack.

"Nat!" she exclaimed. "Oh, Nat, I always *knew* you could be likable if you only gave yourself a chance."

"Oh, I say!" he said, thoroughly embarrassed. An elderly gentleman on the pavement opposite was winking broadly at him. "I believe we should walk on, Lavinia."

They did so in a companionable silence. She was doubtless dreaming of living a life of independence, he thought. And he was dreaming of a blissful life at home without women. Though he did wonder what Bowood would be like with Sophie in it. In the house—he pictured her in each of the main rooms in turn, and in his bedchamber, in his bed. In the nursery, bending over a cradle. In the park, walking with him, her collie and his dogs running on ahead, a little toddler stopping every few feet to pick the heads off the daisies.

Alarming things were happening to him, he decided, catching the direction of his daydreams. Perhaps most alarming of all, though, was the fact that he was not alarmed.

The day continued busy, with a picnic to attend during the afternoon. There were letters on the desk in his study, his butler told him when he arrived home with Lavinia, but it was not a day for business. The reports from Bowood and anything else could wait. Georgina would have sifted out the invitations that arrived in considerable number every day and taken them upstairs.

The afternoon was perfect for a picnic, and the rural setting of Richmond Park could not have been better chosen. Perhaps it was a setting particularly conducive to romance, or perhaps what happened during the afternoon was inevitable anyway. Georgina strolled along one of the grassy, oak-lined avenues with Lewis Armitage for an hour before tea, and for half an hour after tea.

They were being a little indiscreet, Nathaniel thought, and wondered if he should do something to part them. But he did nothing. They were not so unwise as to step out of sight even for a moment and they looked comfortable together—and perhaps a little more than comfortable.

It was an impression that was borne out by Georgina's reaction when they arrived home later to being asked how she had enjoyed the picnic. They were alone, she and Nathaniel, Lavinia having gone straight upstairs to change her clothes. Georgina flung her arms about his neck—the second young lady to do so in one day. No, the third—there had been Sophie early in the morning.

"Oh, Nathaniel," Georgina said, tears of what was obviously sheer joy shining in her eyes, "I am *so* happy."

"Are you, Georgie?" he asked, hugging her. He felt a little uneasy. He would hate to see her hurt. "Lewis Armitage is the cause, I gather. Has he said anything?"

She colored up prettily. "How can he have," she said, "when he has not spoken to you yet?"

"Quite so," he agreed, and found himself exchanging a grin with his sister. She and Armitage had an understanding, then?

"Lord Perry has asked to call upon Lord Houghton tomorrow morning," she said. "I daresay he is going to ask for Sarah's hand. Lewis—Mr. Armitage, that is—says that his mother and father should be given a day or two to recover from that."

"I see," he said.

"But I am so *happy,*" she said.

"Then I am happy too," he told her, kissing her forehead. "I will expect a call within the next week or so."

She smiled brightly and turned to run up the stairs.

How many hours until midnight? Gazing after her, he drew his watch from his pocket. Five o'clock—seven hours. An eternity. Seven hours less seven minutes. He had been that early last night and she had not minded. She would not mind tonight.

It was still an eternity.

This was the evening when he was to have dined with Lady Gullis and then attended the theater with her small party, Nathaniel remembered. Fortunately she had written to him the day before to beg to be excused as she had been invited to a house party in the country for a few days. Perhaps some other time?

Nathaniel guessed that his reluctance to enter into an affair with her had become an annoyance to her and she was putting an end to the acquaintance in an amiable manner.

He could have gone to a concert that Georgina and Lavinia were to attend with Margaret and John, but he was glad of a free evening for a change. He was going to sit with his feet up in the library, he decided, with a book. He might even close his eyes and have a sleep. Even if the night ahead was not going to be quite as sleepless or as energetic as last night, there would still be *some* expenditure of energy, he did not doubt, and some wakeful hours.

He remembered after seeing his family members on their way after dinner, of course, and after settling to his quiet evening that there were letters on the desk in his study. He would read them in the morning, he decided. But in the morning he was going to call upon Pinter with his friends— Eden had found out the man's address and Kenneth had already delivered Nathaniel's copy of the statement against Pinter. Ken should be a full-time politician, Nathaniel had decided after reading it. He certainly knew how to make dirt appear filthy indeed.

He would read his letters in the afternoon, then, he decided, finding his page in his book. But tomorrow afternoon he had promised to take Lavinia and Georgina to the Tower of London, weather permitting. Lavinia wanted to the see the armory while Georgie wanted to see the crown jewels. Besides, tomorrow would bring its own pile of letters.

He sighed and got to his feet. If he was fortunate, he thought as he made his way to the study, there would be nothing from Bowood today, or at least nothing that needed much time and attention. He yawned noisily. He might not have felt tired earlier in the day, but he was deuced sleepy now.

There was nothing from Bowood. He took the few letters there were back to the library with him and settled thankfully into his chair.

There were a couple of bills Georgina and Lavinia had incurred during the past week—both modest. There was a letter from Edwina at the Bowood rectory, doubtless written in her small cramped hand and crossed so that the words would be next to impossible to read. And when he made the effort to read them anyway, he would find the letter as dull as one of her husband's sermons. He felt guilty. At least she had made the effort to write. He forced himself to spend fifteen whole minutes proving that he had been right in the first place.

There was another letter. He opened it and read it. And dropped it to his lap while he set his head back and closed his eyes.

Was this too, he wondered, because she feared Pinter?

She had not feared him last night. And Pinter could not know about last night unless he kept a constant surveillance on her house—an absurd idea even for him, surely.

Why then? If not because of fear, why?

Because she did not want him?

She had wanted him last night.

*I must thank you again for every kindness you have shown me.*

She might as well have slapped his face. Was that what

last night had been all about? Had she been thanking him
for returning her ring and her pearls?

*I will remember you fondly.*

Oh, Sophie. The letter sounded so very like her—calm,
practical, cheerful. Somehow the image he had of her in
his mind now was of the old Sophie, plain, rather dowdy,
slightly disheveled—Walter's wife.

He could not associate this letter with last night's vibrant,
passionate lover.

Had she merely wanted a night to remember? Had she
known even this morning before he left that she would
write this letter? Had she used him—as he had used countless women years ago?

There would be some justice in such a thing, he was
forced to admit.

But not Sophie. Not *Sophie*.

They had decided, he and his friends, that they would
not let her know of their visit to Pinter tomorrow. She
would discover she was free, but she would not know that
they—that *he*—had had any hand in it. There would be no
excuse to call on her.

He would never see her again, then, unless he ran into
her by accident.

He would see to it that that did not happen, he thought.
If Georgina became officially betrothed within the next
while, she would perhaps wish to return to the country to
prepare for her wedding there. Perhaps they could all return
to Bowood. He did not believe Lavinia would object to
being deprived of the rest of the Season.

Or if Georgina preferred, then perhaps she could stay in
town with Margaret and he and Lavinia could return to
Bowood and begin the process of setting her up on her own
somewhere reasonably close. She would surely be eager
now that he had mentioned the possibility to her.

He was desperate to leave town. To be back in the tranquil security of Bowood.

*Sophie,* he thought, realizing suddenly that he did not
need to rest now as there was nothing and no one to rest

himself for. *Ah, Sophie. It was such a pleasant dream, my love. I thought perhaps you were dreaming it too. How foolish of me!*

But he stayed where he was, his eyes still closed. There was nothing else to do.

# NINETEEN

BORIS PINTER HAD HIS lodgings on the second floor of a house on Bury Street, behind St. James's Street. Sophia arrived in the middle of the morning, alone and on foot. Those facts did not endear her either to the servant who answered her knock or to the woman who came out of a downstairs room to examine her appearance—presumably the landlady. But Sophia had dressed with care and wore the voluminous cloak she had always worn in the Peninsula—it had a somewhat military look, she thought. And she introduced herself with cool confidence as Mrs. Sophia Armitage, wife of Major Walter Armitage, come to call upon Lieutenant Boris Pinter.

Somehow, Sophia thought with what might have been amusement under other circumstances, she awed both of them into submission. The landlady even preceded her up the two flights of stairs to the second floor, just as if she were a servant herself. She knocked on the door that presumably opened into Mr. Pinter's rooms and waited until his man answered her knock.

Mrs. Armitage, the valet informed the landlady, was expected. He opened the door wider, and Sophia stepped inside. Her heart, which had been thumping for some time, threatened now to rob her of all breath. She declined to allow the valet to take her cloak. She would not be staying long, she told him. He showed her into a salon, a large square room with heavy furnishings and dark draperies. She was left alone there for a while.

She was standing a little to one side of the door when it opened again. She had been tempted to cross the room to take up her stand before the window or the fireplace. She could not bear the thought of being anywhere close to him. But she did not want him between her and the door either.

"Ah, Sophie, my dear," he said, closing the door behind him, "what a pleasant surprise it was to know that you were coming here—and sooner than you might have. But you have come alone without even a maid?"

He looked rather handsome, she thought dispassionately, dressed in well-tailored clothes, his dark hair freshly brushed, his face smiling. A new acquaintance might consider him a charming young man.

"You have no answer," he remarked. "Will you have a seat?" He gestured toward a sofa.

"No, thank you," she said. "Where is the letter?"

"Here," he said, patting the right side of his chest. "But you do not want to read it, do you, Sophie? Have you not put yourself through enough of such torture? You may see it, of course, if you do not trust me and wish to verify its authenticity. One hates to be vulgar, but do you have the money?"

He had crossed the room as he spoke and sat down in a low chair close to the window, though she had not sat herself. A deliberate discourtesy, of course.

"No," she said.

He raised his eyebrows, crossed one leg over the other, and swung his booted foot. "Oh?" he said softly. "No money, Sophie? But you have come for the letter? And what, pray, do you have to offer in exchange for it? Your less-than-delectable person? I am afraid that would be worth less to me than one corner torn from one letter." He smiled his most charming, white-toothed smile at her.

She understood something then, something that explained everything, something that she should have realized far sooner—the reason Walter had blocked his promotion, the reason for his intense hatred of Walter and all who had been close to him, the reason for his determination to use these letters in any way he could for their destruction.

Most villains, she supposed, were not just blackhearted incarnations of evil. Most of them had some justification for what they did, however misguided. She understood his justification.

"I want all the remaining letters," she said. "Every one of them. For a simple price. I will take them in exchange for your life."

His foot stilled and his smile became immobile. "My dear Sophie," he said, sounding amused, "where is your gun?"

"Here." She drew Walter's gleaming pistol from one of the large pockets inside her cloak, holding it steady with both hands and pointing it at the center of his chest, both arms extended.

There was one big problem, she realized. He had only one letter inside his coat. The others would be in another room. She was going to have to go with him, the pistol trained on him the whole way, to get them. And there was that large valet in the rooms somewhere. But she had thought of all that ahead of time and had been unable to think of any way to simplify matters.

She must simply be firm. She must not lose her resolve by one single iota.

His boot had resumed its swinging. His smile had broadened. "By Jove," he said, "I can almost admire you, Sophie. You had better put it away, though, before I come over there and take it from you. I might feel constrained to send you home with a few bruises to remind you not to so waste my time in future."

"You forget, Mr. Pinter," she said, "that I am no ordinary woman. I followed the drum for seven years. I have seen battle and death. I have handled guns and used them. I am not squeamish at the thought of shedding a little blood.

If you believe I am bluffing, you may come over here and take the pistol from me. But you may get only a hole in your heart for your pains. Now. I will take that letter first— the one you have on you. Toss it across the floor.''

He still looked almost insolently at his ease. But Sophia, sighting along the barrel of the gun, her eyes intent on him, could see beads of moisture above his upper lip and on his forehead. He shrugged and chuckled and reached inside his coat. A letter came spinning across the carpet toward her.

''I will humor you for a few moments,'' he said. ''I must say I find this vastly diverting, Sophie. It is, of course, the last letter. I suppose I might be generous this once and allow you to have it. Shall we shake hands on it?'' He half rose from his chair.

''Sit down!'' she commanded him.

He sat and folded his arms. He was grinning.

''In a few moments,'' she said, ''we will go to fetch the other letters. I am well aware of the fact that you will try to keep back at least one or two of them so that you may continue your game in future. But I wish you to know something first. I have grown tired of keeping this secret to myself. I have written a letter of my own and made several copies. They are all with a lawyer I visited yesterday. He has instructions to have the letters delivered immediately on my instructions or on my death or unexplained disappearance. I will give those instructions as soon as your next attempt at blackmail is made or as soon as you publish one of these letters for all the world to see. And that, Mr. Pinter, is no bluff.''

''But the scandal would be just as scandalous, my dear,'' he said. She wondered he had not grown tired of chuckling.

''Yes,'' she agreed. ''And I believe that my brother, Viscount Houghton, Sir Nathaniel Gascoigne, Lord Pelham, Viscount Rawleigh, and the Earl of Haverford would be interested to learn the identity of the author of that scandal. I would not wish to be in your shoes on that day, Mr. Pinter. It might be kinder if I were to shoot you now.''

Her conviction that he was nothing more than a coward

and a bully had been well-founded, she could see. His posture and manner had not really changed, but he was clearly uneasy. His foot was jerking rather than swinging freely. His eyes were darting about, seeking ways to distract or disarm her. Perspiration was beginning to drip into his eyes and onto his cravat.

"You have been remarkably eager so far to keep all this to yourself, Sophie," he said. "I do not believe you have written those letters at all."

"You may well be right," she said. "Indeed, it seems very possible that you are, does it not? But you will not know for sure until you put the matter to the test, will you? Is it a bluff or is it not? Do you think you will be able to sleep easily from tonight onward?" She smiled grimly, though she did not relax her concentration on his person. "Am I bluffing, Mr. Pinter, or am I not?"

"Now, Sophie," he said, "I believe we should talk this over."

"You will get to your feet now," she said, "your hands out to the sides where I can see them. I am an angry woman, Mr. Pinter. Not passionately angry, you will understand, but coldly so. I believe I would rather enjoy being given an excuse to shoot you. Perhaps you should be careful not to tempt me. Up!"

She should have practiced, she realized then. She had not thought of it. Her outstretched arms were growing tired. The pistol seemed to weigh a ton. And this was not over yet by a long way. She dug deep inside herself for the fortitude she would need. She would find it. She always had when facing adverse circumstances during the wars.

And then the totally unforeseen happened just as he got to his feet and raised his arms to shoulder height, palms out. Someone knocked on the outer door.

He grinned at her again. "This could be a trifle inconvenient for you, Sophie," he said.

"Stay where you are." She did not take her eyes from him for a single moment. If she was fortunate, it would be a tradesman or someone else whom the valet could deal with without consulting his employer. If she was not fortunate, well . . . She had no plans.

There was the sound of voices from beyond the door. Not just two. More than two. And they were inside the outer door. Sophia drew a steadying breath. Boris Pinter's eyes had resumed their darting. His smile had grown a little more assured.

The door opened.

"It *is* Sophie," Kenneth said. "She has a gun."

"Don't do it, Sophie." Rex spoke sharply. "Whatever you do, do not shoot."

"Put it down, Sophie," Eden said. "There really is no need to use it even if he *does* deserve to die."

"Well," Boris Pinter said, lowering his hands, "the Four Horsemen of the Apocalypse to the rescue." But his pleasant tone was utter bravado. His eyes showed more fear than they had shown so far, a fact that Sophia found considerably annoying.

"Get those hands up!" she snapped, and felt a moment's satisfaction as they jerked upward again. She had made him look foolish, if nothing else.

And then Nathaniel stepped into her line of vision, so that her pistol was suddenly trained right at *his* heart.

"Give me the gun, Sophie," he said, reaching out one hand.

"Careful, Nat," Eden said. "She may not know quite what she is doing."

"He is not worth it," Nathaniel said, taking one step toward her. "He is not worth what you would have to live with in your waking life and in your dreams until your dying day. Believe me, my love. I know what I am talking about. Give me the gun." He took another step toward her and clearly meant to keep coming.

Sophia did not wait for the ignominy of having the pistol removed from her nerveless fingers. She put it back into the pocket inside her cloak.

"An unloaded gun does little damage," she said, "except perhaps to a man's nerves."

Someone was breathing with audible relief.

"She is a madwoman, I tell you," Pinter was saying. "I was returning something of Walter's to her, thinking she might wish to have it. Unfortunately it is a love letter old Walter wrote to someone else and Sophie cut up nasty. Taking it out on me, I suppose, because Walter is beyond her reach."

"Save your breath, Pinter," Kenneth said. "You are going to need it in a short while. Are you all right, Sophie?"

She was staring into Nathaniel's eyes just a few feet away. She was despising herself for the knee-weakening relief she felt. She tried not to show it. She had not even begun to wonder what had brought the four of them here.

"I could have managed alone," she said.

"There is no doubt of that," Nathaniel agreed. "But friends stick together, Sophie. And we are your friends whether you like it or not."

"So you really did it, Sophie." Boris Pinter was chuckling yet again, though it was not a merry sound. "Not even by letter. You told them."

"Was this the letter, Sophie?" Kenneth asked, bending and picking it up from the floor.

"Yes," she said.

"There are more of them?"

"Yes."

"They will all be in your possession," he said, "before many more minutes have passed."

"They would have been even if you had not come," she said, her eyes on Nathaniel. Did they *know*? And did it matter any longer? Soon now she would not have to face the torment of seeing him—any of them—any longer. She would be gone.

"Sophie," he said, and he stepped forward, set his arms about her, and drew her against him. She felt his lips brush across one of her cheeks. It was only at that moment she realized that she had begun to tremble. She had shown her relief after all. "Would one of you take her home, please?"

"No." She drew her head back, but it was a weak protest.

Why would he not take her home himself?

"Come, Sophie," Rex said after a short pause.

None of them, it seemed, wanted to leave and miss what was about to happen here. And what was that to be? she wondered. What were they doing here? Why had they come? What were they going to do to Boris Pinter? Had they stopped her from killing him—not that she could have done so with her unloaded pistol—only so that they might have the satisfaction of doing it themselves?

Did they *know*?

"Come, Sophie," Rex said again. "Catherine is at Rawleigh House with Moira and Daphne. Let me take you to them."

Nathaniel's arms had dropped from about her and Rex's arm came firmly about her shoulders.

"Come," he said again. "You have nothing more to fear. You could have done it alone—that was clear to all of us as soon as we came in. But let your friends finish it off for you."

*Finish it off.* He did not elaborate, but she did not care. Not any longer. Even if they did not already know, they soon would. She did not care about that either. All she cared about was that it was over, that she was going to be free—even if after all she needed the Four Horsemen to help free her—and that within a few days she was going to begin the life that had so excited her as she had planned it yesterday.

The excitement would return, she told herself as she allowed Rex to lead her from Boris Pinter's rooms and down the stairs and outside to his waiting carriage. She was feeling depressed only because she had not been allowed to end it her way—depressed and also immeasurably relieved.

Rex handed her into the carriage and followed her inside and it jolted immediately into motion. Sophia set her head back and closed her eyes.

"What is going to happen?" she asked.

"They will recover your letters," he said. "They will bring them to you at Rawleigh House and it will be all over. Friends *do* stick together, Sophie. When I had a certain matter of honor to settle a few years ago, those three stood by me just as the four of us are standing by you today. Their support meant a great deal to me."

She half smiled, though she did not open her eyes. "I take your point, Rex," she said. "I will not again accuse you of interference. What else will happen?"

"He will be punished," he said after a short silence.

"Three against one?" It seemed not quite right.

"One against one," he told her. "We all wanted to be that one, Sophie. We should have drawn straws, perhaps. But Nat would not hear of it. But then neither would I hear of anyone's taking my place a few years ago—I was avenging a wrong to Catherine."

Sophia opened her eyes and looked at him. He was looking steadily back.

Nathaniel, she remembered then, had put his arms about her and kissed her cheek. He had called her his love.

*Believe me, my love*, he had said.

She closed her eyes again.

"Now, Pinter," Kenneth said briskly when they had all heard the outer door close behind Rex and Sophie. "The rest of the letters, if you please."

Boris Pinter laughed. "There was only the one," he said. "I was giving it to her, but I suppose she was so upset to know what sort of letter it was that she imagined I was somehow threatening her with it. You all know about women and their fits of the vapors—especially when they discover that their men have been having a little bit on the side."

Kenneth strolled across the room to stand almost toe-to-toe with Boris Pinter. He towered ominously almost a whole head taller than the other man. "I do not believe you have understood the nature of the order, *Lieutenant*," he said. "I am loath to raise my voice since we are not on a parade ground. I will accompany you while you fetch the rest of the letters. Do you understand now?''

''Yes, sir,'' Pinter said, the tone of camaraderie gone from his voice. When Kenneth stepped to one side and gestured toward the door, he went toward it smartly enough.

Nathaniel and Eden looked at each other when they were alone.

''Damn it,'' Eden said, ''she looked magnificent. Who would have suspected that the pistol was unloaded? I would not.''

''Help me with the furniture?'' Nathaniel suggested, and they set about moving back a few chairs and small tables that occupied the center of the room.

''Nat.'' Eden straightened up after they had moved a sofa together. ''A kiss? On the face? *My love?*''

Nathaniel looked assessingly at the empty center of the room. It should do. He had had his back to everyone else and had been unnerved by that gun pointed right at him—and by the thought of what might have happened to Sophie if Pinter had wrested it away from her before their arrival. He had forgotten for a few disastrous moments that they were not alone.

''Is that why you would not play fair and give any of us the chance to do this?'' Eden asked, gesturing to the empty space.

Nathaniel looked back at him but said nothing.

''Sophie?'' Eden looked and sounded intrigued. ''*Sophie*, Nat? Not Lady Gullis?''

But Ken and Pinter were coming back. Ken was carrying a bundle of what looked to be another eight or ten letters, all resembling the first in appearance.

''Old Walter was quite the boy,'' Pinter said heartily.

''*Major Armitage,*'' Eden told him, ''will remain out of all your conversations and correspondence from this moment forward, Lieutenant. As will these letters and all matters pertaining to them. We will not ask for your word on this, as frankly we do not trust your word. Let it simply be said, then, that disobeying orders on this matter will be somewhat injurious to your health. I will not ask if you understand.''

''That is a threat,'' Pinter said. ''Sir.''

''And so it is.'' Eden regarded him coolly. ''It is also a promise. So is this.'' He reached inside his coat and drew out a folded sheet of paper, which he tossed onto one of the tables he had moved to the edge of the room. ''It is something that will be made public, Pinter, unless for the rest of your natural days you are a very good boy indeed. It outlines certain interesting facts about your sexual preferences.''

Pinter visibly blanched. ''It is all a lie,'' he said.

''What is?'' Eden asked him. ''But it does not matter, does it? None of it will ever have to be made public. *Will it?*'' He barked in a manner that had even Nathaniel jumping.

''No, sir.'' Boris Pinter's bravado had disintegrated as they had all known it would. Though not entirely, Nathaniel hoped.

''There *are* several copies of that document, by the way,'' Eden said. ''We all have one. We do not have the power to impose any sentences of banishment, Pinter, but we do strongly suggest that you remove yourself from this country for a year or ten. You understand me?''

''Yes, sir,'' Pinter said.

''Good.'' Eden stood aside. ''Your turn, Nat.''

Pinter had been eyeing him uneasily for the past minute or two. Nathaniel had been methodically removing his coat and waistcoat and rolling up the sleeves of his shirt.

''You are not going to die, Pinter,'' he said conversationally. ''Unless it is from fright, of course. And you are not going to be tied down, you may be disappointed to learn, since that was always your favorite form of punishment. You may remove some of your own garments for greater ease of movement—I will give you time—and then use your own fists as much as you like. I will be using mine.''

Pinter backed up a step. "You have the letters," he said. "And you have my promise of silence. I will even leave the country. What is this for?"

"This?" Nathaniel raised his eyebrows. "This is for Mrs. Armitage, Pinter. Our friend. You have one minute to get ready. After that it will be either a fight between you and me or else simple punishment. Take your choice. It is all the same to me."

"There are three of you." To his discredit, Pinter's voice was almost a squeak.

"But fortunately for you, Pinter," Nathaniel said, "we are honorable men. If you can succeed in avoiding your punishment by knocking me insensible, Major Lord Pelham and Major Lord Haverford will not lay a finger on you." He smiled. "Thirty seconds."

Perhaps Boris Pinter thought he had a chance. Or perhaps he was too frightened to take the coward's way out. Or perhaps he simply did not understand that he was dealing with an honorable man, who would not have continued hitting him once he was down.

However it was, he stayed on his feet for a satisfyingly long time. Not that it was in any way an equal contest. One of his punches landed rather painfully against Nathaniel's shoulder blade and another wild one drew blood from the corner of his mouth. Everything else glanced harmlessly off or missed altogether.

Pinter himself, by the time he went down, completely unconscious from a crushing blow beneath the chin, had a broken nose, which was bleeding copiously, an eye whose surrounds were puffed up to twice their normal size and would soon be black, two raw-looking cheeks, and two broken front teeth. The bruises on the rest of his body, all from the waist up, were invisible beneath his shirt.

Nathaniel flexed his fingers and looked down ruefully at his raw knuckles. There were other people in the doorway, he noticed for the first time—Pinter's valet, the landlady from downstairs, the servant who had opened the door to them.

"If you are his valet," Nathaniel said, pinning the man with his gaze, "I would suggest that you fetch some water and throw it over him."

The valet disappeared at a run.

"My card." Kenneth held one out to the landlady. "If there has been any damage to your property, ma'am, you may have the bills sent to me."

"There is *blood* on my carpet," she said, apparently unconcerned with the unconscious and bloody person stretched out on top of it.

"Yes, ma'am," Kenneth said, "and so there is. You are dressed again, Nat? Good day to you, ma'am."

"You are slipping, Nat," Eden said as they descended the stairs and stepped out onto the street. "Out of practice. Rusticating too long. You actually allowed him to punch you in the face. I could have expired from shame."

"He has to have some trophy to take home to Sophie," Kenneth said. "Nat? Is there something you care to tell us, old chap? Something to get off your conscience?"

"Go to the devil," Nathaniel instructed him, mopping at the corner of his mouth with his handkerchief.

"As I understand it, Ken," Eden said, "Lady Gullis is as innocent as the day she was born. White as the driven snow. Nat has been leading us a merry dance."

"You may go with him," Nathaniel said.

# TWENTY

CATHERINE, MOIRA, AND
Daphne, Lady Baird, were in the morning room at Rawleigh House, playing with their children. But the game was
instantly abandoned when the door opened.

"Rex," Catherine said, hurrying toward it. She stopped.
"And Sophie?"

Young Peter Adams toddled toward his father, clamoring
to be picked up so that he might impart to him some news
in the incoherent babble that only a parent could understand. Young Amy Baird went close to Rex, tugging on the
tassel of one of his Hessians to attract her uncle's attention.
Jamie Woodfall, forgetting that he was a big boy now, first
put his thumb in his mouth and then leaned against his
mother's legs and raised both arms above his head.

Sophia felt awkward. But she was not ignored. Catherine
caught her up in a hug and then laughed and looked down
at the swelling of her womb.

"I am having to learn that I must keep my distance from
people again," she said. "Sophie, how *lovely* it is to see
you again. See who is here, Moira, Daphne?"

"Hello, Sophie," Moira said before picking up her son.
"When everyone stops talking at once, sweetheart, we will

ask Uncle Rex where Papa is. Is that what you want to know? I daresay he will be back soon.''

''Amy,'' Daphne was saying at the same time, ''Uncle Rex has two ears, darling, but he can listen to only one person at a time. Do let Peter finish what he has to say and then you may have your turn.'' But Peter was no longer babbling. He was giggling—he had hold of his father's ears and looked as if he was trying to bite his nose. ''Sophie, you have come to a madhouse.''

If she had been thinking straight in the carriage, Sophia thought, she would have asked Rex to set her down outside her own door. Why had she allowed him to bring her here?

''Do sit down, Sophie,'' Catherine said, linking an arm through hers and leading her toward a chair. ''I shall ring for Nurse to take the children up to the nursery for milk and biscuits and for the tea tray to be brought in here. We will soon have a measure of sanity restored, I do assure you.''

She was very gracious, Sophia thought, sitting stiffly on the chair that had been indicated, and watching the children being led from the room by the nurse—after Peter had been set back on his feet and Rex had gone down on his haunches to look at Amy's new tooth and Jamie had been assured that his papa would be back soon and would come to the nursery to take him home.

''We have all been dreadfully worried,'' Moira said, looking from Rex to Sophia, ''fearing that something would go wrong. Where is Kenneth? And Nathaniel and Eden, of course. And Sophie? How did you learn of this? We were all going to be so careful to keep it from you.''

''Sophie was there ahead of us,'' Rex said. ''She had a pistol pointed at Pinter's heart.''

Daphne gasped and Catherine clapped both hands to her mouth.

''Good for you, Sophie!'' Moira said. ''Oh, well done. I would wager it was not loaded, though.''

''No, it was not,'' Sophia said.

''Women!'' Rex shook his head. ''Do you not realize

the danger of pointing unloaded pistols at villains?''

"It is the principle of the thing," Moira said. "I am so glad you got there first, Sophie, and showed everyone that you are no abject victim. Now tell us everything that happened. And if you are going to do the telling, Rex, you may not give us a laundered version. Sophie is here to set you right.''

"I feel so dreadful," Sophia said, looking down at the hands she had spread in her lap. "I would not admit you when you came to call on me, Moira and Catherine, although it must have been clear to you that I was at home. I *scolded* Rex and the others for interfering in my life and broke off my friendship with them. Yet you continued to try to help me. And you are being kind to me now. I am so ashamed.''

"Oh Sophie," Catherine said, "we understood. And I am glad you went to Mr. Pinter's this morning even though it was a remarkably rash thing to do. If you had not, none of us would have told you why the blackmail had suddenly stopped, and we would have been reluctant to try to see you soon lest you suspect. But we have never stopped being your friends, have we, Rex?''

"Of course not," he said, "and never will. Ah, the tea tray. I daresay Sophie could use a cup.''

"*Where* are Kenneth and the others?" Moira asked, sounding a little exasperated.

Rex proceeded with an account of what had happened in the rooms on Bury Street. Sophia accepted her cup of tea gratefully and sipped on it, hot as it was.

They had been going to *punish* Boris Pinter. *Nathaniel* was going to punish him. Not with a gun or a sword. With his bare fists, then. Not in order to get back the letters—she did not doubt that just the presence of the three of them would be sufficient to pry them from Mr. Pinter. But for her sake—because of what Pinter had done to her.

Nathaniel was doing that for her.

Nathaniel was also discovering the truth. They all were.

They would know now. By the time they came here, she would see the knowledge in their faces.

She would see it in *his* face.

She should have gone home. She should have thanked Rex and sent her thanks to the others for what they had done for her, but she should have gone home.

Was he hurt? Had Mr. Pinter hurt him? She did not doubt that it would have been a fair fight. Not really punishment but a fight in which Nathaniel might as easily have been hurt as Mr. Pinter.

Her hands were beginning to shake. She set her cup down in the saucer.

"It is all over, Sophie," Daphne said kindly. "But what a dreadful experience for you."

"Yes." Sophia smiled. "But how fortunate I am to have such friends."

"Did you know," Catherine asked her, leaning forward in her chair, "that Harry—my brother Harry, Viscount Perry—is to call upon your brother-in-law this morning? None of us can even begin to guess the reason why, of course. Perhaps it is just that spring is in the air."

Sarah? To marry the very handsome and amiable Lord Perry? So soon? But they were so very *young*. Or else she was getting rather old, Sophia thought.

"Oh," she said. "No, I did not know. And I cannot guess the reason either." She laughed. "But if the approval of a mere aunt is important to Sarah, then she has it."

They all conversed on a variety of topics for half an hour before the sounds beyond the door of new arrivals proved just how tense they all were. Moira leaped to her feet, Rex got to his and strode to the door, Catherine and Daphne leaned forward expectantly in their chairs, and Sophia pressed back into hers, her hands gripping the arms tightly.

Everyone was talking at once. Moira was in Kenneth's arms and—for some reason—weeping. Rex was asking in feigned disgust if that was a *wound* at the corner of Nat's mouth or merely a cold sore. Eden was proclaiming the debilitating influence of a life of rustication on a man's instincts for self-defense. Nathaniel was inviting him to go to the devil—at the risk of repeating himself and becoming tedious. Catherine was demanding to know what had *happened*.

And then Nathaniel detached himself from the group at the door and came across the room to stand in front of Sophia's chair. He reached out a hand and she placed one of her own in it.

"Sophie," he said, "it is all over, my dear. He will not be bothering you again, and the information he held will never be published. You have my word on it, and the word of your other friends here."

"Thank you," she said as he raised her hand to his lips—and she saw his knuckles.

Kenneth was right behind him, Moira holding to one of his arms. He held out a bundle that was even fatter than Sophia had expected it to be. There might be ten more letters there—enough to have beggared both Edwin and Thomas before the last one or two had been used to bring about the scandal she had no doubt Boris Pinter had intended from the start.

"They are all here, Sophie," Kenneth said. "Including the one that was on the floor. And even on the remote chance that he dared keep one or two back, I can assure you that he would never dare to let them come to light. Walter did not call us the Four Horsemen of the Apocalypse for nothing."

She stared at the bundle, feeling rather faint.

"There is a fire in here," Kenneth said gently. "Shall I set them on it, Sophie, and we will watch them burn?"

"Yes," she said, and watched as he tossed the letters into the heart of the fire. There was an instant blaze about them, and they curled into golden and brown ashes. "Thank you."

"We did not read them, Sophie," Eden said from across the room. "We do not know who she was and we do not want to know. All that needs still to be said on the topic is that I for one think old Walter had execrable taste and I would tell him so if he were still alive. But I'll not say more. He was your husband and I daresay you were fond of him—and your marriage is really none of our business, is it? There—end of topic. Do you have only lukewarm tea to offer us, Catherine?''

They did not *know*. They had not read the letters, and apparently Boris Pinter had said nothing. Sophia closed her eyes and heard a buzzing in her ears at the same time as she felt a blast of icy air in her nostrils.

''She has fainted,'' someone was saying from very far away. ''No, she will be all right. Just keep your head down, Sophie.'' Something firm was pressed against the back of her head, holding her face down almost on her knees. ''Let the blood flow back.'' It was Nathaniel's voice.

Someone was chafing her cold hands with warm ones. ''Oh, poor dear Sophie,'' Catherine said from close beside her ear. ''This has been *such* a strain on you. Nathaniel, do carry her upstairs to one of the guest rooms. I will go ahead of you.''

But Sophia lifted her head, pressing back against the resistance of Nathaniel's hand. ''No,'' she said, ''I am all right now. How terribly foolish of me. I must go home. Please, I must. I am more grateful to you all than I can say, but I need to go home.''

''Of course,'' Rex said. ''I will have the carriage brought back around. Nat will accompany you.''

It did not occur to Sophia to wonder why he had named Nathaniel rather than anyone else. All she wanted was to get home, where she could think herself back into yesterday's mood and yesterday's plans.

She was free. Totally free—they did not even *know*.

But while she should have been feeling euphoria, she was actually feeling mortally depressed. How perverse human emotions could be!

She needed to be at home. She needed to start packing her belongings. She needed to pull herself free of the past, to detach herself from the present, and to look forward to the future.

To the bright future.

•   •   •

He had set her hand on his arm in the carriage and held it there with his free hand. He looked at her several times to make sure that she was not going to faint again. But they did not converse. She stared ahead and downward to the seat opposite.

How must it feel, he wondered, for a woman to discover that her husband had conducted a long-term love affair with another woman and had left behind him a large pile of love letters? And to have salt rubbed in the wounds by a blackmailer threatening to expose the infidelity of her hero husband and her own corresponding shame?

What did such knowledge and such an experience do to her confidence in herself, to her sense of self-worth? Did it send her into hiding behind a facade of plainness and placid amiability?

But why had she broken off her friendship with them rather than enlist their help? Was she ashamed to have even them know that Walter had been a bounder after all? It was still difficult to think of Armitage engaging in what must have been a passionate affair—and writing *love* letters.

He wished he could say something to console her. But anything he said on the topic would only make matters worse. Besides, Eden had promised her that the topic was permanently closed. And Ken had tossed those letters onto the flames.

Why had she written that letter to him yesterday? he wondered. Because she knew what she was going to do this morning and had not wanted to be distracted? Because she just did not want a continuance of their affair? Because she did not care for him at all except perhaps as a friend?

He could not even ask her at the moment. She still had too much of a burden on her mind after the events of the morning. Devil take it, what would have happened to her if they had not arrived when they had? Sooner or later Pinter would have got that gun away from her.

The carriage came to a halt outside the house on Sloan Terrace.

"Shall I come in, Sophie?" he asked. "Or would you rather be alone?"

He expected that she would wish to be alone. But she looked at him as if she had just remembered that he was there with her.

"Come in," she said.

She excused herself when they had arrived in her sitting room and was absent for a few minutes. When she returned, she was carrying a bowl of water with a towel and a cloth over her shoulder. There was a jar of some ointment in one of her hands.

"Sit down," she told him as he looked at her in some surprise.

He did so and watched silently as she took one of his hands and lowered it into the water—it was warm—and proceeded to cleanse his knuckles with the cloth. Her touch was infinitely gentle. He felt very little pain, even though his hand had been devilishly sore and the other one still was. She patted his hand dry with the towel and smoothed some of the ointment onto his knuckles. She started on the other hand.

She was wearing a dark-colored walking dress that he knew now was about one size too large for her. Her hair had been dressed severely for the morning's activity. She had obviously not combed it since leaving for Pinter's lodgings. Unruly curls had sprung all about what had probably been a smooth chignon for perhaps five or ten minutes. Her face was intent on what she was doing. It was still rather pale.

She looked beautiful to him.

She got up without a word or even a glance at his face after she was finished and took everything back to wherever she had found it. He flexed his fingers rather gingerly. His knuckles shone from the ointment. They felt considerably soothed.

He raised his head when she came back into the room. She stood looking down at him—it had not occurred to him to get to his feet.

"Thank you for what you did, Nathaniel," she said. "I am sorry I ever called it interference. I recognized it today for what it was—friendship. It is good to have friends."

"Sophie," he said, "will you marry me?"

She stared at him for what seemed a long while, her eyes filling with tears. The whole of the rest of his life hung in the balance, he knew, scarcely daring to breathe. But her answer came even before she spoke. She shook her head slowly.

"No," she said. "Thank you but no, Nathaniel. I am going away—within the week. I am selling my house. I was not sure I could, but apparently it is mine without any conditions attached. I am going home to Gloucestershire to stay with my brother and his family until the sale is final. Then I am going to buy a cottage of my own and begin a new life with old acquaintances and friends. I believe I needed to be here for a while to recover from all those years without roots. But I know now that I will be happiest in the country. I am really looking forward to going, to beginning afresh."

He swallowed. Perhaps he had not really believed until now that it was all over, that she simply did not want him. He had served a purpose in her life—though he did not believe she had deliberately *used* him—but that was now in her past. She was planning her future and looking forward to it. It did not include him.

"Well." He got to his feet and smiled at her. "I had to ask, Sophie. Forgive me. I wish you well. I wish you all the happiness in the world. We can part friends?"

"Of course," she said. "Oh, of course, Nathaniel. You will always be dear to me. You must know that. Always."

He held his smile and felt the raw ache of tears at the back of his throat and up behind his nose.

"Yes," he said. "Always."

Though it would be a friendship only in the sense that they would always think kindly of each other, he thought. They would not correspond with each other. They would probably never meet again. He hoped they would not.

"I will leave you, then, Sophie," he said. "If I were you, I would rest for a while."

"Yes." She nodded.

"Well." There was a moment of awkwardness, a moment of almost unbearable panic. "Good day to you, then."

"Good day, Nathaniel," she said.

She stood where she was, not far from the door, her back to it, while he let himself out without touching her. He dismissed Rex's carriage and set out on the walk home.

What they had really been saying was good-bye.

"You are going to Gloucestershire," Lavinia said unnecessarily, since Sophia had already told her so, and indeed she had arrived with the knowledge—Nathaniel had told her yesterday when he had returned home. "And you are going to buy your own cottage and live an idyllic life in the country."

"Yes," Sophia said.

There were a few boxes lying open in various parts of the room, into which she had started to pack ornaments and books and the contents of the escritoire. Lavinia was wandering idly about, peering into boxes, though absently rather than inquisitively.

"I am so happy for you," Lavinia said. "But not as envious as I might have been. Nat and I are going back to Bowood soon. Georgina will stay with Margaret and John. Nat is going to allow me to live alone somewhere on the estate. It is a great triumph for me."

"I am glad." Sophia smiled, though she did not fail to notice that *Lavinia* was not smiling. "Are you quite sure, though, that it is what you want? A life of solitude sometimes sounds idyllic. In reality it is frequently lonely."

"Are *you* sometimes lonely?" Lavinia was looking at her, frowning.

"Sometimes," Sophia admitted. "Not often, it is true, but on occasion one wishes there were someone to talk with during the quiet hours at home, apart from a dog." Someone to lie with at night, someone with whom to mull over the events of the day while one lay cozily in his arms. Someone to snuggle close to so that sleep would come more easily and be deeper when it came.

"I thought you were happy." Lavinia was still frowning. "You do not look happy, Sophie. You are pale. You look as if you have not slept. Are you sure you are doing the right thing?"

"Oh yes." Sophia smiled brightly. "It is just that there is so much work to uprooting oneself and moving across a country. I was accustomed to it once, but those days are long gone. Besides, I had very few belongings in those days."

"What were they *like*?" Lavinia asked. She picked up the handkerchief that was lying on the arm of a chair—*the handkerchief!* "Nat, I mean, and Lord Haverford and Lord Rawleigh." She made as if to put the handkerchief down again, but she spread it, folded, across her open palm instead. "And Lord Pelham. Were they horridly obnoxious?"

"No." Sophia could scarcely concentrate on what she said. She wanted to snatch away the handkerchief. "They were dashing and brave and bold and charming and funny and outrageous—and very good officers. Their superiors were always exasperated with them—but sent for them whenever there was real work to be done. Their men trusted them and were devoted to them. The women—all of us— were in love with them."

"They were not—conceited?" Lavinia asked. Her finger was tracing the outline of the embroidered letter *G*.

"They had a great deal to be conceited about," Sophia said. "There was something—oh, larger than life about them. But they never *seemed* conceited. They were the best of friends to me. My father's name was George, you know." Her father's name had been Thomas.

"Mmm?" Lavinia looked up at her with blank eyes.

"The handkerchief," Sophia said. How foolish that lie had been. Lavinia had not even been noticing the handkerchief. But she looked at it now.

"Oh," she said, and set it down on the arm of the chair again.

Sophia went toward the chair, picked up the linen casually, and put it into the pocket of her apron.

"I suppose," Lavinia said, "men who are too handsome for their own good are not necessarily conceited, are they? They cannot help their looks and their physique and their— experience with life."

She was in a strange mood, Sophia thought. Restless. She had not sat down at all, though Sophia had invited her to sit and have some tea.

"Georgina has an attachment to your nephew," Lavinia said, picking up a china ornament that had not yet found its way into the box beside which it stood. "And your niece is going to marry Viscount Perry. It certainly did not take them long to make up their minds, did it? Is it possible, Sophie? To know someone for such a short time and yet know for certain that he is the only man in this world with whom one could contemplate spending the rest of one's life? And that life without him would be unbearably empty? It is not possible, is it? Yet they seem so happy."

What was this all about? Sophia sat down and looked closely at her guest. "Whom have you met?" she asked quietly.

Lavinia looked at her, startled, and flushed deeply. "Oh." She laughed. "No one. I was not talking about me. I was talking theoretically. Is there such a thing as love, Sophie? As that one man who seems like part of one's very soul? It sounds like ridiculous rubbish to me, even though I suppose I have always dreamed . . ."

Sophia remembered her sleepless night. Remembered Nathaniel's sitting on this very chair yesterday, asking her to marry him. With quiet, kind courtesy. Because he felt sorry for her and responsible for her. Because he had lain with her. Because he was genuinely fond of her. Because he was an honorable man. She remembered the temptation, worse than any physical pain. She remembered the stark knowledge the night had brought. Never again. Two of the bleakest words in the English language when put together. *Never again.*

"Yes," she said softly, "there is such a love."

"Have you known it, Sophie?" Lavinia asked, eagerly.

"Oh, yes," Sophia said. "Oh, yes." She got to her feet abruptly and crossed to the bellpull. "I feel like tea, if you do not."

"Sometimes," Lavinia said with a sigh, "I wish life were simpler. I wish it could be lived with the reason alone. Why do we have to be plagued with emotions?"

"Life would be very dull," Sophia said, "without love and friendship and joy and hope and all the other positive emotions."

"Yes." Lavinia chuckled and sat down at last. "It is all the negative ones I object to. I want to be sane and sensible and free and independent."

*But you have fallen in love,* Sophia thought, and wondered who the gentleman was. She could not imagine any man not reciprocating feelings Lavinia had for him.

However, Lavinia was clearly not ready to confide in her and she would not pry.

The tea tray arrived.

And then there was all the distress of parting. Sophia was going to Gloucestershire the next day. Lavinia and Nathaniel were going to Bowood in Yorkshire soon after.

They would write to each other, the two women agreed. But they both seemed aware that it was unlikely they would meet again.

# TWENTY-ONE

SOMETIMES SOPHIA LOOKED back with nostalgia on the settled, tranquil life she had lived on Sloan Terrace in London. In the three months since she had left there life had been anything but settled. The sale of her house had taken a little longer than she had expected, with the result that though she now had the money with which to buy a home in Gloucestershire, she still had not done so. She was still nominally living with Thomas and Anne and their children.

Now she was no longer sure she wished to buy a home just there. Perhaps, she thought, she would go elsewhere, farther away, where no one knew her, where she could really begin all over again. But the prospect was dreary and a little frightening. Sometimes she was tempted to take a more obvious path.

She had delayed making the decision. First there had been Sarah's wedding to Viscount Perry to attend in July. Sophia had gone with the idea of spending just two weeks with Edwin and Beatrice, but they had wanted her to stay on so that she might travel with them to Yorkshire late in August for Lewis's wedding to Georgina Gascoigne—Sophia had, naturally enough, received an invitation. No one had been able to understand her hesitation about going.

How could she go? It had been bad enough seeing Rex and Catherine at Sarah's wedding. Wounds that had barely filmed over had been ripped raw again, especially when Catherine, heavy with child, had strolled with Sophia one afternoon and told her that they had been convinced during the spring, she and Rex, that there had been something between Sophie and Nathaniel.

"It was wishful thinking, of course," she had said, laughing. "We like to have our friends all closely linked together. And the fact that it was Nathaniel who fought for you seemed wonderfully romantic. You will shake your head at us for trying to manage your life again, Sophie. You are happy in Gloucestershire?"

But how could she not go to Lewis's wedding? She would be able to offer no reasonable explanation for not going. Everyone would be hurt and offended if she did not.

Except Nathaniel. Although he had sent her an invitation, he must surely be hoping that she would refuse.

But her dilemma had been solved for her—or partly so. Lavinia had written to her each week since they had parted. She was now living alone—except for a few servants—in a cottage in the village of Bowood and claimed to be idyllically happy. She had invited Sophia to stay there with her when she came for the wedding. It would be so much more cozy, she had written, than staying at the house, which would be crammed with other guests.

And so Sophia was traveling into Yorkshire with her brother- and sister-in-law and wishing she was going anywhere else on earth—though that was not exactly true, either, she admitted to herself as they drew close to their destination. Edwin and Beatrice were both asleep.

She was looking forward to seeing Lavinia again. She was looking forward to seeing the village and the house and park. Forever afterward when she thought of him— perhaps there would come a time when that would not be almost every single hour of every single day—she would be able to picture him in the right setting. And of course she wanted to see *him* again—dreaded it and longed for it.

She was missing Lass, she thought suddenly—that warm, constantly loving presence of another living being. She had left the collie in Gloucestershire, where Thomas's children were spoiling her dreadfully.

The carriage rounded a curve in the road and she could see a church spire in the distance ahead. Could that be it? It must be. Bowood was the next village along their route, was it not? There was a strange lurching in her stomach and she spread a hand over it to keep the feeling from escalating into panic.

"Is that the village ahead?" Beatrice asked, waking Edwin with the sound of her voice. "I do hope so. My bones are as weary as bones can be. Are yours, Sophie? Oh, it will be wonderful to see Lewis again. Is he nervous, do you suppose, Edwin?"

"He will be soon, m'dear," he said with a chuckle, "once he has you to fuss over him and remind him that he is about to be a *bridegroom*."

"I wonder," she said, not taking up the bait, "if Sarah and Harry will have arrived ahead of us. I am longing to hear about their wedding trip to Scotland and the Lakes. Dear Sarah—it is still difficult, I declare, to realize that she is a married lady. Viscountess Perry. She has done well for herself, has she not, Sophie?"

Sophia smiled and nodded. They had arranged to set her down at Lavinia's cottage before proceeding on to Bowood Manor. Perhaps, she thought, life at the house with all the wedding guests would be so busy that she would scarcely see Nathaniel except at the church and wedding breakfast. He could be no more anxious to see her than she was to see him, after all.

But then she *was* very anxious.

The hand she held over her stomach was doing nothing to quell the turmoil and growing queasiness the proximity of their destination had brought on.

"One shudders," Eden said, "to discover what changes can overtake a man's life when he does not watch himself.

When I *think,* Nat, of the way we envisioned our lives when we sold out of the cavalry.''

''We were boys, Ede,'' Nathaniel said, ''even if we were closer to thirty than twenty, all of us. We had been living in an artificial environment that made us grow up in a hurry in one way and kept us back from maturity in other ways.''

''And that is the worst of it,'' Eden said. ''You never used to be a philosopher, Nat.'' He shuddered theatrically.

With only two days to go to Georgina's wedding Bowood was teeming with guests and with all the extra servants hired for the occasion. The stables and coach house were full to overflowing. And a mood of only-just-controlled hysteria had settled over the female members of the family as the day approached—except Lavinia, who wisely stayed at her cottage.

Eden had arrived the day before. He and Nathaniel had escaped from the house for an afternoon stroll in the park.

''There are Ken and Rex, married men this long time,'' Eden continued, ''and Rex in the letter that arrived this morning writing about nothing but *babies.* I ask you, Nat. Could you picture Rex a few years ago writing a lengthy missive about his anxiety over his wife's going into labor one month early, about his insistence on remaining with her through the whole lengthy ordeal—Rex!—about his idiotic wonder at having fathered a small but perfectly healthy daughter, about his terror over Catherine until the physician informed him that she was out of all danger? Is *this* what we have come to?''

Nathaniel chuckled and turned when they were halfway down the long lawn before the house to look back up at it. He never tired of the joy he felt in knowing it was home—a joy that had somewhat tempered the unwelcome depression and lethargy that had threatened him since his return from London.

''It would appear so, Ede,'' he said.

''And you, Nat.'' Eden gestured toward the house. ''We would have had a collective shuddering attack if we could have pictured *this*—all this wedding business, all this domesticity. And you the host of it all.''

"I took Georgina to London in the hope of finding her a husband,'' Nathaniel said. "I succeeded—or rather she did—and I am happy for her.''

"And so you are going to be alone,'' Eden said.

"Yes.'' Nathaniel waited to feel the satisfaction he had expected to feel on such an occasion. It just would not come.

"And the worst of everything,'' Eden said with what seemed to be a gloom that matched Nathaniel's own, "the very worst, Nat, is that I might just be caving in too.''

Nathaniel looked at him.

"I went home for a couple of weeks last month,'' Eden said, "or rather to the house and estate I have owned since my father's death. I have never lived there. Neither did he. I went out of curiosity. The house was mostly shut up, of course, with everything draped in holland covers. But the housekeeper, who has been there forever and obviously loves the place, has it all clean and gleaming. And the steward, who has been there just as long, has everything shipshape—he even has the park looking like a damned showpiece. I knew I was wealthy, Nat, but when I looked over the books, I discovered that I am something of a nabob. And all the neighbors started organizing balls and assemblies and dinners and treating me as if I were someone's long-lost brother. It was deuced embarrassing.''

"And deuced tempting?'' Nathaniel suggested.

"And deuced tempting,'' Eden agreed. "What is happening to me, Nat? Am I growing senile?''

"Growing up, I suppose, like the rest of us,'' Nathaniel said. "Shall we keep walking?'' They had been standing gazing at the house.

"Sophie is at your cousin's?'' Eden said. "Should we walk over there and pay our respects to her, Nat? I suppose I should pay mine to Miss Bergland too, though doubtless she will bite my head off and accuse me of treating her like a charity case or calling there only so that I might condescend to inform her how quaint her cottage is—or something like that. I wonder you did not find her somewhere altogether farther away than the village to live. For your peace of mind, old chap.''

The Houghtons had arrived the day before, having set Sophie down at Lavinia's cottage. He should have walked over there last evening, Nathaniel thought now. Or this morning at the very latest. He had made the excuse to himself that he had houseguests to attend to. He had convinced himself that she would not wish to see him any more than he wished to see her. But that fact was immaterial. She was to all intents and purposes his guest, since she had come for Georgina's wedding to her nephew. He owed her the courtesy of a visit.

He dreaded seeing her. He had scarcely begun to get over her. Now he would have to start all over again.

''Lavinia and I have been remarkably in accord with each other since we returned from town,'' he said as they resumed their walk and directed their footsteps toward the village. ''Yes, we really should pay our respects to Sophie.''

They walked in silence—and in gloom. Nathaniel was sure that Eden shared his mood. It was unusual to find him either silent or in low spirits. Perhaps they would both cheer up when Ken and Moira arrived—they were expected later in the day.

Lavinia's cottage was larger than its name suggested, and though it was part of the village, it was situated somewhat apart from the general cluster of buildings around the village green. It was set in a large garden that was almost a little park of its own. It had been the home of a retired rector and his wife until the two of them had conveniently decided to move away early in the spring in order to be closer to the rest of their family.

Nathaniel found an excuse to call there most days. He had called yesterday morning. He might not have come today unless Eden had prompted him. He would do anything, he thought as the two of them went through the gate and up the gravel path toward the front door, to find an excuse not to call today after all. Perhaps they were out. Perhaps Lavinia had taken Sophie on a walk or on a visit to some of the village's inhabitants.

But he was not to be so fortunate. They were in the rose arbor behind the house—Lavinia's manservant directed them there. They were sitting on a stone bench inside, talking and laughing together, their backs to the house so that they did not know of the arrival of guests until those guests were upon them. They both looked up, startled.

Nathaniel bowed to Lavinia and then turned his attention to Sophie. She had changed, he noticed in the second or two before he bowed to her. She was wearing a light sprigged muslin dress—new, he thought, and made to enhance her figure rather than disguise it. She must have had her hair cut. It was not short, but it was dressed prettily in a style that allowed for loose curls. Her face was fuller—she must have put back on the weight she had lost during those stress-filled weeks in London. And her eyes were large and luminous.

"Sophie," he said, bowing to her. "How are you? How lovely it is to see you again, my dear. You are looking well."

"Nathaniel," she said. She did not say anything else. She smiled and gazed back at him.

She really was looking well. Any faint hope he had had that she might have regretted her rejection of him and have been looking faded and unhappy as a result died. How ridiculous of him. Had he really been hoping that?

"Oh, it is you, is it?" Lavinia had been saying to Eden.

"It is I," Eden agreed, "stepping into your rustic idyll, Miss Bergland. But have no fear. I shall be stepping out of it again as soon as I have greeted Sophie and spent the obligatory half hour with the two of you, conversing about the weather and the health of every acquaintance we have in common."

Those two had the most extraordinary verbal exchanges, Nathaniel thought, becoming aware of them as Eden was turning his attention to Sophie and greeting her with a great deal more warmth and courtesy.

And so they sat, the four of them, surrounded by the sight and perfume of roses and other summer flowers, with a blue sky above them and the warmth of the August sun beaming down on them, conversing about very little more than Eden had suggested. They were all very agreeable. They all talked and smiled.

Half an hour after their arrival he and Eden took their leave. The ladies walked with them to the gate, Sophie with Eden, Lavinia with Nathaniel. They parted with bows and curtsies and smiles.

"Well, *that* is over," Eden said, sounding as relieved as Nathaniel felt. "She is in remarkably good looks, I must say."

"Yes," Nathaniel said. "Yes, she is." He still could not believe that she had hidden her beauty so successfully for so long behind the dark, unfashionable, ill-fitting clothes and the heavy, unbecoming hairstyle and the cheerful, comradely expression. "She is, in fact, quite beautiful."

"I did think," Eden said, "that perhaps she would have discovered that living alone in the country did not suit her after all."

"Yes," Nathaniel said with a sigh, "I thought the same thing too."

"I wondered if she would have lost some of her bloom," Eden said.

"She has not." Indeed, Nathaniel thought, she had bloomed gloriously, though she must be close to thirty years old. He wondered what she had been like before she married Walter. Had she been like this then? Had she ever before been like this? Or was it something quite new?

Eden chuckled. "I suppose," he said, "I hoped she would have. It is somewhat lowering to know that one has had no affect whatsoever on a female even when one has no wish to have any affect."

Nathaniel's hands had curled into fists at his sides. What *was* this?

"She is not for you, Ede," he said stiffly. "Hands off if you know what is good for you."

"*Eh?*" Eden stopped walking—they had just left the village behind them and had turned onto the tree-lined driveway to the house. "What the devil? She is of age, Nat. *If* I were interested. *Which* I am not. Heaven forbid. I have some sense of self-preservation."

"Sorry, Ede," Nathaniel mumbled. "We are a sorry pair, are we not? About to come to fisticuffs over a woman who has made it very clear that she wants neither of us." He laughed and started to walk on.

Eden caught up to him and they walked in silence for a while. Then Eden cleared his throat.

"Just for the record, Nat," he said, "about whom were we talking back there?"

"About whom?" Nathaniel frowned. "Why, about Sophie, of course."

"Ah," Eden said. "Quite so. Yes, indeed. She is in good looks. She has done something with her hair."

What the devil? Nathaniel was thinking. Ede had been talking about *Lavinia*? He might have felt amused if he had not been inwardly grimacing over what he had just revealed about his feelings for Sophie.

How would he ever be able to call upon Lavinia in the future without feeling the presence of Sophie there—even after she had gone? She would be at Bowood too a few times. His home would be haunted by her presence for a long time to come, perhaps for the rest of his life.

How would he bear it?

An invitation to take tea at Bowood Manor was delivered the following morning. Sophia would have been quite happy to make some excuse if Lavinia had been so inclined. But Lavinia was of the opinion that it might be discourteous not to go.

"There are some social niceties that even I cannot ignore, alas," she had said with a sigh.

She had done a fair deal of sighing since Sophia's arrival,

especially since the visit of the afternoon before. They had both agreed that it was very civil of the gentlemen to have called, though if they had come because they thought male company essential to female happiness, then they were sadly mistaken. But Lord Pelham had always struck Lavinia as one of the most conceited gentlemen of her acquaintance—he thought altogether too much of the power of those blue eyes of his. And Nat always thought he must call on her at least once a day lest she fall into some dreadful indiscretion out of which she would never be able to fall out again without his assistance.

They had spent the rest of the evening assuring each other, as they had been doing since Sophia's arrival, that living alone and independently of male interference was really heaven on earth. At least that was what they seemed to imply, Sophia thought, even if they did not use those exact words. It was almost as if they had to reassure each other so that they would convince themselves.

Lavinia, Sophia had come to suspect, had a strange fondness for Eden, even though the two of them could scarcely be civil to each other. He was, Sophia guessed, the gentleman about whom Lavinia had been unhappy during that last meeting in London. Poor Lavinia. It did not seem likely that Eden shared her feelings. He was, Sophia feared, uncatchable.

They walked to Bowood, the weather being fine, though not as lovely as the day before. But the park and the house did not need the enhancement of blue sky and sunshine in order to appear splendid indeed to her eyes. The park was all woodland and green lawns. If there were flower gardens, they were at the back. The house itself, solid and imposing even if not one of the more massive mansions of England, was at the top of a steady rise. Below the slope to one side of it was a lake, shaded by willows and sturdier oaks.

And it all might have been hers, she thought with a heavy heart as she approached the house. She might have been mistress of Bowood.

Nathaniel's sister Margaret, Lady Ketterly, received them

on their arrival and took them to the drawing room, where they were served tea and Sophia was introduced to other houseguests and to the other sisters. Edwin and Beatrice were there too, of course, as were Sarah and Lewis. Moira and Kenneth, who had arrived the day before, came to speak with her. She felt less awkward than she had expected to feel—until Nathaniel appeared in the room.

Was he too feeling aware, she wondered, that she might have been mistress of all this? Or had his two offers of marriage been forgotten since they had been made out of a sense of honor and obligation? Perhaps he did not feel the awkwardness at all. Certainly he had shown no sign of any yesterday at Lavinia's. He had even called her *my dear* in that kindly, friendly tone he had always used.

And then he was at her side, smiling at her.

"Sophie," he said, "would you like to see the house after tea? I have not given Moira and Ken the guided tour yet either."

She could feel herself flushing. But there could be no harm in it if Moira and Kenneth were to come too. And she did, perversely, long to see the whole of the house, to store away memories so that she would be able to picture him here—so that she would be able to torture herself with details.

"Thank you, Nathaniel," she said. "I would like that."

But Moira and Kenneth, when applied to, explained that they had promised to walk back to the rectory with Edwina and Valentine. Eden was going with them.

"We will take Lavinia too, if she will come," Moira said. "I long to see her cottage. Margaret says it is very picturesque."

"Oh," Sophia said quickly, "perhaps I should go too, then."

"I believe, Sophie," Kenneth said with a grin, "that Nat's nose will be severely out of joint if we all desert him. You must stay and be suitably impressed with the house. We will see it later, Nat." He winked at his friend.

Sophia looked at Nathaniel in some dismay.

"I will walk back to Lavinia's with you later, Sophie," he said. "Please do stay."

It was true, she thought. There was no awkwardness in his manner at all. Had she hoped there would be? That what they had shared in the past would at least have made him a little embarrassed with her? He had probably almost forgotten about that too, or at least had relegated it to the category of unimportant memory. He could hardly, after all, remember every woman with whom he had ever lain.

What a humbling and humiliating thought!

"Thank you," she said.

"Nicely done, Ken," Eden said as the six of them set out on the walk to the village. The Reverend Valentine Scott and his wife strode on a little ahead of them. "I doubt they even suspected."

"Thank Moira," Kenneth said. "She has a more devious mind than mine. But getting them alone together amidst these hordes is no easy matter."

"I am really not sure anything can be accomplished anyway," Eden said, "unless she can be made to feel the same way as he obviously does. It seems doubtful. Good old Sophie would probably not recognize a romantic situation if it punched her in the nose."

"But looking at it from a female perspective," Moira said, "one can see quite clearly that he is well-nigh irresistible. He has the loveliest smile."

"*Irresistible,* Moira?" Kenneth was looking down at her with raised eyebrows.

She tossed her glance to the sky. "To those ladies who have not already succumbed to the charms of someone even more so, of course," she said.

"Of course," he agreed, and they grinned at each other.

"Pardon me," Lavinia said sharply, "but do I understand that I have somehow become involved in a *plot*? Are you by any chance trying to get Nat and Sophie matched up?"

Eden sighed. "I should have warned you," he said, addressing Moira and Kenneth, "not to say a word in present company. Men, to Miss Bergland's way of looking at the world, were created merely as a punishment to be imposed upon ladies by other men. And since Nat is the man who has oppressed her with his guardianship for years and Sophie is her friend, she will doubtless have a fit of the vapors at the very idea of trying to promote a match between them."

"Do *you* have fits of the vapors, Lord Pelham?" Lavinia asked. "Must *I* merely because I am a woman? Do try not to be ridiculous."

Moira laughed. "You asked for that, Eden," she said. "Bravo, Lavinia."

"Actually," Lavinia said, "Sophie *does* have a fondness for Nat. More than a fondness, I suspect."

"She does?" Eden and Kenneth spoke together.

"She was severely discomposed by his visit yesterday," Lavinia said.

"Sophie does not become discomposed by visits from her friends," Kenneth said, frowning. "But she was disturbed by Nat's?"

"But it is a harebrained notion to draw from that mere observation the conclusion that Sophie is fond of him," Eden said.

"Thank you," Lavinia said curtly. "I have better evidence than that, sir. She has one of Nat's handkerchiefs."

"By Jove," Eden said, smiting his forehead with the heel of one hand. "Proof positive. What better evidence could any man ask? She has his *handkerchief*."

"Ignore him, Lavinia," Moira advised, still laughing. "He is being quite ill-mannered. Do tell us more."

"I called on her in London just before she left for Gloucestershire," Lavinia said. "Almost everything was packed, but there was a handkerchief lying on the arm of a chair. I picked it up absently and held it in one hand, hardly seeing it until Sophie said that her father's name was George. She was indicating the handkerchief, and sure enough there was a letter *G* embroidered across one corner.

But the shape of the letter was very distinctive. It was the same as Nat has embroidered on all his handkerchiefs and printed on his ring. It was Nat's handkerchief. It was nothing in itself, perhaps. But if it really was nothing, why did she make up that story about her father and then snatch it away from the arm of the chair after I had set it down and put it into her pocket?''

"Why indeed?'' Kenneth agreed.

"It would appear that old Nat has some hope yet, then,'' Eden said. "Is this the lowest level to which we can sink, Ken? We have become nothing better than *matchmakers*?''

"Sophie and Nat.'' Kenneth was shaking his head. "It still does not quite seem possible.''

"Well I think they would be quite perfect together,'' Moira said with some spirit. "They are both amiable and kind.''

"And Sophie really is in good looks,'' Eden said. "Nat remarked on it yesterday and I took a good look today. One might even say she has gone into a second bloom.''

"How delightful!'' Lavinia said. "A woman is only eight and twenty years old and yet when she is looking handsome she must be in *second* bloom.''

"It is when one talks of third blooms that offense might be taken,'' Eden said.

Lavinia clucked her tongue.

# TWENTY-TWO

"I AM SO SORRY, NATHAN-iel," Sophia said as they left the drawing room together.

"For what?" He offered her his arm.

She was almost overwhelmed with embarrassment—and awareness. "For all this," she said, shrugging her shoulders. "For feeling obliged to come here. For making *you* feel obliged to invite me. For this tête-à-tête."

"Sophie," he said, leading her down the stairs to begin the tour on the ground floor, "have we come to this, my dear? To being awkward with each other after all? We were once close friends. Nothing has happened really to change that, has it? Can we not simply be friends again?"

"Yes, I suppose." She smiled at him, though she was feeling suffocated by that part of their relationship that was not friendship. "Beatrice and Edwin would have been hurt if I had not come, and Lewis too, I believe. And I wanted to see Sarah again now that she is returning from her wedding trip. She and Harry look very happy, do they not?"

"Indeed yes." He opened a door, having waved away the servant who had crossed the tiled hall toward them. "This is the library—my personal domain. My favorite room."

Yes, it would be. It was a large and elegantly furnished

room. Three walls were lined with books. There was a huge oak desk covered rather untidily with papers and inkwells and pens. There was a fire laid, though not lit, in the hearth. There was a large and comfortable-looking leather chair on either side of it. It was an impressive room but also a cozy room that looked lived in. It was very masculine.

This was his favorite room, Sophia thought, releasing her hold on Nathaniel's arm and walking farther into it. This was where he spent much of his time—alone. He sat here in the evenings, reading a book. She touched the headrest of one of the chairs, the one that looked more worn than the other—and there was a book on the small table beside it. She picked it up.

*"The Pilgrim's Progress?"* she said.

"Yes." He was still standing just inside the door, watching her. "It is a book I have always intended to read and never have read until now."

He sat here working, she thought, moving to the desk, running her hand over the surface closest to her. He read his letters here and wrote letters. To all his friends. To Rex and Kenneth and Eden and others she did not know. She was his friend, he had just said. But he would never write to her here or read any letter from her.

The tall windows looked out over the tree-dotted lawn that sloped down to the lake. He would stand here, she thought, standing there herself and gazing out, when he wished to think over some problem or when he simply wished to relax.

"It is a beautiful room," she said.

"Yes."

He had not moved from just inside the door, she noticed. He had not pointed out any features of the room. He had just stood there in silence, watching her. He had probably intended to have her just peep into this room and move on. They would take all day seeing the house at this pace. She turned her head and smiled at him.

"I'll show you the music room next," he said.

He asked an abrupt question when they were in the conservatory later, looking at tropical plants that must make it a veritable paradise during the winter.

"Does Lavinia appear to you to be in good spirits?" he asked.

"Oh." She smiled at him. "You really must not worry about her, Nathaniel. She is almost five and twenty and she has made her own choices about the sort of life she wishes to lead."

He nodded. "She was annoyed, I suppose, at Eden's calling on her yesterday?" he asked.

She searched his face. "Irritated," she said, and smiled.

"Hmm." He smiled too. "It would be the most unlikely match in history."

"An exaggeration surely," she said. "But I am afraid she will suffer heartbreak—not that Lavinia is the sort to invite quite that disaster. She has firm control of her feelings, I believe. Eden is not ready yet to settle down. I doubt he ever will be."

"He is rattled," Nathaniel said. "I believe he feels an attachment to her but is fighting the feeling every step of the way."

"Oh," she said. "And Lavinia too."

"Perhaps they need some help?" he suggested. "A shove in the right direction? If I contrive with Ken over the coming day or two to get them alone together, you will not feel obliged to chaperon her, Sophie?"

She raised her eyebrows and then laughed. "You—the very proper cousin and guardian—are plotting to leave her *un*chaperoned?" she asked.

"Well." He chuckled. "I am still determined to be rid of her by hook or by crook before her thirtieth birthday, you know."

"I will not feel obliged to chaperon her," she assured him. "I never have, if you will recall, Nathaniel. The very idea! I am only four years older than she."

They grinned conspiratorially at each other and Sophia felt herself relax for the first time that day. Perhaps that other relationship could be forgotten after all. Perhaps they could be just friends again—*matchmaking* friends. She was not at all sure their schemes would work. If left alone together, Lavinia and Eden would probably have a massive quarrel and never speak to each other again. But that would be their business. At least it was worth trying to make them understand that perhaps they could make a match of it.

It was half an hour later before Sophia and Nathaniel came to the gallery, a lovely room that ran the whole width of the house on the upper floor, long windows at each end. It was bathed in late-afternoon light as they moved from portrait to portrait and she learned some details about the Gascoigne ancestors.

She was particularly charmed by a family portrait of a youthful Nathaniel with his parents and his sisters, the youngest of them—Eleanor—a bonneted baby on her mother's lap.

"You must have been a happy family," she said. Nathaniel was standing at his seated father's shoulder, smiling at the artist, his chest puffed out with pride.

"We were." He chuckled. "But I can remember my growing disgust as my mother continued to produce nothing but sisters for me."

"But now the last of them is about to be settled," she said, "and you will have peace and independence. No more women underfoot. You must be very happy."

"Yes," he said. "Sophie, are *you* happy?"

The uncomfortable tension between them returned instantly, though it seemed an innocent enough question.

"Of course," she said too quickly.

"You have set up your new home?" he asked her. "Describe it to me. I would like to be able to picture it."

"No, not yet," she told him, turning away from the painting, the last to be seen. "I am still with Thomas. I—I have not yet seen quite the house I want. And I may go somewhere else where I can have more independence—Bristol, perhaps, or even Bath. I do not know. I have not quite made up my mind."

"You do not—regret the way everything turned out in London?" he asked her.

She shook her head firmly and moved toward the window at one end of the gallery. And there—oh, yes, *there* were the flowers at the back of the house, banks and parterres and meadows of them, a glorious profusion of bloom and color.

"Sophie—" he said quietly. He had come up quite close behind her, she could tell. She hunched her shoulders and said what she had in no way planned to say, what she had not dreamed of saying ever to any living soul.

"I need to tell you something," she said. "About those letters."

There was a short silence. If he did not break it, she thought, the silence might stretch forever. She might never know the release she had not realized until this moment she had always craved.

"The letters Ken burned?" he said then. "You do not have to say anything, Sophie. None of us looked at them. I do not care who she was. I care only that Walter did that to you. Perhaps it is as well for all of us that he is not still alive."

"They were not written to a woman." She closed her eyes and bowed her head.

The silence stretched longer this time.

"His name was Lieutenant Richard Calder," she said. "I did not know him. Perhaps you did. Or perhaps you remember the name."

"The man he died trying to save." Nathaniel's voice sounded almost shockingly normal.

"Ironic, is it not?" She chuckled without humor. "Walter was decorated posthumously and I was awarded a house and a pension because of his great bravery in dying to save an inferior officer—his lover."

"Sophie," he said.

She should not be burdening him with this. He would at best be dreadfully embarrassed. At worst he would be horrified and disgusted. The latter was what she had always

feared in London, during the spring, while Boris Pinter was
still blackmailing her. Somehow it did not seem to matter
now. She felt compelled to tell him.

"I did not know," she said. "Those letters were written
over a two-year span, Nathaniel. They were tender, passionate letters that made quite clear the fact that a physical
love affair existed between them. But he was very discreet.
I did not even suspect. He would have to be discreet, of
course. He would have been disgraced as an officer if the
truth had been discovered. And—it is a criminal offense.
He could have—one can be hanged for it, can one not?"

"Yes," he said.

"If Lieutenant Calder had been equally discreet," she
said, "I would have been none the wiser. Neither would
Boris Pinter have been. But he was the one to sort through
the dead man's effects—and he had kept the letters."

"Oh, Sophie." He did not *sound* disgusted, she thought,
reaching out to grip the window ledge with both hands.
"He must have loved you too. Perhaps—"

"Oh, I did know," she said quickly, "about his—preferences. How could I not? He married me when I was eighteen and still naive enough to expect a happily-ever-after.
He was not a cruel man. I do not believe he intended to
make me suffer. I believe he married me only partly to give
himself respectability. He also, I think, wanted to convince
himself that he was—normal. He—I—oh, Nathaniel." She
buried her face in her hands. "On our wedding night—
afterward—he ran across the room and behind the screen
and—and *vomited*."

The gallery was uncarpeted. She could hear behind her
the click of his booted feet as he walked away from her.
She gasped against her hands. She had had *no idea* she was
about to reveal those intimate, nightmarish details of her
shame. How could she have just said that aloud—to Nathaniel of all people?

She could hear his footsteps coming back again until they
stopped a short distance behind her. She did not believe she
would ever again be able to move or look up.

"Tell me the rest now," he said. "Tell me whatever you need to tell me, Sophie. I am your friend."

She could say nothing for a while. She was biting hard on her upper lip, fighting the ache of tears in her throat. Could anyone have ever said anything more purely precious to her?

"After a week like that or almost as bad as that," she said eventually, "I asked him to send me home to my father. That was when he told me. He begged me to stay with him. And I could not bear the thought of going back home and admitting my inadequacy. And so we struck a bargain. We would live together as man and wife in the eyes of the world—or of the *army*—but in reality we would be each other's companion. We both promised to remain faithful to our vows and live celibate lives. I kept my promise. I believed he had kept his—until Boris Pinter came to me with one of those letters."

There was a lengthy silence again. But she knew he was still there. She would have heard him walking away.

"And so," he said, "after the first week of your marriage when you were eighteen, there was no one—until me?"

"No." She shook her head.

"And I suppose," he said, "it was after that first week that you went into hiding."

"What?" she said. She was holding to the window ledge again and watching Lewis and Georgina strolling in the garden among the parterres. They were holding hands. They looked young and innocent. They looked as if they expected a happily-ever-after to be awaiting them after tomorrow's ceremony. She prayed with all her heart that they were right.

"Was it then," Nathaniel asked, "that you started dressing in clothes that did not become you and that you cultivated the placid, cheerful, comradely manner of a woman twice your age? Was it then, Sophie, that you began to hide your beauty and your femininity from the world? And even perhaps from yourself?"

"My reason told me," she said, "that even the most

beautiful, most charming, most fascinating woman in the world would not have tempted Walter. He explained to me—and I believed him—that admiring and wanting other m-men came as naturally to him as admiring women came to most men. It was not something he chose to do out of any sense of perversity or out of any lack on my part. It was the way he was created. I did not hate him, Nathaniel, or even dislike him. But—oh, but I *felt* so inadequate. I *felt* that if only I had been a little lovelier or a little more fashionable or a little more experienced . . . Or if I had been a *lady,* perhaps. He could not bear to *touch* me.''

''It is damned well not *fair,*'' Nathaniel said, surprising her with both his choice of words and the fury with which he spoke them, ''that you were then made to suffer what you were suffering when we met you this spring, Sophie. Why did you do it? Why did you not simply laugh in Pinter's face and tell him to do his worst? Or come to us for help once you had met us again?''

She turned at last to look at him. His face was set into hard lines, the way she had sometimes seen it after battle, when there were dead and wounded soldiers to be seen to. It was also very pale.

''He was my husband, Nathaniel,'' she said. ''He was a decent man—yes he was, despite his infidelity. And he was a good officer. He always did his duty. He fought bravely even if he was never brilliant as the four of you were. By a strange twist of fate he achieved great fame after his death—but he *did* save the Duke of Wellington and other men of prominence. And he *did* give his life in an attempt to save a comrade. There would have been a dreadful scandal if the truth had then come out. He would have achieved a notoriety to surpass the fame. His name would have been spoken with abhorrence and scorn.''

''And yet he betrayed you,'' he said.

''That would have been no excuse for me,'' she said. ''Besides, there were the living to think of and they were perhaps even more important to me. Edwin and Beatrice are good people. Sarah has just made a good marriage, which she would not have made if the truth had come out and scandal had broken. Lewis is about to make a good marriage with your sister—that would not have taken place. My brother's business is thriving, a good thing, as he has four young children to support. The business might have faltered if his connection to such a notorious—criminal had been made known. And there was me too." She smiled fleetingly. "It feels good to have an independence and a good name."

"Why did you not at least tell *us*?" he asked her. "We could have helped you long before we did, Sophie."

"I did not want you to know," she said. "You were gods to me, Nathaniel—and that is only a little exaggerated. You were all very precious to me—you most of all. I could not bear the thought of seeing the disgust on your faces. . . ."

"Sophie." He frowned. "Dear God, Sophie, do you know so little of the nature of friendship?"

"Keeping secrets," she said, "trusting no one with my deepest self became second nature to me, you know. I had to stand alone from the age of eighteen on. I do not complain. I believe that in some ways I have become a stronger person than I would otherwise have been. But I have always valued the few close friendships I have had. I did not see any of you for three years. But the letter you wrote me after the Carlton House business was very precious to me. And when I saw you again that morning in the park, I knew all of a rush that you had been—well, unforgettable. And that even if I were not to see you again for another three years, or ever, I could not risk losing your friendship."

"And yet," he said, "you told us all to go to the devil—in more ladylike words, of course."

"I know why Boris Pinter hated Walter so much," she said. "And why Walter blocked his promotion."

"Yes." He held up one hand. "It does not take too much imagination to put together the pieces, does it? Sophie, thank you for telling me all this. I know you are dredging up all you have kept ruthlessly suppressed for years. And

I know you could do it with no one but a special friend.
Thank you for trusting me.''

"Do you hate me?'' Tears sprang to her eyes despite all
her efforts to stop them. "Do you hate the thought of Georgina marrying Lewis—Walter's nephew?''

"Lewis is simply Lewis,'' he said. "He is a young man
who has won my sister's heart and who is eligible enough
and amiable enough to have won my approval. I am happy
for them both. And you, Sophie? I believe you know my
feelings for you. They are certainly not hatred. You look
drained. Let me hold you?''

What did he mean? she wondered. No, she did not know
what his feelings for her were. *What did he mean?* But the
answer did not seem to matter too much at the moment.
He was right. She was weary right through to the marrow
of her bones. She took the few steps that separated them
and let his arms come about her and draw her against him.
She rested her face among the folds of his neckcloth and
breathed in the familiar, comforting scent of his cologne.

For now he was her dear friend and it was enough.

"I did not mean to burden you with all that,'' she said
after several minutes had passed.

"It is no burden,'' he said. "It is a privilege.''

"Nathaniel.'' She looked up into his face—ah, so very
dear. "You are the kindest man I have ever known.''

He bent his head and kissed her briefly on the lips.

She drew away from him when he lifted his head again.
She was still feeling as if someone had picked her up and
squeezed her dry—though she felt strangely calm and com-
forted after all the embarrassing admissions she had made
to him.

"I need fresh air,'' she said. "I am going to walk back
to Lavinia's. Do you mind if I go alone?''

His eyes searched hers. "Not if it is what you wish,'' he
said.

"It is.'' She smiled ruefully. "And you have a wedding
to prepare for tomorrow, Nathaniel. I have taken enough of
your time. I hope all will go well, but I am sure it will.''

"With four sisters even apart from Georgie herself, and all of them claiming to be authorities on weddings," he said, "how could it fail?"

They smiled at each other until she turned determinedly away and hurried back along the gallery, leaving him where he was.

He would have kissed her again, she thought, if she had not turned the moment. And perhaps he would have offered for her again out of the deep sympathy he had been feeling for her—how could she have ever feared that Nathaniel of all people would have reacted with disgust?

If he had offered, she might have been weak enough this time to accept. She hurried down the stairs and out into the brightness of the near sunshine—the clouds rode high in the sky. She had seen his home, she had seen *him* again, she had shared her deepest self with him, and she had felt the gentle strength of his arms.

And she *needed* him.

No, she did not, she thought, lifting her face to the sky and striding down the slope in the direction of the village. She did not *need* anyone. And she loved him too dearly to burden him with herself.

Sometime between now and tomorrow, she thought, she was going to have to get herself in the mood for a wedding. She put a spring in her step and a smile on her lips. Unconsciously she put on the old Sophie.

The sun had merely been taking a breather, as Margaret put it the following day. The wedding day itself was brilliantly sunny, a perfect day in every way. Though she would not have noticed, Georgina said through her tears as she hugged everyone good-bye on the terrace before being handed into the carriage by her new husband and driven off on her wedding trip—she would not have noticed if it had poured with rain all day, or even if it had *snowed*.

"Thank you. Thank you for everything," she said, clinging to Nathaniel's neck. "You are the best of brothers. Oh, Nathaniel, I am so *happy*."

"I am glad you told me," he said, chuckling. "I would never have guessed it. Away you go now."

"Oh," she said, "I wish, I *wish* you will find the same happiness one day soon."

And then she was gone and waving, smiling and tearful, from the window as the carriage lurched into motion, Lewis by her side. Half the wedding guests, it seemed, had come out onto the terrace to see them on their way. There was a great deal of noise and laughter—and tears from Lady Houghton and Lady Perry, her daughter, and from Nathaniel's sisters.

It would not take a great deal to draw a few from him too, he thought, feeling foolish. He turned to go back into the house.

"A walk, Nat?" Kenneth asked him with a wink. "Eden has already agreed that the house is to be avoided at all costs for the next hour or so. Too much sentimentality for him, I believe."

"Weddings are enough to put the wind up the hardiest of fellows," Eden said.

Moira, Nathaniel saw at a glance, had her arms linked through Lavinia's and Sophie's. She had been roped into this conspiracy too, then. It did not seem today that it was one likely to succeed. Eden and Lavinia had stayed as far from each other all day as the occasion had permitted. But then so had he and Sophie.

He ached for her. Yesterday he had cheered himself with the belief that he must be special to her if she had confided all that to him. She need not have done so—they had told her in London that as far as they were concerned the whole matter of Walter and his love affair was a closed book. And he had thought of those words she had spoken: *You were all very precious to me—you most of all.* He had remembered her telling him in London that he had always been her favorite.

Yesterday the situation had seemed promising to him. Today she had kept her distance. But then so had he. He was afraid to bring on the moment only to have his hopes dashed yet again—and finally this time. Sometimes it was better to live in painful hope.

They walked toward the woods below the house, toward the quiet privacy and welcome shades of the paths that had been set out through them. Lavinia walked with Kenneth, Eden with Sophie, he with Moira.

"Now," Moira said to him after a couple of minutes, her voice shaking with amusement. "This is the perfect place, Nathaniel."

He cleared his throat. "I say," he called ahead, turning everyone's attention his way. "I want to show the folly down at the lake to Moira and Ken—and Sophie has not seen it either. You have, Ede. Perhaps you and Lavinia would like to keep walking and we will catch up to you."

"Splendid idea," Kenneth said, a little too heartily for theatrical brilliance. "It should not take long."

"Oh yes," Sophie said. "Margaret told me to be sure not to miss seeing the folly."

Amazingly it worked. Lavinia and Eden went striding off toward the woods without protest, three feet of space between them, and the four conspirators struck off in the direction of the lake.

"If they do not come to blows," Nathaniel said, "perhaps it will only be because they will be too far apart to trade insults."

Three of them chuckled.

"Oh dear," Moira said, stopping in order to set one hand to her brow.

Kenneth was all instant concern. "What is it, my love?" he asked, setting an arm about her waist.

"I fear it is the heat," she said. "How very provoking."

"You never could stand direct sunlight for more than a few minutes at a time," Kenneth said. "I should have run up for your parasol."

"I just need a few minutes somewhere cool," she said. "I will return to the house alone. You go on, Kenneth."

"I most certainly will not," he said. "Lean on me. We

will be back there in no time. You carry on to the lake, Nat. And Sophie, of course.''

She was all wilting weariness and he was all tender concern as they walked away—at least that was the story their backs told. In reality they were both laughing softly.

''I feel positively *sinful*,'' Moira said. ''And it probably will not work with either couple, Kenneth. But Eden was so eager to follow the plan to isolate Nathaniel and Sophie, and Nathaniel was so eager to isolate Eden and Lavinia. Oh, we will surely burn in hell for this.''

''If it *does* work,'' he said with a sigh, ''we might well have a couple more weddings to attend, love. And we will have no one but ourselves to blame. We already have to go to Kent to admire the new baby and to make sure that Rex is bearing up well enough under the strain. Will we ever get back to Cornwall and Dunbarton, do you suppose?''

''Absence really does make the heart grow fonder,'' she said.

''When we *do* get back there,'' he said, ''we are going to get to earnest work on number two at last. Be warned.''

''Mmm,'' she said. ''It sounds like bliss. If there *are* to be two more weddings, one must at least hope that Nathaniel and Eden are impatient enough to rush out for special licenses.''

''I suppose we could suggest it in some innocent, roundabout manner,'' he said, and they both laughed again.

''Don't forget to wilt,'' he said. ''I doubt they are still watching, but they may be.''

Moira wilted.

# TWENTY-THREE

"WELL," LAVINIA SAID AF-
ter they had walked some distance in silence and with a
ridiculous amount of space between them. "It had better
work today, that is all I can say. It certainly did not work
yesterday. Sophie came back to the cottage looking more
placidly cheerful than ever. She did not mention Nat even
once during the evening."

"A promising sign?" Eden suggested.

Lavinia tossed her glance toward the sky. "On the assumption that all women are contrary creatures, I suppose,"
she said, "and must say and do the exact opposite of what
they mean?"

"One must confess," he said, "that it can be unnerving.
One never knows where one stands with females."

"Perhaps if *men* were not so devious," she said,
"women would not need to be."

They strolled onward, forced to within two feet of each
other when the path narrowed as it entered the trees. There
was also a delicious coolness there and a shady, fragrant
sense of privacy.

"We should always speak our minds, then," he asked
her, "and risk having our faces slapped?"

"You seem," she said, "to feel a terror of having that

happen to you, Lord Pelham. Could it be that you do not have the confidence in your charms that you affect to have?''

"It could be," he said, looking sidelong at her, "that I have naughty thoughts that no true lady would wish to hear expressed aloud.''

"Oh goodness," she said, spreading one hand over her bosom. "Pardon me while I have a fit of the vapors. But I have forgot—I believe we have already established, sir, that I am not a true lady. At least it is what you have accused me of on more than one occasion.''

"Have I?" he said, raising his eyebrows and fingering the ribbon of his quizzing glass. "Could I possibly have been so ungentlemanly?''

"I do believe," she said, "you are as little the gentleman as I am the lady.''

"Dear me," he said. "We *are* speaking our minds today. Are you happy in your role as village spinster?''

She looked at him scornfully. "Are you happy in yours as society bachelor?" she asked.

"Touché." He twirled his quizzing glass on its ribbon and looked about him. "This place seems designed for dalliance, does it not?''

"Oh, decidedly," she agreed. "God created the trees and the forest for that sole purpose, I daresay.''

"It would be a shame to confound the plans of the Almighty," he said.

It was Lavinia's turn to look at *him* sidelong. "Nat will be along soon," she said. "He would blacken both your eyes if he found you six inches closer to me.''

"Oh, I think not," he said. "I do not think he will be coming along behind us, that is. He will be too busy with Sophie. And if I were you, I would not expect Ken and Moira either. They are leaving you and me alone. It was a double plot. They think I do not know, but I know my friends every bit as well as they know themselves, I believe.''

Lavinia had stopped in her tracks and was staring at him.

"They are leaving *you and me* alone?" she said, aghast.

"You and me, as in us," he said. "You ought to train yourself not to blush quite so deeply, you know. The color of your face clashes with your hair."

"I am not blushing, sir!" She glared at him. "I am furious. Whoever would think that you and I should be left together?"

"Nat and Ken apparently," he said. "Oh, and Moira too. She is no innocent. It was probably all her plan. I wonder what excuse she used to get Ken back to the house."

"Well!" Lavinia drew an audible breath. "I am going back to my cottage, sir. I would suggest that you too return to the house. Good day to you."

"Lavinia," he said, and raised his glass to his eye.

"I do not recall," she said, "giving you leave to make free with my name, sir."

"To steal a phrase," he said, sounding infinitely bored, "do try not to be ridiculous, Lavinia."

"Well!" was all she could think of to say. She seemed to have forgotten that she had taken her leave and could now turn and hurry away. He was not detaining her by force.

"Precisely," he said. "If our friends—including your *guardian*—believe that we might make a match of it, do you not think we should give the matter some consideration? Find out what makes them think so?"

"I would as soon be matched with a toad," she said.

He pursed his lips and considered her words. "I doubt it," he said at last. "I believe you wish to be persuaded."

"You may believe what you wish, my lord," she said. "I shall have a word with Nat tomorrow."

"Kiss me," he said.

Lavinia drew breath to speak but snapped her mouth shut again. "Why?" she asked warily.

"Because I have been wanting you to since the last time," he said. "Because I have not been able to forget it or you. Because if I leave here tomorrow without settling something with you, I might well be haunted by you for the rest of my life. Because if anyone is ever to tame me, you are the one. And if anyone is going to tame you, I suspect it will have to be me. Because I lo—oh, the devil, now *that* is too much for me to say. Kiss me.''

"To how many women have you delivered this speech?'' she asked, her eyes narrowing on him.

"To one," he said. "You."

"I am no wild animal to be tamed," she told him.

"Neither am I," he said. "Are you going to kiss me?"

"I do not know," she said.

"What are you uncertain of?" he asked her, and took one step toward her. She took a step back, realized what she had done, and stepped forward again so that they were almost toe-to-toe.

"I do not trust you not to mock me afterward for falling into the trap," she said. "If you want a kiss, then *you* kiss *me*."

He did so.

And then, after they had come up for air a minute or so later, both panting, he kissed her again.

And after they had drawn an inch apart another few minutes later and gazed at each other as if to verify each other's identity, *she* kissed *him*.

"That does it," he said when their mouths were free once more—but still almost touching. "You are not going to tell me after that that you are indifferent to me."

"It was just a kiss," she said shakily.

"No," he said. "Allow me to know more about such matters than you, Lavinia. That was more than a kiss. And it was more than just physical. Are you prepared to see me leave here tomorrow never to return?"

She stared at him.

"I could not quite face it myself," he said. "I have this terrifying notion that I should return to my estate, which I visited for almost the first time in my life a month ago, and make a home of it. I have this even more dizzying idea that I should take a wife there and start rusticating in earnest—and even, heaven help me, setting up my nursery. I'll do it too, if you will come with me and do it all with me."

"How ridiculous," she said without any of her usual spirit.

"Yes." He gave her no argument. He kissed her instead.

"Well," he said at last. "Are we going to do it? Or are we going to stand here forever, wearing out our lips?"

"Oh," she said, "I think we are going to do it, my lord. Just do not expect me to be a biddable wife, that is all."

"A biddable wife?" he said in disgust. "What a ghastly notion. I will expect—no, I will insist upon—at least one argument a day. Starting at breakfast. Call me Eden."

"Eden," she said.

"What a biddable woman you are." He grinned at her— and kissed her again before she could mouth her protest. "Now I think we ought to go slinking off to the lake to see if Nat and Sophie have finished their tête-à-tête. If they have, we had better hint to Nat that I will be making a formal appearance in his library tomorrow morning or sooner. I daresay he will be so amazed that we could knock him down with the proverbial feather if we felt so inclined."

"Eden," she said, tightening her arms about his waist when he would have drawn away, "say it."

"It?" He grimaced.

"What you would not say earlier," she said. "Say it. I want to hear it."

"You certainly enjoy taking your pound of flesh, do you not?" he said, frowning.

Lavinia smiled her dazzling smile at him.

"Lord," he said, "you had better not do too much of that until we are standing beside—or better yet lying in— our marriage bed. I have enough to cope with. Now let me see—*it*." He cleared his throat. "Here we go, then. I love you. Was that it? I hope I have not been through that torture only to find it was something else you wanted to hear."

"No, that was it," she said. "It sounded lovely. You can say it every day after we are married so that it will come more easily to your tongue—at breakfast each morning, I believe. I love you too, you know.''

''Unfair,'' he said. ''You did not even find it difficult, did you?''

She set her forehead on his shoulder then and his arms tightened about her.

''Yes, I did,'' she said. ''Oh, yes I did. I have always been terrified of love, Eden. I never wanted just marriage as other women seem to do and perhaps a little romance to make it palatable. I have wanted the stuff of poetry and of dreams. I would rather settle for nothing at all than a mere shadow of the real thing. This has to be the real thing. It *has* to be. Tell me now if it is not and we will part and go our separate ways. Just never come back, that is all, even to see Nat. If you leave now, stay away forever.''

He held her for a long time, saying nothing.

''Now you have *really* put the wind up me,'' he said at last. ''It feels real enough to me, Lavinia. I never expected this to happen. I never *wanted* it to happen. It is not the sort of thing I would imagine merely because I wanted a wife. I have never *wanted* a wife. It is real, right enough. I love you right enough.''

''I knew,'' she said into his shoulder, ''that I would squeeze the words out of you again if I tried.''

They both laughed. But they both knew that her words had not been spoken out of anything less than the very depths of her heart. And they both knew that he would not have surrendered his freedom for anything except a deep and abiding love.

''Let's go and find Nat,'' he said.

''Yes.'' She drew away from him and smoothed out the folds of her dress. She looked at him and smiled sheepishly. ''Oh, it is you, is it? All that close stuff was being done with you?''

''It is I,'' he agreed meekly, offering his arm. ''We had better get this wedding out of the way as soon as we can. You know absolutely nothing yet, my love, about close stuff. Ah—I knew I could get you to blush again if I tried.''

• • •

"Hoist with my own petard," Nathaniel muttered.

"What?" Sophia turned her attention from the retreating backs of Kenneth and Moira to look at him.

"Nothing," he said. "Let me show you the lake and the folly. This was always my favorite part of the park. I always loved swimming and boating here. I also love just sitting and dreaming."

"Yes, I can see why." They were approaching the bank of the lake and the trees that grew beside it or overhung it. "You have a beautiful home, Nathaniel."

And now and at last it was all his. He had longed for this day. To know that his sisters were all well settled in homes of their own and Bowood was his alone. To know that he could do as he pleased here and come and go as he pleased. Today it seemed an empty triumph.

And he was afraid to hope.

"There it is," he said, pointing to their right. It was a small Greek temple of gray stone, complete with columns and carved pediment. "Foolish, is it not? But that is why such buildings are called *follies,* I suppose."

"It is charming," she said, and she smiled as they walked toward it.

It had been built in a carefully chosen spot so that it was hidden by the slope and the trees from the house above. And when one sat on the stone bench inside, one could see only the bank in front and the lake and the trees beyond. One felt surrounded by wilderness.

Sophia stepped inside and sat down. Nathaniel stood outside, his hands clasped behind him, watching her look about at her surroundings. The gardener always kept well-tended pots of flowers inside the folly during the summer.

"Sophie," he said, "you are looking so very pretty, my dear. I love these light dresses you have been wearing. And you have cut your hair. It is very becoming worn like that, though I suspect it might look less glorious when worn down than it used to look."

She turned her eyes from the lake to look at him briefly and smile.

"And you have gained weight," he said. He chuckled. "That is not usually a tactful thing to say to a lady, is it? But it looks good on you."

She smiled again, though she was looking now at the lake.

"It was a lovely wedding," she said. "Georgina looked beautiful and was very obviously happy. You must be happy for her—and also very glad to have all the busy festivities over."

"By this time tomorrow," he said, "almost all the guests will be gone. In a few more days I will have Bowood to myself."

"That must be a pleasant thought," she said.

"Sophie." He leaned his shoulder against the column to one side of the doorway. "Are *you* happy? Does the thought of returning to Gloucestershire and choosing a new home, perhaps in a place where you know no one and will have to start all over again—does the thought excite you?"

"Of course." But she did not look at him.

The same question, the same answer as they had exchanged yesterday.

"Do you know why I brought you here?" he asked her. "And why I showed you around the house yesterday?"

She looked at him then, though she did not answer him.

"I did not want you here at all, you know," he said. "I sent you an invitation and of course it seemed very likely that you would accept for Lewis's sake and for the sake of his family. But I hoped you would find some way of refusing."

She jumped to her feet.

"I did not want to call on you at Lavinia's," he said. "I did not want to have to invite you to tea yesterday. I did not want you inside Bowood."

"Let me pass," she said. "I must get back to Lavinia's. I must pack my things. Edwin wishes to make an early start in the morning."

She could have passed him without his moving, but she might have brushed against him had she tried. He did not move.

"But once you were here," he said, "I knew that I had wanted it all the time. I knew that I wanted to saturate my home with memories of you. I wanted to be able to picture you in every room. You touched the headrest of my chair in the library. You ran your hand over the top of my desk. You stood at the window there admiring the view."

She sat down again and spread her hands in her lap.

"I wanted you just here," he said, "so that for the rest of my life I can come here and sit where you are sitting now and feel your presence."

"Nathaniel," she said. "Please—"

"Yes, I know," he said. "I am being dreadfully ill-mannered. I am hanging a millstone about your neck with this self-indulgence of a confession. I will feel guilty, fearing that I have upset you. But I believe I would feel worse if I let you go from here without telling you that I will always be thankful that you came."

Her head was bent downward. She said nothing. But watching her, he saw a tear splash onto the back of one of her hands. She lifted the hand and brushed at her cheek. He lowered his head to avoid bumping it on the low doorway and stepped into the magical shade of the folly. It always seemed lit from within—something to do with the light from the lake reflecting off the ceiling, he believed. The folly was fragrant with the scents of sweet peas and other flowers.

"I *have* upset you." He set one booted foot on the bench beside her and draped one arm over his raised thigh. He bent his head closer to hers.

"Nathaniel," she said, "what are you *saying*?"

"That I love you," he said.

"It is sympathy, pity, affection," she said. "Think of who I am, Nathaniel. I am the daughter and sister of coal merchants. I have never had any claim to beauty, accomplishments, wit, charm. Whereas you . . . You have everything—gentility, wealth, property, elegance, charm, good looks. You could have . . . Have you *seen* the way women—ladies—look at you? Beautiful women? Your peers?''

He touched her at last. He cupped his hand softly about one of her cheeks, the heel of his hand beneath her chin. He did not raise it. He ran his thumb across her lips.

''Terrible harm has been done to you, Sophie,'' he said. ''I wish I had known you when you were seventeen years old. Would I have found a wide-eyed, lovely girl who considered herself worthy of the best life had to offer? Would I have found a girl who believed that she had everything to offer the man who would love her? And would I have known even then what a priceless treasure I had found? Perhaps not. Perhaps I needed to be older. Perhaps you did. Perhaps you needed to suffer what you have suffered so that all the perfection of your beauty could shine through you. Don't let the harm be irreparable, my love. Trust yourself. Trust love. Perhaps you can never love me. But there will be someone for you. Someone who will perhaps be almost worthy of you. Meet him as an equal.''

She lifted her hand and set it over the back of his against her cheek.

''Nathaniel,'' she said, her voice revealing the fact that she was still very close to tears, ''I have something I must tell you, something I must burden you with, though I promised myself I never would. Oh, forgive me.''

He lifted her face to his then and gazed into her tear-filled eyes. ''Sophie?'' he whispered.

''I told you I knew how to prevent it,'' she said. ''I told you it simply would not happen. But that last night—I knew it would be the last—I wanted it to be the most wonderful night of my life. It was too. But I forgot about practical matters. Nathaniel—''

He stopped her mouth with his own.

''My God,'' he said. ''My God, Sophie. You are with *child*?''

''It does not matter,'' she said. ''I will go somewhere where I can say I am a recent widow. And I really do not *mind*. I am really rather happy. I will have a tangible memory for the rest of my life. What are you doing?''

He was swinging her up into his arms. He strode out of the folly with her into the sunshine. He set her down on the bank, hidden from the house, sheltered by the trees. A little piece of wilderness fragrant with trees and grass and water, loud with birdsong and insect chirpings, warm with the late August sun. He stood beside her, looking out across the lake.

''I want to know something,'' he said. ''You will be marrying me now, of course, as fast as I can procure a license. I told you when we began our affair in London that you would have to marry me if there were a child. But I want to know your feelings for me. I *need* to know. The truth, please, Sophie.''

She did not speak for a long time. He steeled himself. She would be honest now, he knew. But she was a kind woman who cared for people. He knew that she cared in some special way for him. She would be choosing her words in order to give him as little pain as possible.

''I remember the first time I saw you,'' she said at last. ''It was at a party in Lisbon given by Colonel Porter. Walter had introduced me to all the other officers. I thought Rex and Kenneth and Eden particularly handsome and charming. You were speaking with someone else, your back to me. But you turned when Walter spoke your name and you looked at me when he presented me—and you smiled. You have been told, I suppose, that you have a quite irresistible smile. My heart was yours in that moment. It has been yours ever since. You lent me a handkerchief once and I never gave it back. I used to keep it between lavender bags and take it out frequently to look at it and hold it to my face. I was in a way, you see, unfaithful to Walter. I put the handkerchief away after his death. I thought I would never see you again. I thought you had become merely a wistful memory until you wrote me that letter two years ago and until I saw you again in Hyde Park this spring.''

He turned his head to look at her. She was looking back.

"I am not sure," she said, "if for even one mad moment I convinced myself that having an affair with you would help me get over you. I believe I knew from the start that I was wreaking dreadful havoc on my life. I dreaded coming here, Nathaniel. I dreaded seeing you. Yet since I have been here I have been storing memories so that for the rest of my life I can picture you in the setting where you will live your life. I touched your chair where your head rests, and the top of your desk, where you work. I sat inside the folly, where you sit, and looked out at the lake, on which you gaze."

He smiled slowly at her and reached out a hand for hers.

"Come, my love," he said.

She placed her hand in his and he drew her to her feet and into his arms. But he did not hold her close at first. He set his hands at her waist and moved them inward and down, looking into her face as he did so. He could feel the soft beginnings of swelling in her womb. He slid his hands upward and about her breasts. They were fuller, heavier. They would suckle his child.

She was smiling at last, softly, dreamily.

"It is a good thing you like my extra weight," she said. "There is going to be much more of it."

"Oh, I like it," he assured her. "And it terrifies me. What have I done to you?"

"You have made me feel like a woman again," she said. "Like a desirable, even beautiful woman. Years ago you gave me a dream to dream against the bleakness of reality. And now the dream has become reality. You have made me fruitful. And you love me too. Nathaniel, you *do* love me? You were not just—"

He kissed her hard.

"I have a feeling," he said, "that healing is not going to be instant with you, Sophie. You are going to doubt yourself for a long time to come, are you not? I will be your healer, my love. This is going to be your medicine every time you voice your doubts.'' He kissed her again. ''I love you.''

She wrapped her arms about his neck and laughed as he picked her up off her feet and twirled her once about. It was a rash thing to do. They were not far from the water's edge. He laughed too.

Someone was loudly clearing his throat.

''We are not interrupting anything of, ah, importance, are we?'' Eden asked.

His fingers, Nathaniel was interested to note, were laced with Lavinia's.

''When a man and a woman are in a secluded spot wrapped in each other's arms,'' Nathaniel said dryly, ''they must be merely waiting with impatience for someone else to come along to make life more interesting, Ede.''

''Quite so.'' Eden grinned. ''You have two witnesses, Sophie. If I were you, I would demand that Nat make an honest woman of you.''

''She never was dishonest.'' Nathaniel frowned. ''And that is my *ward* you are clutching, Ede.''

Eden's grin did not falter. ''And so it is,'' he said. ''Muzzle me if I am speaking out of turn, but would we save a great deal of time and energy if we celebrated a *double* wedding? Within the week?''

''I have not heard anyone asking me for Lavinia's hand,'' Nathaniel said.

''Nat.'' Lavinia was engaged in that activity she normally avoided at all costs—she was blushing. ''Do try not to be ridiculous.''

''I have not heard you ask for Sophie's either,'' Eden said. ''Not that you need to, of course. But I will stand her friend. Has he asked you, Sophie? Nicely? On bended knee?''

''*You* did not go down on one knee, Eden,'' Lavinia said.

''I make it a practice never to make a spectacle of myself,'' he said. ''Well, Sophie?''

''You, Eden,'' she said, wagging one finger at him, ''may mind your own business.''

Nathaniel set an arm about her waist and drew her against his side. "Shall I let him have Lavinia?" he asked her. "And *shall* we make it a double wedding? Our families can remain here instead of having the tedium of bringing themselves back in a few months' time. We can send for your brother in haste—ah, and he can bring Lass with him, since I daresay she is there and you are pining for her—and any of Ede's family that he has always stayed very quiet about. I daresay Moira and Ken will stay, though I suspect they are longing to return to Cornwall. But they will have to stay. This is all their doing after all. What do you say, love?"

Sophia and Lavinia had been smiling at each other.

"I say yes," Sophia said, tipping her head sideways to rest on his shoulder despite the presence of an audience. "I say yes, yes, yes." She was laughing softly.

"I rather think, Lavinia," Eden said, "our presence here is severely *de trop*. They had not finished kissing when we interrupted them. Shall we slink off back to the house and see if Moira has recovered from her sprained ankle or her headache or torn hem or whatever it was that took her back there?"

"Sunstroke," Nathaniel said.

"Ah. Nasty." Eden led Lavinia away.

"I am not at all sure about those two," Nathaniel said, lowering his head to Sophia's.

"You do not have to be," she said, wrapping her arms about his neck. "They have their own lives to live and their own marriage to forge, Nathaniel. As we have. You must stop worrying about people who are old enough to see to their own futures."

"Soon enough I will have new people to worry about," he said. "A new person anyway. Will it be a daughter, do you think?"

"Heaven protect her from an overprotective father," Sophie said, laughing. "Perhaps it will be a son. You can teach him to smile."

He laughed with her until laughter faded as they felt

again all the wonder of having discovered a love they had shared without knowing it for some time and would share with full awareness for the rest of their lives.

They moved together to close the distance between their mouths.

**E**nter the rich world of
*historical romance*
*with Berkley Books.*

Lynn Kurland

Patricia Potter

Betina Krahn

Jodi Thomas

Anne Gracie

*Love is timeless.*
**penguin.com**

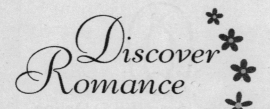

*Titles by Mary Balogh*

**HEARTLESS**
**TRULY**
**INDISCREET**
**SILENT MELODY**
**UNFORGIVEN**
**THIEF OF DREAMS**
**IRRESISTIBLE**

**TIMESWEPT BRIDES**
*(an anthology with Constance O'Banyon,
Virginia Brown and Elda Minger)*